In Search of Love

Dianne Johnson

A catalogue record for this book is available from the National Library of Australia

ISBN-13: 978-1-923174-36-8

Linellen Press
265 Boomerang Road
Oldbury, Western Australia
www.linellenpress.com.au

Dedication

I dedicate this book to Marlene, my sister, friend, and mentor, who has been a constant encouragement to me while I was writing this book. She would often say, "Have you finished yet?"

The characters in this book are fictional.
Any resemblance to real people,
living or dead is purely coincidental.

Acknowledgements

I would like to thank all those who have encouraged me to write this book. To my friends and fellow writers at the Warnbro Writers' Group, especially Kate Stanford who spurred me on to finish it

To Beryl Stone who proofread the first draft, thank you for your valuable input.

For my daughter-in-law Mary and my sister Marlene for your kind comments and enthusiasm after reading the final draft. Thank you.

To my publisher, Helen Iles, thank you for the time and expertise you put into bringing this novel to fruition and for your kindness and patience with me on the journey.

Chapter 1

Claire's lips quivered; her hands shook. 'Mum,' she said, 'I just wanted to tell you that I've moved back in with Eddy.'

Sonia frowned. She looked at her daughter and heaved a long, frustrated sigh. 'Oh no, here we go again! I thought you'd finished with that brute of a man – if you can call him that. Why have you gone back to him – again?'

'Because I love him,' Claire sobbed. 'But I knew you wouldn't understand. I shouldn't have told you.'

'Even if you hadn't told me, it would have soon become obvious, with all your cuts and bruises.'

'Oh, Mum, he's not like that anymore. He's changed. He had counselling, quit drinking, only smokes *one* pack of cigarettes a day and he's given up gambling forever. You'll see; he's a changed man.'

'Well, that I'd really like to see! But didn't he promise all those same things last time? And the time before, and the time before that?'

Claire reached for another tissue, dabbed her eyes, and sniffed. 'Yes, but ...'

Sonia's heart ached for her daughter. She took her in her arms and held her close. 'Oh darling, I only want the best for you. Dad and I love you and we don't want to see you hurt again.

'Come into the lounge room and we'll talk.'

Sonia led the way; she sat on the sofa, fluffed the cushion, and patted the seat beside her. Afternoon sun flooded the room, creating a warm and welcoming atmosphere.

Claire flopped down on the chair beside her mother.

'And Mum, there is something else I want to tell you.'

Sonia's mind wandered. She frowned, unable to figure out why on earth her daughter would want to go back to such an abusive situation. *It's the old pattern starting all over again! Well, at least there are no children involved.* She shook her head, realising she'd been daydreaming. 'Sorry, darling, what was that you said?'

'I said there is something else I want to tell you.' Claire rolled her eyes and tutted. 'I'm pregnant, and Eddy's the father, so you see, I have to stay with him.'

Sonia's head pounded and her heart ached. She tried desperately to control her emotions, but the silence in the room was more than she could bear. 'I thought you didn't want to have children. What changed your mind?'

Claire shifted uneasily in the chair; she grabbed a cushion, held it tight to her chest and began to rock back and forth. 'But I do want this baby, Mum. It's not an accident. Eddy and I talked about it. He says it's just what our relationship needs.'

Sonia shrugged. 'What can I say? If you planned it, all I can say is, congratulations. And when is this baby due?'

'July sixth the doctor thinks, but I'll know more when we have the ultrasound next week.'

'We? You mean you and Eddy?'

'Yes. You can come too if you like,' Claire added hopefully.

'I don't think so dear, I'll leave it to you.' It was all too much for Sonia. She shuddered at the thought of being in the same room as that horrible man, let alone sharing such an intimate moment.

'What's wrong, Mum? Aren't you happy for me? I'm going to have a baby! Your grandchild – your first grandchild!'

Sonia turned her face away, hot tears threatened to spill over. She blew her nose and sobbed. 'Oh darling, if only you knew! If only you realised how much I love you, and yes, of course I will love your baby. I already love the baby but ...'

Claire finished her mother's sentence. 'I know you don't like Eddy! You can't stand him – you've never liked him. That's what it is, isn't it?'

Sonia reached for her daughter. Emotions torn; she smiled a sad smile. 'It's just that I don't want you to get hurt again and I know he will hurt you.'

'Okay, Mum, it seems we can't agree on that, so I suppose I'd better be going. I'll be in touch.' Claire headed toward the front door.

'It was lovely seeing you, darling, but please give me a little time to process this latest news – won't you – please?'

'Yeah, it's okay, Mum.' Claire kissed her mother goodbye and took off.

The sun hung low in the clear summer sky as Sonia watched her daughter's car disappear around the corner.

When Bill Martin returned home from work that evening, he was just as shocked and disappointed as his wife when he heard of their daughter's news. He took Sonia in his arms, and they both found comfort in a loving embrace. 'It will be all right, darling,' Bill said. 'I know it will.'

Sonia waited each day for word from Claire; she dared not try to phone her in case Eddy answered, and she definitely didn't want to speak to him.

The week dragged on. Then, late Monday the telephone rang. Bill answered it. 'Hello, darling, how are you?'

Sonia hurried over and stood by her husband. She extended her hand toward the receiver, as Bill listened. 'Excuse me, dear,' Bill interjected, 'just a minute; I'll put your mother on. Lovely to hear from you, bye.'

Sonia tucked her hair behind her ear and grabbed the phone. 'Hello, darling, how did you get on with the ultrasound?'

'Oh Mum, the baby is beautiful; I can't wait to show you the photos. They're gorgeous! You should see his little toes and fingers and … oh, Mum, can I bring them over tomorrow?'

'Of course you can., I'd love to see them.' It was in that instant Sonia realised her deep love for her unborn grandchild. Her heart warmed. 'Claire, did I hear correctly when you said *his* toes? Is it a boy?'

'I don't know, Mum, it's too early to tell. Besides, I'm not sure if I really want to know if it's a girl or a boy. But Eddy wants them to tell him as soon as they know.'

'Does he now!' The old hatred stirred again in Sonia's chest. How she detested that monster of a man. But she wasn't about to let it stop her from enjoying this precious moment.

The next day, Claire arrived at her mother's house bright and early. The morning soon passed, and the two of them went over old and new photos. First, the 3D ultrasound proofs of Claire's baby, followed by the old baby photos of Claire herself. Sonia gazed in awe at the images of her grandchild, amazed at the clarity and detail.

'Wow, it's like an actual photograph. Look the baby's even sucking its little thumb! I just can't believe it. They didn't have anything like this when I was expecting you.'

'Well, these are the first photos to go into our baby's album,' Claire announced with delight.

Months went by and the young mother-to-be busied herself preparing for the baby. Eddy tried to be on his best behaviour and Claire endeavoured to ignore the negative signs. He didn't actually hit her, but there were times when his words and body language wounded her deeply. On one such occasion, during a severe bout of morning sickness, Claire moaned in distress. Eddy responded unsympathetically. 'Well, don't complain. What else do you expect – you were the one who wanted a baby!'

Claire was hurt and disgusted by his words. She knew full well that it was actually Eddy who wanted this baby, but she chose not to say a single word in her own defence; instead, she comforted herself, rubbed her aching stomach and cradled her precious baby bundle in her arms. 'We'll be all right, darling. I'll look after you,' she whispered.

At thirty-four weeks the pain started. First Claire thought she had wind, but the wind pains intensified to the point of panic. Anxious and upset, she rang her mother. 'Mum, I think the baby is coming, but it's too early. Oh, Mum, what will I do? I've tried to ring Eddy, but it just went to his message server. I'm scared!'

Sonia could feel the fear in her daughter's voice, but she tried to stay calm. 'Don't worry, darling, you just relax. I'll be there as quickly as I can.' Sonia's heart ached for her daughter.

Claire felt alone. She looked around. She knew she needed the bag she'd packed to take to the hospital, but there were more things to go into it, and she couldn't think clearly. Then another pain hit. She cringed and leant forward. Her face flushed. A warm fluid trickled down her leg and onto the floor. She felt dizzy but couldn't let herself fall; she must sit down.

The doorbell rang. 'Claire, it's Mum. Are you there?' Sonia pressed a sweaty finger on the buzzer again and knocked loudly with her other hand. 'Claire, Claire, can you hear me?'

A low moan came from inside the house. 'Can you come to the door, darling. It's locked, and I can't get in.'

Sonia waited.

It seemed like time stood still, yet each minute felt like an hour. Sonia reached for her phone and rang triple zero. A soft voice answered. 'Emergency. Can I help you?'

Sonia took a deep breath and hurriedly explained the situation.

'Just hold the line, I'll put you through to ambulance services.' There was a click and a hum, then a male voice; 'St John's Ambulance Service, Officer Corry speaking.'

Once again, Sonia explained the situation and gave clear directions for the driver.

'We'll be there as soon as possible. The police will gain access to the property for us. So, try not to worry. You've done everything you can. Okay?'

'Yes, thank you, Officer.' Sonia breathed a sigh of relief; she put the phone back in her bag, sat down on the doorstep, dropped her head to her knees and wept.

The police arrived first, closely followed by an ambulance. They forced the front door and entered the house. Sonia shivered. The house felt cold. She blinked, trying to focus in the darkness. By that time, curious neighbours appeared, but thankfully kept their distance.

In the corner of the sparsely furnished room, Claire was slumped on an old chair. Sonia rushed to her side, but the paramedic gestured her toward his assistant.

'Your daughter will be all right, dear. She's in good hands.' The assistant pulled over a rickety chair and sat her down.

Sonia licked her dry lips. 'Thank you,' she said and smiled.

The tall medic slid an oxygen mask onto Claire's face and placed her on the stretcher. Claire reached out for her mother. Sonia went to her side, took her by the hand and kissed her moist forehead. 'I love you, darling,' she said as she trundled alongside the trolley. 'Everything's going to be fine,' she added, trying to reassure herself as much as her daughter.

The driver turned to Sonia. 'Would you like to sit in the front seat or ride in the back with your daughter?'

'In the back, please, if I can. Are you sure there's room for me?'

'Yes, of course,' he replied as he helped her into the rear of the vehicle.

When they arrived at the hospital, a doctor and nurse whisked Claire through to the maternity labour ward.

'Oh, Mum,' Claire called, 'would you ring Eddy for me please? I couldn't reach him when I tried.'

'I don't have his phone number,' Sonia replied as she trotted alongside the hospital trolley.

'You can get the number from the receptionist, Mrs Martin,' the nurse informed her.

Sonia stroked Claire's arm. 'I'll try to get through to him,' she said, not relishing the thought one bit. She did try – once. The phone rang and rang and just as she was about to hang up, the answering machine cut in. 'Eddy's phone, leave a message.' *Beep*.

'Um, it's Sonia here. Claire's been taken to hospital. Could you get there as soon as possible,' she hesitated, added 'please,' and hung up. Sonia's heart thumped hard, and her face flushed. Oh, how she detested that man. She was relieved. At least she didn't have to speak directly to him, and she'd done what her daughter had asked.

Suddenly, her mind went back to Claire. She looked at her watch and hurried back to the ward. 'Is there any news of my daughter, Claire Martin?' she inquired at the nurse's desk.

'The doctor is with her now, Mrs Martin. I'll let you know as soon as they finish the assessment. Would you like a tea or coffee?'

Until then, Sonia hadn't thought about eating or drinking; the adrenaline and nerves had been her sustenance. *But yes*, she thought, *a cup of tea would be nice*.

Sonia went to the visitors' lounge and made herself a cuppa. The warm, sweet beverage was a welcome friend, and she savoured every sip.

A young lady walked toward her. 'Hi, I'm Sharon. I'll be looking after your daughter, assisting Doctor Carlson.'

Sonia looked anxious. 'How is Claire doing?' she asked, and noticing her name tag added, 'Miss Read.'

'Just call me Sharon,' she said with a gentle smile. 'Claire's labouring hard but is making little progress. And baby is starting to show signs of distress. So, we've decided it best to do a caesarean section.'

'Oh no! Is she going to be all right?'

Sharon put her hand on Sonia's shoulder and smiled. 'Yes, she'll be fine. Now don't you worry. You can go in and see her now if you like.'

Entering the room, Sonia noticed her daughter was shaking and looking rather pale. She leant over and kissed her head. 'Don't be nervous, darling,' she said.

'I'm not nervous, Mum; it's just the effects of the epidural they have given me. But ...' she hesitated momentarily, 'it's just that it's all happening too quickly, and I don't feel ready to have my baby today.' She sobbed. 'And where is Eddy? He should be here!'

'I couldn't get through to him; I just left a message on his phone.'

Claire sighed.

Sharon Reid manoeuvred the trolley to the right side of the bed, rearranged some tubes and disconnected others. She and the orderly carefully transferred Claire to the trolley and covered her with a fresh warm blanket.

'We're off then,' the orderly announced as he slowly reversed the trolley.

Sharon glanced back over her shoulder, checking to see if she had all the necessary paperwork. 'You can come too, Mrs Martin,' she said.

Sonia walked beside the trolley, holding Claire's hand. Claire smiled up at her mother. 'Just think, you are going to be a grandma today, Mum.'

'Yes, I am,' sighed Sonia, pleased to think that her daughter seemed now to have accepted the fact that her baby was on its way.

They arrived at the waiting area outside the operating theatre. 'You will come in with me, won't you, Mum?' Claire pleaded, 'I can't do it by myself; I really need you; please stay with me.'

The midwife nodded. 'Yes if you'd like to, Mrs Martin. I'm sure Claire will appreciate the support.'

Tears welled in Sonia's eyes. 'Of course, I'll stay. I'll be with you all the way, my darling.'

Sonia put on a gown and facemask and sterilised her hands.

The nurse nudged open the door with her generously endowed rear end and guided the trolley through into the cold operating room. She and the orderly then transferred Claire to the table, attached cables to monitors and set up a screen.

'Are you comfortable, dear?' asked the midwife.

'Yes, but I can still feel pain,' Claire replied.

Nurse Reid frowned and spoke to the doctor. 'I'll just check your tummy,' she said. 'You might feel a little pressure. Just relax.'

'Oh, your hands are cold!' Claire shivered.

And that's the very reaction they look for to indicate the epidural hasn't taken full effect.

The anaesthetist, Doctor Anderson, entered the room and explained that he would be administering a full anaesthetic.

'Does that mean I won't be awake to see my baby?' Claire asked.

'Yes, that's right, Ms Martin, but you'll see your baby just as soon as you wake up and we'll all be here to look after you and baby, so don't worry, just relax.' He took Claire's hand, flicked his finger on a vein and wiped it with a cool swab. 'You'll just feel a tiny prick.'

And that is the last thing Claire heard before she fell asleep.

'Sorry, Mrs Martin. We'll have to ask you to wait outside. This has become an emergency procedure, and only medical staff are allowed.'

'An emergency! Is she going to be all right? Is the baby all right?'

'Yes, yes, she's in good hands. We will let you know when it's all over. Okay?'

'Yes, thank you, you've been wonderful.'

Sonia was led from the room and pointed in the direction of the lounge area.

Still in the gown, she slipped the facemask under her chin and was about to make herself a cup of tea when she heard the commotion as Eddy bellowed his demand to see his partner.

Sonia quickly ducked down the hall and into the ladies' toilet. The last thing she needed was an encounter with him.

The tranquillity of the maternity ward was broken. Eddy Simpson had arrived!

On hearing the kerfuffle, a male orderly and a senior nurse quickly ushered the troublemaker into a private room.

'Now what's all this fuss about?' Nurse Myer asked.

'Me baby's comin', and I need to be there,' he demanded.

'Well, that's no way to behave, mister.' She paused. 'What is your name?'

'Edward Simpson,' he slurred. 'And I'm gonna cut the baby's cord.'

'Well, that won't be happening today, Mr Simpson.'

Plunged into the cloud of Eddy's stinking, intoxicated breath, Nurse Myer turned away, covered her mouth and coughed. The air hung thick in the stuffy room.

The drunken man became aggressive. He lashed out, arms flying. One fist made contact and the young orderly fell to the floor unconscious.

Nurse Myer tried to reach the door, but Eddy grabbed her and threw her back against the wall. She cringed in pain. Before she could regain her balance, he kicked her hard and her leg crumpled under her.

A young nurse's aide heard the bang and ran toward the room. She almost collided with Sonia who was coming out of the ladies' toilet.

'Sorry,' she said nervously. 'I don't know what's going on in there, but I heard a terrible noise!' The poor young nurse looked pale and scared.

Sonia knew full well what was going on.

'You'd better not go in there, dear,' she said. 'Best to call Security.'

Eddy staggered from the room. The young nurse took one look at him and hurried back to the nurses' station, locked the door behind her and phoned Security.

Sonia stood her ground; she wasn't going to let this monster of a human being ruin the day. She looked him straight in the eyes and, with a boldness that surprised even her, drummed her index finger on his chest and said, 'Right, mister. Pull yourself together and be quiet!'

He hung his head and sobbed.

Moments later, two burly security officers arrived and escorted the troublemaker away while a doctor tended to the injured staff members.

But Eddy didn't go quietly; his voice echoed down the corridor as he was dragged away.

Sonia sighed. Her legs began to shake. She looked at the young nurse, forced a shaky smile, and, in a barely audible voice, tried to express her gratitude. It had been a stressful time for them all, and, at least for now, they didn't have to contend with the unruly intruder.

Meanwhile, downstairs, the commotion continued with Eddy throwing his weight around. Two policemen arrived, arrested him, handcuffed him, and took him into custody.

Finally, back in the maternity ward, Sonia stood by her daughter's bedside. Having caught only a momentary glimpse of the tiny premature baby girl before she was whisked away for specialist care, tears filled Sonia's eyes as she looked at her own little girl. Her mind drifted back to the day Claire was born, just as if it was yesterday; the feel of her soft pink skin against her own skin, the little whimper she made, the frown that formed on her forehead as she tried so hard to focus those tiny blue eyes.

Sonia was lost in thought when Doctor Carlson entered the room. He drew back the curtain, placed a folder on the table and extended his hand toward Sonia.

'Congratulations, Mrs Martin.' He spoke softly. 'You have a beautiful granddaughter.'

'How is Claire?' she asked.

'She had a pretty rough time of it and has lost quite a lot of blood. We are going to keep a close eye on her and do more blood tests tomorrow. Hopefully, she won't need a transfusion. She'll be very tired for quite some time and will need a lot of rest. However, with time she should be fine.'

'And the baby?' Sonia asked.

'Baby came through fine. Although it was touch and go there for a while. She had to be revived and helped with her breathing. But she's a good colour now and I don't expect there to be any problems.'

There was a pause. A stray tear trickled down Sonia's cheek.

Doctor Carlson smiled reassuringly as he picked up the file and checked the notes. 'Do you have any more questions, Mrs Martin?'

'I don't think so,' she replied.

Just then Claire moaned and tried to open her eyes. Sonia kissed her forehead and the doctor spoke.

'How are you, Claire? It's all over now. You have a baby girl.'

A pained smile crossed her pale face before she drifted again into a drowsy sleep.

'I'll leave you now, Mrs Martin. She should sleep for a while. The nurses will check on her regularly, and the buzzer is here; just ring if you need anything or you're worried. Okay?'

'Thank you, doctor,' Sonia sighed. 'Thank you for everything.'

With just the two of them alone in the recovery unit, and Claire fast asleep, Sonia allowed herself to cry. She rested her head softly on the bed, put one hand on her daughter's arm and sobbed. A warm glow covered her like a cloud. At last, she felt at peace.

Minutes later, a midwife entered the room, tapped Sonia on the shoulder and whispered, 'Mrs Martin, would you like to go down to the nursery and see the baby? I think it will be a while before Claire wakes up fully, so you might as well take the opportunity while you can.'

Having asked directions, Sonia picked up her bag, swung it over her shoulder, turned around and left the cubicle. She squinted in the bright light that illuminated the passageway and was glad to be free of the mixture of anaesthetic and antiseptic smell in the recovery ward.

Arriving at the special nursery, she peered through the glass panel in the door and knocked. Soon, a nurse, clad in a sterile gown, shoe coverings, headgear and face mask, ushered her into the gowning room. Sonia put on her special coveralls, washed her hands as instructed and followed the nurse into a room lined with incubators. 'How is Claire's baby doing?' she asked.

The nurse smiled and pointed to an enclosed crib. 'Come and see for yourself. She is beautiful.'

Of course, Sonia agreed; just one look at her newborn granddaughter had captivated her heart. The nurse opened a small round window in the side of the incubator and touched the tiny baby. 'Sorry we can't take her out of the crib, but would you like to touch her?'

Sonia reached into the warm enclosure and gently rubbed the side of her granddaughter's little leg with the back of her fingers. 'Oh, she's so tiny,' she exclaimed.

The baby stretched her arms and opened both hands. Sonia reached her finger toward the baby's palm and a little hand folded around her finger.

'Look at that!' the nurse said. 'She knows who you are already!'

Sonia smiled. 'Isn't she just beautiful?'

'She certainly is. Does she have a name?'

'No, I don't think so. Claire hasn't mentioned it. Everything happened so quickly, the baby wasn't due for another six weeks.' Sonia looked at the small hand still clinging to her finger. 'I didn't realise how tiny she would be. Look at her fingers; they are so fine you can almost see through them. I think she'll just swim in the clothes we've got for her. We might need to buy doll's clothes!'

The baby loosened her grip on Sonia's finger, her tiny chest rising and falling with every breath.

A buzzer sounded.

Sonia gasped. She thought the baby's lips were turning blue.

'Don't worry, Mrs Martin.' The nurse adjusted one of the tubes in the humidity crib and the noise stopped. 'Buzzers go off all the time in here. You get used to it after a while. Everything's okay.'

'She seems to be having trouble breathing and she's blue around the mouth,' Sonia said.

'That's quite normal for a premature baby; her little lungs haven't had time to fully develop. That's why she's getting a continuous flow of oxygen to help with her breathing.'

Sonia sighed with relief. 'Thank you, dear, you have been a great help, but I had better get back to my daughter. Hopefully, she's awake, and I can tell her all about the baby.'

Sonia de-gowned and left the nursery contented.

When she arrived back at the recovery ward, she found the bed empty and was told that Claire had been transferred to the maternity ward.

Sonia hurried down corridors, through heavy swinging double doors, and passed a nurse's station until she finally reached Claire's room. Entering the dimly lit room, she paused and took a step back. Voices could be heard coming from behind the curtain screen, so she backed out of the room and waited. It was then she realised how tired she was. The day had been long and traumatic.

As she waited in the corridor, she heard footsteps and a familiar voice.

'Hi, darling. I got your message. Came as soon as I could.' Bill Martin put his arms around his wife in a loving embrace, and as she lingered in his strong arms, the strain of the day seemed to seep away, and Sonia wept.

'It's all right, darling,' he said. 'How is Claire?'

Sonia wiped the back of her hand across her tear-stained face. Bill pulled out a white handkerchief from his pocket and gently mopped her eyes.

'Oh, honey,' she sobbed. 'Claire's only just come out of recovery, and I haven't had a chance to speak to her yet.' Sonia blew her nose. 'I saw the baby, and she is beautiful. She's very small and in a humidity crib, but so strong! She held my finger and I thought she would never let it go.' Sonia smiled.

Just then two hospital staff came out of Claire's room. 'Oh hello, you must be Mr and Mrs Martin?' They nodded yes. 'I'm Nurse Simmons and this is my assistant, Jane. We'll be looking after Claire tonight.'

Bill extended his hand and thanked them both then asked after Claire.

'She's doing fine, although she is in a bit of pain, but we will make sure she is kept comfortable. You can go in and see her now if you would like.'

'Thank you, we will,' they said, not needing any further persuasion.

Claire was drowsy and quite flushed. 'Where's Eddy?' she asked. 'I thought he'd be here by now.'

Sonia hesitated. She looked at Bill and cleared her throat, not knowing quite what to say. 'He was here earlier, but he got held up this afternoon. Um, he'll probably come in tomorrow.' That was the best answer she could come up with on the spur of the moment and she hoped Claire wouldn't ask any more questions. Sonia sighed with relief and quickly changed the subject. 'I saw the baby,' she said.

'What does she look like? How is she? What does she weigh? Is she beautiful?' The questions came thick and fast.

Sonia laughed. 'Yes, she is beautiful, and no, I don't know how much she weighs, I didn't think to ask. She is very tiny but strong and doing well.'

'The nurse said they would take me down to the nursery in a wheelchair to see her when I'm ready. I can't wait. I'm ready now! Do you want to come with me?'

'That would be great. I'm sure Dad would like to see his brand-new granddaughter too, wouldn't you, Bill?'

'Sure would,' he replied. His chest swelled like a balloon and his face beamed a smile so broad that one could almost skate across it.

Claire reached for the buzzer but was restricted by the fluid drip tube attached to her hand. 'It's all right, darling, I'll get it for you.' Sonia reached over and passed it across to Claire.

It took a great deal longer than expected to transfer Claire from bed to wheelchair. Claire's head began to spin, colour drained from her face. 'It's quite normal to feel that way,' the nurse explained. 'It'll soon pass; just sit quietly in the chair until you feel better. Okay?'

Claire nodded.

Chapter 2

When they entered the special care nursery and were shown to the baby's crib, Bill's face beamed. Sonia watched her daughter as Claire laid eyes on her newborn baby for the very first time.

Claire just stared blankly.

'Isn't she the most beautiful baby ever?' Sonia exclaimed, hoping to get some response from her daughter. But there was nothing.

'She looks just like you when you were a baby, Claire,' Bill added, 'only in miniature.'

'Take me back to my room, get me out of here!' Claire demanded, an angry scowl on her face.

'Whatever's the matter?' Sonia asked. 'Aren't you feeling well, dear?'

Claire didn't reply; instead, she tried to turn the wheelchair around herself but, in her weakened state and with tubes attached, was unable to do so. She became more agitated and angrier.

Noticing the fuss, the nurse came over and spoke quietly to her patient. 'It's all right, Claire; we'll take you back to your room. You can come and visit again tomorrow when you're feeling better. Okay?' Claire hung her head and said nothing.

'There we go,' the nurse said as she settled Claire back into her bed. 'We probably got you up too soon. Never mind I'll give you something to make you feel better.'

Having been given a sedative, Claire turned her face to the wall and said nothing.

'That should settle her for the night,' the nurse explained.

Bill and Sonia looked anxious.

'The doctor will be in early tomorrow to check on her, so don't you worry,' Nurse Simmons assured them. 'You should go home and get some rest yourselves; it's been a stressful day for all of you.' She smiled and reached her hand toward Bill. 'Tomorrow will be a better day, Mr Martin.'

'Thank you,' he said, tears threatening to spill from his eyes.

Then she put her arms around Sonia and gave her a comforting hug. 'See you both next time I'm on duty.' She smiled and said goodbye.

'Thank you, dear,' Sonia replied, and hand in hand they left the hospital.

Bill and Sonia had a restless night, sleep evading them. They talked. They worried. They prayed. But nothing took the pain away.

The next day, Bill phoned his boss and explained the situation. 'Congratulations, Grandfather.'

Bill gave a sad smile. 'Thanks, Phil, much appreciated, I'll let you know when I'll be in. Bye.'

Bill put the phone back in its cradle. He thought about Phil Haynes, his business associate and close friend. He'd worked with Phil at the same engineering company for over thirty years and had come to value his work ethic and his personal integrity. Their respect for each other was mutual and Bill appreciated Phil's kind words.

The next day, in a private consulting room at the hospital, Bill cleared his throat, reached over, and, taking Sonia's hand, smiled a sad smile. 'It has been difficult, Doctor,' he explained, 'but we are bearing up under the circumstances.'

Doctor Carlson folded the stethoscope and placed it in the side pocket of his lab coat. 'Yes, I can appreciate that it would be an extremely difficult time for you both.' He lowered his voice. 'And I heard what happened in the nursery yesterday, and I'm so sorry.'

He paused a moment, leant back on the chair and, clasping his hands behind his head, added, 'Would you like to come with me while I look in on Claire?'

Sonia smiled. 'Yes, please, Doctor, I'd like that.' She turned to Bill.

He nodded in agreement.

Sonia entered the room first. 'Hi, darling,' she whispered, 'how are you feeling today?'

'All right.'

'Dad's here, and Doctor Carlson has come to see you.'

'Hi, Princess,' Bill said. He leant over, brushed a loose, wispy curl from her forehead, and kissed her.

Doctor Carlson drew the curtain around the bed. 'Do you mind if Mum and Dad stay while I check your tummy, or would you rather they left?'

'That's all right,' she sighed, then lifted her t-shirt.

After finishing the examination, Doctor Carlson took Claire's hand and asked about the baby.

Tears filled her eyes. 'It's that baby they showed me yesterday. They told me it's mine. But how do I know? I was asleep. Everyone is trying to trick me. Nobody is telling the truth. My baby is dead!' she shouted.

'No, Claire, that dear little baby girl in the nursery is yours,' Doctor Carlson said. 'She is small, but she's healthy. And, Claire, she needs you.' He touched the armband on her wrist. 'See this ID number here; it is identical to the one on your baby's ankle. I delivered your baby, and I made sure procedure was followed to the tee. Besides, the midwife, as well as her assistant, double-checked before baby left the theatre. So, there is absolutely no need for you to worry. That baby is yours.'

Claire sobbed. Sonia turned away and wiped her eyes.

'We're all here for you, darling,' Bill said, trying to hold back the tears that threatened to overflow. He took Claire's hand in his and kissed her forehead.

'Everything is going to be fine,' the doctor reassured her. 'Now, look, I'll just leave you with your Mum and Dad and I'll be back to see you later this afternoon.' He gave her a little pat on the back of her hand and left the room.

Bill stood and drew back the curtain. A soft ray of morning light touched a glass vase on the window ledge, sending a rainbow of colours across the room.

Claire squinted and covered her eyes. Sonia moved the vase over to the bedside table. 'Sorry I haven't brought you any flowers. Everything happened so quickly. I didn't even think about flowers.'

The breakfast trolley could be heard trundling down the hallway.

'Something smells good,' Bill said, rubbing his well-endowed tummy.

'Err, Yuk, hospital food. I don't want any. I'm not hungry.' Claire scowled.

'But you must eat something; you need to keep up your strength, not only for yourself, but for your baby.' As soon as the words were out of her mouth Sonia knew she shouldn't have said it. *I must be more careful*, she thought.

After the breakfast tray was taken away, untouched, Sonia excused herself and left the room under the pretext of needing the toilet. She went directly to Reception and spoke with the nurse in charge, expressing her concerns about Claire.

The nurse looked up the notes Doctor Carlson had left. 'We are watching her carefully, Mrs Martin, and I will make sure the doctor knows that she's not eating. He has ordered more blood tests for today and, depending on the results, may start her on medication to make her feel better.'

'Do you think it could be postnatal depression?'

'I can't really say, Mrs Martin, you will need to ask the doctor about that.'

Sonia was worried. 'Thank you dear,' she said and returned to her daughter's room.

Tossed between staying with Claire and going to see her granddaughter, Sonia suggested they all go down to the special care nursery together.

'No!' replied Claire abruptly. 'I don't want to.'

Taken aback by Claire's attitude, Sonia began to protest when Bill interrupted.

'I'll tell you what, you go down, dear, and I'll stay here with Claire.'

Dressed in a hospital gown, Sonia spent the remainder of the morning enjoying her granddaughter.

Just as she was about to leave, a sinister figure swaggered toward her. His beady eyes pierced her soul. She shivered. The hospital mask covering his mouth couldn't cover the putrid stench of stale tobacco that wafted toward her.

Released from custody, having spent the night in the local police lock-up, Eddy demanded to see the baby.

He ignored Sonia. Looked in the crib. Turned. Pointed. And in an accusing voice, yelled. 'That is not my baby! I knew it! It's that bloody guy at the gym.' He pointed at Sonia, his face inches from hers. 'Your daughter! Your bitch of a daughter has been at it behind my back.' As he staggered back, he bumped into the crib.

The baby whimpered.

Sonia rushed to the other side of the crib and reached out to stabilise the unit. 'You get out of here! How dare you come in here spitting your venomous lies.'

Eddy snarled and hissed. But when Sonia stood her ground, he turned and stomped off without a backward glance.

Shaken to the core, Sonia flopped into the chair beside the crib.

One of the nursery staff came to her side and put her arm around her. 'What a terrible man! Don't you worry, we won't ever let him in here again.' She placed a box of tissues on Sonia's lap.

'Would you like me to make you a cup of tea?'

'Yes, please,' she replied through trembling lips.

When Claire finally fell asleep, Bill ventured down to join Sonia in the nursery. Relieved to see him, Sonia fell into his arms, cried on his shoulder and then, little by little, relayed the awful "Eddy drama" to him.

Bill could hardly believe his ears. 'That fellow has a real problem,' he said, as he held her lovingly in his arms.

The baby stirred, opened her eyes and whimpered. Both grandparents turned their attention to the newborn.

'You poor little darling,' sighed Sonia.

The nurse added more formula to the baby's nasal tube. She made sure the baby was receiving the correct measure for her age and weight. 'By feeding premature babies this way it puts a lot less stress on their tiny bodies,' she explained in reply to Sonia's unspoken question.

Sonia and Bill watched the baby being fed, changed, and resettled. The small door on the side of the incubator open, Bill reached in and gently stroked the soft, warm skin on his granddaughter's little arm. His hand looked so big beside her tiny body.

'Look, she's responding to your touch,' the nurse said. 'It is so important for premature babies to have that human contact because, as studies have shown, they need it to thrive.'

'I noticed your daughter hasn't been in to see the baby today. Is everything all right?'

Sonia shifted uneasily in the chair. 'No, not really; she isn't at all well.'

'That's a shame; maybe she'll come down tomorrow when she's feeling better. It's good that you are here for her.'

'Thank you, dear,' Sonia sighed.

Bill put his arms around his wife and held her close. 'Why don't you go off to the cafeteria and get a bite to eat; you look tired and beside you haven't had anything since breakfast. I'll stay here until you get back.'

'Why don't you come with me while the baby is asleep?' Sonia suggested. But then she noticed the longing expression on Bill's face and realised that he wanted to spend more time with his little granddaughter.

'Oh, it's all right, darling,' she said, 'you stay as long as you like. I forgot you haven't had as much time with the baby as me. I'll see you when I get back.'

All was peaceful. The only sound to break the silence was the hum from the humidity cribs and the occasional alarm buzz. Bill, sat alongside his granddaughter's crib, overwhelmed with a feeling of love for this tiny little child. Tears filled his eyes as he watched her breathing. 'Welcome to the world, little one,' he said, 'I love you and I always will.'

By the time Sonia returned, Bill had regained his composure. 'Change of shift,' he said, with a cheeky grin.

'Go on now,' Sonia replied, digging him in the ribs, 'it's your turn; you had better go and get something to eat.'

With that command, Bill clicked his heels, saluted, turned on the spot and marched toward the door. 'Okay, boss.'

Chapter 3

Claire remained in the hospital for ten days, having been diagnosed with postnatal depression. She was prescribed medication and, although she slept a lot, day-by-day her health improved. Occasionally, with Sonia by her side, she would reluctantly venture down to see her baby.

Doctor Carlson was kind and understanding; he explained Claire's condition and the care she would need when she left the hospital.

Sonia and Bill were happy to have her come home and stay with them until she was strong enough to look after herself.

'Have you chosen a name for your baby yet, Claire?' Doctor Carlson asked.

'I was thinking Ella,' she replied, looking to her mother for approval.

'That's a nice name,' the doctor said.

Sonia smiled and nodded her head.

'Of course, Ella will need to stay in hospital for some time yet, Claire, but you are free to go home if you feel up to it. What do you say?'

'Can I go home with Mum and Dad? Today?' Her eyes lit up.

'If that's okay with them, I don't see why not.'

Claire smiled. 'What do you think, Mum?'

'Yes, of course you can. We've already got your old room ready for you.'

The doctor signed the necessary paperwork, wrote a prescription, and turned to leave the room. 'Nurse will be in shortly with your discharge papers, together with the final instructions. So, you can start packing and get ready to go. And I'll see you in the surgery in about four weeks. My secretary will be in touch with you about the appointment.' He patted Claire on the shoulder, wished her well, said goodbye, and left the room.

A cool early winters' breeze surprised them as they walked from the warm, air-conditioned hospital. Claire pulled her coat around her body and shivered.

'We'll soon be in the warm car, dear,' Sonia said just as the car pulled into the pick-up bay.

Bill got out from the driver's side and hurried around to open the back passenger door. 'There we go, darling,' he said, and supporting Claire's arm, helped her into the car.

Overcome with exhaustion Sonia wondered how she could maintain the pace. In addition to caring for her sick daughter and the everyday running of the household, there were her daily trips to and from the hospital where she would spend precious hours with the baby.

Whenever Sonia left the house, Bill stayed home with Claire, for fear, if left alone, she might do herself some harm. Both he and Sonia had to tread carefully. At night they sometimes found Claire wandering through the house in a zombie-like state, or she would keep them up, talking like a threshing machine until the early hours of the morning. Then she would fall asleep, causing them to tiptoe around so as not to wake her.

'You must tell the doctor what's happening, Sonia,' Bill said. 'We can't go on like this.'

Sonia nodded. 'I'll arrange to see Doctor Carlson today.

Bang! Bang! Bang! There was a loud knock at the front door. Claire woke with a start, staggered from her room, and wandered down the stairs.

'Someone's at the door!' she said, her eyes wide with terror.

'You go back upstairs, Claire, I'll answer it,' Bill said as he unlatched the door. 'Who's there?'

'It's me, Eddy. I want to see Claire,' came the demand in a drunken slur.

Holding the door ajar, Bill sent up a quick prayer and then replied. 'Listen here, you are in no state to talk to Claire or anyone. Go home, sober up and clean yourself up, and then, maybe, we will talk.'

Eddy turned, mumbled some obscenity, and staggered down the pathway and out of sight.

Bill's heart quickened. He checked the time: 11:17 am.

Phew! He breathed a sigh of relief. 'I'm glad Sonia isn't here,' he whispered.

Claire sauntered down the stairs, her face wet with tears. 'Oh, Daddy,' she cried, 'I'm so scared.'

'It's all right, darling. You're safe here. We won't let anything happen to you.' He held her gently in his arms, swept a stray strand of hair from her face and kissed her forehead. 'My little princess, everything is going to be fine,' he assured her.

Ten minutes later, the sound of a key unlocking the front door caught their attention.

'Hi. I'm home,' Sonia announced as she opened the door. 'Oh, it's nice to see you both down here.' She was pleased to see Claire downstairs, as she spent most of her waking time in her bedroom.

Bill frowned. 'We had a visit from Eddy,' he said.

Sonia put her hand to her mouth. 'Oh no!'

'Don't worry he didn't come inside. I told him to go home and pull himself together. Something to that effect anyway.'

Sonia sighed in relief and, overcome with exhaustion, flopped down onto the nearest armchair. 'Well, I hope he doesn't come back anytime soon. That's all we need.'

Bill asked, 'How is little Ella today?'

Sonia closed her eyes. A contented smile crept across her face. 'She's just beautiful. I fed her again today and she took every drop.'

'Did you get to see the doctor?'

'Yes. I told him the latest,' she hesitated and looked up at Claire. 'Umm, everything's okay.'

Bill got the message and said no more.

Claire was confused. She knew things weren't right. *Surely having a baby isn't meant to be like this*, she thought amid the fog that filled her brain. She banged the side of her face trying to clear her head. That didn't help. 'It's like my stupid head is stuffed with cotton wool,' she muttered and burst into tears.

Doctor Carlson was concerned about Claire and arranged to see her early the next day.

Claire and Sonia arrived at the surgery, and the doctor ushered them into his consulting room. 'I believe you haven't been feeling so good, Claire. Tell me what's been happening?'

Claire felt comfortable with Doctor Carlson and knew she could trust him, but her tears began to flow again. Between sniffs and sobs, she poured out her heart. Then, plucking another tissue from the box, wiped her eyes, blew her nose, and sobbed. 'I'm sorry, Doctor.'

'It's all right, Claire; you don't have to apologise. You have been through a tough time. And you're not alone. Did you know that, in Australia, about one in seven new mothers are diagnosed with postnatal depression? And sadly, there are many more cases that go undiagnosed every year and those poor women have to battle on without the help that is available to them if only they realised. I know it is tough for you now, but let me assure you, Claire, with support, you will come through. Okay?'

Claire smiled through tear-filled eyes. 'Yes, Doctor.'

'You've got wonderful parents to help and support you, and there are counsellors and support groups out there.' He paused and thought for a moment. 'Actually, I'd like to recommend you see a colleague of mine who specialises in this area. Her name is Doctor Emily McInerney. I'm sure you'll like her, Claire. Not only is she a doctor who knows all the theory, but she is a mother herself and understands.' He looked over his glasses, 'What do you think, Claire?'

Claire agreed. *After all,* she thought, *anything would be better than nothing.*

He wrote the referral and made out a new prescription, adjusting her medication. 'Leave off the other tablets and start on these tonight. I'm sure that in a couple of days you will feel better. But if you have any problems just let me know.'

Doctor Carlson stood up, opened the door, and followed them through to Reception. 'I'll see you in a couple of weeks,' he said and placed the folder in its slot.

Days passed without much change, Claire retreating to her room preferring her own company, not wanting to see the baby, and generally being gloomy.

Bill and Sonia worried.

The one ray of hope and sunshine each day for Sonia was her visits to the hospital to see her little granddaughter.

Ella was doing nicely. She was feeding well and starting to gain weight. Sonia treasured every opportunity to hold her, feed her, and just sit and gaze into her baby-blue eyes. The bond between them grew stronger, and Sonia longed for the day she would take her home.

Claire attended her first appointment with Emily McInerney. It was a long session, but it seemed fruitful. Sonia noticed a definite change for the better in her daughter's demeanour.

Sonia took a deep breath, her heart warmed with renewed hope.

Bill had almost finished decorating the nursery in preparation for the new baby, Ella Claire Martin. *What a lovely name,* he thought. He was happy that Claire had chosen to register the baby's family name as Martin instead of Eddy's name, Simpson.

Bill felt sad for Eddy. Deep down, he had a soft spot for him. Knowing that Eddy had been brought up in a poor household with an alcoholic father who beat him then left him to fend for himself.

Poor bloke, Bill thought. *I think I'll give him a call.*

Eddy's mobile phone rang. 'Ugh,' he grunted.

'Bill Martin here. I thought I'd give you a call just to see how you're going, mate?'

Eddy, rather taken aback, replied, 'Yeah, ugh, okay, I s'pose.'

Bill paused. 'Something else I'd like to ask you. How would you like to go out for a coffee with me sometime?'

'Yeah.'

'How about this afternoon?' Bill looked at his watch. I could drop by and pick you up, say, about four?'

'Okay, I'll be ready,' he said a bit more enthusiastically.

'Bye then.' Bill pressed the *end call* button and replaced the phone in its cradle. He scratched his head. *Well, at least Eddy sounded sober.*

Just as Bill was about to leave the house, the two women returned home.

'Where are you off to in such a hurry?' Sonia asked.

'I've arranged to take Eddy out for coffee.'

'What! I can't believe it.' She shook her head and tutted in disgust. 'Why on earth would you do that?'

Bill knew she disliked the man but was shocked by her reaction. 'I thought it would be the right thing to do,' he said. 'I want to try and help the guy … you know, try to build a bridge somehow.'

'Oh, I can't believe you would do such a stupid thing!' Sonia said and stomped off in a rage.

Claire ran up the stairs into her room and slammed the door. She hated it when her parents were mad at each other. It didn't happen often; her dad was very placid, and it took a lot to get her Mum upset, but today was one of those days and Claire hated it.

I'm to blame, she thought, *it is all my fault. If I weren't here, Mum and Dad wouldn't be fighting.* With that she sniffed, wiped her nose with the back of her hand and, grabbing her clothes, bundled them up and stuffed them into her duffel bag. *I'm off!* she thought. *Out of here!*

Bill drove away from the house puzzled and hurt at Sonia's outburst. But brushing the thought aside, he shook his head and drove on.

Arriving at Eddy's, he walked up the uneven pathway, dodged overgrown bushes, and was just about to knock when the door opened. A whiff of stale musty air wafted through the open door.

Bill covered his mouth, turned his head, and coughed. 'Sorry, mate, something must have caught in my throat.'

Eddy grunted, pulled the door behind him, and followed Bill to the car.

'Would you like to go to the Dome for coffee?' Bill asked as he wound down the window remembering how much he hated the smell of cigarettes.

'Yeah, whatever,' came the reply.

Bill began to doubt his decision and wondered if Sonia had been right after all.

They ordered a cappuccino and found a table toward the back of the café. Bill swung his jacket over the back of the chair and sat down. 'Well, what's been happening?' he asked.

'Nothin' much.'

Bill sighed. 'The baby is doing well,' he said, trying to break the ice.

'Don't talk to me about that baby,' Eddy snarled. 'It's not my kid. Looks nothin' like me. Your bloody daughter went off behind my back, I know she did.' He banged his fist on the table, sending the cutlery flying. 'And who wants a girl anyway? I wanted a boy.'

The waitress arrived with their coffees. 'Cappuccino, sir,' she said and, gathering the cutlery, backed away cautiously.

Bill took a handkerchief from his pocket and wiped his forehead. 'Just calm down, Eddy,' he said. 'What makes you think Claire was unfaithful to you?'

'It was the guy at the gym; he was always lookin' at her.'

'That doesn't mean anything. Lots of guys look at girls.'

Eddy's face darkened. 'Yeah, but …'

Bill stood up. 'I don't believe Claire was interested in anyone but you. And if you doubt that you know what to do. Easy fixed. These days there are tests to prove it one way or the other. So, it's up to you. If you're man enough, front up for the test. If not, don't blame Claire!'

Eddy hung his head.

Bill resumed his seat, took a deep breath, and continued. 'You can't have this hanging over your heads. You must get it cleared up once and for all. Do you understand?'

Eddy huffed and, with down-turned eyes and a surly pout, mumbled, 'Mmm, I might think about it.'

'Right. Now that we understand each other, let's drink our coffee before it gets stone cold.'

Claire was breathless when she arrived at Eddy's front door, her mind in a haze. No one was home. She rummaged through her bag, desperately searching for her keys, which, in the panic to get away, she'd left behind. She shivered, pulled her cardigan around her thin body and, squatting down on the cold front step, rocked herself back and forth.

The last rays of the sun cast eerie shadows across the house, and storm clouds swirled overhead. Claire waited, and with every blink of her eyes, the darkness seemed to thicken around her.

Suddenly headlights from an approaching vehicle startled her. Her eyes widened. Her heart pounded. Leaves rustled in the tree above her head. A bird, disturbed by a barking dog, took flight. She jumped up. Then, looking this way and that way in panic, she ran around the side of the house and crouched in the shadows.

Someone entered the house. It must be Eddy. A light shone from inside the kitchen. Creeping cautiously along the side of the house, she peered through the window. It *was* Eddy. She sighed in relief. *Home at last.*

Hurrying to the door, she knocked and waited. The door opened and she smiled up at the man she loved.

Eddy looked at her, his eyes ablaze. 'Oh, it's you,' he said. 'What are you doing 'ere?'

'I've come home to you, Ed. Aren't you pleased to see me?'

'No, you dirty bitch, get out of here. I don't ever want to see you again.' He slammed the door.

Claire stepped back and, as she did, tripped over something on the landing. She fell hard and gasped. 'Oh, my head,' she cried and sat stunned. Blood streamed from a deep gash on the back of her head and an intense pain, like a lightning bolt, shot through her leg.

It was late when Bill arrived home, and Sonia turned away from him in calculated silence. He tried to apologise. 'Sorry, darling, I didn't mean to upset you. You were right, I should have just let things be.' He put his arms around his wife and drew her gently to him.

'Oh, Bill!' she said, pushing him away. 'You have not only upset me but, just when Claire was starting to come good, you've unsettled her again. She hasn't left her room since you went. I think you had better go up and apologise to her.'

Bill's heart sank. *I've really messed things up this time*, he thought. *How could I have been so insensitive.* And with that he climbed the stairs and knocked on Claire's door. 'Are you awake, darling?' he whispered, but there was no reply. Thinking she was asleep, he went back downstairs and into his study.

Claire dragged her aching body through dirt and rubble. Cut, bruised, and bleeding she went on, her eyes blinded with tears. Once clear of Eddy's place, she tried to stand, but a searing pain shot through her leg, and she crumbled to the ground. Everything went black.

Lights from a passing car picked up the shape of something in the gutter. The driver stopped, got out of the car, and shone his torch on the object. To his horror, he discovered the battered body of women. He reached out and touched her arm. It was cold. He went back to the car, grabbed an old rug from the boot and covered her. Then he took out his phone, dialled triple zero and, with quivering lips, relayed the information through to emergency.

After a couple of brief questions regarding the patient, and instructions as to how to place the injured into the recovery position, the operator assured him that the police and ambulance were on their way. 'Will you wait with her until they arrive, sir? They shouldn't be long.'

'Yes, of course,' he answered and ended the call.

A distant sound of sirens soothed his fear. Help was on the way.

All was quiet at the Martin house. The table was laid and the evening meal was ready to serve.

'Bill,' Sonia shouted, 'go and tell Claire dinner's ready.'

Bill wandered out of his office. 'Something smells good,' he said as he passed by the kitchen. He hurried upstairs and stopped on the landing outside Claire's room. He knocked on the door. 'Time to come down for dinner,' he called, but there was no reply. 'Claire, are you awake?' He knocked again Still no answer. Shrugging, he hurried downstairs. 'That's odd,' he said, 'I can't rouse her and there's no light coming from under her door.'

Sonia frowned and tutted and then stomped up the stairs. *I wish she'd snap out of this stupid depression and stop just thinking about herself. It's about time she started to think about her baby, and us.* 'Come on, Claire,' she shouted. 'Get yourself down for dinner right now!' She swung the door open with a bang and switched on the light. The room was in a shambles, but no Claire.

'Bill! Bill, come quickly,' she called.

Bill bounded up the stairs two at a time. 'What's wrong now?' he asked as he entered the room.

'She's not here! She's gone!' Sonia yelled as she thumped her clenched fists on Bill's chest. 'It's all your fault. You upset her and now she's gone.'

Then, exhausted with worry, she flopped her head on Bill's shoulder and cried bitterly.

Bill tried to comfort her. 'It'll be all right, darling,' he said, his own heart doing cartwheels in his chest. He swallowed. 'Where do you think she would go? Could she have gone to the hospital to see the baby?'

'I doubt it,' Sonia replied.

Bill tapped his fingers on his forehead. 'Think, think,' he repeated to himself. Then he decided to phone the hospital just in case she had gone there.

Releasing himself from Sonia's grip, he turned to go.

'You'll have to ring the police,' Sonia demanded and followed him downstairs.

Bill whispered a quick prayer, picked up the phone and pressed triple zero.

The operator answered promptly, and Bill explained the situation.

'Hold on and I'll put you through to the police,' she said, followed by a click and a pause.

'What did they say?' Sonia asked.

'I'm on hold. They're putting me through to the police,' he replied in a broken voice.

The telephone line clicked to life. 'Sergeant Jones here, can I help you?'

Again, Bill relayed the information. The officer noted the details and said he would get back to him if anything came to light. 'We can't file an official missing person report until she has been missing for at least twenty-four hours, but we have the details and will keep an eye out for your daughter,' he assured him.

The call ended.

Sonia shuffled nervously from one foot to the other. 'Well, we have to do something. We can't just wait around here doing nothing while our daughter is out there somewhere!'

'We'll take the car and drive around,' Bill suggested, 'but before we do let's check her room again. She might have left a note, or we might find a clue of some sort.'

They searched the room – inside the wardrobe, in the desk, under the bed, even in the en suite – to no avail.

Bill grabbed his keys. 'Come on, let's drive over to the hospital. She just might have gone there.'

The night was dark. An icy wind blew from the south. The ten-minute drive to the hospital passed in a blur as they sat side by side in deathly silence.

Bill parked the car. They went inside. How different it was to walk the dimly lit corridors so late at night – void of people coming and going, no sound of voices or the clatter of hospital trolleys. The only sound to be heard was the squeak of their shoes on the polished vinyl-tiled floor.

The nursery staff were surprised to see them at such a late hour.

Nurse Reid came out of the nursery to meet them. 'Hello, Mr and Mrs Martin, is everything all right?'

'Sorry to disturb you, but we were wondering if Claire has been in to see the baby this afternoon?'

'I don't think so,' she said. 'Just wait a minute and I'll check.' Nurse Reid went back into the secured enclosure. Bill and Sonia could see her lips moving as she spoke to the others. The nurse in charge looked at the visitors' register, ran her index finger down the page and shook her head.

Nurse Reid returned and spoke with them again. 'Sorry, Claire hasn't been in today, in fact she hasn't been in at all since she left the hospital.'

Sonia lowered her eyes.

'Is Claire all right?' the young nurse asked.

Bill put his arms around his wife and answered for her. 'We really don't know – she's missing.' He took a handkerchief from his pocket and blew his nose.

'I'm so sorry. If there is anything I can do, please let me know, and if Claire does come in, we'll contact you. Okay? And don't you worry about the baby. We'll look after her.'

Sonia sniffed. 'Thank you, dear,' she said, and they turned and headed off.

Worried and confused they drove through the town, up streets, and alleys, through parks and playgrounds. Round, and round they went in search of their daughter.

Back at their home, the ring of the telephone echoed through empty rooms.

Darkness of night gave way to dawn when Bill and Sonia finally returned home.

The phone blinked, signalling three messages.

Sonia sprang to action. 'Oh, it might be Claire!' she said and quickly pressed the *playback* button.

'You have three unanswered calls,' came the familiar monotone voice. Then the first message, 'Sergeant Jones here, would you please ring the station when you get this message. Thank you.'

The monotone voice cut in again announcing the time of the call; '3:41 am. If you want to return this call, press the hash key now; if not simply hang up.' Sonia held the phone close to her ear and was about to call back when Bill stopped her.

'Wait!' he said, 'We need to hear the other messages first.'

The second call was just a dial tone and the third another message from the police, similar to the first. That one came through at 4:55 am.

Bill took the phone from Sonia, rang the police station, and spoke to Sergeant Jones. Sonia clutched both hands close to her chest and waited.

'Yes, Sergeant, we'll go straight away and meet you there.' Bill returned the phone to its cradle.

'What is it?' Sonia asked anxiously.

'We need to go straight to the hospital. A young woman, matching Claire's description, was brought in during the night.'

'Is she hurt? Is she all right?' Sonia asked.

'Whoever the woman is, she's injured and unconscious, but they think she is going to be all right. We don't know if it's Claire, or not; we just have to get down there. Come on, let's go!'

Sonia looked for her handbag. 'Where is it?' she said and burst into tears.

'You've got it on your shoulder,' Bill replied impatiently. 'You didn't put it down when you came in.'

Bill was already standing poised to open the door when Sonia looked back. She saw the table still set from the previous night, food cold and uneaten. But that was the least of her worries.

Chapter 4

Bill and Sonia stepped through the sliding glass doors into the busy Emergency Department of the hospital where Sergeant Jones and the duty doctor were waiting for them.

Doctor Wallace introduced himself, showed them through to a private room and briefly explained the situation. 'I'm sure you will understand that I can't give you much more information until it is confirmed that she is, in fact, your daughter. So, if you are ready, I can take you through to view her now.'

Sonia's heart sank. *I don't think I'll ever be ready*, she thought, *and why did he say to 'view' her, as if we are about to see a dead body?*

Bill took her hand. They hesitantly nodded their agreement, braced themselves and followed.

Sonia wept when she saw her daughter's motionless body, pale against the sterile blue hospital sheets, her head covered in bandages.

Bill turned to the sergeant and nodded. 'Yes, this is our daughter.'

The doctor reassured them that Claire was comfortable and her condition was stable, and briefly outlined the extent of her injuries. 'I'll leave you for a moment,' he said. 'Take as much time as you need. I will come back to ask you some more questions shortly, but for now I'll just confirm your daughter's full name and age.'

Bill stepped aside and gave the doctor the information he wanted then returned to Sonia's side. 'Are you all right, darling?' he asked, putting his arm gently around her waist.

'I think so,' she whispered her reply.

After about ten minutes of silence, Sergeant Jones approached them. He cleared his throat. 'Sorry to disturb you, I just need to ask a few questions.' He paused. 'And I'm sure that you will have questions to ask me too.' He directed them back to the interview room. 'Would you like me to order coffee?'

'Yes please, we haven't actually eaten since …' Bill looked at his watch, 'I can't remember when.'

'Yesterday afternoon,' Sonia added.

'Well, you guys could do with coffee. Milk? Sugar?'

'Milk and one sugar for me and white tea, no sugar for my wife,' Bill replied.

The sergeant left the room just as the doctor entered.

He nodded and looked down at his notes. 'I have accessed Claire's medical records,' he explained and, adjusting his stethoscope around his neck continued. 'As you know your daughter was brought in by ambulance this morning at approximately 3:30 am. She was unconscious with a deep gash to her head and suffering hypothermia. Her temperature has stabilised, and she is on oxygen and receiving fluids via an intravenous drip. Shortly we will transfer her to our Intensive Care Unit for further tests and ongoing care. Do you have any questions?'

'How did she get these injuries?' Bill asked.

'We're not sure at this stage. Perhaps Sergeant Jones may be able to answer that question.'

The police officer entered the room juggling four steaming mugs and a plate of sandwiches.

'Here we go,' he said and placed the tray carefully on the table. 'Tea for the lady, white coffee with one, Mr Martin,' and pointing to the blue cup, he said, 'and that one is for you, doctor.'

'How did you know I like my coffee black and strong?'

'Aha,' he said with a cheeky grin and a finger tap to the side of his nose, 'it's a policeman's job to suss out relevant information, Doctor.'

That helped to ease the tension and the four of them smiled, if somewhat tightly.

'Thank you for the coffee, but I'm afraid I'm going to have to leave you, so I'll take it with me.' Doctor Wallace left the room, mug in hand.

'Now, I just need to ask you a few more questions,' Sergeant Jones said and flipped open the cover of his notepad. 'Firstly, when did you notice your daughter was missing?'

Bill looked at Sonia.

'Umm, we were about to have our evening meal, so that would have been around 8:30,' Bill replied.

'Right. So, when was the last time you saw her?'

Sonia put her hand to her mouth and sniffed. 'It was just before four. Claire and I had returned home from an appointment and Bill was about to leave the house.' She gave Bill a sideways glance, and then continued. 'Claire went upstairs and into her bedroom and that was the last I saw of her.'

The police officer scratched his head. 'That means she would have left the house somewhere between the hours of 4:00 pm and 8:30 pm.'

Sonia interrupted the interview. 'Excuse me, but we have some unanswered questions too.'

'Sorry, Mrs Martin, please go on.'

'We want to know exactly what happened to our daughter.'

'You do understand that this is an ongoing investigation,' the sergeant replied.

'Of course we do! And do you understand this is our daughter you are talking about, not just a case number.'

Bill put his arm around Sonia. 'It's all right, darling, I know you're upset, but he's just doing his job.'

Sergeant Jones paused, drained the last of his coffee, and then leaned forward. 'Just take your time,' he said. 'I realise it has been a long and stressful day for you both.'

Bill turned to him. 'Would you fill us in with what actually happened to Claire?' he asked calmly.

'As you know we are still looking into it, but we suspect it might have been a hit and run. A young man found her lying unconscious in the gutter, and presuming her dead, called us.'

Sonia gasped.

Sergeant Jones explained. 'The young man called triple zero and stayed with her until we, and the ambulance, arrived.' The sergeant paused, cleared his throat, and asked, 'Can you tell me why your daughter would have been in the vicinity of Paxton Avenue? Does she know anyone there?'

Sonia screamed. 'That's where Eddy lives!'

'Who is Eddy?' Sergeant Jones asked.

'Edward Simpson, Claire's partner,' Bill replied.

Sonia interrupted, 'Ex-partner you mean, well at least I hope so.'

'This Edward Simpson, you say he lives in Paxton Avenue, is that right?'

'Yes.'

'What is the house number?'

'Fifty-two,' Sonia said without hesitation.

The sergeant noted the address, closed his book, and thanked them both for their help. 'I think that's all I need for now. I will let you know of any further developments as they unfold and if you think of anything else that could help with our enquiries, please let us know.'

Bill and Sonia returned to Claire's side.

'How is she?' Sonia asked the nurse.

'There's been no change; she's still stable, and we will know more when the test results come through.'

Bill looked at his watch. 'Why don't you go and have a little time with the baby? I think it will do you good. I'll stay here with Claire.'

Sonia wandered down the corridor in a blur. She stopped and shook her head, trying to get her bearings. *Where am I?* she thought.

Eventually, she found her way to the Special Care Nursery. Good news at last. Little Ella was out of the humidity crib. Sonia smiled and looked down at her tiny granddaughter. 'Hello, darling,' she said.

A young nurse approached. 'Good to see you, Mrs Martin,' she said as she checked the baby's formula was the right temperature. 'You are just in time to feed her if you would like to.'

'Oh, yes please. That would be lovely.'

'Sit down and make yourself comfortable and I'll bring her to you.'

The baby felt warm in Sonia's arms and, as their eyes met, Sonia thought she detected a little smile. It was probably only wind, but that little wind smile melted her heart. Sonia held her close, breathed in the sweet fragrance of her new granddaughter and kissed her tiny cheek. How she loved the feel of the baby's soft skin against her lips.

Ella drank the milk, right down to the last drop. Sonia looked at the empty bottle. 'What a good girl you are,' she said. To which the baby replied with a big burp.

The young nurse returned and was surprised to see the baby's bottle empty. 'Did she drink all of that? And so quickly! Wow! You really do have the right touch. She fusses for me when I try to feed her, and she always leaves at least this much,' she said, spacing thumb and index finger as an indicator. 'Aw, look she's fallen asleep on your shoulder. Would you like me to put her back into her crib?'

'I don't want to spoil her, but do you mind if I hold her just a little longer?' she said, clinging tightly to her tiny bundle of joy.

The nurse smiled. 'Of course not. She looks so comfortable there, and besides, you can't ever spoil a newborn baby with too many cuddles.'

'Thank you, dear,' she said, savouring every precious moment. Sonia marvelled at how such a little one could bring the joy and peace that she felt at that moment. The tension and stress of the last twenty-four hours seemed to drain away as she cradled the baby in her arms.

The police cordoned off the crime scene and continued their investigation. They detected traces of blood leading to number fifty-two Paxton Avenue, the home of prime suspect, Edward Simpson.

Sergeant Jones, accompanied by two officers, knocked on the door.

There was silence.

Then came a shuffling sound from inside.

The door opened a smidgen, and Eddy appeared squinting and shading his eyes.

'Are you Edward Simpson?' the sergeant asked.

Eddy frowned. 'Yeah.'

Sergeant Jones shoved the door open. He gripped Eddy's shoulder and pronounced: 'Edward Simpson, I am placing you under arrest for the suspected attempted murder of Claire Martin.'

'What!' he exclaimed. 'No way! You got the wrong bloke.' He pushed the policeman's hand off his shoulder, shook himself, and stepped back from the doorway.

The sergeant blocked the entrance with his foot. 'You will need to accompany us to the Police Station for further questioning, Mr Simpson. And I'm warning you, you had better come quietly, or you will just make things worse for yourself. We don't want any trouble. Do you understand?'

Eddy grunted.

The two assisting officers handcuffed Eddie, led him to the paddy wagon, bundled him into the back of the vehicle and drove off to the Police Station.

Word reached the Martins of Eddy's arrest.

'See, I told you he was no good,' Sonia said as she paced the corridor outside Claire's hospital room. 'How dare he lift a finger to our daughter?' she shouted in disgust.

Bill put his finger to his lips. 'Shh! Keep your voice down. We're in a hospital, remember.'

'How could I forget?' Sonia replied with gritted teeth. 'Forget that we're in the intensive care unit of a hospital? Forget that we are standing outside the door of the room where our only daughter is, at this very moment, lying in a coma, kept alive only by machines? And *you*,' she poked her finger at Bill's chest, 'tell *me*, to remember where we are!'

Bill took her in his arms, his face ashen. 'Believe me, my darling, I do remember. I feel it too.' He held her tight as tears rolled down Sonia's flushed cheeks.

Eddy denied the accusations furiously. How dare they accuse him of such a crime? When questioned he answered truthfully, even admitting that Claire had come to the house that night. But they didn't believe his story.

'Ask Claire,' he insisted. 'She'll tell you what happened.'

'I'm afraid that's not possible,' the officer informed him. 'The young lady you put in hospital is unconscious and can't talk to anyone.'

Eddy banged his fists on the table. 'Why won't anyone believe me?'

'Why should we? One look at your record shows us what you're capable of, and the evidence speaks for itself.'

'I want a lawyer,' he demanded.

'You'll get more than a lawyer. Mark my words, the judge will throw the book at you.'

On bail and under strict conditions, Eddy was released from custody with a date set for his preliminary hearing. Witnesses were summoned to attend the hearing. Bill and Sonia were called, together with James Cowan, the young man who had been first on the scene of the accident.

Bill read the notice and handed it to his wife.

'I don't want to go,' she said, 'I can't stand the thought of even being in the same room as that detestable man.'

'Sorry, my dear,' Bill replied, 'but neither of us has a choice in the matter. I'm afraid we must attend.'

James Cowan, who was on a business trip from Adelaide, delayed his return flight from Perth to attend the hearing.

Chapter 5

The day of the hearing arrived. Five people waited in the foyer of the courthouse – Sergeant Jones, Eddy's lawyer Michael Harrison, James Cowan, and Bill and Sonia – but no Eddy.

The lawyer tapped his foot impatiently and frowned as he looked at the large wall clock ticking away the seconds. He stood and began to pace the room. Suddenly, the heavy wooden door swung open, and Eddy staggered in, unshaven and reeking of stale beer.

Sonia gasped. *On no, he's drunk,* she thought and, plucking a tissue from her bag, covered her nose.

The lawyer grabbed hold of his client's arm and took him through to another area. 'Pull yourself together, mate. You can't go into the courtroom in this state. Besides, look at the time, you're late. Right then, you just sit here, and I'll get some coffee into you.'

Michael Harrison left the room and hurried to the nearest café. 'Give me a strong, black coffee, as fast as you can please.'

The young waitress knew Michael well. She smiled and quickly prepared the order. 'Trouble at court?' she asked, handing him the steaming coffee. 'And I guess you will be wanting plenty of sugar with that, sir.'

The lawyer snatched a handful of sugar sachets and a spoon. 'Just add that to my account.' He rushed out the door.

Fortunately, for all concerned, there had been a delay in court proceedings that morning.

Sergeant Jones introduced James to Sonia and Bill.

Bill put his hand on the young man's shoulder. 'Thank you for what you did for our daughter. If you hadn't been there who knows what could have happened. Thanks, mate.'

James smiled shyly and asked after Claire, his soft blue eyes sparkling at the news of her progress.

What a lovely young man, Sonia thought, raising her eyebrows and rather impressed with this quietly spoken gentleman.

The foyer door opened, and the court clerk cleared his throat. 'Calling all parties involved in the case *Simpson versus Martin*.'

They entered the musty courtroom and took their places on the hard wooden pew.

Bill looked around but couldn't see either Eddy or his lawyer.

Where is the Defendant? The court clerk returned to the foyer area now crowded with people waiting their turn. Again, he cleared his throat and, in a loud and clear official voice, called for Edward Simpson. But there was no movement among the crowd. He opened the front door and repeated the call.

From a side alcove lawyer Michael Harrison tried to hurry his client.

Eddy scowled. 'Don't push me. I gotta go for a leak first.'

'You don't need to go again; you've already been four times in the last half hour.'

'It's your fault, all that coffee you gave me.'

'Coffee! What about all the alcohol you consumed before you even got here. Anyway, you can't go to the toilet now. We have to go into the court; right now! Do you hear?'

He grabbed Eddy by the arm and marched him into the courtroom.

'Sit here beside me and keep quiet. Remember what I told you?'

Eddy hung his head and grumbled under his breath.

'All stand. Magistrate Stone presiding in the case of *Simpson versus Martin.'*

The magistrate took his seat. Silence filled the room.

'All be seated.'

After perusing the written evidence, the magistrate looked up, peered over his glasses, and scanned the faces of those present.

'Who represents the accused?'

Michael Harrison stood. 'I do, Your Honour.'

'Sit down. Let the accused stand.'

Michael Harrison nudged his client.

'What?' Eddy retorted.

'Stand up.'

Slothfully, he dragged himself to his feet and leaned on the rail.

'Edward Simpson, you have been accused of attacking one Claire Martin, causing grievous bodily harm. How do you plead? Guilty or not guilty?'

'Aw, you gotta be kiddin' … that stupid bitch is lyin', again 'n I ain't …'

Bang! The gavel striking the block echoed in the courtroom.

'Order in the court. I will repeat the question once more. You will reply guilty or not guilty. Do you understand?'

Eddy sniffed, wiped his nose across his shirt sleeve and mumbled. 'Yeah.'

'Edward Simpson, you stand here today accused of attacking Claire Martin, causing her grievous bodily harm. Do you plead guilty or not guilty?'

'Not.'

'Not, what?'

'Not; it wasn't me.'

'Do you mean not guilty? Well, say it.'

'Not guilty.'

Next, Sergeant Jones was called to the stand and questioned, followed by witness James Cowan, architectural engineer from Adelaide.

Sonia breathed a sigh of relief when the session came to an end and neither she nor Bill had been called to give evidence.

The magistrate ended the hearing. Eddy was released on bail. His conditions included presenting himself daily to the Police Station, good behaviour, and a restraining order forbidding him to go within 500 metres of any member of the Martin family. The magistrate set a trial date and anticipated that the victim, Claire Martin, would be able to give her evidence then.

Days stretched on and Claire remained in a coma.

Doctor Wallace was on his daily hospital rounds when he met up with Bill and Sonia. 'Just the people I want to see,' he said and directed them to a side room. 'Your daughter is doing quite well. As you know, at first, we hesitated to reset her fractured leg, but fortunately, the orthopaedic surgeon, Doctor Ryan, was able to realign and set the limb successfully without the need for anaesthetic. And it's looking good. The head wound is healing well, and the swelling has subsided. So, we expect that she will soon wake from the coma. It's just a matter of time.'

Grasping the doctor's hand in his, Bill shook it vigorously. 'That's great news.'

Sonia couldn't contain herself; she put her arms around the doctor and gave him a big kiss. The doctor blushed slightly and nodded.

Bill returned to work, which in some respects distracted him from the pressures he was under.

Day after day Sonia visited the hospital. She had developed quite a routine. First stop, the nursery to feed, change, bath, and cuddle the baby, followed by a quick morning tea at the cafeteria. Then up to ICU to spend time talking to her own "sleeping beauty." Most days she didn't feel too uneasy sitting there by Claire's bedside conducting a one-way conversation. Doctor Wallace had reminded her of just how important touch and talk is for someone in a coma. Apparently, after they wake up, they often recall some of the conversations spoken while they were still unconscious.

After having lunch, Sonia would return to her nursery duties, although of course they were never a chore or burden to her. Then, after a final visit with Claire, she would make her way home to prepare the evening meal for herself and Bill.

Every day on his way home from work, Bill would stop by the hospital to see Claire and his baby granddaughter. It always warmed his heart to see the little one thriving and his daughter improving.

One morning Sonia woke early. An amazing feeling of expectancy swept over her. She blinked, and in the pale light of winter's dawn, she checked the time. *Oh, it's much too early to get up yet*, she thought, and turning over, tried to go back to sleep. But sleep evaded her. Not wanting to disturb Bill, whose rhythmic snoring confirmed his deep sleep, she carefully pushed aside the doona, slipped out of bed, and crept down the hall and through to the kitchen.

The alarm sounded. Bill yawned and stretched and, reaching his arm over to Sonia's side of the bed, patted the vacant hollow. Rolling out of bed, he rubbed his blurry eyes and wandered out to find her.

To his surprise she had already packed his lunch for work, prepared a delicious breakfast, fed the cat and was leisurely sitting sipping a cup of tea.

He took the cup from her hand, placed it on the table and, wrapping his arms around her waist, lifted her off her feet and twirled her around. 'Good morning, my darling, what got you up so early?'

Sonia giggled. 'I really don't know. I just feel so good today.'

'Well, my darling, you look good to me too, today and every day!' he said and kissed her forehead.

Sonia failed to notice the flicker of Claire's eyelids as she sat chatting to her about the baby. It was the first faltering words coming from her daughter's trembling lips that were like music to her ears.

'Baby … my baby?' Claire whispered.

Sonia fumbled for the buzzer and pressed down hard on the red button. 'Come quickly,' she shouted to everyone within earshot.

The head nurse hurried in. 'Welcome back, sleeping beauty,' she said with a somewhat mischievous smile.

Claire responded with a look of bewilderment as she tried hard to speak through dry cracked lips.

'Just take your time, Claire. Don't tire yourself,' the nurse said while checking Claire's vital signs.

Hardly able to contain her joy, Sonia clasped her hands over her heart and breathed out a sigh of relief.

'Don't get too excited, Mrs Martin. Remember this is ICU and we have a lot of very sick people here,' she said, and then returned to the observation desk.

Sonia sat quietly beside Claire and kissed the back of her hand. 'Oh, there is so much to tell you, I don't know where to start.'

Claire blinked several times as she tried to focus. 'Where am I? What happened?'

'You're in hospital. You had an accident, but you are going to be all right.'

'I don't remember,' Claire said and closed her eyes again.

Nurse Hughes returned to Claire's bedside. 'Claire, I have spoken to Doctor Wallace, who's been looking after you since you were admitted, and he will be in to see you shortly. Meanwhile, I have a few questions to ask you if you are feeling up to it.'

She nodded in response.

'Can you tell me your full name?'

Claire licked her lips. 'Claire Elizabeth Martin.'

'Good. And who is this sitting next to you?'

'My mother.'

'That's good, Claire; you're doing well. Just a couple more questions: What is your mother's name?'

Claire frowned. 'Her name is Sonia Martin, of course.'

'Thank you, my dear. I think that will be all for now.'

Nurse Hughes jotted down some notes and closed the patient file. 'I'll leave you two now,' she said and moved away.

Claire kept her eyes closed and Sonia detected a slight restlessness in her.

'Are you all right, darling?'

'Yes.' Yet she moaned and tears flooded her eyes.

Sonia stroked her arm. 'Everything is going to be all right. You've been through a lot, and it will take time to piece it all together. But you'll be fine.'

Claire smiled through her tears. 'Oh, I've got so much to tell you, Mum,' she said and fell asleep.

Sonia looked at her watch. It was lunchtime but there was no way she could even consider eating food at a time like this. *I must phone Bill*, she thought.

Looking around, she caught the nurse's eye and beckoned her over.

'Is everything all right?' Nurse Hughes asked.

'Yes. She's just gone back to sleep. Will it be okay if I go outside and phone my husband?'

'Of course, that's fine. We're expecting Doctor Wallace early this afternoon. Do you think you'll be back before he comes?'

'I'll make sure I am,' she replied.

Bill was thrilled to hear news of Claire's recovery and, after receiving the phone call, found it hard to concentrate on his work.

His boss slapped him on the back. 'Go on, Bill. Go see your girl. I'm sure we can manage here without you for the afternoon.'

Bill quickly gathered his belongings and rushed off.

Arriving at the hospital, he entered on the ground floor, pressed all six of the lift buttons and waited. He watched as the indicator lights showed where each lift was on its journey. Up and down, they went, sometimes stopping so long on one floor that he thought they must be stuck. *Oh blow*, he thought, *I'll take the stairs, I need the exercise anyway*. So off he ran up the stairs two at a time.

Having reached his destination, he took a deep breath. *Mmm, not as fit as I used to be*, he thought.

The doctor was still there when Bill came in puffing.

Sonia looked up in surprise.

Bill leant over and kissed her and then, turning to his daughter, let out a sigh of relief.

'Hi, my princess. It's so good to see you awake.

Claire's eyes sparkled and her face lit up at the sound of his voice. 'Oh, Daddy,' she said, 'I have so much to tell you.'

Doctor Wallace was pleased with Claire's progress. He answered all her questions, updated her on her current situation and explained the ongoing care plan.

'We will keep you here in ICU for now, at least overnight anyway. And I'll get Sister to remove those tubes; that should make you feel more comfortable.' He looked at his notes. 'I see you have already eaten something. That's good.' He lifted the jug from the bedside table and gave it a swirl. 'Try to drink as much as you can manage but take it slowly. Just suck through the straw, a sip at a time. If you can't manage water, Sister will give you ice to suck. That will give you the fluids you need and keep your mouth moist and fresh.'

He smiled and, with a little stroke of his hand on Claire's cheek, said his goodbyes.

Claire dozed on and off throughout the afternoon and into the evening, her parents by her bedside. When eventually she settled for the night, reluctantly they pulled themselves away, made a quick visit to the nursery then headed home, happy, content, relieved and thankful. It had been a long and tiring day for them all.

Chapter 6

The next day, Sonia woke bright and early.

'Saturday, hooray!' She threw her hands in the air. It was Bill's day off so he could go with her to visit Claire and the baby.

Claire was sitting propped up in the bed when Bill and Sonia poked their heads around the side of the curtain. 'Hi, darling,' they said in unison.

'Mum, Dad, I'm so glad you're here. Come and sit down I'm dying to tell you about the dream I had. I wanted so much to tell you yesterday, but I just couldn't get the words out.'

Bill pushed the curtain aside, brought another chair over and sat down beside his wife.

Claire took a deep breath. 'I had a dream,' she said. 'It seemed so real. But I don't know if it was a dream or a vision, or something else. I saw my baby Ella, but she wasn't a baby anymore; she looked to be about two years old. I saw her standing in front of me. Her chubby arms reached out to me. "Mummy," she said. "I need you, Mummy." Her eyes were so sad.'

Sonia sobbed and blew her nose and was about to say something when Bill stopped her. 'Shh, let her go on.'

An all-encompassing peace filled the room.

Claire cleared her throat and continued. 'I tried so hard to get to my baby, but something kept dragging me back. I strained to reach her. The more I pushed forward the further she seemed to drift away.

'In the distance, I could hear your voice, Mum. You were telling me about Ella. I tried to open my eyes. I desperately wanted to get back.'

Claire paused and closed her eyes. 'Then I prayed. I cried out to God. "Please, God, help me. I can't do it by myself. I need you, you're the only one that can help me." Right then something broke. Whatever it was that was pulling me back snapped, and I was released. I felt free, light, totally in control and I knew God had answered my prayer.'

Bill pulled a handkerchief from his pocket, wiped his eyes, and put his arms around her. He held her close and wept on her shoulder. 'Oh, my darling.'

Lost for words, Sonia cupped her hands, buried her face and howled like a baby.

Nurse Hughes made a stage-like entrance to Claire's room. 'Claire, it's good to see you looking so much better. We have decided to move you down to the maternity ward,' she said as she packed Claire's personal belongings. 'You'll be in a room next to the nursery, so you will be able to pop in and see your baby whenever you would like to. Oh, and Doctor Wallace and Doctor Carlson will come in to see you when you get settled.'

A huge smile spread across Claire's face. 'Thank you for all you've done for me; you've been so kind.'

'You're welcome.'

The orderly arrived with a wheelchair. 'Your carriage awaits you, madam,' he said with a bow.

No sooner had Claire settled into her new hospital room than both her doctors came to see her.

Doctor Wallace looked around. 'This is a lovely room, Claire, a big improvement on the one you just came from, don't you think?'

'It sure is, and it won't be as noisy as ICU either, at least I hope not.'

'That's for sure,' Doctor Carlson added.

Doctor Wallace perused his notes. 'Well, Claire, you have made great progress, and you're looking well. How are you feeling?'

She sniffed and pointed to her nose. 'My nose is sore and red raw from where they had that horrible oxygen tube up my nose, and my throat hurts, and my leg is still painful.'

'That's understandable; it was a bad break. It will just take time to heal. Are there any other problems?'

'No, I just want to get better and go home.'

'That's good, Claire. We'll see what we can do about that.'

Doctor Carlson moved to the bedside. 'How's your tummy healing?' he asked.

Claire had completely forgotten about the caesarean section she'd had only a few weeks before. 'I think it's all right,' she said.

He placed his hand gently on her abdomen. 'That's good,' he said then continued. 'Doctor Wallace and I have consulted together, and we both agree that you no longer need the antidepressant medication you were on before the accident. You seem to have come right through that bout of PND. However, I would like you to have at least one more follow-up session with Doctor Emily McInerny. Will that be all right with you?'

'Yes, I like Emily; she is so easy to talk to.'

'Right then … we'll leave you for now and one of us will be in to see you again tomorrow.'

The lunch trolley arrived. Claire lifted the cover on the main meal and grimaced. Although she was hungry, she wasn't *that* desperate. She replaced the cover, peeled open the yoghurt and allowed the soft, cool dessert to slide down her still-raw throat.

'Umm, that was good.'

Sharon Reid, the midwife who had assisted in the delivery of Ella, popped in to see Claire. 'Hi there,' she said. 'Doctor Carlson told me you were here. I just had to come and see you. How are you?'

'Much better now, thanks, but did you hear what happened?'

'Your accident? Yeah, that was terrible, you poor thing.' She put her arms out and gave Claire a hug. 'Ella is doing nicely; she is so beautiful. Have you been in to see her today?'

'No, not yet.'

Nurse Reid looked at her watch. 'It's almost baby's feed time. Look, I'm going to the nursery now. Would you like to come with me?'

Claire's face beamed, and then she hesitated; she pulled back the bed cover and pointed to the plaster cast on her leg. 'I'd love to, but I can't walk yet.'

'No problem at all,' Sharon replied and dashed off to find a wheelchair.

She soon returned and transferred Claire from the bed, pushed the wheelchair down the hall, through the sliding door and on into the gowning area where they scrubbed up, donned their coveralls, and entered the nursery.

When Claire laid eyes on her little daughter, her heart melted.

Ella looked up, her soft blue eyes seeming to focus on her mother's face. Tears of joy rolled down Claire's cheeks. She gently touched her baby. The little one stretched out her arm and wrapped her tiny hand around Claire's finger.

Sharon quietly backed away, leaving mother and baby to bond. *What a moment. What a joy.* Still feeling overawed and almost speechless by what she had just witnessed, she met Bill and Sonia in the hallway. 'Come look at this,' she said and guided them across to the window.

Tears flowed freely as all three gazed in wonder at the scene.

Bill blew into his handkerchief. 'I think we'll go away and come back later,' he suggested, and, taking Sonia by the hand, turned to leave.

Sharon beckoned them back. 'Just a minute, come. Look!'

They turned toward the window once more, and there, in the special care nursery, sitting in a wheelchair, they saw their daughter, holding her baby for the very first time. They watched as she lovingly cradled the little one in her arms, fed her, and burped her.

Bill stood behind Sonia, his arms around her waist. She leaned her head back against his shoulder and smiled contentedly. Bill's heart threatened to explode from his chest.

Next morning, Sergeant Jones arrived at the hospital to interview Claire. He introduced himself and the other young man with him. 'This is James Cowan – he found you on the night you were injured.'

'Hi,' James said, nodding in response.

Claire smiled up at him. 'Thank you,' she replied, and blushed slightly.

'Claire, I'd like to ask you a few questions if I may.' The sergeant flipped open his notepad, licked the tip of his pencil, and then continued. 'I don't know how much you remember of the night of the accident, the night of June twelfth. But would you tell me in your own words what happened?'

'Yes, Sergeant, I'll try. It's all still a bit hazy, but I'll do my best.'

'Just take your time.'

Claire paused for a moment, her heart rate quickening – not so much with the thought of the accident but more because of an acute awareness of the handsome young man standing beside the police officer.

She swallowed and cleared her throat. 'My memory of that night is fragmented. I get flashes of memory, but they are like still photos and all fuzzy.'

'That's all right, Claire; just tell me what you see.'

Claire squeezed her eyes closed and tried to focus. 'It was dark. I was cold and scared,' she began. Then suddenly she cringed, her facial expression contorted, 'I see headlights. I see Eddy's angry face. My leg hurts. I've got to get away. I must run. Oh, my leg!' Claire frowned.

Sergeant Jones interrupted. 'It's all right, Claire; you're safe now.'

Claire opened her eyes. She saw James and smiled. 'I'm sorry, I didn't mean to …'

'Don't worry, I didn't mean to upset you,' the sergeant said, 'but I've just got one more question if you don't mind. Did Eddy hurt you, Claire?'

'I don't know,' she said with a pained sigh.

'Don't worry, Claire. I think we'll leave it there for today, but, if you do think of anything else, anything that might help us with the investigation, would you please let your father know and he will pass the message on to me. I've given him my number.' He could tell that she was beginning to stress.

Sergeant Jones closed the notepad, slipped it back into the top pocket of his shirt, and buttoned down the flap. 'Well, thank you for your cooperation, I know it couldn't have been easy for you, Ms Martin, but whatever information you can give us will be most appreciated.'

The two men started to leave the room when James looked back. 'Bye, Claire,' he said. 'Nice to meet you.'

And they were gone.

Would she ever see James Cowan again?

Claire had many questions she wanted to ask her parents: questions about Eddy, about the accident, about the investigation, and about James.

Her opportunity came that evening when Bill and Sonia arrived.

'A policeman came this afternoon,' Claire said, puzzled. 'He asked me about the accident.'

They were surprised and rather annoyed to hear that the police had been in to interview her so soon.

'Oh, that's a bit tough on you, Claire. We haven't even had time to explain what's been happening since you've been in here,' Bill said as he dragged an extra chair across to her bedside.

'The sergeant talked about an investigation. What's that all about?'

'They suspect that Eddy beat you up and tried to kill you.'

'What!' Claire responded. 'Eddy wouldn't do that. What makes them think such a thing?'

'Because you were found injured and unconscious in Paxton Avenue, not far from Eddy's place,' Bill explained.

Sonia quickly added her bit. 'And there was blood leading up to *his* back door,' she said. 'And your duffel bag was on Eddy's back porch!'

'Oh, my goodness,' Claire sighed.

Bill took Claire's hand in his and continued. 'Eddy was arrested the next day and released on bail. There was a preliminary hearing, and a trial has been set for early next month.'

'Poor Eddy.'

'Poor Eddy, my foot!' Sonia rebuffed. 'Don't feel sorry for him. Think about what *you* have been through.'

Claire sighed and lowered her head. 'I can't remember much about what happened. But I don't think Eddy hurt me.'

Sonia tutted.

Claire wiggled about, readjusted her pillows, and then asked about James Cowan.

Sonia's demeanour lightened instantly.

The following day Nurse Myer was on the early shift. Partway through her morning rounds, she stopped in to chat with Claire. 'Has Doctor Carlson mentioned when you'll be going home?'

'No, not yet, but I hope it will be soon. I can't wait to get back to a normal life again.'

'Normal? What's that?' she said tongue-in-cheek.

Claire laughed. 'Yes, I know what you mean.'

The nurse wrapped the blood pressure cuff around Claire's arm and pumped. With the stethoscope in place, she slowly released the pressure, watched the gauge, and listened.

Suddenly, there was a rapid increase in Claire's pulse rate. Nurse Myer hadn't noticed the young man enter the room, but Claire had.

James Cowan excused himself and was about to leave when Nurse Myer called him back. 'Come in. I was just about to leave,' she said. Loosening the cuff from Claire's arm, she squeezed out the excess air and gave a subtle wink.

'I'll see you later, Claire,' she said, with another wink, and quickly disappeared around the corner.

James walked slowly into the room and apologised again. He smiled shyly. 'These are for you,' he said and held out a bunch of colourful flowers and a box of chocolates.

'Oh, thank you,' she said and graciously accepted the gift. 'That's very nice of you. You didn't have to do that.'

'It's the least I could do for you; besides, it's my pleasure.'

'Would you like to sit down?' Claire asked, clutching the sheet, and raising it a little higher to her chest.

He sat in the armchair closest to the bed and Claire breathed in the soft fragrance of his aftershave. *I think it is the same one Dad uses*, she mused. *I've always liked that musky smell.*

'So, you didn't bring the sergeant with you this time?'

'Nope. Thought I'd leave him back at the station, he seems to be a pretty busy guy.'

It felt like the conversation was exhausted, neither of them knowing what to say next. Eventually, Claire broke the silence. 'Where do you live?' she asked.

'I'm from Adelaide,' he explained and clasping his fingers together, looped them over one knee. 'Came to Perth on business, but I need to stay around until after the trial. So, I thought I'd come to see you.'

'Wow! Adelaide. You're a long way from home. Sorry you have to stay back on my account,' she said, crossing her fingers behind her back. 'Tell me more about what happened the night you found me.'

He looked concerned. 'I don't want to upset you by talking about it.'

'I won't get upset. I'm trying to piece it all together in my mind.'

'I understand. Okay then, I'll tell you, but promise to stop me if it bothers you.'

Claire nodded, and James continued.

'It was a dark windy night … seemed like a storm was brewing. I was driving slowly along Paxton Avenue when I noticed something on the side of the road. I stopped the car and went over to see what it was. It was you, Claire – you were lying there, motionless. I touched your arm; you were cold. I was scared. There was no one else in sight. I popped the boot, found a blanket, and covered you. Then I phoned emergency and waited for help. That's all I know, Claire.

'I've given my statement to the police, so I don't understand why they need me to stay for the trial. I can't add any more to that.'

He looked into Claire's eyes. *Maybe I do know why I'm here*, he thought.

'What about you, Claire? Have you remembered any more since yesterday? Or don't you want to talk about it? I understand if you don't, it must have been terrifying for you.'

'They're blaming Eddy. They say he hurt me, but I don't believe he did.'

James shuddered at the mention of Eddy. *Oh no, she still has feelings for him. How could she? I met the fellow.* He exhaled a puff of air through pursed lips. 'Eddy was drunk when he arrived at court for the hearing. It's a wonder they didn't lock him up there and then. But his lawyer did all the talking for him and he got away with it – this time,' he said firmly.

Claire put her hand to her forehead and, resting the elbow in the palm of her other hand, lowered her head. 'I wish I could remember what happened that night. I think I fell over something outside. It was dark. I heard a bang, then a crack. And my leg hurt, and my head was throbbing. I was scared. I had to get away.' She paused. 'But I'm sure I would remember if Eddy had hit me. I'm positive he didn't,' she said, shaking her head.

'Sergeant Jones wants you to make a statement. He's hoping you will lay charges against Eddy.'

'What! No way!'

'Promise me you'll think about it, Claire.'

'I'll think about it,' she said, lowering her gaze.

James felt uneasy. 'I'm sorry if I've upset you. It was wrong of me to bring up the subject.'

Claire looked at him. She, too, was sorry – sorry about her bad reaction – but she dared not admit it. 'That's all right,' she said. 'I have to face it sooner or later.'

James stood and moved toward the door. 'I'll head off now,' he said. 'Can I see you again?'

'Yes,' she replied and, not quite knowing what else to say, added, 'Thank you for the flowers and chocolates and thank you for coming.'

James smiled from the doorway. 'You're welcome,' he said, and then he was gone.

He did visit her again –the next day, and the next, and the next.

Claire recovered enough to leave hospital and, following her discharge, returned each day to spend time with Ella. The bond between mother and baby grew stronger, and Claire longed for the day she would take her baby girl home.

Sonia kept busy taxiing Claire to and from the hospital and keeping up with her household duties. She smiled to herself when, from time to time, she caught a glimpse of young James on one of his frequent visits to the hospital where he would meet Claire and take her for coffee.

Home alone, Bill picked up the phone and called Eddy. He was about to hang up when a gruff voice answered. 'Yeah, what-d' want?'

Bill's heart pounded in his chest. He took a deep breath. 'Hi, Eddy. It's Bill Martin.'

Eddy grunted.

Bill continued, 'I was wondering if you've taken the blood test that I suggested you have; the one to determine if you are Ella's father?'

'Yeah, I had the bloody test. They tried to kill me. Stabbed a huge needle in me arm and drained me blood.'

Bill smothered a chuckle. 'You poor thing,' he said. 'That must have hurt. But have you got the results yet?'

'Yeah, they recon the kid's mine.'

'In that case, congratulations, Eddy,' Bill said.

'Whatever,' Eddy replied, and ended the call.

The day of the trial arrived. Claire hobbled into the courtroom on crutches accompanied by her parents. And, to everyone's surprise, Eddy arrived early and sat quietly beside his lawyer, clean, neatly dressed and sober. He looked across to Claire, smiled, and mouthed, 'I love you.' Claire smiled back.

One by one the witnesses were called to give their statements and answer questions.

Claire stood, as best she could, repeated the oath and gave her account of the incident.

'Did Edward Simpson attack you?' the lawyer asked.

Claire straightened her back and, in no uncertain terms, answered the question. 'No, sir.'

'Are you sure? Think carefully. Did Edward Simpson harm you in any way?'

'No, sir, he did not.'

'Tell the court then how you sustain those injuries.'

Claire hung her head. 'I can't recall, sir,' she mumbled.

The lawyer tutted in frustration, and said, 'You may take your seat.'

Satisfied, the judge gave his verdict. 'In the case before me today I find the accused, Edward Simpson, not guilty.'

'Yes!' Eddy exclaimed, jumping to his feet.

'Quiet, please. Order in the court,' came the directive. 'All stand.'

After the judge had left the room, the court was dismissed.

Eddy threw his arms around Claire almost knocking her off her feet. 'Thank you for helping me,' he said and held her tight.

Bill asked the lawyer where they stood now regarding the restraining order. 'Does the outcome of today's hearing cancel the existing restraining order?' he asked.

'I'm afraid so. Sorry about that, mate. I did all I could.'

Outside the courthouse, James stood back, forlorn.

'Why don't you come home with us?' Sonia suggested.

'Thanks, Mrs Martin, I'd rather not. I had better get back to the hotel and start packing,' he replied. He didn't want to be around if Eddy was going to be there. So off he wandered.

As he drove away, he glanced across and saw Claire and Eddy emerge from the building together, Eddy's arm slung lazily over Claire's shoulder and a smug expression on his face. Claire smiled up at Eddy.

Tears filled James' eyes as he thought of what might have been.

Sonia fumed. How she detested Eddy. And to think that now he was free to harass their daughter again. That was the last straw.

Hating to see Sonia upset, Bill put his arms around her and gently rubbed her back. 'Come on, darling. I'll take you home.'

'But what about Claire! We can't leave her with him,' she snarled.

He guided her over to a bench. 'You just sit down here; I'll go and ask her what she plans to do.'

Claire decided to return home, pack her things, and shift back in with Eddy.

Bill found it hard breaking the news to Sonia. And her reaction was predictable.

'I don't want him in the house,' she said through clenched teeth.

'Okay, I'll keep him talking outside while Claire gets her things,' he promised. 'I don't want her to go either, but there is nothing we can do about it. She's an adult and we have to let her make her own decisions.'

'But she's making the wrong decision, again!' Sonia sobbed. 'I know she is.'

'Come on, darling. I'll take you home.'

The air in the car hung thick as they drove home. Sonia's annoyance was palpable. Bill remained quiet as he focused on the road ahead, while at the same time trying to reign in his own emotions.

He'd no sooner stopped the car than Sonia jumped out, slammed the door, and ran up the pathway and into the house.

The garage door lifted slowly. Bill then inched the car forward, brought it to a stop, pulled on the hand brake and turned off the ignition. His head flopped forward and rested on the steering wheel. When the garage door lowered and he was alone at last, he allowed his tears to flow.

The sound of screeching brakes broke the silence alerting him to the arrival of Eddy and his own precious daughter.

He pulled himself together, climbed out of the car and went to meet them.

Eddy remained in his vehicle revving the engine impatiently.

Claire struggled from the car, tucked the crutches under her arms and hobbled towards her dad. Her face beaming with happiness, she threw her arms around him and kissed his cheek. 'Oh, Dad, I'm so happy. Eddy and I will be a real family now.' She stepped back and looked into her father's face.

Bill couldn't hide his disappointment.

'Aren't you happy for me, Dad?' she asked in surprise.

Bill sniffed and lowered his eyes, his face wet with tears.

'My princess,' he pleaded, 'your mother and I love you so much, and we don't want to see you hurt again. Are you sure you want to go back to Eddy?'

'Oh, Daddy, don't worry about me. Eddy is going to look after me.'

Eddy revved the engine and shouted, 'Come on, luv. We gotta get going. Hurry up and get your stuff.'

'Coming,' Claire replied and hurried as best she could.

'Mum,' she called. But there was no reply.

Gathering her few things together, Claire paused, glanced back over her shoulder then left the house.

At first, Bill hadn't noticed his daughter struggling out of the house, a backpack slung over one shoulder and trying to balance two overstuffed bags, one in each hand while manoeuvring on wooden crutches. He hurried to help her. 'Let me take those,' he said. 'Where would you like me to put them? On the back seat or in the boot?'

'Don't open the boot,' Eddy commanded. And Bill wondered what he might be hiding.

Bill pulled open the back passenger door with a *crunch*, pushed aside empty beer cans and a pile of unsavoury-looking magazines and rubbish, and piled the luggage on the seat.

'Claire, when you get to Eddy's, don't you go trying to carry those bags by yourself,' he said, hoping Eddy would get the hint. He helped her into the car and closed the door.

Claire wound down the window and smiled. 'Thanks, Dad. I'll be in touch.' But before he could reply the vehicle took off, tyres screeching and smoke pouring from the exhaust.

Bill scratched his head and frowned.

Entering the house, he found Sonia in a state of exhaustion. She had cried until there were no more tears left to cry. He put his arms around her and held her close. 'It's all right, darling,' he said and stroked her tear-moistened hair. 'Let's put it all into God's hands, shall we?'

Sonia blinked. Her eyes stung. 'That's about all we can do now,' she sighed.

They both agreed that it wasn't so much "all" they could do, but it was the very best thing to do.

So, they prayed.

Chapter 7

James sat alone in the hotel room, his head in his hands. He had packed his bags, but it was too early to leave for the airport. His heart was heavy as he thought of Claire. How he longed to see her, to talk to her, to rescue her from Eddy. But his hands were tied, there was absolutely nothing he could do. Then he thought about the baby; the little one who had, in such a short time, won his heart.

I may not be able to see Claire, he thought, *but nothing can stop me from seeing Ella.* So, after checking out of the hotel, he headed to the hospital.

He parked the car and followed his usual daily route through to the special care nursery and waited at the viewing window.

Nurse Myer spotted him and smiled. 'Want to see Ella?' she mouthed from inside the room.

'Yes please,' he replied silently.

She wheeled the baby's crib across to the window, turned it around to face him and pulled the little rug away from Ella's face.

James stood gazing in wonder at the tiny baby whom he'd grown to love so much. Tears spilled from his eyes.

Ella opened her little eyes and stretched an arm toward him as if waving goodbye.

Nurse Myer frowned with concern for James; he didn't seem quite himself, so she went out to see him.

'Are you all right?' she asked.

James didn't answer.

'Where's Claire? She hasn't been to see the baby today. Do you know when she's coming in?'

James cleared his throat and wiped his eyes. 'She had to go to court today,' he explained.

'Oh, how did that go?'

'Not good. Her partner Eddy was exonerated, and it looks like she's gone back to him again.'

'Oh no. I can't believe it!' Nurse Myer put her arms around James and breathed in the soft fragrance of his aftershave. 'I'm so sorry,' she said, 'I really thought she was finished with that disastrous relationship. And I thought that you two had a thing going.'

'That's what I thought too,' James replied sadly.

'What are you going to do now?' she asked.

'Go back to Adelaide.' He looked at his watch. 'My flight is due to leave in just under two hours, and I have to return the car before check-in, so I'd better get going.'

'I could keep you up to date with the baby's progress if you'd like me to,' she suggested, hopefully.

'Would you really do that for me? That would be much appreciated,' he said and, reaching into the inside pocket of his jacket, he pulled out his business card and handed it to her.

'Yes, I'll be happy to do that for you,' she said and held the card to her chest.

James said goodbye and thanked her for all she'd done for them. Francine smiled up at him, threw her arms around his neck and held on longer than usual. He pushed away. Embarrassed, she retreated, gave a wave, and went back inside.

James, lingering at the nursery window and with tears in his eyes, blew a kiss and whispered his final goodbye.

Claire flopped exhausted into a rickety chair in the dingy lounge room thankful that at least Eddy had carried one of her bags into the house.

She took a few minutes to catch her breath then asked Eddy if he would take her to the hospital to see baby Ella.

'No need to go today, luv,' he said. 'You just take it easy. The nurses will look after the kid for you; that's what they're paid for.'

'Okay, if you say so,' she replied reluctantly.

Eddy stretched out on the tattered recliner, stubby in one hand, a cigarette in the other. He flicked a head of ash onto the floor.

'When we gonna eat?' he demanded.

'What is there to eat?' Claire asked.

'I dunno. You're here now, that's your worry.'

Claire struggled to her feet, tucked a crutch under each arm and hobbled off to the kitchen.

Balancing on one crutch, she pushed aside rubbish strewn across the floor with the other. Having made a pathway, she ventured to the sink that was stacked full of dirty dishes. The smell caused her to gag. Clearing more debris, she manoeuvred her way to the fridge and opened the door. There was nothing edible inside, only a green furry mould covering something that could have once been bread or cheese. *Who knows? Perhaps there's food in the cupboard,* she thought, and to her surprise there was one tin of baked beans, some stale cracker biscuits and, right at the back of the shelf, a packet of two-minute noodles. *Good,* she thought, *I'm sure I can make a meal out of that.*

Clearing a space on the bench top, she began the food preparation.

'Eddy,' she called, 'do you know where the tin opener is?'

'It's in the sink.'

Claire sighed. She made her way cautiously across the kitchen and then, balancing on one crutch, began to move aside dirty dishes, pots and pans, mugs, and other things, until she finally reached the cutlery at the bottom of the pile. Rummaging around, she tried to find the tin opener. Suddenly she let out a scream as her finger caught on the blade of a sharp knife. Blood poured from a deep gash. She grabbed a tea towel, shook out the resident cockroaches and wrapped her hand, trying desperately to stem the flow.

Eddy stomped into the kitchen, scowling. 'What are you doing now, woman?'

Clutching the side of the sink, Claire began to sway. Her one good leg crumbled under her, and she fell to the floor.

Eddy sighed. 'I s'pose I better take you to the hospital or they'll blame me for bashing you again.' He nudged her with his foot. 'Come on, wake up you crazy bitch.' She didn't move, so he filled a bowl with water and tipped it over her head.

Claire spluttered. 'Where am I?' she cried.

'Looks like you hurt your hand, so get up. I'm taking you to the hospital.'

Claire moaned and tried to sit up.

Impatiently, Eddy held out his rough, nicotine-stained hand and yanked her to her feet. 'Come on, you're dripping blood on my floor,' he said and thrust the crutches at her.

The engine of the old car spluttered and coughed before finally bursting into life. The tyres screeched as Eddy took off.

Claire felt woozy and didn't remember much of the trip to the hospital. Eddy parked in the "Ambulance Only" area at the front door of Emergency. He left Claire sitting in the car, went straight up to the nurse's station and demanded they come and get her from the car immediately.

'You just wait your turn, mister,' the receptionist retorted.

'But she's bleedin' all over my car.'

'Just a moment, I'll get someone to take a look at her,' she said and messaged the nurse in charge.

Claire was put in a wheelchair and taken to an examination cubicle while Eddy supposedly shifted the car to an authorised parking bay. But instead, he took off, leaving Claire to fend for herself.

Having had the wound cleaned, sutured and dressed, Claire was told she could go home.

Home, she thought, *where is home?* Could she face returning to the squalor she'd just left? *Why did Eddy go? Why didn't he stay with me when I needed him? Dad would have stayed.* Claire's mind went back to her parents; she thought of their love for her, their constant support and how they were always there for her no matter what she did. But then again, she reasoned, *Eddy is the father of our baby and I know he will change; he just needs a bit of love and understanding. And I'm sure it won't take me long to clean up the house.*

Claire took her mobile phone from her pocket and tried to ring Eddy. The call went to voice mail. 'Hi Ed, it's me; I'm all through at the hospital; could you come and pick me up, please?' She finished the call and waited.

Eddy never came for her; he didn't even answer her message. With tearful eyes, she called home.

Sonia answered the phone. There was a crackling noise on the line, but the sound of Claire's voice warmed her heart. She hadn't expected to hear from her daughter so soon. Sonia cleared her dry, parched throat and swallowed. 'Hello, darling, is everything all right?'

Claire sniffed. 'I'm ringing from the hospital, Mum.'

But before she could explain further her mother cut in. 'Oh, that's good. It's nice of you to phone me. I haven't got up there to see Ella today. How is she?'

'I don't know, Mum,' Claire replied impatiently. 'Actually, I'm waiting in Emergency.'

'Emergency! What's wrong?'

'I just cut my finger and needed a few stitches, that's all.'

'Is Eddy with you?'

'No. I tried to phone him, but he mustn't have got my message yet. I've been waiting here for a long time, and I was wondering if you or Dad would mind coming to pick me up.'

'Of course we will, dear. You wait right where you are, and we'll be there in a jiffy.'

'Thanks, Mum, I love you.'

'I love you too darling. See you soon.'

Bill knew by the smile on Sonia's face that it was good news. 'What's happening?' he asked.

'I'll tell you on the way,' she said as she grabbed her coat and bag.

Bill collected the car keys. 'Where are we off to this time?' he asked.

Sonia talked like a thrashing machine filling in the details.

'That's all well and good, my darling, but did she say where she wants us to take her?'

Sonia looked puzzled. 'No, not really,' she said hesitantly. 'But I thought she would want to come home, here, with us.'

'Maybe. But let's not jump to conclusions. She might want us to take her to Eddy's.'

'I hope not,' Sonia replied then fell silent.

Claire was in the waiting room when the sliding glass doors opened, and Bill and Sonia entered. She stood slowly and, balancing on her one good foot, smiled. 'Thanks for coming,' she said, fumbling for her crutches. Just as she grabbed one of them, the other slid off the plastic chair. 'Oh, what a nuisance,' she mumbled.

'Don't you try and get it,' Bill said, and bending over he picked up the other crutch and gave it to her. 'There we go, darling. Now are you ready to go home?'

'Yes, please, Dad.'

'Home to our place?'

'Yes.'

Arriving home, Claire breathed in the sweet smell. 'I'll try Eddy's phone later,' she said and sat in the closest recliner.

It had truly been a tumultuous day for all of them.

Claire never did get to ring Eddy that day; or the next, or the next and Eddy failed to contact her, much to Sonia's relief.

And they didn't even bother to go back to retrieve Claire's belongings. Instead, mother and daughter enjoyed a great shopping spree and bought new clothes for Claire and the baby.

Bill and Sonia were happy and content to have their daughter home with them.

Chapter 8

Nurse Myer seized the opportunity to contact James. First, she sent a simple text message.

HI JAMES, I HOPE YOU HAD A GOOD FLIGHT BACK TO ADELAIDE. BABY ELLA IS DOING WELL.

REGARDS, FRANCINE MYER.

She waited, hoping for a reply.

James checked his phone and read the message. He was pleased to hear good news about the baby, but his heart ached for Claire. He pressed Reply and punched in a short acknowledgement.

THANKS, JAMES.

Francine waited a whole day before sending another message.

HI JAMES, ELLA IS GAINING WEIGHT AND SHOULD BE RELEASED FROM HOSPITAL SOON. HOPE YOU ARE WELL. She paused. *How should I sign off?* She wrote LOVE. Then quickly deleted it and settled for CHEERS, FRANCINE.

How she would have loved to add kisses, hugs, and a love heart. *Not yet*, she thought, *it's a bit soon.*

James returned to work, his heart as heavy as his workload. He tried to concentrate, but his thoughts were miles away. He thought about Claire and wondered how she was coping with Eddy. Anger boiled in him at the mere thought of the man. How could Claire even consider being with him? But she was – well, so he thought.

Claire settled in at her parent's home, and Sonia, always the mother, enjoyed every minute of it. Claire's health improved; her hand injury healed, and her leg recovered enough to enable her to walk without crutches, albeit with a slight limp; her cuts mended, and the bruises faded. All in all, she looked a picture of health.

Their daily visits to the hospital were happy times. They took turns in cuddling and caring for the baby. Ella thrived.

Nurse Francine Myer felt desperate. She had heard from Sharon Reid that Claire was no longer with Eddy. *I wonder if James knows about that,* she pondered. Adding to her frustration was the fact that the baby, her one link with James, would soon be discharged from her care. *Drats,* she thought. *What am I going to do?*

So, she launched her final missile.

DEAR JAMES, she wrote. ELLA IS DOING WELL, WILL KEEP YOU UP TO DATE WITH HER PROGRESS. INCIDENTALLY I WILL BE IN ADELAIDE SOON, NEVER BEEN BEFORE AND DON'T KNOW ANYONE THERE. PERHAPS WE COULD MEET AND MAYBE YOU WOULD SHOW ME THE ROPES? I AWAIT YOUR REPLY.

YOUR FRIEND,

FRANCINE.

Sonia and Claire both noticed how evasive Nurse Myer had become. She used to be friendly and bubbly, but lately, she'd been giving them the cold shoulder for some reason. *Oh, well, maybe she's just overworked or has personal problems,* they concluded.

But others had noticed it too.

Sharon, who was probably her closest colleague, had tried to find out what was wrong with her, but without success. 'You really need that holiday, I think that's what it is,' she suggested.

Francine blushed. 'Yes, I think you're right.'

'You're going to miss little Ella when she goes home. I think she's your favourite. You give her more attention than all the other babies put together,' she said light-heartedly.

Francine nodded. 'It's strange how some win your heart more than others.'

Reading the text message, James scratched his head. *Nurse Myer coming to Adelaide? That's a strange coincidence*, he thought quite innocently. A half smile lifted his face. *Perhaps she'll have news of Claire*, he hoped.

Francine checked her phone again. There was still no reply from James. She paced the floor. *He might be out of credit*, she thought, *or maybe he's in a meeting and has the phone switched off.* Her heart thumped hard against her ribs. *Or*, she hated the thought, *maybe he thinks I'm too forward.* She re-read the last message she'd sent. *I'm stupid. I should never have asked him to show me the ropes. Why did I do it?*

Just then her mobile phone pinged. *A message!*

HI FRANCINE,

RECEIVED YOUR MESSAGE. PLEASE LET ME KNOW WHEN YOU WILL BE ARRIVING, AND I'LL ENDEAVOUR TO MEET YOU.

REGARDS, JAMES.

She smiled. *Well at least he didn't ignore me*, she thought and breathed a sigh of relief.

The Martin household was full of excitement. The day had come at last for them to bring little Ella home. It was a beautiful day; the winter sun shone brightly, casting soft shadows through the still, bare branches.

Claire arrived at the hospital hardly able to wipe the smile off her face. Bill and Sonia walked along beside her, Bill carrying the baby capsule and Sonia clutching her camera.

After Ella's bath and feed, Claire dressed her in a little white 00000 Wonder suit, the smallest size made! She just swam in it; her little feet disappeared right up into the leg piece and, even when the sleeves had been rolled several times, her hands were nowhere to be seen.

'You poor little darling,' Claire chuckled. 'One day you will grow into it.'

Claire slipped the tiny pink doll's bonnet onto Ella's head – it fitted perfectly.

'Oh,' Sonia gasped, 'doesn't she look beautiful? Now let me take some photos before you put her in the capsule.'

So out came the camera.

The photo session was drawing to a close when Claire called to Nurse Myer. 'Come on, we must get a picture of you with the baby,' she said, beckoning her over.

Reluctantly, she stepped forward. 'Just one photo. I have a very busy morning,' she said with a poker face and, taking Ella in her arms, posed for the camera.

'Smile.' Sonia focused the camera. 'That's better, thank you, dear.'

Francine's heart was in her mouth. She was the one on duty and the one assigned to escort the mother and baby to the vehicle. She hastily bundled the baby into the capsule, fastened the safety straps, picked it up and, straightening her back, moved efficiently toward the door. Claire followed in close pursuit with Bill by her side.

Sonia looked back, scanning the area to make sure they hadn't left anything behind. She quickly thanked the nursing staff for all they'd done, slung the camera bag over her shoulder and hurried to catch up with the others.

Francine, still annoyed with herself for not getting a copy of the photo of her holding the baby, arrived in Adelaide and, to her delight, James was there to meet her.

'Hi there,' he said and reached out to take one of her bags. 'It's good to see you. How was your flight?'

Francine caught her breath and smiled. 'Good to see you too,' she said coyly, 'I had a good flight, thank you.'

'Is this all of your luggage?' he asked.

'No, I've got one case to pick up from the carousel.'

'Well, in that *case*,' he said, 'we have time for a coffee. Would you like one?'

'Yes, please,' she answered eagerly even though she wasn't thirsty.

James took her to the café and, resting his hand gently under her elbow, guided her toward a table. He placed the bag down and pulled the chair out for her.

Francine smiled up at him. *Wow, what a gentleman*, she thought.

He ordered their coffee and returned to the table. 'I can't wait to hear about Ella,' he said. 'How is she doing?'

'I believe she's doing fine since being released from hospital,' Francine replied abruptly.

'And Claire? How is she?'

'I haven't seen her, or her partner Eddy since she took the baby home.'

James went quiet.

Francine felt uncomfortable and slightly ashamed for the way she'd deceived him. But she justified herself in that she hadn't actually told a lie.

James collected the order and brought the coffees to the table. 'Here we go,' he said.

Francine emptied two sachets of sugar into her mug and stirred vigorously. 'Thanks, James. I owe you one,' she said.

He took a sip of coffee. It was hot. *Oh blow, this is going to take forever.* He turned to Francine. 'Would you like some cold milk for your coffee?' he asked.

'No, thank you, I like to drink mine hot,' she replied.

And so, they sat in silence and sipped their *hot* coffee.

Finally finishing their drink, they made their way to the luggage carousel. The crowd had dispersed leaving only a few lingering passengers.

Francine pointed to her case, one of only a handful still circling on the conveyor belt.

James was surprised at the size and weight of it. 'How long did you say you are planning to stay?' he asked seriously. 'I thought you were only coming for a week.'

'A girl needs to bring what a girl needs to bring,' she replied with a frivolous grin.

'I'm glad it has wheels,' he groaned, and stacked the other bags on top. 'Well, we're off then,' he added and headed for the exit.

Arriving at the car, James popped the boot, stood back, scratched his head, and wondered how he was going to fit it all in.

He transferred his own gear onto the back seat. Then, with a mighty heave, lifted the largest suitcase up and over the edge of the boot, letting it drop with a thud. Next, he managed to squash another bag in beside the case. Then, placing his hands on the small of his back, he stretched to relieve some of the stiffness from his spine. Eventually, with the boot closed and the last of the luggage stowed on the floor of the back seat, James opened the front passenger door for Francine and wondered with a sigh just what he'd gotten himself into.

Driving carefully from the airport, James turned onto the main highway and, keeping his eyes on the road ahead, tried to make light conversation. 'So, you've never been to Adelaide before,' he said.

'No, this is my first time.'

'And what brings you here?'

Francine adjusted the seatbelt strap on her shoulder and tried to think of an appropriate answer. 'Umm, actually I thought it would be a nice place to visit,' she said and bit her bottom lip. *That was a stupid answer,* she thought.

'Well, I hope you enjoy your visit,' James replied.

Just then the GPS sounded. In two hundred metres, turn right on the roundabout, and take the third exit.

'It's not far to go now. We're almost at the hotel. Just around this corner and you'll be able to see it.' James flicked the indicator to turn right. 'There it is,' he said, pointing to the sandstone building up ahead. The sun glistened on its glass panels, giving the illusion of a golden palace.

'Oh, it's beautiful!' Francine exclaimed. 'Thank you so much.'

'You're welcome.' James pulled the car into the circular driveway, turned off the engine, popped the boot and walked around to the other side and opened the passenger door.

'Thank you again,' she said, showing a bit of knee as she climbed from the car.

James turned his head away.

A porter arrived and welcomed them.

'Oh no. I'm not staying,' James quickly explained. 'It's just the lady here.'

James started to unload the luggage.

'Here, let me do that,' the porter said, and, taking the large case, he hoisted it onto the trolley.

Francine stood back and waited until all her things had been unloaded.

James thanked the porter and was about to get into the car when Francine called to him.

'When will I see you again?' she asked.

'I'll pick you up from here and take you to the airport when you're ready to go. Just send me a text message when you're ready.'

Francine's expression changed. 'I thought we would be able to catch up while I'm here,' she said, putting on her best puppy-dog face.

'I've got a very busy week at work,' James explained. 'I'll be in the office all day tomorrow, then off to the country for four days. Sorry.'

'Oh, I can go with you. I'd love to see the country.'

James felt rather sorry for the poor girl, all alone in a strange city. 'I'm afraid it would be against company policy to take you along. But I tell you what, I'll phone you on Friday when I get back and we'll see what can be arranged. Besides, there's lots for you to do in Adelaide – there's the beaches, the city, and the bus service is really great. Check at the reception desk … I'm sure they'll have a map of the city, and the Tourist Bureau has lots of information about tours and places to go.'

James waved goodbye, started the car, and, with a sigh of relief, pulled away from the kerb. The car felt stuffy. He wound down the windows in an effort to eliminate the after smell from Francine's perfume. He coughed. *I'm so glad I've got a busy week,* he thought.

Francine flopped onto the plush king-size bed, disappointed that her plans for the week had been quashed. *Now how am I going to fill in this stupid week in Adelaide?* she thought.

Chapter 9

When James returned from his trip to the country, he was tired and hungry, but satisfied with the result; the business was doing well. And, after a good meal and a long hot shower, he was ready to relax, but he'd promised to phone Francine. He looked at his watch. *If I wait another hour or two, it will be too late to arrange anything for tonight and then there is only the weekend to get through.* So, he waited.

Having endured five days of utter boredom, Francine paced up and down the room, phone in hand, waiting for James to call. *He's not going to ring*, she thought and, picking up the remote control, turned on the television. She flicked from channel to channel. There was nothing worth watching. It was late. She had to do something. Anything! *Friday night in Adelaide … surely the place comes alive.*

She slipped into a slinky black dress, reapplied heavy glamour makeup and wiggled her feet into the highest of her high heels. She looked in the mirror with approval, grabbed an evening bag and jacket and hobbled out of the room, slamming the door behind her.

The nightclub's atmosphere was thick, and many of the patrons were already intoxicated. Francine wandered across to the bar.

'What's you having, dear?' asked the barman.

'Surprise me,' she replied with a couldn't-care-less attitude.

'Surprise you? Well, that's an invitation.' He mixed the brew and handed it over the counter. 'Here you go … try this.'

Francine turned, but as she did a bulbous man knocked her arm causing the entire contents of her glass to spill over the front of her dress. 'Now look what you've done, you stupid man,' she yelled.

'Sorry, luv. Here let me fix it for yu,' he said, wiping his filthy hand down her front.

'Get away from me,' she yelled and pushed him so hard that he fell and lay motionless on the wet floor.

Francine backed slowly away, her heart beating hard in her chest. In the commotion that followed, she made a hasty exit.

Making her way along the darkened street, Francine opened her purse and fumbled for her mobile. It wasn't there. *Oh no*, she gasped, *I must have dropped it in the pub, but there's no way I'm going back for it.* She sniffed and shivered in the night air. Tears welled in her eyes and cascaded down her mascara-stained cheeks. She started to run.

The pavement was uneven, and the heel of her shoe caught. Her body lurched forward. She heard the crack. *Oh no,* she thought, clutching her burning leg. But it was only the heel of her shoe that had broken and snapped completely off.

Forlorn, she hobbled the rest of the way back to the hotel.

Fortunately, there weren't any guests in the brightly lit foyer when she limped through the door.

The receptionist took one look at the bedraggled girl, lowered her eyes and with a slight smirk, played ignorant.

Francine rummaged through her bag, found the swipe card, and entered her room; she kicked off what remained of her best shoes, dumped her bag on the bed and went straight through to the en suite. Stripping off, she soaked her dress in the washbasin and took a long hot shower.

After such a disastrous night out, she decided to go to bed and read a book. But, as she pulled the doona back, something hard and cold slipped from the bed and hit her sore foot. *What now!* she thought. She looked down and there on the floor was her mobile phone. Thank goodness, at least something has gone my way at last. She opened the phone and noticed a message. It was from James.

Hi Francine,

I'm back. It's too late to go out tonight. Would you like to meet for coffee tomorrow afternoon?

Regards, James.

She checked the time: 2:53 am. It was too late to ring back, so pressing reply, she tried to formulate an appropriate response.

Dear James … *Stop. Delete 'dear.'*

Sorry I missed your call. She deleted *'call'* and changed it to *'message.'* Will ring you in the morning.

Love, *delete 'love.'* Cheers. *That's better.* Francine.

She reread the message and pressed, "Send."

Early next morning, James' mobile phone rang. He cringed, took a deep breath, and reluctantly swiped his finger across the screen.

'Hi Francine.'

'James! I was just wondering what your plans are for today?'

'Busy this morning. I have a bit of paperwork to catch up on plus business reports due in on Monday. What about you?'

'Oh, nothing planned. Is it still on for coffee this afternoon?'

'Yes, that'll be fine. And I was thinking about going to an Art Exhibition later. Would you like to join me?' There was silence on the other end of the line. 'Francine, are you still there?'

'Yeah.' A loud gulp was audible. 'But I'm not really into art.'

'That's all right. Would you rather go to the movies?'

A smile swept across her face. 'Oh yes. That's more my scene.'

'I don't know what's showing,' James said.

'That's okay. I can check it out and get back to you.'

'I'll tell you what, you decide which show you want to see, and I'll pick you up … say 2:30? You can just let me know then.'

'I'll be ready. Thank you, James,' she said in a saucy tone. 'I'll

be waiting out the front for you. I'm never late you know. See you.'
She sighed and ended the call.

James felt flustered. But reassuring himself that it would only be an afternoon matinee, he wiped his brow and returned to the business at hand.

For James the morning seemed to fly, but for Francine, it dragged on like a never-ending story. She caught the bus to the city, sat and drank coffee for half an hour then wandered up one side of the main street and down the other, bored. Any other time she would've enjoyed shopping, but not today – her mind was on other things, actually on another person – James.

She looked at her watch. *Only 11:52. It's not even lunchtime! Oh, blow this*, she thought. *I might as well go back to the hotel as waste more time here.*

She climbed up the bus steps, flashed her ticket to the driver, and slumped into the closest seat.

As the bus neared her stop, Francine wondered if she should stay on board and do the circuit again just to fill in time, but she pressed the red button, stood up and, grabbing the overhead handle, waited for the bus to come to a halt. 'Thanks, driver,' she said unenthusiastically and got off.

James checked the time. *Don't know how I'm going to get all this finished*, he thought. *At least I've done Monday and Tuesday's reports; now for Wednesday's.* He closed his eyes, leaned back in the chair and, placing his hands behind his head, tried to formulate the next sentence. *I can't repeat the same words*, he thought, *must put it a different way.* But try as he may nothing jelled. Frustrated, he closed the folder and pushed it aside. *I know what I need, another coffee.*

Francine tried another outfit and frowned at what she saw in the mirror. 'No, don't like it,' she said and stripped off again! She tossed the clothes on top of the ever-growing pile of discards on the floor. 'I need something smart but casual, not too over-the-top – it's got to be just right.'

She looked through what remained in the wardrobe. 'Maybe I need something a bit dressy just in case he takes me to dinner after the movie. Oh, what a dilemma.' Finally, she decided to wear black pants and a flimsy red low-cut blouse together with high-heeled shoes, a matching handbag and her black suede jacket. 'Yes! I like it. That's the one,' she said, meeting the approval of her reflection.

James pulled into the circular driveway of the hotel and looked at his watch; it was 2:25 pm. He drove slowly around and pulled into one of the allocated parking bays.

Francine was waiting. She ran toward the car. 'Hi, James,' she mouthed, waving the movie tickets in the air. But before he could get out of the car, she opened the passenger door and smiled. 'I told you I'd be early. And here I am!'

'Hi, Francine. I see you've already got the tickets!'

'Yeah, I picked them up when I was in town this morning,' she said and flopped into the seat.

'So, what time does the movie start?'

'Three o'clock.'

'That's good. Thanks for getting the tickets, at least we won't have to line up and wait for them when we get there, and we'll still have time for coffee before we go in.'

Francine secured her seat belt and wiggled into the seat. 'Yeah, that's what I thought too.'

'Did you enjoy your morning in town?' James asked as he pulled into the traffic.

'Yeah.' Francine lied and then changed the subject. 'Did you finish all that work you wanted to get done?'

'Unfortunately not,' James sighed. 'I just couldn't concentrate properly.'

Francine grinned and rolled her shoulder seductively. *I wonder if he was thinking of me*, she thought. 'Never mind, James, you can just relax and enjoy yourself for the rest of the day.'

James parked the car in the cinema car park and then took Francine for coffee. The picture theatre was packed for the afternoon matinee.

'Umm, the popcorn smells great! Would you like some?' he asked as he ushered her past the ticket box and through to the counter.

'Yes please,' she replied.

James shuffled forward and placed his order. 'Two medium popcorns, please.'

'Why don't you make that, one large box,' Francine suggested. 'That's better value.'

Turning back to the girl, he apologized, 'Sorry, would you change that to one large popcorn. And is there anything else you would like? A drink? An ice cream?'

Francine shook her head. 'No, thanks. Not just now. I might want something more at interval or after the movie,' she suggested hopefully.

Theatre Three was packed. James looked around to see if there were any other guys in the room, then he spotted two fellas sitting on the other side of the aisle. *Phew!* he thought, *at least I'm not the only male in the place.* Then he looked again and noticed the two fellas were holding hands. He gulped. *Oh, not a chic-flick! Why did I let Francine choose the movie?* he asked himself. But it was too late.

Francine chose seats near the back, right in the middle of the row. Good for viewing, but not so good for escaping! Francine sat on his left. On his right sat a rather large, loud-mouthed, female in her mid-forties; she reeked of strong body odour and garlic.

Francine rested her hand on James' leg. 'Isn't this exciting? It's the movie I've been waiting to see. And I couldn't have picked a better friend to share it with.'

James couldn't agree – less! It was not the way he expected to spend his Saturday afternoon, but he was stuck with it – for now anyway.

The movie went on and on and, sharing popcorn proved a bad idea. Each time he reached into the box, Francine's hand just happened to brush against his. As much as he tried to focus on the story, it just wasn't his style. His mind drifted to the other side of the country, to Perth and what might have been.

At last, the credits began to roll.

'Wasn't that just the best movie ever?' Francine exclaimed. 'I've never gone through so many tissues in my life. Thanks for bringing me, James. You're a pal.'

Thankfully, James didn't have to answer the question, and before he had time to take a breath, Francine was already onto another subject.

'What are we going to do now?' she asked as the crowd inched toward the exit.

James looked at his watch. 'Let's wait until we get out into the fresh air, and we can think about it then,' he said, his head throbbing like a bongo drum.

Eventually, outside, James took a deep breath and rolled his shoulders. 'That's better,' he said and pointed out a quiet restaurant further along the café strip. 'That's a good place to eat. Would you like to have dinner there?'

Francine jumped at the offer. 'Yes, please. I'm famished.'

'We can leave the car and walk if that's okay with you.'

'That's fine,' she said with a grin as wide as a chasm. She leaned close and wove her arm through his. 'Isn't this nice?'

James remained quiet as they made their way through the press of people out for a good time Saturday night.

The waiter showed them to a table for two, unfolded the linen napkins and placed one on each lap. 'Would you like to look at the wine list, sir?' he asked.

James looked at Francine. 'Do you drink?'

'Oh yes,' she said and grabbed the list from the waiter. 'How about you, James. What are you having?'

'No alcohol for me, thanks; I'll just have water.'

What a goodie, goodie, Francine thought as she pondered the list.

James poured water into both glasses and waited.

'I'll have a glass of Sparkling White,' she said, pointing to the most expensive wine on the list.

James signalled the waiter and ordered. 'And what would you like to eat?'

'Since it's my last night in Adelaide, I think I'll have the Lobster and salad.'

The waiter brought Francine her drink and took their dinner order: Lobster and salad for two. 'And would you like to order dessert now, or shall I bring the list back later?'

James was about to delay the second-course order, but before he replied, Francine cut in. 'Yes, please, I'll have pavlova and cream and ice cream with strawberries.'

Turning to James, the waiter asked, 'And for you, sir?'

Not wanting to delay the evening's procedures, James ordered the fruit salad.

The meal was pleasant enough, with not too much of a wait between courses. Francine's wine glass was topped up several times during the evening, and James was glad he had a generous credit card limit.

Draining the last of his coffee, he folded his serviette and placed it on the table, and covering his mouth, he gave a little cough. 'Are you just about ready to go, Francine?'

'I need one last drink to wash it all down.'

'Shall I order coffee?'

'Oh no!' she slurred. 'I need something stronger than that.'

James poured water into her glass. 'I think that will wash it down for you. Besides, it's time for me to take you back to the hotel.'

Francine rolled her bottom lip. 'But it's Saturday night! My last night here! I can't go back yet.'

James' patience was thinning. 'Well, I have to get home. I've got work to finish.' He checked the time. 'And it's getting late.'

Francine pouted. 'I don't want to go.'

James stood. He walked around the table, put his hands on the back of Francine's chair and coaxed her up. She grabbed her jacket and handbag and staggered toward the door. James steadied her. 'Wait, I need to pay the bill,' he said.

'I like you, James. Do you like me?' She hiccupped. 'You can come back to the hotel with me.'

'Let's just get you back to the car,' James said as the waiter handed back his credit card. 'Thank you, sir, the food was great!'

'Good luck to you, sir,' the waiter smirked.

They arrived back at the hotel relatively unscathed. James parked the car and helped his passenger into the hotel foyer. Francine leaned heavily on his arm. 'There we go,' he said, 'back safe and sound.'

'You'll have to take me to me room,' Francine mumbled.

James steered her to a plush leather couch. 'There, now you just wait here while I get someone to help.'

She slumped back into the seat and let out a long loud belch. 'Yes, James. Whatever you say.'

The reception desk was busy, and James joined the queue. While waiting he kept glancing over his shoulder to check on Francine.

'Can I help you, sir?' asked the receptionist.

'Yes, I've just dropped off one of your guests. I'm afraid she is a little intoxicated and may need assistance to get to her room. She's sitting over there,' James turned and pointed to where Francine should have been sitting. 'Oh, looks like she's gone. She must have made her own way up to the room. Sorry to bother you.'

'That's no bother. Thank you for caring. Have a good evening, sir.'

'Phew!' James let out a whispered sigh.

As the hotel doors opened, a wisp of fresh air soothed his burning face.

Exhausted and relieved, he climbed into the car, wound down the window and moved off slowly.

Suddenly something caught his eye. He froze. Was it a flashback? Like a nightmare rising from the dark?

James sat transfixed, his hands frozen on the steering wheel. He blinked, and as he did, the image came into focus; a pair of startled eyes stared back at him like a rabbit caught in the spotlight.

Just then a car sped past and came to a sudden stop alongside the frightened figure.

James jumped from the car. 'No, no, she's with me!' he yelled as he sprinted toward Francine.

The car took off.

James stooped and gently helped the fragile girl to her feet. Then, flinging her arms around his neck, she cooed, 'Oh, James, you rescued me. I knew you loved me.'

'Shh, don't you worry now; everything's going to be all right. Just give me your arm, lean on me and I'll help you back to your room.'

'Thank you, James.'

Together they staggered through the foyer and caught the lift to the third floor. Francine rummaged through her handbag, found the swipe key, and, handing it to James, asked, 'So what are we going to do tomorrow?'

James unlocked the heavy wooden door and held it open for Francine. 'I'll pick you up from the hotel at three o'clock and take you to the airport.'

'What about the morning?'

'I'll be busy all morning, and into the afternoon.'

Francine pouted. 'But it's my last day in Adelaide and I have to do something! Why can't you take me somewhere?'

'There's plenty of things for you to do to fill the time,' he said, and noticing the pile of discarded clothes on the floor added, 'and you'll need time to finish off your packing as well. Besides, I take my mother to church on Sunday morning, and she always cooks lunch for me, then we go for a little drive. It's what she looks forward to all week, so you see I can't change that.'

'I could go with you,' Francine suggested. 'Anyway, I'm supposed to check out of the hotel by ten o'clock, and I can't drag my bags around town all afternoon!' she exaggerated.

James scratched his head and tried to think quickly. He knew that if he mentioned "bringing a girl home" to his mother, she would probably jump to the wrong conclusion. The mere thought of bringing this particular girl home almost paralysed him with fear.

'I'm sure the hotel would have a room where you could leave your luggage for a few hours,' he suggested.

'Dunno.' She shrugged.

James backed toward the door and rested his hand on the knob. 'Look, I'll go down and check with Reception and let you know.' He opened the door and, holding it ajar, added, 'I'll have a little think about tomorrow, see what we can do, just leave it with me.'

He approached the desk in the lobby with his query and was told that, not only could the luggage be left securely for the time required, also an eleven o'clock, late check-out could be requested. He thanked the Receptionist, pulled out his mobile phone and punched in a message.

HI FRANCINE,

GOOD NEWS! YOU CAN LEAVE LUGGAGE AT HOTEL, CAN REQUEST LATE DEPARTURE, 11:00AM!

REGARDS, JAMES

Ping! Francine's phone sounded. She read the message and pressed 'Reply'.

James was driving home when the message came through to his phone. He didn't stop to read it. *Can wait 'til I get home*, he thought. *Besides, I've got a lot of figuring to do — about tomorrow. Francine is the problem. I don't want her upset. I can't afford to have her upset; I need to ask a favour - BUT what about Mum?*

Umm...

I could delay taking Mum out for a drive. Mm... Maybe? What if I put it off until after I drop Francine at the airport, say about five, five thirtyish? It might work. I could make it a surprise! Yes, that's what I'll do. Tell her she needs to have rest in the afternoon, like a "Nanna nap", and be ready for something special later. I'd make it something memorable like taking her out for coffee (although I know she only drinks tea) then I could take her to see the city lights. And I've got an idea there might be a cruise ship in port. I could take her down to the docks she'd enjoy that. Yes! That should work out.

James parked the car in his unit's driveway, his brain still sparking with ideas. He looked at his watch. It was too late to message Francine now. I'll do it in the morning. I hope *it suits her,* *h*e thought.

Alert and excited with ideas, he decided to put his energy into finishing off the business reports for Monday and worked late into the night.

Satisfied and with reports finished and tomorrow organised, he fell asleep.

Chapter 10

Sunday, at 8:00 am, James took his phone, swiped the screen, scrolled up, and hovered over the name. He pressed 'Call' and waited. After a few rings, voice mail cut in: "Sorry, I'm not available to answer your call. Leave a message, and I'll get back to you."

'Morning, Francine. James here. Just wondering if you organised the late checkout. If you get this message before nine ring me back. Oh, no don't ring me; I'll ring you when I'm free. Bye.'

Having parked the car, James ran up the path and rapped on the door.

'Coming,' Gloria called as she hurried down the hall to answer the door.

'Hi, Mum, you look lovely.' James put his arms around his mother and held her in a tight embrace. He was her only son and the only one in the family who lived close enough to visit her regularly. Their father had died four years earlier and his older sister and her husband lived in Melbourne with their three children and only came to visit during school holidays. His younger sister was doing her first year of teaching in the country and was planning to come home for Christmas.

James checked his watch. 'Are you ready to go?' he asked with a mischievous grin.

Gloria Cowan turned to her son. 'Of course I'm ready. You know I'm always ready and waiting for you,' she chided him.

'Yes, I know you are Mum. Come on, I've got something exciting to tell you.'

Gloria's face lit up. She turned, pulled the door to and locked the security screen. 'Come on, don't keep me in suspense, spit it out.'

James took hold of his mother's hand. 'It's a surprise and you'll have to wait 'til we get in the car, then I'll tell you. Do you think you can wait?'

'Yes, if you hurry,' she said and pulled him along faster.

'Oh, Mum, you're a wag.'

The drive to church was always pleasant, Mum asking lots of questions and James talking about his week at work. On this morning, however, time passed quickly with James sharing his plans for the evening.

'Well, yes, that sounds wonderful, dear, but why don't you stay with me for the afternoon. That'll save you going home and driving all the way back again to pick me up.'

'Actually, there are things I need to do this afternoon,' he said and quickly added, 'Remember, I've been working away all week, and I need to catch up.'

'Okay, but don't be late.'

As they pulled into the church car park, his mobile phone on the dashboard rang. Gloria reached forward. 'Would you like me to answer that for you, dear?'

'No, no, just leave it to voice message. I'll look at it later.' James suspected Francine was ringing, and he didn't want his mother to find, out about her.

They were ten minutes early for the service and Gloria headed over to chat with a couple of her friends. Once James saw she was occupied he ducked back to the car, retrieved his phone, and checked the message. Sure enough, it was Francine. He didn't reply. Instead, he put it on mute and slipped it into his pocket.

It was a good thing he had put the phone on mute because he felt it vibrate three times during the service. He gritted his teeth and silently cursed. *That silly girl. She knew I was taking Mum to Church, and I told her not to ring. She'll just have to wait!*

The doxology concluded, the blessing was given, and people began to move out of the auditorium. James accompanied his mother to the adjoining hall for morning tea and left her with her friends. Gloria enjoyed catching up with "the girls" as they called each other, and as soon as they were engrossed in conversation, James excused himself.

He sat in the car and replied to Francine's messages.

HI FRANCINE,

SORRY COULDN'T REPLY SOONER. HAVE RESCHEDULED MY AFTERNOON. WILL MEET YOU AT HOTEL 1PM. TAKE YOU OUT FOR THE AFTERNOON THEN TO AIRPORT WHEN YOU'RE READY IF THAT'S OK WITH YOU. REGARDS, JAMES

He pressed 'Send' and waited.

He didn't have to wait long before the reply came.

OH JAMES, THANK YOU SO MUCH. WILL BE WAITING OUTSIDE THE HOTEL. CAN'T WAIT TO SEE YOU. YOUR FRIEND, FRANCINE XXX

He didn't reply. He didn't need to.

Back in the Church Hall, Gloria and "the girls" chatted on. James finished his coffee and hovered around their table trying to catch his mother's eye. He didn't want to rush her, but at the same time, he had a tight schedule and couldn't afford to dilly-dally.

Anna, one of "the girls", noticed James standing behind his mother. 'I think your son is ready to go Gloria. I wish I had a handsome son to take me home.'

James blushed. *Why do they always have to say things like that?* he thought with embarrassment.

Gloria gathered her belongings, said goodbye to her friends and took hold of her son's arm.

'Bye, Gloria dear,' Chrissie said, 'see you next week.' And the others added their farewells.

James led his mother to the car, opened the door and held her bag while she got in and settled.

'Thank you, son,' she said and fastened the seat belt.

'Now, wasn't that a lovely service, James? Did you enjoy the message?'

'Yes,' he answered automatically without thinking it through. *Did I enjoy that message?* he asked himself. *I can't even remember what it was about.*

'Did *you* enjoy the sermon, Mum?'

'Oh yes, it was great.'

'What part did you like the best?' he asked, fishing for clues.

'I liked the bit he read from the Bible about how God sees every tiny sparrow that falls to the ground. Then he said, "If God cares so much for the birds, then know that He loves you much more." Wow! God loves us so much that He sent Jesus, who had never sinned to take the blame and punishment for our sins, so we can be forgiven by God and become friends of God! That's great!'

'Yes, I remember the pastor saying that bit about the birds and something about flowers as well. I think it was in relation to how, because the birds don't worry about their next meal and the flowers aren't worried about how they look, then we shouldn't worry either. Is that right, Mum?'

'You got it, son, and here's me thinking that you weren't listening.'

'I was a tiny bit distracted, I must admit. It really has been a full-on week. But never mind … we'll have a nice quick lunch together, then I'll leave you to have a rest and I'll come back about five.'

James didn't want to eat much lunch at his mother's place; he had to leave room for a second meal with Francine.

'Come on, you can have a second helping,' Gloria coaxed.

'No, Mum, really, I'm not hungry.'

'It's not like you, James; you always go back for more. You're not sick, are you?' She felt his forehead.

'No, Mum, I'm not sick. I'm just tired.'

'All right then. You just leave the dishes; I'll do them later. You go home and get some rest.'

'Thanks, Mum. You sure you don't need a hand with those dishes?'

'No, go on, off you go.' She kissed his cheek and shooed him out. 'See you later.'

James put his arms around her, held her tight and kissed her tenderly. 'Bye, Mother dear.'

James was running late. The traffic seemed heavier than usual for a Sunday, and of course, he caught every red light.

Francine sat on her overstuffed suitcase surrounded by an odd assortment of other baggage.

Oh no, he thought. *How am I ever going to fit all that in the car?*

He pulled into the nearest pick-up bay and walked around the car. 'Hi, Francine. Sorry I'm late; the traffic was murder.'

'That's okay, James, I haven't been waiting long,' she lied.

'You must have done a lot of shopping while you were here,' he said and popped the boot. 'I'm not sure how it's all going to fit in. I'll put the big case in first. You might have to give me a hand. You take that end and I'll lift here. Are you ready? Right. Lift.'

James balanced his end of the case on his knee and manoeuvred it up onto the edge of the boot. 'Now you'll need to swivel your end around so it will go over the lip.'

'I can't do it,' Francine yelled and dropped her end.

James flinched in pain and let the case slide slowly to the ground. He grabbed the edge of his shirt, wrapped it around his hand and held it tight.

'Oh, I'm so sorry. Are you hurt?' Francine cried crocodile tears.

'Yes, I'm hurt,' he said, blood oozing through the fabric of his shirt.

He sat down on the kerb, put his head on his knees and waited.

Francine wrapped her arm around his shoulders and crouched on the path beside him. 'Are you all right?'

'Obviously not,' he said abruptly. 'You might need to get help.'

'Oh, does that mean you're not going to take me out tonight?'

James lifted his head and slowly unwrapped his hand. 'You have a look and tell me what you think.'

'Oh James, I didn't realise it was that bad. Quick, wrap it up again.'

As she turned to go for help a hotel porter came over to see what was happening. He took one look at James and beckoned for assistance.

'What happened?' he asked.

Francine answered, leaving out a few minor details. 'I'm a registered nurse,' she added. 'That wound will need stitching. Where's the nearest hospital?'

'Just a minute, Francine,' James interjected. 'Just how do you plan we get to the hospital?'

'I'll take you in your car of course.'

'Oh, I see. And what do you plan to do with your bags?'

She turned to the porter. 'Can I leave them here and pick them up later?'

'Under the circumstances, we should be able to work something out. Just leave it with me.'

He helped James into the car and gave directions to the hospital.

'I know how to get there,' James said, 'but are you sure you can drive my car?'

Francine adjusted the seat and revved the engine. 'Of course, I can. No trouble at all.'

The Emergency department of the local hospital was busy. Francine sat with James while they waited for an assessment.

'Next please,' the Triage Nurse called.

James stood. His head began to spin. He paused momentarily before moving toward the window.

'Name please.'

'James Cowan.'

'And what's the problem?'

'He's hurt his finger,' Francine answered.

The nurse frowned and looked directly at James. 'Mister Cowan, would you tell me how you sustained the injury.'

'I was lifting a suitcase into the car boot, and it fell on my finger.'

'I'll get you to uncover your hand and I'll take a look at it.'

James carefully peeled away the covering, and as he did, his head spun. He saw flashing lights, and then darkness enveloped him.

The next thing he remembered was being wheeled along a corridor on a hospital trolley, Francine by his side. 'Now my head hurts too,' he said.

'Keep your hand elevated,' Francine instructed. 'You must keep it above your heart.'

'Excuse me, Ms Myer, we give the instructions here.'

'I'm a nurse too you know, and I was with him when the accident happened, and I brought him into the hospital.'

'All the same, he's under our care now. So let us get on with the job.' The young man introduced himself. 'I'm Chad,' he said, and manoeuvred the trolley into the cubicle and drew the curtains. 'Do you think you will be able to move across to the bed?' he asked.

'I think so.' James tried to sit up.

'Just a minute, I'll give you a hand.' Chad slipped one arm under James' shoulder and slowly eased him to a sitting position. 'Just take your time Mister Cowan.'

'I could help you; you know?' Francine tutted.

'Yes, I know, you already told me.' He pointed to a chair in the corner. 'You can sit there,' he said.

Francine snubbed her nose and plonked herself down.

'The doctor will be in to see you shortly,' Chad said, wrapping a blood pressure cuff around his patient's right arm.

'Meanwhile, I'll take your Obs.' *I know. Don't say it. You could do it too,* he thought.

After completing the observations and filling in the relative information, he left them alone.

James looked at his watch, 'Well this isn't the way I planned to spend the afternoon. Sorry,' he said, 'I hope we won't be here too long. I'd like to at least be able to take you out for coffee before you head home.'

Francine sighed. 'I suppose I had better think of a plan B just in case you're not out of here in time. How long would it take to get to the airport from here?'

'About thirty-five minutes, I'd say, but you'd be best to allow three-quarters of an hour just to be on the safe side.'

'I have to check in by four-thirty, so if I have to get a taxi, I'd better order it for about three forty-five.'

'Don't forget you'll need to allow time to go back to the hotel to get your bags.'

'Oh drats! That means I'll have to leave here at three-thirty! What's the time now?'

'I make it two-twenty-two.'

'That leaves just over an hour. Well, we won't be going out for coffee.'

'Sorry, Francine, and you must be starving – you haven't had lunch.'

'What about you? You'll be hungry too.'

'No, I'm not hungry. Okay!'

The curtain moved. A young doctor and a nurse came in.

'Hello, I'm Doctor Bradley and this is Nurse Corrie.' The doctor extended his hand and James did a left-handed sideways shake. 'So, tell me, what have you been up to?'

James repeated the story, with Francine adding details.

'Right then, let's have a look at this finger.' Removing the gauze Doctor Bradley squeezed the edges gently. 'Mm, you've got quite a nasty gash there. It will need sutures, and I will have to irrigate the wound, but before that, I'll send you around to x-ray. How are you feeling?'

'Not too bad … a bit better than when I first came in.'

'That's good, because I heard all about the fuss you made in Reception.'

'Sorry about that, Doctor. I'm not usually given to fainting.'

'Never mind; we'll look after you. Wait here while I fill in the paperwork, and then the Nurse will take you to the X-ray in a wheelchair.

'Thanks, Doctor.'

Francine sat with her arms folded. 'What's the time now, James?' she asked impatiently.

'Two-forty-three. Do you want to go and get something to eat? There should be one of those food dispensers out there in the waiting area.'

Francine rubbed her tummy. 'Yeah, I suppose so. I'll see you soon,' she said and disappeared around the curtain.

James closed his eyes, pleased for a little peace and quiet.

'Wake up, Mister Cowan.' The nurse touched his arm. 'Time to go for your x-ray.'

Loaded into the wheelchair, he was whisked off to the X-ray Department. James shivered. The air-conditioning was so much cooler in the empty sterile X-ray room. The nurse introduced James to the Radiologist and handed the paperwork to him.

'Sit here and rest your arm on this,' he said. The radiologist moved his hand this way and that until he settled it in position. 'Now hold your arm still until I tell you.' He ducked behind the screen, clicked the button twice then re-appeared and re-arranged the arm once more. 'Same again,' he said, 'hold still.' Two more clicks and it was finished. 'You're free to go now, Mister Cowan.'

The nurse was waiting to take him back to the treatment room. 'Here we go. How was that? Not too uncomfortable?'

'It wasn't too bad, but I couldn't stop shaking, I was so cold.'

'Yes, it's always much cooler in there than in the consulting/treatment rooms. Anyway, when we get back, the doctor wants me to take some blood from you. Hope you don't mind.'

'Do I have a choice?'

'Well, actually you do, but I'll try to be gentle, I promise.'

'That's okay then.'

Francine was already sitting in the cubicle when they returned. 'I booked a taxi to pick me up from out the front at three-thirty.'

James looked at his watch it was two-fifty-seven. 'That means you've got just over half an hour!' he said.

The nurse helped James out of the wheelchair and back onto the bed. 'Are you warm enough, or would you like another blanket?'

'A blanket would be nice if you don't mind, thank you.'

'I'll be back soon.'

She'd no sooner left than Francine turned to James and made a snide remark. 'What do you mean, saying; "if you don't mind, thank you," that's their job, that's what they're paid for.'

'It doesn't hurt to be polite. Good manners cost nothing.'

Francine hung her head. 'Sorry, James. I'm just so disappointed with how today has turned out. I thought we'd have a lovely afternoon together, just the two of us. And here we are stuck in this awful place.'

'These things happen. It couldn't be helped.'

Just then the nurse came to do the blood test. Francine sat in the corner sulking.

James flinched slightly and turned his head. The nurse loosened the rubber tourniquet, removed the needle, and applied a pressure wad to the puncture spot. 'There, that wasn't so bad, was it?'

'Not too bad, I 'suppose, but I feel like a bit of a pin cushion.'

'Sorry to tell you, but the doctor has put you down for a tetanus jab as well.'

'When?'

'I might as well do it now, and get it over with.' She flicked the vial.

'Oh, you had it there all the time.'

'Yes, once we start jabbing, there's no stopping us,' she joked. 'Which arm?'

'Well, not the sore one,' James said and tried to push up his sleeve.

'Here, I'll do that,' Francine tutted.

'There you are, Mr Cowan,' Nurse Corrie said, 'all done.' She gathered her things and headed off.

'All this fuss and they haven't even fixed my finger yet.'

James checked his watch again. It was 3:08 pm. He turned to Francine. 'It's almost time for you to go and there's something I want to ask you.'

Francine sat bolt upright. 'Yes, James,' she replied enthusiastically.

'I wanted to ask a favour.'

'Anything at all.'

'Do you think it would be at all possible for you to try and find out Mr and Mrs Martin's address or phone number for me? Even their email would be great.'

With disappointment written all over her face, she sighed. 'I don't know about that. It wouldn't be right for me to look up medical files.'

James was quiet.

Francine sensed his disappointment and, not wanting to leave on a sad note, added, 'Just leave it with me, and I'll see what I can do.'

'Would you? I'd so appreciate your help.'

'Oh, James, when will I see you again? Will you be coming back to Perth any time soon?'

'Not as far as I know. But we could keep in touch. You've got my phone number and I've got yours. And would you let me know if, and when, you find the Martin's contact, please?'

Francine agreed, reluctantly.

Doctor Bradley poked his head around the edge of the curtain. 'Sorry to disturb you two lovebirds, but I'll have another look at that finger now.'

'Can I stay? I am a nurse and I've seen it all before.'

'Yes, you may.' *And I've heard it all before*, he thought.

The wound was cleaned, stitched, and dressed and James was given the all-clear to leave the hospital.

'Here, James, take my arm. You might be a bit unsteady on your feet for a while.' Francine smiled up at him.

'Thank you,' he said and looked at his watch. 'You'll be just in time to catch your taxi. I'll wait with you 'til it comes.'

'Do you think you'll be all right to drive? Or should you order a taxi and leave your car here until tomorrow?'

'I should be okay. I'll get myself a coffee and just sit for a while before I head off. Don't worry, I won't drive if I'm not up to it.'

Beep! Beep!

'Here's the taxi. Oh, James, I wish I didn't have to go. I feel like I should be staying here to look after you.' She threw her arms around his neck and kissed him passionately.

James pulled away. 'You'd better not keep the taxi driver waiting or he'll start the meter.'

Tears filled her eyes. 'Bye, James. I'll be in touch.'

He waved as the taxi drove away.

With just over an hour to fill before he was due to meet his mother, James thought about phoning her but changed his mind. He didn't want to mention the accident, she'd only worry, so he left the arrangements as they were. *I might as well go home for coffee. It's no point hanging around here. I'll go home, have a bite to eat, change out of these grotty clothes, tidy up and then go over to Mum's.*

Francine off loaded her baggage – at a cost – she was charged excess! That, plus the unexpected taxi fare and, to top it all off, her flight was delayed. She phoned James. It went to voice message. 'Hi James, it's me. You're not going to believe it, the flight's delayed. I could have stayed another hour, instead I'm stuck here twiddling my thumbs.'

James couldn't get to the phone when it rang; he was in the shower, his hand wrapped in a plastic bag. Checking the message later, he was pleased he hadn't had to talk to Francine – the message was enough.

James arrived at his Mum's with time to spare. He climbed the stairs and tapped out his signature knock on the doorpost.

Gloria opened the door. 'Whatever happened to you?' she gaped.

'I had a little accident.'

'What! How?'

'I was helping someone lift a case and accidently dropped it on my finger.'

'Is it all right?'

'Yes, it's not broken, just bruised, and cut. I got a couple of stitches but it's going to be fine. Nothing to worry about.'

James was relieved when his mother didn't quiz him further about the accident. She was more concerned about *him* than the details of how it happened.

'Well, are you ready for your big night out?' he asked.

'Oh darling, are you sure you're up to it? We don't have to go anywhere; we can just stay here, I don't mind. In fact, why don't you stay the night?'

'I can't do that, Mum. Thanks all the same, but I have work tomorrow.'

'How are you going to be able to work with your sore finger?'

He hadn't thought about that. He would just go in and do what he could.

'Come on, Mum, let me take you to see the city lights. There's a nice little café in the mall that specialises in handmade chocolates! That's going to be our first port of call. Oops! I think I might have given you a clue to our next stop.'

Gloria pulled the door to, locked the security screen, and, looping her hand through the crook of his arm, gave the okay. 'Onward, James, and don't spare the horses.'

'You used to say that when I was a little boy, but I think it was; "Home, James, and don't spare the horses," do you remember?'

Gloria chuckled. 'Of course I do. That was a long time ago, I'm surprised you still remember it.'

The night was still. City lights flickered in the crisp night air. James parked the car and took his mother by the arm.

'This is lovely, James. I can't remember the last time I visited the city at night. I think it was with your father. Yes, it was. It was on our Silver Wedding Anniversary.' Gloria's eyes glistened with delight as she relived those happy memories.

James stroked her hand. 'The café is just around the next corner,' I'm sure you'll like it.' The *clip, clip* of her shoes on the pavers echoed as they slowly walked arm-in-arm.

'Here it is, Mum.'

Gloria stopped and gazed in awe at the beautiful display of handmade chocolates in the window.

'Now, Mum, before I order the drinks, I want you to select ten, or more, of the chocolates you like best. I'll ask the young lady to put them in one of their exclusive carry bags. It's my shout tonight; my shout, your treat.'

'Oh, they're all so lovely, it's hard to choose.'

'Just take your time, we've got all night.'

James got so much pleasure from just watching his mother's face. She was like the proverbial "kid in a candy shop".

With her bag of treasures in one hand and holding on to James with the other they climbed the stairs to the mezzanine floor. From their rustic, old-world-style wooden table-for-two, they watched pedestrians as they scurried to and fro along the brightly lit mall.

'This is charming!' exclaimed Gloria. 'It's so quaint. I didn't know such a place existed.'

'Then I'll have to bring you here more often,' he said.

The waitress came with their order. 'A pot of Lady Grey tea-for-one for the lady, and cappuccino in a mug for the gentleman. And there's a chocolate éclair and our special triple-chocolate-slice. Would you like anything else with that order?'

'Thank you, dear, but I'll be surprised if we get through this lot.' Gloria laughed as she lifted the lid of the teapot. 'Oh, that smells divine.'

James poured milk into the fine China cup for his mother. 'Would you like me to pour your tea now or wait awhile?'

'You can leave it a minute, but I'll get you to cut the cake in half. I can't possibly eat all that.'

'Sure, you can! Wait 'til you taste it, it'll melt in your mouth. You'll eat that and look for more, just wait and see.'

James was right. Nothing was left on the plate except a few crumbs.'

'Well, did you enjoy that, Mother?'

Gloria wiped her mouth and placed the serviette beside the plate. 'That was absolutely delicious,' she said, draining the last of her tea.

They left the café, walked along the mall, and headed back to the car.

James' finger throbbed. The effect of the anaesthetic had worn off. He tried to ignore the pain and keep going for his mother's sake; she was so enjoying herself.

They took the thirty-minute scenic drive through the city, passed the Torrens River and on to the Outer Harbour Port where a large passenger cruise ship was berthed. Coloured lights reflected on the calm water creating a fairy-like atmosphere.

Gloria was awestruck. 'This is amazing! I'm so glad you brought me out here. You really spoil me.'

James reached toward his mother and pulled her close. 'You deserve to be spoilt after all you've done for us kids.'

Tears filled her eyes.

'What's wrong, Mum? Don't cry.'

Gloria clasped her hands together and lowered her head.

'Are you thinking about Dad?'

She nodded.

'Oh Mum, I didn't mean to upset you.'

Gloria smiled a sad smile. 'No, darling, I'm not really upset, just recalling happier times.'

'Come on, Mum, I'll take you home.'

As they drove back, a warm silence filled the car. There was no need for words; just being there, together, was all they needed.

Chapter 11

Bill and Sonia didn't want to spoil their new granddaughter, but she was so cute, and they couldn't just let her cry.

Ella thrived and Claire seemed thankful to have her parents help, especially at night. Sonia often took on the two or three hourly night feeds.

All was going well until Claire became restless. Bill and Sonia noticed the change in her. She grew moody and irritable and seemed to resent them for the time they were spending with the baby.

'What's wrong, Claire?' Sonia asked. 'Are you unwell?'

'No, I'm just fed up.'

'What do you mean?'

'I want to go back to Eddy.'

'Oh, Claire.' Sonia's heart sank. 'But what about Ella? She needs a good home.'

Claire looked daggers at her mother. 'What do you mean? Don't you think Eddy and I can give our daughter a good home?'

Sonia turned and left the room. She went downstairs, picked up the phone and rang Bill's work number. He answered on the second ring.

'Bill Martin here, can I help you?' There was silence, then a sniff and a muffled voice. 'Sonia, is that you? Are you all right?'

'No, I'm not all right. It's Claire, she wants to go back to Eddy and take Ella with her.' Sonia blew her nose and swallowed.

Bill sighed. 'Is she there?'

'Yes, she's upstairs.'

'Can you put her on the phone for me?'

'I'll try.' Sonia placed the phone on the table and tiptoed up the stairs. She tapped gently on the door. 'Claire, Dad's on the phone. He wants to talk to you.'

'Tell him I'm busy.'

'But, Claire, he's worried about you.'

'Tell him not to worry. I'm not his little girl anymore.'

Sonia knew it was no use trying to reason. Claire had made up her mind. She crept downstairs and passed the message on to Bill.'

'I'll talk with her when I get home. That's if she's …'

Sonia finished the sentence for him, 'Still here!'

'Now don't you go worrying. I'll try to get away early.' He checked the time. 'I'll just finish off here and be home as soon as I can. Okay? Are you going to be, okay?'

'Yes.'

'Are you sure? It's no good worrying you know, that's not going to help.'

'Yes, I know – well my head knows, but tell it to my heart.'

'I understand, my darling. My heart hurts too.' There was a pause and then a sad 'goodbye.'

Sonia hung up the phone. She turned around and flopped into the closest chair and sobbed bitterly. Ella began to cry, softly at first, just a few baby whimpers.

'You, poor little darling,' Sonia whispered. 'You don't want to leave us, do you?'

As if answering her question Ella's cry got louder, and Sonia's heart beat faster. She held off until she could wait no longer and then she rushed to the nursery and lifted the baby from her crib. Ella stopped crying. Sonia held her close and rocked her gently in her arms. *Hush, little baby, please don't cry...* Her voice cracked; she could sing no more.

When Bill pulled into the driveway, Eddy was already there, sitting in his car, revving the engine.

Bill parked his car in the garage, pressed the remote-control button for the roller door and took a long deep breath. 'Please,

Lord, give me strength and wisdom in this situation. I don't know what to do.'

Before he had time to gather his thoughts, two simple words went through his mind – keep loving. He shook his head. 'Wow!' he whispered, 'if that's you, God, thanks.'

Sonia dashed out through the internal garage door. 'Eddy's here! And Claire's packed her things! You've got to do something. Quick!'

Bill got out of the car and took her in his arms. Sonia wept bitterly.

'Don't worry. Everything's going to be all right.'

'How can you say that?'

Sonia pulled away and thumped her fists on his chest and with every beat re-emphasised each word; 'How – can – you – say – that?' With each thud, her energy seeped away until she slid slowly to her knees.

'Oh, my darling,' he said, tears pooling in his eyes. 'Come inside and we'll sort things out.' He helped her to her feet and guided her into the house.

Claire stood in the passageway, her things packed and ready to go. She turned to her father. 'Well, are you going to help me, or will I get Eddy to come in and get the things?'

Stunned, Bill led Sonia to the sofa. She looked up at him, her eyes red and swollen and her cheeks stained with tears. He kissed her forehead. 'I'll try and talk to her,' he whispered and ran his hand down her arm.

Bill turned. Claire was facing the other way. He walked over and stood in front of her. 'Where's Ella?' he asked.

'She's asleep in her cot.'

'Are you planning to take her with you?'

'Of course I am!'

'It's a shame to disturb her. Can't you wait until she wakes up?'

'But Eddy's waiting for me.'

'Why don't you ask Eddy to come in? He could have dinner with us.'

'No!' shouted Sonia.

'Mum doesn't want him to come in the house.'

'You just sit down and wait here. I'll go and talk to him.'

Claire stood firm, arms folded, defiant. 'Okay, if you must.'

Bill walked down the path to the car. He tapped on the passenger-side window. Eddy stubbed his cigarette on the dashboard, flicked the butt out through the window and opened the other door.

'Hi, mate, how're you going?' Bill tried to be civil.

'Aw' right, I s'pose,' Eddy replied.

'What's happening?'

'Dunno.'

'Looks like Claire's moving in with you. She's all packed.'

'Yeah, that's it.'

'How do you feel about having a baby in the house?'

'Yeah, long as it doesn't cry.'

'All babies cry, Eddy. That's a fact, you will have to accept it.'

'Yeah, s'pose.'

Bill looked at the back seat, cluttered with rubbish. 'You'll need to have a baby capsule fitted on the back seat.'

'Can't, haven't got one.'

'Well, you'll have to have one; it's the law. You can't travel with an unrestrained baby in a car. So, there's a problem, wouldn't you agree?'

'S'pose.'

'Look, Eddy, I'll go and talk to Claire. She probably hasn't thought about the capsule. I'll ask her what she wants to do.'

By the time Bill entered the house, Ella was awake and crying. Sonia hadn't moved from the sofa and Claire stood where she'd been when he left the house.

'Who's going to get Ella?'

No one moved. No answer came.

'I'll go up and get her, shall I?' Bill looked from one to the other. Still no response. 'It's all right, darling, I'm coming,' he said as he climbed the stairs two at a time.

Bill opened the nursery door, switched the light on low and walked over to the cot. Ella looked so tiny in her little crib. He leaned over and picked her up. She felt soft and warm. He held her close. 'I love you, my darling,' he whispered. Her crying stopped. She snuggled her head into his neck. 'How can I let you go?' he said as he breathed in her sweetness.

Beep, beep, beep! The blast from Eddy's horn broke the silence and Ella started to cry. 'Shh, don't cry, darling,' Bill said, and wrapping her in a soft rug, he carried her downstairs.

He handed the baby to Sonia. She took her in her arms, cuddled her close and began to gently rock her back and forth.

Daylight ebbed. Bill walked slowly to his daughter's side. He put his arm around her. 'Claire, Eddy doesn't have a baby seat for his car. I could take the one out of the back of my car, but it's getting dark, and it would be hard to see to be able to fit it properly. So, I suggest you wait until morning to do your move.'

Claire sighed. 'But Eddy's come all this way and he's been waiting so long; he'll be upset if he has to go home and come back tomorrow.'

'I'll go out and explain to him. I'm sure he'll understand.' Bill didn't wait for a reply; he hurried outside.

Bill leaned his elbows on the open window ledge. 'Hey, mate, it's getting late, and we think it would be best all round to leave the move 'til tomorrow.'

Eddy put the car into gear and, looking straight ahead, and with a pressure-flow of fowl obscenities, took off in a cloud of smoke.

Almost knocked off his feet, Bill staggered backwards clutching his arm. *Lord, you said, "keep loving," but how?*

The front door swung open, and Claire rushed out. 'What did you do to him?'

'I did nothing to him; it's what he did to me.'

Claire noticed he was holding his arm. 'Oh Dad, are you hurt?'

'It's my arm. It got knocked when Eddy sped off. That guy doesn't think of anyone but himself.'

The smell of car fumes lingered in the air as they made their way to the house.

Inside, Sonia sat nursing Ella. 'So, he's gone! Good!' She scowled.

Claire ran up the stairs and into her bedroom. The door slammed.

'Please be careful what you say,' Bill pleaded. 'Claire is in a very vulnerable state.'

'What about me? Do you care about my state?'

'Of course I do. You know I do,' he said and reached out his hand toward her.

Sonia noticed he was favouring his right arm. 'What's wrong with your arm?'

'It got knocked.'

Sonia leaned over and touched his arm. Bill winced. 'It's swollen; I can feel it through your shirt! Let me see!'

Bill carefully rolled his sleeve up revealing a lump the size of a chook egg.

'Did Eddy do that?'

'No, I bumped it on the side of the car when he took off.'

'You sure he didn't swerve to hit you on purpose?'

'Of course not! I was in the way, that's all.'

'I wouldn't put it past him. Nothing would surprise me as far as that …' she hesitated, '*thing* is concerned.' Ella began to wiggle and make a fuss in her arms. 'Bill, you sit down. I'll get an icepack for you.'

Sonia hurried into the kitchen, jiggling the baby on her hip.

Bill removed his shirt and examined his arm more closely. Not only was he sporting a huge lump on the elbow, but a graze extended the full length of his forearm, and bruising had already appeared.

Sonia handed Bill an ice pack wrapped in a light tea towel. 'Here, put this on the swelling.' She stepped back horrified. 'Oh, my goodness, that is bad.'

'It'll be okay. I think it looks worse than it is.'

'Does Claire know that Eddy did this to you?'

'Yes, she knows I'm hurt but, no, Eddy didn't "do this to me."'

'So, what's going to happen now?'

'How do you mean?'

'With Eddy? What's going to happen? Is he coming back?'

Bill shrugged. 'I really don't know. He went off in a rage.'

Ella lay peacefully in Sonia's arms making little baby noises as she sucked contentedly on her bottle. Sonia looked down. 'It's this little one I'm most concerned about. What future does she have if exposed to *his* behaviour?'

'I know, darling, I worry too.'

Bill and Sonia slept fitfully that night, with Sonia doing all the baby's night feeds, again!

When they went down for breakfast the next morning, Claire's baggage stood in the entranceway, undisturbed, but Claire made no appearance.

Bill got ready for work. 'There's no point in me hanging around here,' he told Sonia.

'But what if you-know-who turns up?'

'I don't think he will, but if he does just tell him that he cannot take Ella without a properly fitted baby car restraint. And that's all about it – no arguments. If he gives you any trouble, just ring me and, you can always phone the police.'

He kissed her goodbye and headed off.

By ten-thirty Sonia thought it time that Claire was up. She knocked on her door. 'Claire, it's time to get up, darling.'

'Go away.'

Sonia stood outside the door, stunned. 'But, Claire, Ella is due for her bath. Are you going to come down?'

'You do it. It'll be your last chance.'

Sonia's heart pounded hard in her chest and tears trickled from burning eyes. She turned and followed the baby's cry. 'I'm coming, darling, please don't cry.'

Bathtime was fun. Ella relaxed as the warm, soothing water swished around her tiny body, and Sonia cherished every precious moment spent with her granddaughter.

Sonia took her time to dress and feed the baby. As she did, tormenting questions played over in her mind – would this be the last time she'd get to hold Ella? Would Claire leave and not return? What if Claire cut her out of her life altogether? What if she never saw her granddaughter again? Sonia shook her head. *I mustn't think like that,* she resolved.

Warm and content, Ella fell asleep in her arms. Sonia laid her down in the little rocker and ran upstairs.

'Claire, I need to do some shopping. Ella's asleep; should I leave her here with you or do you want me to take her with me?'

'Whatever,' came the glum reply.

'I'll take her with me then. I should be home by about two. See you then. Love you. Bye.' She listened for a reply, but none came.

Sonia enjoyed taking Ella shopping with her. She was such a good baby, and people would often stop them in the mall and say what a beautiful baby she was, to which Sonia proudly agreed.

Arriving home after their shopping jaunt, Sonia unlocked the house and pushed open the door. The house seemed quiet. She looked around. Claire's belongings that had been in the hallway before she'd left were gone. With Ella in her arms, she ran upstairs. 'Claire!' she called, but no answer came. The door to Claire's room was open, the room empty.

Downstairs, the light flashed on the telephone, indicating a missed call. Sonia pressed 'Play'.

'Hi, darling, Bill here. Would you ring me back when you get this message?'

She returned the call. Bill explained how Claire had phoned to say Eddy had come to take her home with him and that Ella was with you. 'Then she told me to take Ella to their place tomorrow.' Bill choked back a tear. 'Is Ella, okay? Are you all right?' he asked.

Sonia sobbed. 'Yes, we're both safe.'

'I'm coming home, darling; I'll be there soon. Is there anything you need?'

'No, I've just come in from shopping. All I need is you.'

'Okay, I'll see you soon. Love you.'

Sonia placed the receiver back on its cradle and waited.

With a bag of baby clothes in one hand and a large package of disposable nappies under the other arm, Claire hurried through to the spare room. She was pleasantly surprised to see that Eddy had made an effort to tidy the house. The kitchen floor, although dirty, was actually visible and there were only a few dirty dishes in the sink.

In what was to be the baby's room, Claire smoothed and straightened the grotty, old doona, and covered it with a clean sheet. She put the nappies, wipes and baby toiletries at one end and laid Ella's clothes neatly at the other end of the bed. Then she went about making a cosy makeshift bed for Ella in the middle; she rolled up two large bath towels to form the sides and threw a soft flannelette cot sheet over the top.

Happy with her creation, she turned to go, but there, in the doorway, Eddy stood blocking her exit. He grabbed both her wrists and pulled her into him.

'Not now, Eddy,' she protested.

'Isn't that what you came back for?'

'Yes, but ...'

He smothered her lips with his mouth, ripped her shirt and threw her onto the bed.

'You're mucking up the baby's things,' she said, but it was no use resisting. Her body tensed. He was rough and selfish. It finished quickly. Claire lay still. Eddy, energy spent and overtaken with exhaustion, went to sleep. Claire felt the heaviness of his body on hers and, knowing he was asleep, slowly wriggled free. *That's not at all how I wanted it to be*, she thought, and wrapping her shirt around herself she fastened her jeans and shivered.

Claire tiptoed down the hall and opened the bathroom door. The stench hit her hard. He obviously hadn't cleaned that room. Holding her breath, she pried open the window, disturbing thick cobwebs and causing a black-widow spider to flee. Releasing her breath, she stood as close as she dared to the window and filled her lungs with fresh air.

She flushed the toilet. It didn't help. The washbasin sported a ring of grease as black as the spider she'd disturbed. The cake of soap (which Claire had left the last time she was there) was now withered and cracked.

Number one on the shopping list, Claire noted, *Bathroom cleansers! And soap!*

Claire looked for a comb. There was none, so wiping the mirror with the back of her hand, she raked her fingers through her tangled hair and splashed cold water on her face. She felt for a towel with no success, so she chose to air-dry instead.

Claire heard the car pull into the driveway and went out to meet them. Ella looked peaceful and snug as she lay fast asleep in her baby capsule in the back of her grandfather's car. Claire was surprised to see her mother in the passenger seat.

Bill got out and wrapped his arms around her. 'Are you sure this is what you want?' he asked.

'Yes, Dad, I think I'm sure,' she said hesitantly.

'Well, you know that we're always only a phone call away.'

'Thanks, Dad.'

Sonia let herself out of the car and wandered over. 'Are you all right, darling,' she said. 'You look flushed.'

'I'm fine, Mum. Don't worry about me.'

'Look, your blouse is torn and you've lost a button.'

'Yeah, I noticed that.'

Sonia looked around. 'Where's your car?' she asked.

'Oh, didn't I tell you? We needed to pay some bills, so we sold it to one of Eddy's mates.'

'Oh, did *we* now?' Sonia was annoyed; she and Bill had bought that car for Claire. *How dare he sell it to pay* his *bills!* 'So how are you going get around without a car?'

'Eddy will drive me. He'll take me anywhere I need to go.'

'Oh, that's good of him,' she said sarcastically.

'Never mind now,' Bill intercepted. 'Let's get this little one out of the warm car and inside.' He disengaged the locking mechanism and lifted the baby capsule from its housing. Ella remained fast asleep.

Sonia popped the boot and handed Claire a box of goodies. 'There are two tins of baby formula in there plus six bottles. I thought that would be enough to get you through – for a while anyway. I've kept one tin of formula and a couple of bottles at home for when you come to visit,' she said and grabbed another bag full of baby things from the back.

'Thanks, Mum, you've been great. I love you.'

'I love you too,' she said and shut the boot.

It was dark inside the house and Sonia had difficulty adjusting her eyes to the change. 'Will you open the curtains so we can see better?' she asked.

'Eddy likes to keep them shut,' Claire replied.

'Oh, I see!' tutted Sonia. 'By the way, where is Eddy?'

'He's asleep at the moment.'

'Oh, poor fellow. Too much for him, is it?'

Bill, still holding the baby capsule, cleared his throat. 'Where would you like me to put Ella?' he asked.

'Um,' Claire looked around the room and quickly thought; *Oh, my goodness, I don't want to take them into Eddy's bedroom, and they mustn't see him on Ella's bed.* 'You can just put her here on the floor at the moment,' she said, pointing to a reasonably clear spot.

'You sure?'

'Yes, I'll sort things out later.'

'What about a cot? Do you have a cot or bassinette for her?' Sonia asked.

'Not yet, but we will get one.'

'Where's she going to sleep in the meantime? You can't leave her in the capsule too long.'

'It's all right, Mum. Don't you worry, I'll sort it.'

Bill placed the baby capsule on the floor and walked across to Sonia. 'I think it's time for us to head off now,' he said, and turned to Claire. 'Bye, darling, do look after yourself.' He held her in his arms and stroked her hair. 'Say goodbye to your mother,' he whispered.

Claire said her goodbyes, wiped her eyes and followed them to the car.

As they drove away, Sonia felt like her heart was tearing apart.

They had only gone a short distance when Bill tapped his forehead. 'Oh no,' he said, 'I forgot to leave the mounting for the baby capsule. Should we turn back?'

Sonia sighed. 'I couldn't go through all that again. Let's wait until tomorrow because we'll have to take the pram over as well. I'm sure she hasn't got one there. I'll phone Claire when we get home and ask if we can drop them in tomorrow.'

'You're right. She won't need them right away.'

For the remainder of the drive home, Bill and Sonia sat in silence, contemplating the future.

Not wanting to disturb Eddy, and while Ella was fast asleep, Claire went quietly about making up her next bottle in readiness for when she woke.

She looked around the room. It was dark. *Perhaps if I open the curtains just a smidgen Eddy might not notice*, she thought. *Be nice to let a little light in.* Taking hold of both curtains, she carefully separated them, disturbing the dust. She coughed. A beam of sunlight entered the room highlighting a display of tiny dust-fairies in concert. Claire smiled, rubbed her nose and sneezed. 'Oops,' she whispered covering her mouth, 'hope I didn't wake Eddy.'

Ella began to stir while Eddy slept on.

'Hello, darling,' Claire said softly, and lifted her out of the capsule. She sprinkled a few drops of milk onto her wrist; the temperature was just right, and Ella was ready for her feed.

Claire held her close; the warmth from her tiny body reassured her and eased her doubts.

The mobile phone beeped. A text message was from her mother.

HI DARLING, SORRY WE FORGOT TO LEAVE THE THING-A-ME-BOB THAT GOES IN THE CAR FOR THE BABY'S CAPSULE. WOULD IT BE ALL RIGHT FOR US TO BRING IT OVER TOMORROW? WE COULD BRING THE PRAM TOO IF YOU LIKE. LET'S KNOW.

LOVE,

MUM XXX

Claire sent a reply without asking Eddy's opinion.

THANKS, MUM, THAT'D BE GREAT. LOVE, CLAIRE XX

When Eddy finally roused from his *beauty sleep and* stumbled into the room, Claire jumped to her feet, flung her arms around his neck and kissed his cheek. 'Mum and Dad have been. They brought Ella. Would you like to hold her so I can get a photo?'

'No!' came the sharp reply.

'Oh,' she said, taken aback. 'I thought you would have been hanging out to hold your *own* daughter for the very first time.'

'Well, you're wrong.'

For the rest of the day, Claire, feeling like she was treading on the proverbial eggshells, tried to steer clear of Ed. *He'll come round — eventually*, she thought.

Chapter 12

Ella woke just after midnight. At first, Claire didn't hear her cry, but Eddy did. Turning over, he landed an all-mighty kick right in the middle of her calf muscle.

'Stop that kid crying,' he growled and pushed her out of bed.

Blurry-eyed, Claire picked herself up and hobbled through to the baby's room. She flicked the light switch. *Bang! Flash! Fizz!* Then darkness. Ella's cry grew louder. Claire felt her way across to the bed and picked her up. 'Shh,' she whispered and tried to remember the words of the song her mother sang. *Hush little baby* … that's all she knew. Wrapping Ella in a rug, she felt her way through to the kitchen and switched on the light. *Success! Hooray!*

Eddy grumbled, 'Turn that bloody light off!'

'How can I make the baby's bottle in the dark?' she retorted.

'You work it out. I need my sleep.'

Right, she thought, jiggling Ella. *Idea! The microwave!* Before switching the main light off, she opened it; the light inside came on. *Good, that should do*, she thought and quickly turned the main light off. Then, by the dim light from the microwave, she mixed the formula, placed the bottle inside and shut the door. *Blow! Now I can't see the buttons to press.* She opened the door again and memorised the keypad. *Success.* But the noise of the microwave seemed to amplify in the stillness of night. Eddy started to complain once more.

'Sorry, Ed,' she said. 'It won't be long. I'll work out something better for tomorrow.'

The microwave beeped three times, each beep seeming louder than the last.

Ouch! It's too hot! Oh no. Leaving the microwave door open, Claire shuffled over to the sink, turned on the cold water tap, and shoved the bottle under the running water. It seemed to take forever to cool the milk enough for Ella to drink.

With Ella in her arms, Claire crept back into the room and, trying not to wake Ed, slid quietly under the covers. She turned on the night light and started to feed Ella. Before she'd half-finished the bottle, both she and Claire had dozed off to sleep. But suddenly a fierce roar awakened them.

'What do you think you're at bringing that into my bed! Git it out of here!'

Claire jumped out of bed. She couldn't believe what she was hearing. Startled by the noise, Ella screamed.

'Now look what you've done,' Claire protested.

'What I've done? It's what you've done bringing that kid in here.'

'But she's your baby too.' Claire shivered, and tears rolled down her cheeks. She howled like a baby. They both cried together.

In the darkness, Claire did her best to change Ella's nappy and settle her down again. Not daring to go back to Eddy's room, she spent the rest of the night with her daughter.

Mid-morning the next day Bill and Sonia arrived at Eddy's to the sight of him, head under the bonnet, his shorts so low you could see … much more than one would want to see.

'Hi, Ed,' Bill called.

Eddy responded with a grunt.

'How's it going, mate?'

'Got'n oil leak; prob'ly the sump,' he replied and rubbed greasy hands on the seat of his pants.

Bill backed up. 'I won't offer to shake hands then,' he said with a smirk. 'By the way, did Claire tell you we were coming?'

'Yeah.'

'Shall we take the things in for her then?'

Eddy grunted again.

I guess that means yes, Bill surmised, and proceeded to unpack the things. Sonia made her way to the back of the car and went to lift the pram out of the boot. 'No, don't you do that,' Bill said. 'Let me get it for you.' He lifted it out, set it down on the footpath and attempted to unfold the contraption.

'Here, give it to me,' Sonia said, and with one practised motion, had the pram set up ready to go. 'See, easy when you know how!' she boasted.

The front door of the house swung open, and Claire, who was holding baby Ella, came out to meet them.

'Hi, darling,' Sonia said as she reached for the baby. Claire happily handed her over. 'How was your first night?' Sonia asked.

'I didn't get much sleep. Ella kept waking up. I had to feed her three times through the night and Eddy didn't like that at all.'

'Didn't he, dear. Poor Eddy.'

'I hope she sleeps better tonight. I suppose she was a bit unsettled being in a different place and all.'

'Yes, I guess so. But remember she is still very small and will, most likely, need two to three hourly feeds for quite some time yet. I know it's tiring, but she will eventually grow out of demanding so many night feeds.'

'I hope so,' Claire said and breathed out a sigh of exhaustion.

'Anyway, come in, Mum.'

As Claire turned to lead the way Sonia noticed her limping. 'What's wrong with your leg?' she asked.

Claire hesitated. 'Oh … nothing,' and quickly changed the subject. 'You'll have to excuse the mess; I haven't had time to do anything much this morning.'

'Don't worry, darling, I know what it's like with a baby in the house. Anyway, I might be able to help you while Dad shows Eddy how to fit the thing-a-me gadget into the car.'

Stepping into the front room, Sonia noticed the curtains slightly open but made no comment. *I must remember to keep my mouth closed,* she thought. 'What would you like me to do, darling? Ella's asleep. Should I put her down?' she said, hoping to be able to cuddle her granddaughter for a bit longer.

'No, it's all right, Mum. You just sit there and relax,' she said, pointing to a rickety chair in the corner. 'I can take Ella for you if you'd like me to.'

'Oh, no. I really don't mind just holding her for a while, if that's okay.'

Claire gave a little chuckle. 'That's okay, Mum. I'll be in the kitchen. Call me if you need me.'

Sonia was pleased to have a little quiet time alone with the baby. *Well at least they got through the first night unscathed*, she thought.

After removing a pile of junk from the back seat of Eddy's car, Bill fitted the baby capsule device securely in the middle.

'That takes too much room,' Eddy protested.

'Sorry, Ed, but that's the requirement and there's no way around it.'

Eddy muttered some obscenity as he kicked the front tyre. *This bloody baby!* he thought.

'Now, Ed, is there anything else you'd like me to do for you while I'm here?'

'Nup!'

'Well, I'll go and see how the girls are doing.'

Bill stood at the front door. *Knock! Knock!* 'Can I come in?'

'Shh, you can come in, but be quiet; she's asleep,' Sonia whispered.

Bill tiptoed across to where Sonia sat with Ella in her arms; he leant over and placed a tender kiss on the baby's forehead. *She's so beautiful*, he thought and smiled up at Sonia, then asked, 'Where's Claire?'

'She's in the kitchen.'

Bill poked his head around the corner where Claire was busy cleaning. 'Hi, darling,' he said, 'would you like me to take you to the shops? Looks like Eddy's going to be tied up out there playing with the engine for a while yet, and I'm sure your Mum would be more than happy to look after Ella for you. What do you think?'

Claire dried her hands and, flinging the kitchen towel over her shoulder, ran into her father's arms.

'It's not that much of a big deal.' He laughed.

'Oh, yes, it is. You've got no idea. You're a lifesaver, Dad.'

'You go and get what you need, and I'll check with your Mum.'

Claire hurried off, quickly tidied herself up and grabbed her bag. 'I won't be a moment,' she said and, pulling out a notepad, started to write a list: one page, two pages; she almost filled a third page. 'That's it! I think I'm done,' she said and slipped the notepad back into her bag.

'Right, we'll be off then,' said Bill as he leaned over to kiss Sonia. 'See you when we get back.'

Claire slung her bag over her shoulder and headed out the door. Eddy was still tinkering with the car. 'Dad's taking me shopping, Ed, and Mum's looking after Ella. Is there anything that we can get for you while we're out?'

'Yeah. A carton of stubbies and a box of fags.'

Claire gasped. She didn't know what to say.

Bill answered. 'Can't do, Ed. That's your business – we'll leave that to you.'

Bang! Eddy's head hit the underside of the bonnet. He swore.

'I think we'd better get going.' Bill opened the passenger side door for Claire.

They had only gone a short distance when Claire turned to her father. 'Thanks, Dad,' she said. 'Thanks for answering Ed for me. It was silly of me; I should never have asked that question in the first place. I'm so sorry for putting you, and me, in such an awkward position.'

'That's okay, darling. It happens to us all at times.'

'But, Dad, I didn't know if he was just joking or for real!'

'Actually, it caught me by surprise, too, because as I understood it, he was supposed to have given up the booze and cigarettes.'

'Mm, that's what he said, but …'

'It's all right, darling. You don't have to answer for him.'

It was getting close to lunchtime when they arrived at the shopping centre. Bill suggested they eat first. 'It's never good to shop on an empty stomach,' he said. 'What say we go to McDonald's?'

'That'd be great, Dad.'

After their lunch break, with tummies full, they ventured into the supermarket.

'Can I help you with the shopping? Or are you like your mother? She prefers to do it by herself.'

'No, I'm not like Mum, and yes, I could do with your help.' Claire checked the list. 'How about you take this page.' She tore the first sheet from the pad – the Cleaning Products Aisle.

'Yes, I think I can manage that,' he agreed and made his way down to aisle eleven at the far end of the shop.

Claire began in Fruit and Vegies.

Twenty minutes later, with two trolleys full, they met at the checkout.

Claire stacked her items on the conveyor belt, and while Bill took the empty trolley through to the other side, she unpacked the second load. It seemed to work well.

A bit taken aback by the final tally, Claire whisked her credit card from out of her bag.

'No, you put that away,' Bill said and handed the girl his card.

'Oh, Dad, you don't have to do that. You already paid for lunch!'

'It's my pleasure. I'm happy to help out.'

'Thanks, Dad.'

Sonia put baby Ella into her capsule as she slept. She was busting to go to the toilet, but after opening the bathroom door once, she quickly closed it again and waited. *I hope they get back soon*, she thought, crossing everything she could!

She heard the car pull into the driveway. 'Thank goodness,' she said and breathed a sigh of relief.

'We're back!' came a welcome voice. 'How was Ella?' Claire asked as she placed two shopping bags on the kitchen bench.

'She was good as gold, no trouble at all. Is there much more to bring in?' asked Sonia, trying desperately to hurry the process.

'Yes, quite a bit, Mum.'

'I'll help you then,' she said.

They soon had the car unloaded and Bill was just about to use the loo when Sonia warned him.

'Okay, darling, we'd better be off now,' Sonia said and gave Claire a quick peck on the cheek. 'I'll call you tomorrow. Bye! Come on, Bill, hurry!'

Claire had difficulty finding a place for everything. All the perishables were away, and most of the food items were stored, but she so wanted to get in and clean the bathroom before Ella woke for her next feed that she left some things on the kitchen bench.

Donning rubber gloves and a facemask, she tackled the offending area, first pouring bleach in the toilet bowl and then squirting a generous amount of bathroom cleanser on all the other surfaces. While allowing time for those products to do their magic, she cleaned the mirror; it came up beautifully; she could even see her reflection in it!

Just then Ella started to whimper. *Oh, no, please don't wake up, just give me another ten minutes*, she thought and, as if she knew, Ella quietened down. 'Thank you, darling,' Claire whispered and continued cleaning. She scrubbed the toilet bowl, scoured the wash basin, wiped and towel-dried the bench top and cupboards and lastly, she gave the room a light spray of lavender room deodoriser. *That's better*, she thought.

'What's that stink?' Eddy yelled.

'Shh, not so loud. You'll wake Ella. And, if you must know, that pleasant perfume you can smell is a clean bathroom.' Claire was hot and bothered and couldn't deal with Eddy's tantrums, but to her surprise, he made no further comment.

It was just coming on to evening when Claire remembered she still had to change the light bulb in Ella's room. *I hope I got the right type,* she thought; *hope it's a bayonet fitting and not a screw-in.*

Quickly grabbing a chair, she crept into the room, flicked the switch off, unwrapped the new bulb and carefully climbed onto the chair. With fingers crossed, figuratively, she removed the old bulb. *Yes! I was right! A bayonet fitting! Yay!* she exclaimed silently and inserted the replacement bulb. *Now, fingers crossed, it works.*

The remainder of the evening went relatively smoothly. Eddy seemed satisfied with the meal Claire cooked. Although he didn't say so, the fact that he went back for a second helping was a clue. Ella settled down nicely after her final feed and Ed settled himself in front of the TV to watch his favourite programs while Claire cleared the dishes, cleaned the kitchen, and prepared Ella's bottles for the night feeds.

Although thoroughly exhausted, Claire waited up with Eddy. She thought it best to stay and keep him company. She needn't have – he soon fell asleep stretched out on his tattered old recliner.

After checking on Ella and finding her fast asleep, Claire went to bed. According to the digital bedside clock, it was 9:08 pm, and Claire was asleep as soon as her head hit the pillow.

Awakened by Eddy's selfish sexual demands and still half-asleep, Claire moaned.

'Come on, girl, perform,' he demanded and shook her vigorously.

Claire looked at the clock. It clicked 11:14 pm. Reluctantly, she rolled over and allowed Eddy his rough egocentric indulgence. But no sooner had she gone back to sleep when Ella woke.

Claire got out of bed before Eddy stirred. It was 1:16 am!

Ella drained her full bottle of milk and, after a nappy change and final *burp,* settled contently.

The next feed, just before 4:00 am, wasn't quite as easy. Ella became unsettled and restless; she fussed and puked and filled her nappy to overflowing, requiring a complete change of clothes for her, as well as Claire. Claire tried giving her Gripe Water. That didn't help. She laid her on her tummy and rubbed her back, but still she writhed in pain. *What can I do?* she thought. *If Mum was here, she'd know what to do. Perhaps if I offer her another bottle of milk or, I think Mum used to give her boiled water; that might help.*

Fortunately, with the door shut, so far the crying hadn't woken Eddy. But she needed to return to the kitchen to get the things she wanted. So, wrapping Ella in a bunny rug and holding her tight, she ventured out.

By then, Claire was quite efficient at working by the light of the microwave and soon achieved her goal.

Happily, the boiled water did the trick and Ella drifted off to sleep again.

Claire tiptoed through to the kitchen. The blurred luminous numbers on the microwave showed 5:25 am.

Almost daybreak, she crept back into bed, but sleep evaded her. Eddy's demands kept her awake until, being satisfied, he pushed her out of bed.

'Get my breakfast now!' he yelled. 'Bring it to me in bed.'

Claire sighed and, pulling her jacket around herself, shuffled out to the kitchen, prepared the food, and carried it into *his lordship* on a tray. He grunted.

She returned to the kitchen and had just sat down to eat when Ella began to cry. *You can't be hungry again,* she thought, and taking her coffee with her, she followed the sound.

'Oh no, you've been sick again,' she said. 'What a mess! You'll need a bath this time.'

Claire stripped and bathed the baby, then stripped and changed the bed, all before she had time to eat her own breakfast.

After another feed, which Ella managed to keep down this time, Claire laid her on the freshly made makeshift baby bed and then hurriedly ate her own, now cold, breakfast.

Eddy staggered out from the bedroom, used the bathroom, then left the house without a word.

The sound of his car driving off down the road told Claire that he was gone. She didn't mind but would have liked to know where he was going and about what time he'd be back. She shrugged. *Well, he's been living on his own so long that I guess it'll take time for him to get out of the habit of just doing his own thing,* she surmised.

The house was quiet and peaceful, and Claire enjoyed the luxury. She was pleased not to have to tread on eggshells, for the time being anyway. Her mobile phone *beeped*, indicating a message. Swiping the screen, she opened the text: GOOD MORNING DARLING, HOW'S ELLA? HOPE YOU HAD A GOOD NIGHT. DAD AND I ARE MISSING YOU BOTH SO MUCH. LOVE YOU, MUM XXX

Claire replied, HI MUM, HAD A TERRIBLE NIGHT, ELLA WAS SICK, I DIDN'T GET MUCH SLEEP. EDDY'S GONE OUT; I DON'T KNOW WHERE. CAN YOU COME OVER? PLEASE. LOVE, C XXX

Sonia rang back straight away. 'I'm sorry to hear that Ella's sick. Of course, I'll come over. Dad's at work, but I'll be there as soon as I can. Is there anything you need me to bring?'

Tears flooded Claire's eyes, she sniffed. 'No thanks, Mum; I think I'm right at the moment. But it'll be good to see you.'

'Okay, darling, I'll be there as quick as I can.'

'Thanks, Mum, you're the best. Bye.'

'Bye, darling,' she said and pressed End.

Ella was good for Sonia.

'I think she misses you, Mum. That's the problem.'

Sonia held the baby to her shoulder and rubbed her little back. 'I know I'm missing her, and you too,' she said, 'that's for sure.'

'You've certainly got the touch, Mum; she looks so comfortable.'

Sonia smiled. 'And what about you, Claire. How are things working out with you and Eddy?'

Claire flopped herself down on the chair closest to her mother. 'It's early days yet, Mum. We're both still adjusting.'

Reading between the lines, Sonia said no more.

Claire had work to do. Excusing herself, she took the dirty washing through to the laundry, filled the machine, added detergent and pressed start. *Clunk! Clunk! Clunk!* The old clapped-out washer did its best. To reduce the noise, she closed the door and took on the next chore of tackling the kitchen, followed by the bathroom, and finally tidying up the main bedroom.

'Would you like a cup of tea, Mum?' Claire called.

'That would be lovely, but I think little missy here is wanting her feed.'

'I'll put the kettle on and make up a bottle while I'm out here. Would you like to feed her, or shall I?' Claire asked, knowing the answer.

'I can do it,' replied Sonia, 'while you make the tea.'

Claire chuckled to herself. 'It's a deal,' she said.

The day flew by, mother, daughter and granddaughter revelling in each other's company.

Late in the afternoon, Eddy's car pulled into the driveway, the horn blasting.

'Sounds like he's home,' Claire sighed.

'Why is he making so much noise?'

'I don't know.' Claire moved toward the door. 'He might want me to help carry some of his stuff in.'

She hurried to see what the fuss was about and, just as she thought, the boot was full of boxes and cartons. 'Need a hand?' she asked.

'Yeah, here take this,' he ordered and dumped a heavy box of beer into her arms. 'And what's *she* doing here *again?* he said, pointing to Sonia's car.

'Mum's been helping with the baby,' Claire said and staggered off with the load.

She placed the box on the kitchen bench and returned to the living room. 'Mum, I think he's been drinking. It might be best if you leave now.'

'Will you be all right?'

'Yes, but he's in a foul mood and I think it's best that you go.' Claire ushered her mother toward the door. 'But don't you worry, I'll be all right and I'll be in touch. Give Dad my love,' she said and kissed her cheek.

'Ring if you need anything. Promise?'

'I will. Thanks, Mum, thanks for everything.'

Reluctantly, Sonia made her way to the car and with a final wave goodbye, drove off.

Sonia had done a lot to help Claire that day: she'd brought the washing in, folded it up and put it all away, prepared the evening meal and bathed and fed the baby. Claire was extremely thankful but not so Eddy. Railing mad, he banged his fist on the table.

'Don't you ever let me see that witch here again. Do you hear!' he shouted.

'But she's my mother,' Claire protested.

'I don't care if she's queen mother, she's not welcome in *my* house.' He stomped off and banged the door behind him.

Claire's heart pounded against her chest. *Whatever's happened to the man I love*, she wondered. *Did I do the right thing coming back?*

Sitting in the living room, alone and forlorn, she bit her bottom lip and contemplated her next move.

Suddenly the silence broke.

'Where's my food, woman?'

Claire shivered. 'It will be ready in five minutes,' she replied and, hurrying into the kitchen, she turned on the stove and placed two dinner plates on the bench. She knew it wouldn't take long; in fact, it was still warm from when her mother had cooked it. *I hope it's to his satisfaction*, she thought. *I won't tell him Mum made it —*

he'll go off his head.

Claire set the table nicely, well, as nicely as she could with what she had, then placed two steaming hot dinner plates between the gleaming stainless-steel cutlery and, standing back, admired the beautifully presented, well-balanced healthy meal.

'Dinner's ready!' she called.

The door flung open. Eddy stomped in, yanked the chair out from the table, plonked himself down and snarled, 'About time!'

Claire felt unwell as she watched him stuff food into his mouth and slurp like a pig. *Oh, my goodness*, she thought, *I can't put up with this.*

After finishing a second helping, Eddy belched loudly, wiped his sleeve across his mouth, pushed the chair back and left the room.

Claire sat stunned. *Surely, he wasn't this bad before.* She couldn't believe that, after such a delicious meal, he would leave the table with not a word of appreciation. *Right, that's it, I've made up my mind. Tomorrow, I'm out of here!*

She finished her meal alone, cleaned up the mess then, while *his lordship* sat in the living room watching *his* TV shows, she crept into the bedroom and began packing.

With her bags packed, she headed toward Ella's room, checking on Eddy as she passed by. He was sprawled out, beer in hand, on his tatty recliner chair. Claire breathed a sigh of relief.

Finally, with her things and most of the baby's things packed, she prepared bottles for the night feeds, had a shower, and went to bed.

Sleep evaded her. She lay shivering under the covers, wondering nervously how Eddy would be when he came to bed. Frightened, she did not know how to orchestrate her escape.

Ella's cry woke Eddy. Claire quickly jumped out of bed, pulled on her jacket, and wrapped it around herself. But, by the time she reached the baby's room, Eddy was already there and yelling abuse.

He snatched Ella from the bed and squeezing her tightly, shook her tiny body.

'Stop!' Claire screamed. 'You're hurting her!'

Claire tried desperately to rescue the baby. But Eddy pushed her aside. She reeled backwards and fell to the floor. Regaining her feet she lashed out, punching, punching, punching into him. He dropped the baby. Claire reached down to pick her up, but as she did, Eddy kicked her again and again. She could see the baby lying pale and motionless on the floor. With one mighty thrust, she flopped herself over to shield her baby.

'Get up, woman,' he growled.

Still protecting her baby, Claire dragged her aching body to a sitting position and moaned.

'You're useless,' he said and, with one final curse, left the room.

Carefully unfolding the bunny rug from around Ella's body, Claire touched her little face. 'I'm so sorry, my darling,' she said, tears streaming down her bruised cheeks.

Through tear-filled eyes, she could see Ella's tiny chest rise and fall with each steady breath. 'Thank you, God,' she said. Then she heard a tiny whimper, and Ella opened her eyes. Claire was sure she gave a little smile and focused her beautiful blue eyes on her mother.

'Are you hungry, my darling?' Claire said and offered her a bottle. The answer came loud and clear as Ella sucked contentedly, moving her little arms and legs as if nothing had happened.

Again, Claire offered up her heartfelt thanks to God, and then, reaching for her phone, called her mother.

Chapter 13

Bill and Sonia were asleep when the phone rang. Sonia awoke, turned on the bedside lamp, picked up the phone and, seeing the ID answered quickly.

'Claire, are you all right, darling?'

There was a pause. 'No, Mum,' came the reply in a quivering voice. 'I need to come home. Can you come and get us?'

Sonia sat straighter. 'What? Now?'

'Yes, please.'

Sensing the urgency, Bill swung out of bed, pulled on his clothes, and went to the bathroom.

Without another question Sonia agreed, 'Yes, we'll be there as soon as we can.' And ended the call.

Pulling the car into the driveway, Bill shone the headlights to illumine the uneven footpath leading to the front door.

'I'll leave the lights on,' he said, 'but you'll still need to be careful not to trip over. And don't rush. Just take your time. We're here now.'

Sonia was out of the car and halfway up the path before Bill finished his spiel.

He locked the car and remembering his own advice, proceeded cautiously toward the front door and gave a gentle knock.

'I already knocked!' said Sonia impatiently. They listened for signs of life, but all was quiet.

Bill knocked louder. There was a stirring from inside. A light came on.

'I'm coming.' It was Claire's voice. More lights, this time flooding the hallway and entrance. The door opened and Claire stood, half hunched over, holding her baby in her arms.

'Oh, darling,' Sonia cried, 'here let me take her.'

Claire gladly handed over her precious bundle. 'Thanks, Mum,' she said in a pained weak voice.

Bill pushed the door wide open, gasping in horror at the sight of his daughter battered and bruised. 'Where's that monster?' he asked, spitting the words.

He didn't have to look far. Eddy stomped out of his room, 'What the hell's going on?' he demanded.

'I'll tell you what's going on, mate.' Grabbing the front of his shirt, Bill pulled him toward the living room. 'You come with me! I need to talk with you.'

Eddy yielded like a lamb. Bill shoved him backwards, and he landed square in his chair. The recliner jolted back, and Eddy's legs flew in the air. Then the chair righted itself, hitting the floor with a *bang*.

'Now *you* listen to *me!* Bill started with such authority and volume that Sonia and Claire looked at each other in amazement. 'Edward Simpson, *you* have problems. *You* need help.' Eddy cringed. 'Listen to me!' Bill went on, 'For starters: *You* have an anger problem. Number two: *You* are an alcoholic. Number three: *You* are selfish and mean; you don't consider other people; you only think of yourself. Number four: *You* are violent and cruel. And … would you like me to go on?'

Eddy shook his head.

'Well, Ed, it's up to you now. You can face the facts and do something about it, or if you keep going the way you are I hate to think of the consequences – and there will be consequences, mark my word.

'Now, I will take my daughter and granddaughter to the hospital for a check-up, and there will be questions. Claire might even lay charges.

'So, my advice to you, mister, is get cleaned up, have a long hard think about what you have done and don't be surprised if the police come knocking on your door.'

The car loaded with Claire and Ella's things and the baby securely fastened in the back, with Claire by her side, Bill slowly reversed out of the driveway and headed for the hospital.

One look at Claire, the triage nurse ushered them straight through to the examination room.

When the doctor came in to examine Claire, she insisted they check on Ella first.

'Tell me what happened,' the doctor inquired.

Claire described the incident as best she could while the doctor began a physical examination of the baby.

First, he pointed out and noted distinct finger-imprint bruising around the torso area. 'Did she vomit at all?' he asked.

'No, and she's taken a full feed since, and kept it all down.'

'That's a good sign,' he said. Next, he felt her head gently rotating it. 'That seems fine, but I'll order x-rays just to be on the safe side,' he added, and then he checked her limbs. 'All good,' he said and, turning to Claire, added, 'Now let's have a look at you. Seems like you bore the brunt of it.'

'As long as Ella's going to be fine, I don't mind,' she said, endeavouring to smile through swollen half-shut eyes. 'Ouch! That hurt.'

'Yes, I should think it would,' the doctor said. 'And do you have any other injuries?'

'My ribs hurt.'

'Let me see.'

Claire lifted her top. Sonia gasped.

'Are you all right, Mrs Martin? Would you rather wait outside?'

'Oh, no, Doctor. I'll stay.'

'Claire, I won't touch your side. A nurse will take you around to the X-ray department and I'll wait to get the results. Is that okay with you?'

'Whatever you think, Doctor.'

'Right, you just wait here while I organise the paperwork and a wheelchair … shouldn't be long.' He was about to leave the room when Claire called after him.

'Can I take Ella for her x-ray when I go?'

He poked his head around the doorway. 'No, we'll arrange to have the baby's x-rays done later. I'm sure she'll be fine with your mother here.' The doctor reached his arm around the corner and gave Sonia a gentle pat on her shoulder.

'Of course, Doctor,' she said with a proud smile.

The test results showed that Claire had two fractured ribs, multiple grazing and severe swelling and bruising around the rib area, as well as significant facial injuries.

The doctor took Bill aside and spoke privately with him. 'I need to let you know that, by law, it is mandatory for us to report such incidents/injuries.'

'Yes, Doctor, I thought as much.'

'And we will need to keep Claire in hospital for a couple of days just to keep an eye on her. There's not much we can do for fractured ribs, but we do want to make sure there's no internal injuries. Is that okay with you?'

'Yes, thank you, Doctor. We want what's best for her, and the baby.'

'I've checked the baby and, other than a bit of bruising, she seems perfectly fine. She's a tough little one, isn't she?'

'She sure is. But we don't want to risk another episode like that again.'

'No, it's important that we all look out for signs of abuse and do what we can to protect our most vulnerable.'

They made their way back to the girls, where Claire was resting easier having been given strong pain relief.

After the doctor explained the situation, Claire was happy for her parents to take Ella home with them.

Sonia leaned over and kissed her daughter. 'We'll be in to see you tomorrow, darling. Don't you worry about Ella, she'll be fine.'

'I know she will, Mum. Thank you for everything.' Claire closed her eyes and drifted off to sleep.

It was still the small hours of the morning when Sonia and Bill arrived home from the hospital. Ella settled beautifully in her old room.

'I'll leave the curtains closed; she must be exhausted, the poor little thing,' Sonia whispered.

Bill came up behind her and put his arms around her waist. 'Isn't she the most beautiful baby in the world?' he said as they stood gazing in awe at their sleeping granddaughter.

'And it's a good thing we left her cot set up, isn't it?'

'You're right. This is her home; this is where she belongs.'

Claire was discharged from the hospital after three days. She chose not to lay charges on Eddy and made up her mind to leave him for good, much to her parents' relief.

However, as time went by, and Claire's injuries healed, and those bad memories faded, she started to miss Eddy and pine for love.

'Mum, would you mind looking after Ella for me today? I want to catch up with a friend.'

'Sure, darling, that'll be fine. I'm so glad you're feeling up to getting out and about again.'

'Thanks, Mum. See you when I get back.'

Claire planned to surprise Eddy. She caught a bus to the station, a train to the city and another bus out to near where Ed lived. And then she walked the last half a kilometre. Altogether it took her an hour and three quarters. But she thought it would be worth the effort just to see his face.

As she turned the corner into Paxton Avenue her heart did a little skip. Eddy's car was in the driveway. *Great he's home!* she thought. Then she noticed another car out front, a yellow Datsun. *Wonder who that could be?* She frowned and slowed her pace. When she drew near the house, she lifted her head and walked straight on by. At the end of the street, she turned around. *Well, I've come this far, I might as well give it a try,* she concluded.

Claire walked up the path, stood at the front door and was about to knock when the door opened.

'Hello, what do you want?'

Claire stepped back, startled to see a woman standing there; she seemed vaguely familiar, but Claire couldn't think for the life of her who she was or where she'd seen her before.

'Is Eddy home?' she stuttered.

'Ed, someone here to see you,' the uncouth woman yelled.

'What do they want?'

The woman looked at her with a silent question.

Claire cleared her throat. 'Tell him I'm an old friend.'

'An *old* friend to see you,' she replied, emphasising the "old." And as she turned, Claire recognised her.

'Francine!' she said, 'what are you doing here?'

'I live here,' she smirked.

Just then Eddy appeared at the door. 'Ah, you. What are you doing here?'

'I ... I ...' But before she could get another word out Eddy started to rant and rave.

'Git outa here, you basted. I don't ever want to see you again.' He put his arm around Francine. 'This's my missus,' he said, and they both stepped back and closed the door with a *bang*.

Claire could hear their sinister laughter as she made her way down the path. Her heart sank as her whole world crumbled around her.

Having just missed the bus back to the city, to fill the time, she walked to the next bus stop, where she waited another forty-five minutes for the next bus.

During the ride to the city, Claire didn't notice the other people on the bus. A little boy tried to show her his red fire engine. 'It's my birthday,' he said excitedly. Claire just gave a dismissive half-smile. 'Is it,' she responded half-heartedly.

'Mummy, why is that lady so grumpy?' he whispered loudly.

'Shh, darling, she must be sad because it's not her birthday.'

'Ahh,' replied the little boy as he extended the ladder on his fire engine.

It truly was a beautiful day, but Claire failed to see the sparkle of the ocean, or hear the chirping of the birds as they sang their song of joy, and she missed breathing in the fragrance of springtime. All she could feel was the deep sorrow of her own heart.

Sonia enjoyed spending the day with her granddaughter. She took her out into the garden where they felt the warmth of the sun on their skin, heard the birds chirping happily in the trees and watched the clouds as they floated across the sky.

With Eddy out of their lives, the future looked promising – no more violence, no more trips to the hospital and no more worrying about their safety. 'Thank you, God,' Sonia said with a sigh of relief. 'At last, the Martin household has returned to its pre-Eddy peaceful existence.'

Her mind went back to that lovely young man James, from Adelaide. The one who found Claire when she lay unconscious by the roadside. *I wonder what he's doing these days. I wonder if he still thinks about Claire. I'm sure he liked her. I wish we could contact him.*

Suddenly an idea popped into her mind. *The police! They'd have his details.*

Sonia rushed inside and rummaged through the telephone table drawer. 'Here it is!' she shouted. 'I knew I had it somewhere. Yay!'

She dialled the number and waited.

'Sergeant Jones speaking. Can I help you?'

'Oh, you're just the one I want to speak to. It's Sonia Martin here. I don't know if you remember me.'

'Yes, of course, Mrs Martin. How's your daughter?'

'Claire, yes, she's doing well thank you. But what I wanted to ask is if you could give me the contact details of James Cowan, the young man who found Claire that time?'

'Um, yes, he was from interstate if I remember rightly.' He

rubbed his chin. 'Can you leave that request with me, and I'll see what I can do?'

A spring of hope rose in Sonia's heart. 'Oh, thank you, Sergeant. That would be most appreciated.'

'You're welcome. I'll get back to you when I can. Cheerio, Mrs Martin,' and with that he ended the call.

It was the sound of the key sliding into the front door lock that gave Sonia the clue. 'Sounds like your mummy's home,' she said, clapping the baby's hands together.

Ella's face broke into a big smile. Sonia ran to grab the camera in the hope of capturing another gorgeous smile.

Claire came in.

'Hi, darling,' Sonia said as Claire walked past. 'Did you have a good day?'

'All right,' came the glum reply.

'Did you catch up with your friend?'

'Yeah.'

Sensing Claire's mood, Sonia changed the subject. 'We had a lovely day. Ella just gave me the biggest smile ever! Didn't you, darling?'

'That's nice,' Claire said, without even a glance toward her daughter. 'I'm tired, Mum. I think I'll have a rest.'

'Okay.'

The telephone rang. Sonia rushed to answer it. 'Hello,' she said excitedly.

'Sergeant Jones here. I've managed to get the information you wanted. Do you have a pen?'

'Yes, I do,' Sonia replied, and proceeded to write down the numbers. And then she read them back to him.

'That's right,' he affirmed. 'Was there anything else you needed?'

'No thank you, Sergeant, I really appreciate what you've done. Thank you.'

'Glad to have been of help. Bye for now.'

Sonia finished the call. She placed the phone back in its cradle and, holding the sheet of paper with James' mobile phone number on, gave a little skip for joy.

I won't ring him; that wouldn't be right. I'll wait until Bill gets home and get him to phone. Sonia could hardly contain her excitement at the possibilities.

Bill came in from the garage and put his briefcase on the floor. He quickly whisked off his tie, looped it over the chair and undid the top button of his shirt.

'Hi, darling,' he called, 'What's news?'

Sonia threw her arms around his neck and planted a kiss firmly on his cheek. 'Well, do you want the good news first or the not-quite-so-good news?'

'Best start with the good news.'

'Guess what?'

'I don't know, you'd better tell me.'

'I've got James' phone number.'

'James who?'

'You know; that lovely young guy who found Claire.'

'Ah, that James. So what's so special about that?'

Sonia huffed. 'Oh, Bill, don't you remember that he really liked Claire.'

'Yes. So?'

'Can't you see? Now that Eddy is off the scene, maybe,' Sonia's eyes went all glassy.

'But he lives in Adelaide, so how do you think they are ever going to get to see each other again?'

'I thought you could ring him and ...'

Bill interrupted. 'Say what?'

'I don't know. I suppose you could ask how he's going.'

'Yeah, then what?'

'Maybe find out if he's planning to come back to Perth. Or something like that. Just use your imagination.'

'And when were you planning for me to make this call?'

'Tonight. Now.'

Bill looked at his watch. 'They're a couple of hours ahead of us over there you know, that would make it 7:52 pm. I suppose that's not a bad time to ring. But how about I have a cup of coffee first and get my thoughts together.'

Sonia left the room and switched the kettle on.

'Hey, honey,' Bill called after her, 'you said there was other news.'

'I'll tell you when I come in.'

Bill went over to where Ella sat in her little rocker and, taking her tiny hand in his, asked, 'And how are you today, my little princess?'

Ella smiled up at him and his heart melted.

'Here comes your granny with my coffee. Smells good, doesn't it? I suppose I'd better drink it or she might rouse on me,' he chuckled.

Sitting together on the sofa, Bill and Sonia drank their coffee while, in between sips, Sonia expressed her concern about Claire and the bad mood she was in when she came home.

'Perhaps she's just tired. She might have over done it a bit today.'

'Maybe,' Sonia replied, 'but she didn't take any notice of Ella, just went straight up to her room, and she hasn't come down since.'

'Let's not worry. Let's just wait and see how she is in the morning. And with that in mind, I don't think it's a good idea to try phoning James' tonight. How about we hold off for now?'

'Yes, you're probably right. Do you think I should mention James to Claire?'

'It's hard to know,' Bill replied. 'I'm not absolutely sure she's over Eddy yet.'

'Aw,' Sonia moaned, 'I hope she is. I couldn't possibly go around that cycle again. Oh, Bill, surely not. You don't *really* think so, do you?'

'I hope not. But it is her life. She's an adult now, strong-willed too. She will do what she wants to do and there's nothing that we can do about it.' He no sooner got the words out when Sonia reminded him of what he said last time.

'When we feel there's nothing we can do – God can. And we can pray.'

Bill took hold of his wife's hand. 'Thank you, darling,' he said, and they prayed together.

Claire wasn't in a talking mood at dinner that night, so neither Bill nor Sonia quizzed her; instead, they kept the conversation light and easy.

'Would you like to help Dad with the dishes while I feed Ella, or would you rather feed her?'

'Whatever,' Claire mumbled.

'Okay, Dad and I will do the dishes.'

Bill cleared the table and rinsed the plates while Sonia scraped the saucepans. They both worked silently, wondering when Claire would come out and prepare the bottle for Ella.

Sonia took the tin of baby formula down from the cupboard.

'No, don't you do it,' Bill warned. 'Let her come and do it herself.'

Sonia knew Bill was right but, at the same time, still wanting to keep up their proper routine, hesitated, then reluctantly put the tin back in the cupboard.

With the kitchen clean and tidy, Bill went back into the family room. Sonia was about to follow him when she called, 'Shall I leave the light on out here for you, Claire?'

'If you want to,' she answered dully.

'Okay, I'll leave it on. The kettle's full, but I haven't switched it on yet, I'll leave it 'til you're ready.' She was hoping to motivate some action. It didn't work.

Eventually, she made up Ella's bottle.

The evening passed slowly for Sonia. She couldn't concentrate on the TV programs, even the ones she usually enjoyed. All she wanted to do was talk to Bill on his own but, true to form, he'd already fallen asleep in his favourite chair.

And after Claire had fed and settled Ella she didn't come back down again – she just stayed in her room.

Well, I might as well go to bed and read a book, Sonia thought. *It's not much point me sitting here talking to myself and twiddling my thumbs. Okay, I'll be off then.*

Chapter 14

Alone in her room, Claire vividly recalled the events of the day. She visualised the smug look on Francine's face, replayed Eddy's words of hate, and remembered the smell, a mixture of stale cigarette smoke, beer and hatred. She shivered. *I don't need that in my life*, she reasoned, *and I'm not sorry I went there today, at least now I know the truth. I'm strong I can deal with it.*

But she lay awake for hours, thinking, planning, wondering, and questioning what the future might hold for her and Ella. She wasn't afraid, just a bit apprehensive.

She slept well. They both slept well, and as morning light filtered through a small opening in the curtains, Claire opened her eyes and smiled. *It's a brand-new day;* she thought, *a brand-new beginning!* Just then, a Bible verse she had learned as a child came to her mind, and she said it out loud. 'This is the day that the Lord has made, I will rejoice and be glad in it." *Yes, I will be glad and rejoice!'* she determined.

The atmosphere in the house seemed better the next day. Claire came downstairs quite early and, with Ella in her arms, greeted her parents with a smile.

'Good morning, you two,' Bill said, giving Ella a soft pinch on her cheek, to which she responded by blowing a big raspberry bubble.

Sonia laughed. 'Well, you look a happy little girl today,' she said, then, focusing on Claire, asked, 'Did you sleep well, darling?'

'Yes, we both had a good night's sleep. Ella only woke up once!'

'That *is* good. Doesn't it make a difference when you get a decent sleep?'

'Sure does.'

'You sit down and have your breakfast. Dad and I have just finished ours. Here, let me take Ella.'

'Thanks, Mum.'

'Well, who's been a good girl then?' Sonia asked, not expecting an answer. She had become quite efficient at holding Ella in one arm and preparing the formula with the other hand.

Bill excused himself and headed toward the back door. 'It's such a lovely day,' he said, 'I'm off to potter in the garden. I'll leave you girls to chat.'

Sonia returned to the table, sat down opposite Claire, and started to feed Ella.

'She's doing very well. I can tell she's gained weight. When is she due for her next check-up?'

'This Wednesday, I think. I've got it in my diary I'll have to check that.'

'I'm sure they'll be pleased with her progress.'

Claire took a bite of toast and washed it down with a sip of coffee. Then, running her finger around the rim of the mug, she licked her lips and swallowed. 'Mum,' she said, 'I want to apologise for how I was yesterday.' She cleared her throat and continued. 'You see, yesterday I went to visit Eddy. I know I shouldn't've,' she hastened to say, 'and I don't know why, but I just felt I had to see him again.'

Sonia took a deep breath. 'So that's why you were so miserable when you came home. Now I understand.'

'Mum?'

'Yes, darling.'

'He wasn't alone.'

'Oh?'

'Do you remember that nurse from the hospital … Francine something?'

'The name rings a bell.'

'You took a photo of her holding Ella.'

'Oh yes. I vaguely remember her.'

'Well, she's living with Eddy.'

'Living with … as in …?'

'Well, he called her his missus.'

'Really!'

'Yeah. And do you know what I think? Good riddance. They deserve each other!'

'Oh, Claire, I don't know what to say.'

'I think you'd better say that your prayers have been answered.'

'Oh, darling.' Sonia went around to the other side of the table and gave her daughter a cuddle and kissed her cheek. And with tears flowing freely, she said, 'As long as you're not too upset about it, darling.'

'I can honestly say that today I'm *not* upset. Yesterday was a different story; I was devastated. I think it was the shock and all that.'

Grabbling a tissue, Sonia dabbed her eyes and blew her nose. 'I'm so sorry you've had to go through all this, darling, but I must say I'm pleased that you've finally made the break from Eddy. He really wasn't any good for you.'

'I know, Mum, but he is Ella's father, and I did love him – well, I thought I did.'

'But I don't think he ever loved you.'

'I think he did at first.'

'But he didn't treat you right,' Sonia said. And then her thoughts went to another young man. 'And you never know, one day you might meet someone who truly loves you and treats you right, someone who loves Ella and only wants what's best for both of you … that special someone you can love forever.'

'Mum, have you got someone in mind?' Claire said with a knowing smirk.

'Now that you mention it, someone does come to mind.'

'Oh yes, pray tell?'

'That lovely young man, the one who found you on the side of the road that night, the one who stayed with you until the ambulance arrived. Do you remember him?'

'Yes, Mum, I remember.'

'He liked you, and Ella. And I thought you liked him.'

'He was nice.'

'Well? Do you want to ring him?'

'But he lives in Adelaide, and besides, I don't have his phone number.'

'I do!'

'Really? How did you get his number?'

'Oh, never mind. That's another story.'

Sonia went over to the telephone table and opened the drawer. 'Oh, here it is, right on the top!' she said with a laugh. 'James Cowan.'

'Mum, I can't just ring him out of the blue!'

'Why not?'

'It wouldn't seem right. Besides, he might already have a girlfriend. He could even be married.'

'I don't think so,' Sonia frowned. 'Actually, that thought hadn't even crossed my mind.'

'No, but it could be true.'

'I suppose so. Well, what if we get your dad to phone him, just for a friendly catch-up, sort of like a guy thing?'

Claire giggled. 'Oh, Mum, you're such a matchmaker! But I suppose it wouldn't hurt for Dad to ring; we can always ask him and see what he says.'

'Oh, he will. I already asked him.'

'What! You old schemer,' Claire said with a sparkle in her eye. 'And just *when* had you planned for Dad to make this call?'

'I don't know. Maybe today.'

Claire sighed. 'Right-t-o then. I'd better get ready.'

Just then Bill came through the door. 'What's all the racket going on in here?' he asked. 'Sounds like a party or something.'

'Mum was just telling me about your plans to phone James Cowan in Adelaide.'

'Oh, did she now?' Bill said and raised his arms in surrender. 'It was her idea. I was just going along with it.'

'Yeah, I believe you, Dad. Millions wouldn't.'

'But it's true,' he protested innocently.

'Anyway, I've come in for a coffee. I have been slaving away out there in the garden for hours while you girls have been in here talking! And look, you still haven't done the dishes from breakfast!' he joked. 'Come on now, where's my morning tea?'

Sonia looked at her watch. 'Oh, it is morning tea time. I can't believe it. Where has that time gone?' Ella was fast asleep in her arms. 'I'll go up and put her in her cot. If you don't mind putting the kettle on, I'll be down shortly.'

Over morning tea, they discussed further the idea of ringing James.

James checked his phone again, still no message from Francine. He couldn't understand it – she said she'd try to get the Martin's phone number for him. He'd tried numerous times to contact her with no success. *Perhaps she's changed her number*, he concluded in frustration.

There was one more business trip scheduled for Perth before the end of the year, but James held little hope of going since he'd done the previous trip and surely the boss would want to go this time.

With a heavy heart he carried on with his work, taking on an extra hour here and there, trying as best he could to take his mind off Claire and her baby girl.

But try as he did, he couldn't keep them from his dreams.

Saturday afternoon, with no plans for the evening, James was at a loose end. Bored out of his brain, once again his mind drifted back to Claire. *Surely there's a way to find the Martin's phone number; think, think, think.* He closed his eyes and scratched his head.

Bing! Sergeant Jones! If I can find the number for the police station and talk to Sergeant Jones, he just might give me the Martin's phone number or address. Yes!

James opened his laptop, got on to Google and typed in what he wanted and there on the screen was the telephone number of the Police Station.

'Yeah! Success at last.' He breathed a sigh of relief.

He tried the number and followed the prompts.

'Hello, Constable Manning speaking,' came a friendly female voice. 'Can I help you?'

'My name is James Cowan; I'm ringing from Adelaide. I was wondering if I could speak to Sergeant Jones, please?'

'Sorry, Mr Cowan, Sergeant Jones isn't here today; it's his day off. He'll be in on Monday. Could I take a message for him?'

'No thank you. I'll try and phone again early Monday morning.'

'I'll let him know you called.'

'Thank you, Constable Manning,' James said and ended the call.

Well, I suppose that's progress, he thought.

After working in his garden all morning, Bill showered, had lunch, and then put his feet up to relax in front of the television.

Sonia sauntered over to him, put her arms around his neck and kissed the top of his head.

'So, what do you want, my dear?' he asked.

'I was wondering,' she said and perched herself on the arm of his chair, 'how would you like to try phoning James this afternoon?'

'Ow, I just sat down,' he protested.

'Well, what if I make you a nice cup of coffee and warm up a blueberry muffin and pipe lots of cream on the top. I know that's your favourite. How about that?'

'It sounds like bribery to me, but very tempting.' He rubbed his chin. 'Can I consider your request while I eat? Because, as you know, I always think better on a full stomach.'

'Okay,' she said and hurried off to the kitchen.

Shortly afterwards, she yelled, 'Claire, come and get it!' as she balanced a tray of three hot muffins smothered in cream in one hand and three piping hot coffees on a tray in the other hand.

'I'll be with you in a minute, Mum. Umm, something smells good.'

'Hoy! What's this?' Bill protested. 'I can't possibly eat three muffins!'

'Don't be cheeky.'

'But I thought you were doing a special favour just for me!'

'Well, us girls have been working hard all morning too and deserve ...'

'Working your jaws hard is more like it, if the truth be known.'

'Yes, that too,' Sonia said with a cheeky grin, and handed Bill his muffin.'

'I just can't eat this,' he said.

'Why? What's wrong?'

'Well, I can't eat it because I haven't got a spoon.'

'Sorry about that, my darling,' Sonia replied, her bottom lip dropping in a mock pout. 'I shall fetch it immediately, your majesty.' And off she ran to the kitchen.

'Oh, Mum, what are you two up to? I could hear you giggling from upstairs. You sound like a couple of kids.'

'We were just having a bit of fun.'

'Actually, Claire,' Bill intercepted, 'your mother here is trying to get me to ring that fellow in Adelaide.'

'Oh, is she now! Mum!'

'I think it's a good idea for your dad to phone him, to have like a guy-to-guy talk, you know?'

'Well, I can't see what harm it can do.' Claire shrugged. 'Sounds okay to me.'

The girls soon devoured their muffins, scraped the plates, and drained their coffee. Sonia started to stack the trays.

'Don't do that, Mum, you stay here, I'll take them.'

'Thanks, darling, and I'll bring Dad's out when he's finished.'

Claire cleaned up the kitchen and returned to the family room. 'Dad, are you still eating? I thought you would've finished by now! Mum and I finished ours ages ago.'

Sonia gave Bill a nudge. 'I know, you're just stalling, aren't you?'

'Whatever makes you think that?'

'For one thing, your coffee's gone cold, and you're just pushing that last bit of muffin around the plate. Come on, hurry up!'

Bill sighed. 'Okay, then you can take it away.'

Gathering her father's plate and mug, Claire took them to the kitchen and dumped them in the sink.

Bill looked at his watch. '1:10 pm, that would be 3:40 in Adelaide; there's two and a half hours difference – is that right?'

'No, Dad, they're only an hour and a half ahead of us, it's not daylight-saving time over there yet, so that would make it only 2:40.'

'A bit early to ring, don't you think? Maybe we should have our lunch first,' Bill teased.

'No!' responded the girls in unison.

'Oh, all right then, bring me the phone.'

'Here, Dad.'

'You're just as keen as your mother,' he said as he punched in the numbers.

Claire and Sonia sat perched on the edge of the sofa opposite.

'No answer,' Bill said and pressed END. 'Should I try again?'

A resounding 'Yes!' followed.

Bill tried again. The phone rang out. 'There doesn't seem to be a voice message receiver,' he said and ended the call.

'You could send a text message,' Claire suggested.

'No, I couldn't do that. What would I write? No, I'll try again tomorrow. Anyway, you never know, he might have changed his number.'

'True,' Sonia replied. 'Although it's still early over there, so I suggest we have our lunch and try again later. What do you think, Bill?'

He rubbed his tummy. 'Umm, it's hard to make that decision on an empty stomach.'

'Oh, Dad,' Claire said and gave him a friendly backhander on the side of his arm, 'as long as you promise to eat at the proper speed this time.'

'I'll try.'

'Okay then.'

Chapter 15

James heard his mobile phone ring twice while he was in the shower. He quickly dried himself, wrapped the towel around his waist, and reached out and grabbed the phone. The ID was 'Unknown'.

It could be Sergeant Jones returning my call. But no, I don't think so, he argued with himself. *Or could it be Francine? After all this time, I doubt it*, he answered himself.

Still puzzled, and with water dripping down the side of his face, he pressed return call.

Ring! Ring! Ring! The telephone sounded at the Martin's.

'You had better answer it, Sonia. It's probably for you.'

Sonia pushed her chair back from the table and went into the family room where Bill had left the cordless extension phone.

'Hello,' she answered.

'Hello,' came the reply. 'I'm returning your call.'

'Is that you, James?'

'Yes. Who am I speaking to please?'

'It's Sonia Martin here, from Perth. Do you rem ...'

'Oh, Mrs Martin, of course I remember you. Is everything all right?'

'Yes, thank you. And you?'

'Well, thank you.'

Sonia beckoned to Bill.

'James, it was my husband Bill who tried to ring you earlier. I'll just get him for you.'

Sonia handed the phone across the table.

'G'day, mate. How's it going?'

'Good, thank you, Mr Martin. How are you?'

'Not bad for an old bloke, but hey, what's with this Mr Martin business … call me Bill …'

'Hi, James!' Claire shouted in the background.

'Is that Claire's voice I hear? Is she there?'

'Yes. And yes.'

'How is she, Mr Martin? Oops, sorry, Bill? And how's Ella?'

'Claire's fine, and Ella's growing like a mushroom – but look, I'll pass the phone to Claire. She can fill you in with the details better than I can.'

'Thanks, Mr … Bill.'

'Hello.' Claire answered tentatively.

'It's … it's... so good to hear your voice,' James replied, at a loss for words.

'Good to hear you too.'

'How's Eddy?'

'He's got another girlfriend.'

'Really!'

'Yes, and you'll never guess who.'

Ella's cry threatened to interrupt the conversation, but Sonia signalled that she would tend to her.

'Was that Ella I could hear?'

'Yes. Mum's gone up to get her.'

'She must be beautiful …' *Like her mother*, he wanted to say but bit his tongue. 'Your dad said she has grown a lot.'

'She sure has. You should see her; she smiles and blows bubbles. She even tries to talk.'

'Really! Wow! I do miss her, and I think about you and Ella a lot.'

'That's nice.'

'Are you staying there with your mum and dad, Claire?' *Oh, how I love to say that name.*

'Yes, we've been here for quite some time now.'

'That's good. I'm glad you're not with Eddy.' *If only you knew how glad I am!* 'And this girlfriend of Eddy's; is it someone I know?'

Claire tapped her fingernail on the front of her tooth. 'Umm, I think you might know her. She is one of the nurses who was looking after Ella in the hospital. Her name is Francine, do you remember her?'

Do I remember her! He rolled his eyes. 'Actually, I do remember her Claire – Francine, Francine Myer.'

'Wow, you've got a good memory.'

'Mmm.'

'James, are you planning to come back to Perth anytime soon?'

'Unfortunately, not. What about you? Have you ever been to Adelaide?'

'No and I don't see myself travelling anywhere for quite a while yet, what with Ella and …'

'Don't say that. You never know what you can do.'

'Yeah, I suppose.'

'Claire, do you know that all the time I was in Perth, I never did get your address? Do you mind me asking for it?'

'No, not at all.'

James and Claire exchanged contact details then, after a little more chit-chat, finished the call with the promise to keep in touch.

Still wrapped in a towel, James punched the air. 'Yippee!' he shouted. Then glancing sideward, he caught a glimpse of his reflection in the mirror. 'Yikes! My hair! I look like a hedgehog,' he exclaimed and tried to flatten it with his hands, but to no avail. He dampened his hair and, with a bit of coaxing, brought it back to order. Talking to his reflection, he smiled and said, 'I might be able to wet my hair, but nothing can dampen my happiness today! Yay!'

Claire couldn't wipe the smile off her face. She whirled around the room singing, *I've got the joy, joy, joy, joy down in my heart, down in my heart, down in my heart, I've got the joy, joy, joy, joy down in my heart to stay!* Yay!'

'What's going on in here?' Sonia asked and, with Ella in her arms, joined in the dance.

The next day, James pulled into the driveway at his mother's place and went to the door.

Gloria answered the first knock. 'Oh, James, you're here already!'

'Hi, Mum. I know I'm a bit early, but seeing it's such a beautiful day, I thought we could take the scenic drive to church this morning if you'd like to do that. What do you think?'

'That sounds lovely, dear. I'm not quite ready yet but I won't be much longer. Would you mind changing the dog's water for me please, dear, and putting some fresh biscuits in his bowl?'

'No problem,' he said, and with a spring in his step, leapt to it.

James ruffled the dog's ears. 'Hi, Buddy, how's it going?' The Golden Labrador smiled up at him and then rolled over for a scratch on his tummy. James obliged.

'Good dog!' he said, 'Here's your breakfast. Now don't go eating it all at once.'

Just then Gloria came to the back door. 'I'm ready to go whenever you're ready.'

'Okey-dokey.'

Gloria looked at her son curiously. 'You seem very cheery today, James. What have you been up to?'

'Well, I'll tell you when we get in the car.'

'Ooh, that sounds intriguing.'

James reminded his mother of his business trip to Perth earlier in the year and how he'd had to stay longer to attend a court hearing.

'Yes, I remember,' she replied, wondering whatever that had to do with his present mood.

'Yesterday I talked to Claire Martin – you remember … she's the girl who was injured.'

Gloria nodded, 'Yes.'

'Aw, Mum, I've never stopped thinking about her since I came back from Perth. I think I love her. I do love her. I really do!'

'But you said she's got a baby.'

'Yes, she has but she's not with the baby's father anymore.'

'Ooh?'

'Mum, I've never been so happy in all my life, and I want you to be happy for me too.'

Gloria sighed. 'I don't know what to say, son. It's at times like this that I wish your father was still here.'

'You don't have to say anything, Mum. I know it must come as a big shock to you, but I just wanted you to be the first to know.'

'Thank you, son, I appreciate that. It's just that Perth is such a long way away, and besides, I don't want to see you get hurt.'

'I understand that, Mum, but if you could just meet Claire, I'm sure you'd love her too. And Ella, she's such a dear little thing.'

'Well, I hope I'll get to meet them one day.'

'Thanks, Mum.'

They didn't talk much during the remainder of the journey; Gloria just stared blankly out the window, her mind a labyrinth of thoughts while James' mind drifted to things far away.

'Well, here we are,' he said as they pulled into the church car park. He stopped the car and went around to open the passenger door for her. 'Wow! We are early,' he said as he checked his watch. 'I'll take you inside first then come out and make a phone call.'

'Are you going to ring Perth?' she asked, curiosity getting the best of her.

'How did you guess?' James replied with a twinkle in his eye.

'I thought as much,' she tutted. 'Come on then, you'd better walk me in.'

Taking her by the arm, he escorted her into the church, where Anna, one of Gloria's friends, met her at the door. After greeting each other, they continued their conversation right where they'd left off last Sunday.

James hurried back to the car and tried to phone Claire. He was just about to hang up when she answered.

'Sorry, James,' she said breathlessly. 'I was bathing Ella and had to quickly wrap her in a towel before I could get to the phone.'

'Do you want me to ring back a bit later?'

'It's okay. I'll dress Ella, then I'll ring you back. I shouldn't be long.'

'Just take your time, don't rush. Bye, Claire.'

'Bye.'

While he waited, he switched the car radio on and checked his emails.

His mother's friend Chrissie waved to him through the window. 'Where's your mother?' she mouthed.

He lowered the window. 'She's already inside talking to Anna.'

'Thanks, dear, I'll catch up with her then.'

His phone sounded. He closed the window, turned the radio off and answered. 'Hi, Claire, that didn't take too long.'

She gave a little chuckle. 'Comes with practice,' she said, balancing Ella on her hip.

'Sounds like you've been busy this morning.'

'Yes, Mum and Dad went to church; they decided to go to the early service, and it's just been Ella and me at home this morning. Mum and Dad should be back soon.'

'I'm at church too, sitting outside in the car. Mum's gone inside and because we were a bit early, I thought I'd give you a call.'

'That's nice, James. It's good to hear your voice.'

'Likewise, Claire.'

'I used to go to church with Mum and Dad, but I sort of got out of the way of it. I should start going back to church again. I will one day.'

Ella gave a little gurgle.

'Was that a little girl's voice I hear?' James asked. 'Hello, Ella, how are you, little princess?'

Claire was somewhat taken aback. 'That's what my dad used to call me; he still does sometimes. Wow! That was amazing hearing you say that.'

'Sorry, Claire, I'm going to have to go. I can hear them starting the first song … Mum will be wondering where I've got to. Look, I'll ring you this afternoon when I get home; that'll still be quite early for you guys over there, won't it? I look forward to talking to you again soon, Claire. Bye for now.'

'Goodbye, James. Enjoy the service.'

James hurried into church. Excusing himself, he shuffled along the row and took his place beside his mother. 'Sorry, Mum,' he mouthed and joined in the singing. He was ecstatic! Nothing could take the smile off his face.

After church, when Gloria had finished her morning tea and catch up with her friends, James suggested they go home the pretty way. 'Would you like that, Mum?' he asked.

'That would be lovely, especially on such a beautiful day.'

It truly was a beautiful day – in more ways than one.

Gloria wanted to know all about Claire. And James was more than happy to share about the love of his life.

'I am happy for you, darling,' she said. 'I can tell that you do love her, and I hope that she loves you as much as you love her.'

'I think she does, Mum.'

Claire was over the moon when her parents walked in. 'Mum, Dad, guess who rang?'

Sonia raised her eyebrows. 'Was it James?'

'Yes, and he's going to call back again this afternoon!'

'Oh, that's great! What did he have to say?'

"Well, he couldn't talk long. He'd taken his mother to church and was making a quick call before the service started. But you'll never guess what he called Ella.'

'No, what?'

'Little Princess!'

'Really!' Bill intercepted. 'That's what I used to call you when you were little.'

'Yes, I know, Dad. That's what's so amazing. He wouldn't have heard you say that.'

'No, I'm sure he didn't.'

Sonia unfurled the tablecloth and spread it across their dining room table. 'I'm so happy that you two are in touch again,' she said.

'Thanks to you, Mum,' Claire laughed. 'We'll see what happens.'

James was itching to get home and phone Claire. He loved spending time with his mother and always enjoyed her cooking but … today was different – he had other things on his mind.

Claire answered the phone on the first ring. 'Hi, James,' she said cheerily. 'How was church?'

'It was good,' he replied, and Claire could hear the smile in his voice.

'And how's your mother?'

'She's well. And Claire, I told her about you, and she'd love to meet you.'

'Really!'

'Yep.'

'I'd like to meet her too, someday. Wasn't it good that my mum thought to contact Sergeant Jones to get your phone number?'

'What! I thought you must have had my number all the time. You'll never guess what.' But before she had time to even try to guess, he added. 'I didn't have yours or your parents' contact details, and I tried to phone Sergeant Jones myself yesterday to ask if he could give me your address or phone number or something, but Sergeant Jones wasn't there; he isn't in until tomorrow. Wow! What a coincidence, ah!'

'That's just amazing. Wait 'til I tell Mum.'

'Yeah, we must have both had the same idea at the same time. They say, "Great minds think alike"; how about that!'

Claire was so happy; she wanted to know everything there was to know about him. 'Tell me about your family?' she asked.

'Well, sadly, my dad passed away a few years ago, and Mum's living on her own; she seems to be managing quite well, and she phones me most days, and as you know, I see her every Sunday. I have two sisters, one older than me and one younger. My older sister is married with three children; they live in Melbourne, and my youngest sister is single and she's teaching in a little country town in the north of South Australia.'

'That's very interesting, James, but tell me about yourself. What sort of work do you do?'

James cleared his throat and nodded. 'Well, I work for a specialised engineering company. And as you already know, my work takes me interstate and to country towns where I visit clients, then draw up plans to meet their specific building requirements. Does that answer your question?'

Claire blinked.

'Sounds impressive, a bit technical but impressive. And hey! You'd get on well with my dad; he works at an engineering company too, as an accountant. Will you send me some photos of the family?'

'Yes, I'll do that, and will you send me some photos of you and your family so I can show my mum?'

'It's a deal.'

The two of them went on talking for well over an hour before, reluctantly, saying their goodbyes.

'I'll ring tomorrow night,' James promised.

Claire came floating down the stairs, all dreamy-eyed. 'Oh, Mum, he's so lovely,' she said and waltzed around the living room.

'Well, you seemed to have a lot to talk about. I thought you were never going to come down.'

'And he's going to ring me again tomorrow night. And he's going to send me some photos of his family. Oh, it's so exciting,' she said and did another twirl.

Bill took her in his arms and together they danced around the room. 'It's so good to see you happy again, darling,' he said and kissed her on the cheek.

Claire's phone *beeped.* 'That might be James!' she said, and pulled away from her father's arms. She swiped the screen: a message from James. Photos!

'That was quick,' Sonia said. 'Let's see.'

'Wait a minute, I want to look at them first. Aw, that's a lovely photo of James with his mother.' Claire turned the phone for them to see then she scrolled up to show the other two photos. 'That's his older sister, Laurel, her husband Matt and their children, Christopher, Emily and Jake.' Then bringing up the last photo, she pointed out the younger sister.

'Oh, what a lovely family,' Sonia said. 'Don't you think so, Bill?'

'Yes, they seem to be a very close and loving family,' he agreed. 'Claire, have you sent him any photos?'

'Not yet, but I will tonight.'

'That's good. And next time you speak to him or message him would you give him our regards?'

'Yes, I'll do that, Dad,' she said as she scrolled through her gallery of photos.

James checked his mobile. He thought he heard it *beep.* Sure, enough it was a message from Claire.

Dear James,

Here are a few recent photos of Ella I thought you might like to see how much she has grown since you last saw her. Mum and Dad send their regards. Look forward to hearing from you soon.

Love,

Claire xxx

Tears filled his eyes. There on the screen was the love of his life holding in her arms the most beautiful baby girl. He gently touched the screen. 'I love you two so much,' he said, and holding the phone to his chest whispered his thanks to God for bringing her back into his life.

Chapter 16

James arrived at work the next day feeling like he was walking on air. 'Good morning, Mister Goodwin,' he said enthusiastically.

'Well, good morning to you too, James. It looks like you had a great weekend.'

'Yes, I did, thank you,' he replied. 'And, um … Mister Goodwin, I know that we're very busy at this time of the year, but I was wondering if I could take one week of my annual leave in the next month or two?'

'Is it something urgent?' he asked.

'Not especially, but I would like to go back to Perth for another visit if I can.'

'Leave it with me, James, and I'll look at our schedule.'

'Thank you. I really appreciate that,' he said as he turned and left the boss's office.

A week passed with no word back from Goodwin regarding his request. James became anxious. He didn't want to approach his boss again, but at the same time he wanted to know the answer one way or the other before he took off for his country trip the following week. *I'll just have to be patient, again*, he told himself.

James rose early on the Monday morning, loaded the car and headed off before sunrise. A week away in the country was usually something he looked forward to and always enjoyed, but for some strange reason, this time felt different. It was as if he was leaving Claire. He shook himself; *this is ridiculous*, he thought; *I've got my phone with me. I can still ring her every day just as if I was at home, so it's not really any different*. But no matter how much he tried, he couldn't shake the feeling.

The morning passed without a hitch. By lunchtime, he'd clocked up just over four hundred kilometres and had visited two of his regular customers. As he pulled the car into the car park of his favourite Bakery, Mister Kearns greeted him like a long-lost friend. 'You having your usual order, James?' he asked.

'Yes, please. I can't pass through town without sampling one of your famous pies,' he said. 'They smell delicious, and I'm starved. I left Adelaide before six this morning and only stopped briefly for coffee at nine!'

Mister Kearns, the Bakery owner, slipped the potato pie into a white paper bag and, into a separate bag, popped in a cream puff. 'That one's on the house,' he said. 'Enjoy! And have a great day. See you next time you're in town.'

'Thanks, Jack, you're spoiling me again.'

'Can't spoil a good thing,' he remarked as James left the shop.

After lunch and a brief walk around the park, James headed off on the next leg of his journey. He had a three-thirty appointment with a new client at his next destination and he didn't want to be late.

James set the cruise control, tuned in the car radio to the local country station and sat back to enjoy the drive.

It was a beautiful day, the air crisp and clear, and the countryside lush in shades of yellow and green. On one side of the road, canola crops spread like a golden carpet as far as the eye could see, and on the left, fields of green rippled like waves in the gentle breeze.

James switched off the air conditioner, wound down the window, and let the wind tousle his hair. Breathing in deeply, he tapped his fingers on the steering wheel in time with the country music. Kilometres on, the scenery changed. Open paddocks with clusters of shady trees, water troughs and grazing animals covered both sides of the road.

James was whistling one of his favourite tunes when suddenly from the corner of his eye he noticed something odd about one of the dams in a nearby paddock. It looked like an animal floundering in distress in the water and a small black and white dog on the edge barking furiously. Sensing danger, James stopped the car, reversed, and pulled off the road. He jumped out of the car and hurried to the fence. Squeezing between the wires he raced toward the dam. The little dog scampered toward him yapping as if to say, *Help!*

The edge of the dam was slippery, and James fell. He tried to right himself but with no success, so he stayed on his bottom and slid his way right into the cold, murky water. As he inched toward what he thought was a young animal, his heart sank in horror. There, lying face down, was the still form of a young boy.

James grabbed the child and, slipping and sliding, made his way to the bank.

Laying the child face down James tilted his head to the side and checked for signs of life. There was none. So, clearing the airways he began CPR. The little dog circled and continued barking loudly. In the distance, James could hear a woman's voice calling.

'Cooper! Cooper, where are you?'

He lifted his hand and waved in between chest compressions. 'Go, fella.' He shooed the dog. 'Go home.'

Tears ran down his mud-encrusted cheeks as he tried franticly to resuscitate the boy. He felt helpless. Scenes from another time flashed before his eyes; the time when he held Claire's lifeless body in his arms that dark night on the side of the road. 'Please, God, help!' he cried aloud.

Then, with one mighty heave, the child spewed out a fountain of liquid, took a couple of sharp breaths, gave a tiny whimper, and then began to breathe steadily.

'Thank you, God,' James cried with relief.

He stood up and, taking the boy in his arms, headed toward the farmhouse. The boy coughed and cried. James rubbed his back. 'Keep crying, son, that's the best sound I've heard all day,' he said as his shoes squished under his feet.

The boy's mother came running toward them. 'She heard her son's cry. 'Cooper!' she said and threw her arms around them. 'Thank you. Thank God, you found him.'

Seeing the relief on her face, he tried to smile. The dry mud cracked. He spat dirt from his mouth and tried to explain, 'I was driving by. It was your little dog that alerted me to the situation; otherwise, I would never have noticed,' James said and spat out some more dirt.

'Oh, look at you. Come inside. Have a warm shower and I'll make you a nice cup of coffee. My name's Cynthia.' She sniffed.

James introduced himself.

'James, I just don't know how to thank you. Words can't express my gratitude.'

'As long as the boy's okay, that's all that matters,' he replied.

The boy's father, Ken, had just come in from the back paddock. He took one look at the two of them covered in mud and realised what must have happened. 'My worst nightmare,' he said and reached for his son.

'He wandered off, and I couldn't find him anywhere,' Cynthia said, 'and this is James; our hero!'

Ken held his son tight. 'Thank you, mate,' he said in a husky voice then sobbed openly.

'I suggest you phone the hospital. I'm sure they'll want to check the boy and make sure he's all right.'

'Yes, I'll do that. You go and have a shower and I'll soak your clothes in the tub.'

James wiped the dirt from his watch then felt in his pocket for his phone. 'Mmm. Mrs ... sorry, what's your name?'

'Our name's Benson, but please just call me Cynthia.'

'Cynthia, would you mind if I used your house phone? Mine, I'm afraid, is waterlogged. I need to ring to change an appointment, but I'll have to go back to my car to get the phone number. And, while I'm there I'll get myself a change of clothes.'

'Of course,' she affirmed. 'Ken will take you in the ute while I give Cooper a bath.'

'I think we had better phone the hospital first,' Ken said.

'Good idea.'

After a good clean up all around, James phoned through, changed his next appointment, and called his boss in Adelaide to inform him of the situation. Then, after a bite to eat, he followed the Benson's ute to the nearest hospital where Cooper was checked over and given the all-clear.

James' late afternoon appointment with the new company went extremely well. Even before he arrived word of his heroic actions had already reached them.

The small country town was abuzz, and James was inundated with TV and Press Reporters vying for interviews.

It was rather late by the time James finally retired to his hotel room. He pulled out the new temporary mobile phone he'd bought to replace his waterlogged ruined one. His finger hovered over the number pad. He scratched his head. *I should remember her number*, he told himself. 'Um …' He bit his bottom lip. 'Zero, four, nine. No – no. Delete nine. One, nine – that's right. Seven, seven, four, nine, nine, two. Or is it two, nine, nine? Mmm.'

He dialled the number he thought was right.

Six-thirty came. Claire's heart purred in anticipation. James always rang between six-thirty and seven every night. With her phone in her hand, she sat in front of the TV. The nightly news was on, but she really wasn't concentrating, her mind miles away.

Little Ella sat in her rocker, smiling and looking as cute as ever. Bill watched the news, and Sonia continued to potter in the kitchen.

Claire's phone rang. She swiped the pad and frowned. An unfamiliar ID number appeared on the screen. 'Oh blow!' she said. 'One of those stupid nuisance calls, right when I'm waiting for James to ring.' She disconnected the call.

Five minutes later, her mobile buzzed again. 'Great,' she said, but when she swiped her finger across the face of the phone, disappointed once more. She hung up. 'Why do they always have to ring at this time?' she asked, and no one replied.

Ella started getting restless. Claire stretched out her foot, rested it on the edge of the baby rocker and bounced it gently up and down. 'I think you're getting tired, little lady.' She stood, put the mobile phone in her pocket, released the strap and lifted Ella from the rocker. 'Come on, darling, it's time for sleepy byes.' Ella snuggled her head against Claire's neck as they climbed the stairs.

The phone vibrated in Claire's pocket. She quickly laid Ella in her cot and grabbed the mobile. *Oh no, not again!* she thought when she saw the ID. Frustrated, she pressed END. Ella began to cry. 'Shh, darling, it's all right; it's time to go to sleep now.' Claire pulled the covers up around Ella and gently stroked her back as she hummed a lullaby. Soon Ella's little eyes could stay open no longer and she fell off to sleep.

It was well after seven and still no call from James. *That's very strange*, she thought. *I think I'll ring him.*

Claire crept out of the room and made her way downstairs. Scrolling through her list of contacts, she stopped at JAMES COWAN, pressed automatic dial and waited. It seemed to take ages before it started to ring. She waited again, but no answer came and no voice message recording, it simply cut out. *Oh, he might be out of range*, she thought. *I'll send a quick text message.* And she did.

Eight o'clock. Nine. Nine-thirty. Ten. Claire worried. Tears filled her eyes.

'Mum, you don't think he could have had an accident, do you?'

Sonia cleared her throat. 'No, darling, I'm sure there's a perfectly logical explanation. He might have got caught up in a meeting or …'

'No, Mum!' Claire interrupted then cleared her throat. 'Remember they're an hour and a half ahead of us, so that means it's already …' She looked at her watch, 'after eleven-thirty over there; and no meeting goes that late!'

Sonia's heart skipped a beat. She reached her arms toward Claire and pulled her close. 'Come on, darling. We mustn't worry. He might have thought it was too late to be ringing tonight and he'll probably phone tomorrow,' she said, trying to reassure herself as much as her own daughter. Sonia breathed a silent prayer, *Please God, don't let anything bad happen, not now, just when things are turning around.*

'I had a couple of those stupid annoying nuisance calls earlier, just when I was waiting for James to ring,' she said in a husky voice.

'That's unusual. I didn't think you got those sorts of calls on *your* mobile phone.'

'No, I don't usually, that's why it was so annoying.'

'You don't think it could have been James trying to get through on another phone, do you?'

Claire shrugged. 'I don't know. Maybe? I didn't think of that.' She frowned and then, arguing with herself, added, 'No, I don't think it would have been that. Besides I tried to ring him, and I sent a message, but he still hasn't got back to me.'

'He could have lost his phone.'

'I suppose so,' Claire said as she jiggled her leg impatiently.

Just then Bill came into the room carrying a tray holding three mugs of steaming hot chocolate and a plate of cookies. 'Here we go,' he said, 'just sit down and have a nice warm drink, that should make you both feel better.'

'Thanks, Dad,' Claire said as she reached out and took her favourite mug from the tray. 'You always make the best chocolate drink ever!'

Sonia wiped a drip from the bottom of the mug and took a sip. 'Thanks, darling, it's delicious,' she said then placed a soft kiss on the edge of his cheek.

Claire wrapped her hands around the warm mug and, with eyes closed, sipped her drink, savouring every mouthful.

Bill laughed. 'You've got a chocolate moustache, Claire. It really doesn't suit you, you know.'

She licked her lip and giggled. 'You'd better look in the mirror yourself, Dad, mo's don't suit you very much either. And look at Mum!'

The three of them burst out laughing.

'Be careful!' Sonia warned. 'Or you'll spill your drinks. You two are both as bad as each other.'

Tension eased. The three of them sat and talked well into the early hours of the next day.

Bill yawned. 'I don't know about you two, but I'm off to bed to get my beauty sleep.'

'I suppose I had better follow suit. What about you, Claire? Do you want me to stay up with you for a while longer?'

'No, Mum, I'll be right. I think I'll have a warm shower and go to bed too.' Claire was about to collect up the mugs and plate and take them through to the kitchen.

'No, don't do that, darling, I'll take care of them, you just go off and get yourself ready for bed.'

'Thanks, Mum.' Claire hugged her mother, said good night, and meandered upstairs.

After a long hot shower, Claire checked on Ella then climbed under the covers. She tried to settle but sleep evaded her. She tossed and turned and counted, first white sheep, then black sheep, followed by a variety of black and white sheep and lambs, to no avail. She rose and went downstairs, put the kettle on and made herself a cup of camomile tea. *This should do the trick*, she thought. But no, she was more awake than ever. She looked at the clock 3:53 am. *It'll be 5:23 am in South Australia; I suppose it's too early to try phoning James. I'd better wait. I hope he's all right.* Claire rolled her hands.

Just then she heard a little girl's voice coming from the nursery. It wasn't a cry as such, just a tiny sound to let her know she was awake.

Claire prepared the baby's formula and tiptoed upstairs, not wanting to wake the household at such an unearthly hour. She crept into Ella's room, switched on the nursery lamp and leaned over the side of the cot. 'Hello, my darling girl,' she said and received a beautiful big smile in reply. 'You're awake early today – couldn't you sleep either?'

Claire lifted the child from her cot and held her close, finding comfort from her soft warm body.

Ella took the full bottle and fell asleep in Claire's arms.

Relaxed and comfortable in the rocking chair, Claire leaned her head back, shut her eyes and, with her baby snuggled on her chest, gently rocked back and forth.

Claire woke to the sound of the roller door opening in the garage. She shook herself. *I must have dozed off; I didn't even hear Dad get up.* She looked at the time. It was well after seven. *Wow. Dad's off to work, I'd better get going myself.*

Ella was still sound asleep, so Claire gently lifted her over to the cot, pulled the covers up and stroked her back. Ella snuggled down and stayed asleep.

'Hi, Mum. How did you and Dad sleep last night?'

'We went out like a light as soon as our heads hit the pillow. What about you?'

'I hardly slept at all. Just managed to grab a couple of hours while I was nursing Ella in the rocking chair. How was Dad this morning?'

Sonia pushed her cereal bowl to one side and reached for a slice of toast. 'Dad woke up as bright as usual. He's amazing, really; he can survive on minimal sleep, not like me; in fact, I still feel half asleep.' She buttered the toast and spread it with a generous serving of ginger marmalade. 'There's coffee in the pot if want some.'

'Thanks, Mum, I'll have some later; I think I'll try to ring James first.' Claire took her mobile phone from her pocket and pressed *call.* There was a long hesitation before it rang with a strange, muffled sound. Then nothing. Claire pressed End and was about to text when her phone sounded.

Mid-morning that day, James tried the number he thought was Claire's mobile again.

It rang. And someone answered on the first tone.

'Hello?'

The voice was familiar. With a sigh of relief, James replied, 'Hello, Claire.'

'James! Are you all right? I was worried all night when I didn't hear from you.'

'Yes, I'm fine. I did try to phone you a couple of times but couldn't get through. I thought I must have got the number wrong.'

'And I've been trying to ring you too, but …'

'Sorry, Claire, my old phone got wrecked and I lost all my contact numbers and I had to buy another mobile. I tried to remember your number, but thought I got it wrong.'

'Well, you got it right this time.'

'Thank, God,' James replied with relief.

'Anyway, how did you wreck your phone?'

'It's a long story, but if you watch the News tonight, you'll hear all about it.'

'The News! Did you have an accident?'

'No, not exactly.'

'What do you mean, not exactly?'

'Well, my phone got dunked in a dam.'

'What? Who dunked it?'

'I had the phone in my pocket when I went into the water to rescue a little boy.'

Claire gulped. 'What? How? Where? When? When did it happen? Is the little boy all right?'

'Yes, the boy's fine. And it happened yesterday.'

'Yesterday! Well, at least you didn't get hurt. Phew, that's a relief.'

'All's well that ends well. Anyway, Claire, I just wanted to let you know I'm okay and give you my new mobile number.'

Claire grabbed a pen and paper off the bench and jotted down the number. She repeated it back, not wanting to risk losing contact with her beloved James ever again.

'I'll ring you tonight,' James said. 'Please give my regards to your mum and dad and love to Ella. Bye, Claire.'

'Goodbye James,' she said and ended the call.

'Thank you, God,' Claire said, her arms and beaming face lifted heavenward.

Sonia poked her head around the corner. 'Sounds like good news,' she said after overhearing Claire's side of the conversation.

'Best news ever!' she responded unable to keep the smile from her face and the dance from her feet.

'Well, tell me quick.'

'James' mobile phone got ruined when he jumped into a country dam to rescue a drowning boy. He had to buy another phone and tried to ring but couldn't get through. That must have been when I hung up thinking they were prank calls.'

'Is the little boy all right?'

'Yes, he's fine and it seems like James is a hero in the town and quite a celebrity; he'll be on the News tonight!'

'Oh, Claire, I'm so pleased everything's all right.'

That evening, they all sat glued to the television and watched every news report. James looked good on screen and spoke calmly during the interview. The young boy's parents were understandably over the moon with gratitude to James for saving their son's life. TV cameras showed the farmhouse and the little black-and-white dog that had alerted James to the pending danger. Then, the camera panned out and focused on the dam. It was a beautiful story with a happy ending.

There wasn't a dry eye in the Martin household that night; tears of joy, pride and relief mingled with their sincere prayer of thanksgiving.

Claire's mobile rang right on the dot of six-thirty.

'Hi, James,' she said. 'We saw you on TV!'

'That was embarrassing,' he said.

'Well, I thought you did very well, and I was proud of you.'

'Thanks, Claire. It means a lot to hear you say that.'

'Well, it's true.'

It was well over an hour before they reluctantly said their goodbyes with the promise to chat again the next night.

'Oh, Mum,' Claire said dreamy-eyed as she waltzed around the kitchen. 'I think I'm in love. Isn't he lovely!'

'Yes, he really is a kind and gentle hero and I'm sure he loves you and Ella. You couldn't get a nicer young man.'

'Only one problem, Mum – he lives so far away.'

'Never mind, dear. Love will find a way.'

'Maybe, but I don't know how.'

'Let's just wait and see.'

'Mm,' Claire sighed, 'I suppose I have to, not much choice.'

Chapter 17

Night after night, Claire and James talked for hours on their mobile phones, laughing together as they shared their thoughts, desires, and dreams for the future. James was the first to open his heart and voice his love for Claire, and in response, Claire affirmed her love for him. They were officially "an item!"

At 4:12 pm Friday afternoon, James walked into the office to the cheers of his workmates.

'Yeah, for Jimmy boy. Our hero!' And after slaps on the back, handshakes and congratulations, they celebrated with drinks and nibbles. No more work was done that day, and Mr Goodwin dismissed all the employees early, all except James, who he called into his office.

'Sit down, young man,' he began. 'I just want to let you know how proud I am of you, not only because of this recent incident, but because of your honesty, diligence, and hard work. I've had my eye on you for quite some time, James, and I'd like to offer you a promotion. I realise you'll need time to think about it, but I would like to offer you the position of Supervisor/Sub-manager; that would make you second in charge.'

He handed James a document folder. 'This is the full work description and salary package. Please take it, read it and consider it over the weekend – or take longer if you need to. James, I'd be proud to have you as my 2IC.

'And another thing: about the request you made earlier, I am happy for you to take time off to go to Perth, and I would like you to consider taking extra time while you're there to incorporate another business trip. All expenses paid – accommodation, air fares etc.'

James' jaw dropped. 'I'd be happy to do that, Mr Goodwin. When would you like me to go?'

'Whenever it suits you, James; just let me know.'

'I'll certainly do that,' he said with a smile that any friendly circus clown would envy.

Mr Goodwin pushed his chair back, put his hands on the table and made to stand. 'That's all for now, James. Have a good weekend.'

'Thank you very much,' he replied as he stood and reached across the highly polished desk. 'I trust you have a good weekend too, Mr Goodwin.' The two men shook hands firmly.

With a skip in his step, James entered the downstairs car park. He pressed the automatic key button, swung the driver's door open and climbed into his car. Although tempted to sit and read through the proposal there and then, he resisted the urge. *I'll wait until I get home,* he determined and placed the folder on the passenger seat beside him.

He knew he had a lot to think about and a lot to do after his weeklong country trip. But he felt energised. A surge of adrenalin pumped through his veins.

First things first, he told himself as he drove into the service station car wash. Streams of soapy water cascaded down the windows carrying with them a week's worth of country grime. The car shook with the force of the rotating washers as they pounded the vehicle. Then quietness.

A fine film of wax sprayed gently down, followed by the final warm blow-dry.

James parked the car and quickly ducked into the petrol shop for a few essential supplies before heading home.

It seemed that wherever he went people recognised him. Some just stopped and stared while others commented. 'I saw you on TV,' one guy said. And a young lady frowned and asked where she knew him from. Embarrassed, James tried not to make eye contact but found that rather difficult, especially when he arrived at his apartment where, once again, he was treated like a celebrity. *I guess I'll just have to get used to it until it all dies down,* he thought.

He kept to himself most of Saturday but phoned his mother, both his sisters and, of course, Claire, who was thrilled to hear the news of his promotion.

'Don't get too excited,' he said, 'I'm still thinking it all through. Although it is an offer almost too good to refuse.'

'It sounds wonderful. I think it's a job tailor-made just for you.'

James didn't mention his upcoming Perth trip; he thought it best to hold off from telling Claire until he had more concrete plans in place.

That evening, James read and reread the job proposal. He could hardly believe his eyes. 'What an offer!' he exclaimed to his own reflection in the blank television screen. 'Wow! That's amazing!'

The package deal, which included a substantial rise in salary, extra bonuses, company shares, and a company car, was much more than James could have ever envisaged.

He was thrilled with the proposition … But what about Claire? Could there ever be a future for them, with him living on one side of the country and her on the other?

By Sunday, James had made up his mind to accept the promotion. He told his mother, who told her friends, and soon, the news spread not only of his promotion but also of his heroic deed.

'Mum, please don't tell anyone else; I haven't confirmed it with my boss yet.'

'It's all right, dear. Everyone is so excited for you, and I'm proud of you.'

James was embarrassed. He wasn't one for being the centre of attention; he shied away from that sort of thing.

First to arrive at work on Monday, James started to sort his desk. He hoped word of his decision hadn't leaked before he had a chance to inform his boss.

'Good morning, James,' Mr Goodwin said as he walked in. 'It's good to see you so bright and early. Did you get a chance to read through the proposal?'

'Yes. I went over it a few times and I thought it a very generous offer.'

His eyes lit up. 'That sounds promising,' he said and opened his office door. 'Come in,' he beckoned.

James closed the desk drawer, grabbed the folder, and followed him.

George Goodwin flicked the switch. The kettle sprung to life. 'Oops, that sounds a bit dry,' he said, and topped up the water level. 'Take a seat, James. Would you like a coffee? I usually like to start my day, especially Monday, with a quick energy boost.'

'Yes, please. I have white with one sugar.'

The kettle purred happily and Mr Goodwin took two mugs from the top shelf. 'How was your weekend?' he asked. 'And by the way, I think you should call me George from now on.'

James sat further back in his chair and adjusted his jacket. 'My weekend was busy, but good. Had lunch with Mum Sunday then took her for a scenic drive along the coast in the afternoon.' He paused and pushed the folder out of the way to make room on the desk for his coffee. 'What about you? How was your weekend?' He avoided calling his boss by his first name but knew he'd better get used to it.

George placed the coffee mugs on coasters and pushed a sugar bowl across to James. 'I'll let you do your own sugar. I don't want to get it wrong,' he said with a half grin. 'Yes, my weekend was okay – did a few rounds of golf Saturday and went fishing with my son yesterday. Didn't catch anything, but that's not the point of it, is it?' he said with a chuckle.

'As long as you enjoyed it.'

'Well, it was relaxing anyway.'

James sipped his coffee.

'A biscuit, James?'

'Thank you.'

They both reached for a Monte Carlo. 'Are they your favourites too?'

'Those, and Cream Cookies, and Scotch Finger Biscuits, I like most of them actually.'

'You're a man after my own heart,' he said, looking James straight in the eyes as he subtly dunked his biscuit. 'By the way, do you have any questions relating to the job offer?'

James opened the folder on the page marked with a Post-it sticker. 'Not really,' he said as he ran his finger down the page to the paragraph he had highlighted. 'It's all set out very clearly, but there is just one thing I wanted to understand better; that is regarding the company shares. Would you explain what it involves please?'

George pulled out a large folder from a locked cabinet and explained the financial position of the company, including the various share portfolios. 'Does that answer your query, James?' he asked.

'Yes, that's all I wanted to know at this stage.'

George sat back in his chair and folded his hands behind his head. 'Well, James, have you decided to accept the position? Or do you need more time to think about it?'

Closing the folder, James looked up and, with a grin on his face, gave the nod. 'No, I don't need time to think about it. And yes, thank you Mr Goodwin. I am happy to accept your offer.'

George rose to his feet, reached across the desk, shook James' hand vigorously and announced to the empty room; 'Mr Cowan, it is with much pleasure that I welcome you as Sub-Manager and my Second-in-Charge. Welcome aboard!'

Claire rushed down the stairs, breathless. 'Mum, Dad, guess what?' she panted.

Bill swivelled around. 'Is everything all right?' he asked.

'Yes, everything is wonderful!' Claire replied and did a little swirl. 'He's coming over. James is coming to Perth!'

Sonia put her hand to her heart. 'Oh, my goodness. When?'

'Monday week,' Claire said. 'He'll be here for two weeks. How exciting is that!'

'That's great, darling. Do you think he'll want to stay here?'

'No, Mum. He will be working some of the time, so he'll stay at a hotel in town while he's here and he'll be away in the country for a few days. But won't it be great to see him again?'

'That is good news,' Bill said. 'It will be good to get to know him better. I wonder if he likes fishing?'

Claire sighed. 'I don't know, Dad; I've never asked him that question.'

'Oh, Bill,' Sonia tutted, 'you can't go organising him; it is his holiday after all.'

'I thought he'd want to hang out with me and do some guy things,' he replied with a smirk.

'I don't think so, Dad. Anyway, he's going to hire a car and he wants to see a bit more of WA while he's here. He didn't get to see too much the last time he was here.'

'That's true. He had to hang around for that stupid court case.'

When they went to bed at almost 11:30, Claire was too excited to sleep, her mind busy planning what they would do and where they would go while James was in Perth.

Chapter 18

James lay awake tossing and turning. He had so much on his mind, what with his new job and scheduling appointments to fit in before he was due to go away, as well as arranging with clients in Perth, booking flights, accommodation, a hire car, and whatever else needed to be done.

In the darkness, a smile crept across his face as he thought of Claire. His heart beat faster. He thought, *I will be with you soon. I love you.*

The plane touched down in Perth. It was a full flight, but James, being in business class, was among the first to disembark.

'Good morning, sir,' the flight steward said. "Welcome to Perth. I trust you'll have a good stay.'

'Thank you, I'm sure I will.'

He stepped from the plane and walked the pedestrian coverway. Coming through the glass doors into the waiting area, he looked up, and there, in the middle of the crowd, was Claire. She ran toward him, arms outstretched. At that moment everything became a blur. He didn't notice Bill and Sonia standing behind Claire with little Ella in the stroller; he didn't notice the sign welcoming him to Perth. All he saw was Claire. It was as if they were the only two people that existed in the whole world.

James swung his backpack over one shoulder, reached for Claire and enfolded her in a tender loving embrace. Her hair smelt of fresh strawberries and her face was as soft as silk.

She rested her head on his chest, breathing in the warmth of his presence.

Bill and Sonia stood back, not wanting to break the magic of the moment. Sonia felt Bill's arm around her waist. She leaned her head on his shoulder. 'Looks like the beginning of a happily ever after love story. What do you think, Bill?'

'Looks that way and I don't think he'll be wanting to go fishing with me after all.' He looked at Sonia with mock disappointment.

'Never mind, dear, you can always buy fish at the supermarket.'

Claire didn't want this moment to ever end. She felt truly loved and protected. It was as if, at that moment, their very beings, the essence of who they were, blended as one. There was no need for words, their hearts beating as one conveyed all they needed to say.

James, overwhelmed with emotion, said a silent prayer. In all his thoughts and dreams of Claire, nothing came anywhere near the reality of what he was experiencing at that moment. A tear escaped, flooded his eyes and trickled down his cheek. He cleared his throat. 'Claire,' he whispered, 'I love you so much.'

She looked up into his eyes, wiped the tear from his face and smiled. 'I'm so happy to see you,' she said. 'Mum and Dad are here too.'

With their eyes still fixed on each other, hand in hand they made their way toward Bill and Sonia.

'Good to see you, mate. Did you have a good flight?' Bill asked.

James released his grip on Claire's hand momentarily and shook hands with Bill. 'Yes, thank you,' he said. 'The flight was good.' Then taking Claire's hand again, he leaned over and kissed Sonia's cheek. 'Hi, Mrs Martin. It's good to see you.' Then he redirected his gaze to Claire.

Just then little Ella stirred. James looked down. 'Ella,' he said in wonder, 'look how big you are.'

Ella smiled up at him.

'I think she's missed you too.' Claire laughed.

With the waiting area almost empty, Bill suggested they go for coffee.

'Can I push the stroller?' James asked.

Sonia stepped to one side. 'Sure, be my guest,' she said, smiling.

With one arm around Claire and one hand on the handle, James pushed the stroller toward the cafe.

'My shout,' said Bill. 'What are we all going to have?' He looked at Claire.

'I'm not hungry, Dad. I'll just have a small Chai Latte, thank you. What about you, James, what would you like?'

His eyes still fixed on Claire, he said. 'I'm not hungry either.' Then, turning to Bill, he added, 'So I'll have a small Cappuccino, please.'

'And you, my darling?'

Sonia looked up and smiled. 'You can make mine a Mocha please, my dear.'

Bill trundled off to place the order while Sonia, feeling rather the odd one out, fussed over Ella.

She was pleased when Bill returned with their drinks.

'What are your plans for the rest of the day, James?' Bill asked and flinched when Sonia kicked his shin under the table.

'I'm picking up the hire car and was planning to do a little sight-seeing. But I was hoping to have a tour guide if there is one you can recommend?'

Bill looked serious. He stroked his chin, 'I suppose I could send the girls home and show you around the place, Jimmy boy. How does that sound?' He felt another kick under the table, and flinched. 'What!' I'm just being hospitable!'

'Don't take any notice of him, James. I'm sure Claire will be happy to be your tour guide, and Bill and I will be very happy to look after Ella, won't we, Bill?'

'Whatever you say, dear.'

Claire folded her serviette, pushed the mug to one side and cleared her throat. 'Thanks, Mum; that's much appreciated.'

'Yes, thank you, Mr and Mrs Martin. I won't keep your daughter out too late, and I'll bring her home safely.'

'See that you do, young man,' Bill said in his gruff voice, and for his effort received another kick in the shin. 'Ouch! I think we'd better go,' he whimpered, 'otherwise I could end up a cripple.'

'Well, we don't want that, Dad. I think you and Mum had better go.'

'Okay, I can take a hint.'

Claire lifted Ella from the stroller, gave her a big hug and kissed her chubby cheek. 'Bye, little cherub, now say goodbye to James.' She held her out toward him, and the baby placed one big, dribbly, open-mouthed kiss on the side of his face.

He laughed. 'Goodbye to you too, little princess,' he said and kissed her tiny forehead. 'What a little darling.'

Claire snuggled her down, tucked the bunny rug in and gave her her favourite soft teddy bear. 'Be good for Nanna and Grandpa and I'll see you tonight.'

After saying their final goodbyes, they turned to go. Bill hobbled off, emphasising an exaggerated limp.

Sonia rolled her eyes. 'Oh, you poor thing. Come on, I'd better get you home.'

'Are your parents always like that?' James asked as they disappeared down the escalator.

'Usually they're much worse!'

'Really? You must have lots of fun at your house.'

'Yes, I guess we do.' Claire turned her full attention to James. 'They really like you, you know.'

'That's good. I think they're great too,' he said as, hand in hand, they headed down the stairs to the luggage carousel where James retrieved his bag.

'I'd quite like to see Fremantle,' he suggested. 'How does that sound to you?'

'Well, I did offer to be your tourist guide, so if that's where you want to go, Fremantle it is.' Claire looked across at him. *I'd go anywhere with you*, she thought with a smile. She loved everything about him.

James picked up the hire car and settled Claire into the front passenger seat before stowing his gear. Then he slipped in beside her and set the GPS.

'Are you ready to go?' he asked as he started the engine.

She clicked her seatbelt. 'Ready when you are,' she replied and wiggled herself further into her seat.

James drove slowly out of the car park and headed toward the main road leading into the city.

'Golly, they're doing a lot of new road works. I'm sure glad I've got the GPS,' he said as he concentrated on the road ahead.

'Don't you think I could have directed you through this maze?' Claire said with a pretend pout.

With his eyes still fixed firmly on the road ahead he assured her of his complete confidence in her navigational skills. 'I probably needn't have turned on the GPS,' he said, 'I'm just so used to being on my own.'

'That's all right. I'll forgive you this time.'

She looked across the car, her eyes drawn to his hands. *Wow! What lovely hands*, she mused. *I've never taken notice of a guy's hands before, but I could fall in love with those hands*. And so the dialogue with herself continued. She checked out his profile; it ticked the box, his soft curly blond hair; another tick. Fine features and lightly tanned skin, a few freckles scattered across his beautifully shaped nose. *Mmm*, she thought, *I do like this guy*.

The GPS cut in, startling Claire from her daydream. 'In five hundred metres turn left.'

They approached the first set of traffic lights. James brought the car to a stop and looked across at Claire, his blue eyes filled with warmth. 'It's so great to catch up with you in person,' he said. 'I've waited so long for this moment, I can't believe it's really happening.'

'Hey! The lights have changed,' Claire said just as the horn sounded from the vehicle behind.

'Oops!' James refocused, turned left, and joined the flow of traffic.

Claire's heart leaped with joy. 'I'm happy too,' she said. 'It will be great to spend time together and get to know each other more.' She breathed in his fragrance. *Mmm, that's delicious! I could just nuzzle my nose into his neck. I wonder what aftershave he uses. I must ask him, but not now.*

James prepared to veer left onto Canning Highway as directed by the voice on the GPS.

'Where would you like to go first when we reach Freo?' Claire asked. 'It'll be lunchtime when we get there. Do you want to have something to eat before I take you sightseeing?'

'I'm not really hungry at the moment, but how about you, do you want to eat first?'

'No, I'm right, thanks. How about we take a ride on the Ferris wheel? It gives a most beautiful panoramic view of the boat harbour and port and on a lovely day, like today, it's spectacular!'

'Sounds good to me,' James replied.

Claire hesitated. 'That's if it's working when we get there – um, I'm not sure of the operating hours.'

'That's all right. If it's not working there'll be plenty of other things to do.'

'Did you visit Fremantle last time you were over?'

'Yes, I did, once, but only briefly and it wasn't much fun being on my own.' James switched off the GPS and slowed the car as they approached Marine Terrace. 'Should I turn right or left here?' he asked.

'Go left then get ready to turn right up the road a bit.'

James flicked the indicator. 'Well, I like hearing your voice better than listening to the GPS,' he said with a grin, and then he noticed the building on the corner. 'Wow, that's a lovely hotel,' he said.

'Yes, that's the Esplanade Hotel. It's very popular for High Teas and special occasions,' Claire said.

'Well, in that case, I must take you there one day. But I don't think we're quite dressed appropriately for such a venue today, do you?'

'No, it'd be best to wait for another time,' Claire agreed. *Mmm, so he's planning to take me somewhere special; that sounds exciting,* she thought, and her heart skipped a little.

'We turn right just up here and cross the railway line then right onto Mews Road.

'Aw, look! The Ferris wheel is working, yeah!' Claire yelled.

James slowed the car. 'Should I park here or drive up closer?'

'No, this should be fine; if you park here, we can walk up.'

James parked the car, purchased a three-hour parking ticket, and set it on the dashboard. Then, hand-in-hand, they crossed the road and headed toward the park.

Claire went to buy the tickets, but James wouldn't have a bar of it. 'No way!' he said. 'I'm privileged to have you as my personal tourist guide so put your purse away.'

'Thanks, James. I'll let you pay this time, but it's my turn next, okay?'

'We'll see, come on now, the wheel's slowing down, let's join the queue.'

The Ferris Wheel came to a stop. After the last car was vacated the next group of passengers took their seats. Claire and James were the last couple to board and were happy to have a compartment to themselves.

'Sit on this side, James; you'll get the best view from over here.'

He moved across, sat by Claire, and stretched his arm over the back of the seat. 'This is lovely,' he said and snuggled a little closer.

The Ferris wheel swayed slightly as it started its upward path.

'Isn't this beautiful, James? I'm so glad you'll get to see a bird's eye view of the Fremantle harbour.' Claire pointed. 'Do you see that tall structure over there ... that's the Fremantle Port Authority.'

James glanced momentarily in the direction Claire pointed. 'Yes, very interesting,' he said and quickly turned his attention back to Claire.

'James, you're supposed to be taking in the view.'

'I am. I'm taking in the most beautiful view ever, and I could watch it all day.'

Claire's face flushed a brighter shade of pink. 'Oh, James,' she said, 'you paid to see the view, so look out the window!'

He turned his head to the front. 'I can still see your reflection in the glass.'

'James, you're incorrigible! You're not supposed to look *at* the window; you're supposed to look *through* it!' Claire said with a grin and gave him a quick jab in the ribs.

'Ouch! That hurt,' he complained.

'Serves you right for not paying attention – to the scenery that is,' she quickly added.

Their ride came to an end. Claire looked at her watch. 'Hey, if we're quick we can get to the Round House before they fire the cannon.'

James was taken aback. 'What, you mean they actually shoot a real cannon?'

'Yeah, they fire it every day right on the dot of 1 pm.'

'Well, let's go then! Lead the way, tourist guide!'

Claire grabbed James by the hand and started to run.

'Hoy, slow down a bit. How far is it to this Round House anyway?'

'Not far, just up the hill.'

'Okay,' he puffed, 'hope it's worth it.'

'It will be.'

They reached the top of the hill just as the volunteer guide from the Round House started explaining how the signal cannon and the large black time ball were used to assist mariners at sea to set the ships clocks for navigation.

Being a Monday, there weren't too many people there and the man in charge kept checking his watch waiting for the scheduled gunner to arrive.

'I'm sorry,' he said, 'I can't wait any longer. I need a volunteer to fire the cannon.'

Everyone else stepped back, leaving Claire and James standing alone.

'James will do it!' Claire announced, lifting his hand high above his head.

'Would you like to do it, sir?'

'Yes, I guess so,' he said, looking slightly apprehensive.

'We don't actually use a cannon ball these days,' the guide explained and showed James the canister device that they now used 'And this is the control. When it's time, you press this button firmly, okay?'

'Yep,' he replied and held the device, his finger poised, ready for the signal.

'Right, everyone, when I say, I want you all to count down from ten.' He paused. The time ticked down. 'Right,' he said. 'Now! Ten, nine, eight, seven, six, five, four, three, two, one, FIRE!'

James pressed the button, and simultaneously, the Time Ball fell, and the Cannon blasted BOOM!

'Wow!' The crowd stood in awe.

'That was louder than I remembered,' Claire said.

The guide shook James' hand. 'Congratulations, now you are an official honorary gunner, and if you follow me, you will be given a certificate to prove it.'

'Thank you, sir,' he said. 'That was awesome!'

After being presented with an elaborate certificate, he and Claire were given a personal tour and a rundown of the Round House's history, and an hour later they wandered hand in hand down the hill.

'Well, what did you think of that?' Claire asked.

'Very informative. To think it's the oldest building still standing in WA, and it was almost demolished. Phew! That would have been a shame. It's such a beautiful building and I'm glad they decided to preserve it for future generations.'

'I thought you'd like it. And you were so fortunate to be able to fire that canon. Usually, people must book a couple of weeks in advance for that privilege.

'Hey, how about a coffee? My shout! There's a lovely restaurant just down near the beachfront.'

'Yeah, I am a bit thirsty.' James looked at his watch. 'No wonder, it's almost time for afternoon tea! Wow, that morning sure went fast!'

'Time flies when you're having fun!'

'You can say that again,' he said and squeezed her hand.

'Time flies when you're having fun,' she replied with a cheeky grin.'

James took her by the hands, twirled her around and pulled her close. He looked deep into her eyes. 'Oh Claire, I love you so much,' he said and placed a gentle kiss on her rosebud lips.

Left breathless and lost for words, Claire simply licked her lips, savouring the moment.

Chapter 19

Sonia looked at Bill. 'Wonder how they're going? I think I'll give Claire a call.'

'No, don't do that. Just leave them be. I don't think they'd appreciate a phone call.'

'Wonder why she hasn't rang me. She usually likes to check how Ella's going.'

'I don't think she'll be too worried about anything today,' Bill said. 'She'll have other things on her mind.'

'Yes, I suppose you are right. I'll just have to wait.'

The afternoon passed quickly.

Claire smiled to herself. She almost let slip the comment she'd made earlier about how time flies but refrained.

'A penny for your thoughts,' said James.

'It doesn't matter,' she replied.

'Come on, what are you thinking?'

'I'm just thinking how quickly the day has gone.'

'But it's not over yet. There's still this evening.' James covered his mouth and yawned. 'What would you like to do? Got any ideas?'

'Mmm, we could always go to the movies or something.'

He yawned again.

'You're tired. You've had a long day. Would you rather have an early night?' Claire asked.

James looked at his watch. 'Actually, you do have a couple of hours on me,' he said. 'So maybe an early night might be a good idea, because we've still got all day tomorrow, and we have done a lot today. So how about I take you somewhere nice for dinner then drive you home?'

'Sounds good to me,' she said then looked down at what she was wearing. 'We can't go anywhere too flash,' she said. 'Unless we go home and get changed first.'

'Yeah, that's a good idea, we could do that, and I'd love to see little Ella again.'

The doorbell rang. Sonia rushed to open it. 'Hello, you two, did you have a good day?'

'Wonderful!'

'Well, come on in, dinner's ready.'

'We're not planning to stay. James is taking me out for dinner. But we just need to get changed before we go.'

Sonia raised her eyebrows.

James followed the girls through to the lounge room where Bill was watching TV and Ella lay contentedly in her rocker.

'Hi, Dad. Hi, sweetie pie.'

Ella's eyes lit up and a big smile spread across her face; her little arms reached out and Claire lifted her from the rocker.

Bill stood and extended his hand toward James. 'Hi, mate. Have a good day?'

'Yes, Mr Martin – oh sorry, Bill – we had a great day. Fremantle's such an interesting place, there's so much to see.'

'And, Dad,' Claire chipped in, 'you'll never guess what.'

'No, I suppose I won't,' Bill replied in his matter-of-fact way.

'James got to fire the canon!'

Sonia came from the kitchen, tea towel flicked over her shoulder. 'How did you work that one?' she asked.

'The fellow who was booked in to do the honours didn't turn up and James kindly volunteered to fill in.'

James gave a mock cough. 'I didn't actually volunteer,' he said. 'I was conscripted by you-know-who!'

'Yes, I can well believe that,' Bill said.

'Oh, Dad!' Claire complained. And little Ella laughed as if she was in on the joke.

'Can I hold her?' James asked.

'Be my guest,' Claire said and happily handed over her little bundle of joy.

Ella was quite happy to go to James. 'Hello, little princess,' he said, and Ella gave him a big smile.

'How amazing is that! It's like she knows you, James.'

'Well, I think she is wonderful,' he said and whirled her around. 'Wee!' The baby giggled.

'Look, you two, why don't you have dinner here tonight and then go out tomorrow evening instead? Be lovely for us to have some time to get to know you more, James. What do you say?'

James turned to Claire. 'It's up to you … what would you like to do?'

'I don't mind.'

Sonia raised her eyebrows, her face aglow in anticipation. Even Bill put in his bid in an endeavour to have them stay.

It worked.

'Claire, I'll get you to give Ella her bottle while I finish off in the kitchen. The bottle's made up, it's on the bench, it just needs to be heated.'

'Thanks, Mum, you're a treasure.' Claire hugged her mother and kissed her cheek. 'I love you, Mum,' she whispered.

Claire went back into the lounge room. 'Come on, cherub, time for dinner,' she said and reached out to take her baby from James. Ella started to fuss.

Claire pouted. 'Don't you want to come to Mummy?' The baby leaned her face toward James. 'Well, it looks like you've won a heart.'

James looked into Claire's eyes. 'I hope I've won two hearts,' he said, 'because two hearts have definitely won mine.'

Ella gave Claire a knowing smile.

'You cheeky little cherub,' she said and tickled her tummy.

'Would you like me to feed her?'

'If you want to,' Claire said and happily handed him the bottle.

'Come on, little princess,' he said and sat on the couch. He tucked the bib under her chin, put the bottle to his cheek to test that the temperature was right and then offered Ella her milk.

'You're a natural, James,' Claire said. 'Looks like you've done that before.'

'It's been a few years, but yes, I often fed my sister's kids when they were little.'

Claire sat on the armchair opposite, watching, amazed at the obvious bond between them. Ella hardly took her eyes off James, even when her little eyelids grew heavy. They'd start to close, and she'd quickly open them again. But the thing that touched Claire's heart and brought tears to her eyes was when she noticed James wipe a tear from his eye.

Claire stood quietly and backed up. She sniffed. 'Well, I'll leave you two and see if Mum needs a hand in the kitchen,' she whispered.

As usual, Sonia had everything organised. Claire beckoned to her. 'Hey Mum, come and look at this.'

Sonia wiped her hands on her apron. 'What is it?'

Claire put her finger to her lips. 'Shh. Look!'

Sonia poked her head around the corner. 'Oh, isn't that a picture. And Ella looks so content in his arms. Let's leave them be.'

They crept back into the kitchen.

'Mmm, something smells delicious. Is there anything you'd like me to do, Mum?'

'No, I'm fine, thanks, darling. You can just talk to me for a while.'

Claire waltzed around the kitchen as if she was floating on air. 'Oh, Mum,' she said, 'I'm so happy, I can't believe this is really happening to me.'

'Well, darling, after all you've been through, you deserve happiness, and you deserve a nice young man like James.'

'It's strange, Mum, I feel like I'm a different person. It's as if I can hardly remember the person I used to be. When I was with Eddy, I was someone else. I thought I loved him, but I was stupid! I don't even know what attracted me to him. I think it must have been sort of the bad-boy, tough-guy image or something like that, I don't know.' She shrugged. 'But James is so different; he really cares. And being cared for makes me want to care too. Does that make sense, Mum?'

'Yes, darling, it makes perfect sense.' Sonia lifted the edge of her apron and wiped her eyes. 'Why don't you go and tell your dad what you just told me. I'm sure he would like to hear it from you instead of second-hand from me.'

'Okay, I'll go find him,' she said with a smile.

Bill had dozed off in his recliner. Claire entered the room, and not wanting to disturb him sat by James and gently stroked her baby's head as she lay asleep in his arms.

'Do you want me to put her into her bed now?'

'I don't mind holding her,' he said, 'but if she needs to go to bed, I'll carry her upstairs for you.'

'Thanks, James, that'd be great. I think dinner's almost ready anyway.'

'Okay then, you lead the way.'

Claire stood, and James slowly moved from the couch, holding Ella gently in his arms.

They reached the nursery. Claire turned on the Tinkerbell fairy lamp, lowered the side of the cot and folded back the baby doona. James leaned across, placed the little one carefully in her bed and stepped back.

Claire smiled. 'Thanks, James,' she mouthed as she pulled the doona up, kissed Ella's tiny cheek and placed her favourite cuddly toy beside her.

James put his arm around Claire's waist and leaned over. 'Good night, little princess,' he whispered and turning to Claire in the dim light of the nursery, placed a tender kiss on her lips.

Claire looked deep into his crystal blue eyes and revelled in the warmth of his love.

By the time they returned to the lounge room, Bill was awake.

'Claire, there's something I want to show you in the garage.' He beckoned. 'Would you excuse us for a moment, James, we won't be long.'

'Sure,' he said with a knowing grin.

'Well, what is it that you want me to see out here, Dad?'

'Nothing really.'

'So, you brought me out here on false pretence, hey!'

'I just wanted tell you that your mother and I agree that James is a very nice young man, and we both approve of your friendship.'

'Thanks, Dad. That means a lot to me.' Claire gave him a big hug. 'Did Mum tell you what I said?'

'No, what was that?'

'Never mind. I'll tell you later. Can we go back inside now?' she asked.

'Dinner's served!' Sonia called from the dining room.

'Be there in a jiffy,' Bill replied. 'Come on, Claire, we'd better not be late.'

Sonia organised the seating while Bill poured the drinks.

'I'm pleased you decided to stay for dinner; there's no way Mum and I could have possibly eaten all this!' Bill said as he gestured with a sweep of his hand.

'Oh, Dad, don't tell me you're going to start on your jokes again!'

'Who me? Of course, not; we have a guest!'

'Don't change anything because of me,' James said. 'You remind me of my father; he was always one with the dinner jokes.'

Silence filled the room.

Bill cleared his throat. 'This all looks lovely, Sonia,' he said. 'Now let's give thanks.'

They bowed their heads; Bill said grace followed by a sincere 'Amen' that chorused around the table.

'I hope you don't mind pumpkin soup, James. Not everyone likes it.'

'I love pumpkin soup, Mrs Martin,' he replied as he rested a piece of bread roll on the plate. 'And this is absolutely delicious!'

'Yes, she's a good cook, James – that's why I married her.'

Sonia kicked Bill under the table.

'Ouch! What's wrong with that?'

'Well, for one thing, you know that I couldn't cook when you married me, so that couldn't have been the reason.'

'Aw, that's right, it must have been your good looks.'

'I think it was a bit more than that,' Claire added. 'I remember you telling me that it was love at first sight.'

'That's right, now I remember.'

Sonia sighed. 'Oh no! Don't get him started.'

'You want to hear the story, don't you, James?'

'Of course I do; it sounds interesting.'

Sonia rolled her eyes; Claire cleared her throat and Bill began.

'It happened one summer afternoon when my brother and I were sitting on the front verandah of our family home. I looked up and saw this pretty young lady in a beautiful red dress running across the road. I turned to my brother and said, "Do you see that pretty girl over there? I'm going to marry her one day." That's what I said and that's what I did.'

'So, it truly was love at first sight,' James said, 'and I think it's a lovely story, Mr Martin.'

'It's a true story, James.'

'More soup, anyone?'

'Yes, I'll have some more,' said Bill.

'But you haven't finished your first helping yet.'

'It's cold.'

'That's because you've been talking too much. Here give me your plate.'

Bill smiled up at Sonia. 'Thank you, dear.'

'What about you, James? Would you like some more?'

'Yes, please, Mrs Martin. I had better keep Bill company.'

'None for me, thanks, Mum, I'll save room for the main course.'

Claire pushed her chair back, collected the empty plates, and followed her mother into the kitchen. 'I'll take one of those bowls in for you, Mum; you just bring Dad's.'

'No, darling, you go back in and keep that conversation on the right track. Don't let Dad do all the talking.'

'He's all right, Mum. James seems to be enjoying the banter.'

'Here, you take this tray of bread rolls and I'll be in shortly with their soup.'

Claire took the tray, twirled on the spot and marched back into the dining room. 'Here we go,' she said and sat down. 'You both look serious … what gives?'

'I was asking James about his plans while he's in WA. He was telling me he'll be heading up north on Wednesday on business.'

Sonia gave the boys their soup. 'Oh, yes?' she said and sat down.

'I thought it best to get the bulk of the work done this week then be back in Perth for the weekend. I plan to go south the following Monday and Tuesday, so that'll leave Wednesday, Thursday, Friday, and the last weekend free.' He looked sideways at Claire, raised his eyebrows, and winked.

Sonia rearranged her already perfectly aligned cutlery and cleared her throat. 'So, what are your plans for tomorrow?' she asked.

'We've decided to go down to Mandurah for the day and, weather permitting, we'll do the lunchtime dolphin cruise.'

'That sounds nice,' said Sonia then turned and headed for the kitchen. Claire excused herself and followed.

The second course was served, and Bill piped up. 'Lamb chops and vegetables! Mmm, come on everyone, get in for your chop!' Sonia glanced at him with a stern expression and landed a punch on his upper arm. 'Ouch! What was that one for?' he grimaced.

James grinned. 'Don't worry, Mrs Martin, that's another one my dad used to say.' He looked down at the beautifully presented meal. 'This looks lovely.'

Sonia smiled. 'Thank you, James, enjoy!'

Following the second course, Claire and Sonia served dessert. But before placing each plate on the table, and with cheeky grins, they chorused 'We're discussed with the custard!'

Bill looked up. 'Now who's being cheeky?'

'I think it must be catching,' said James. They all laughed.

'We thought we'd save Dad from getting into more trouble,' Claire said as she handed James his sweets.

'Fancy, depriving him of one of his fatherly pleasures! You know how important it is for fathers to pass on their *dad jokes* to the next generation!'

'Well, I think we can survive without them. When you've heard them a thousand times, that's enough, don't you think?'

'Maybe.'

After dinner they retired to the lounge room for coffee. A tiny whimper sounded through the baby monitor.

James leaned forward in his chair. 'Sounds like our little princess is waking up,' he said.

Sonia smiled. *Oh, so she's* our *little princess now, is she? Hmm,* she thought.

'I can't believe it's almost ten o'clock,' Claire remarked with a cheeky smirk and looked across at James. 'Wow! How time flies when you're having fun.'

'I think I've heard that somewhere else today,' he said and waited, expecting someone to go upstairs and bring Ella down. But no one moved. They all just sat comfortably in their chairs sipping coffee. He put his mug on the coffee table and changed position. 'Is Ella due for another feed soon?' he asked as the whimper increased to a cry.

'Yes, I'll go and get her soon. I'll just finish my coffee first,' said Claire.

James appeared agitated.

'Don't worry, James, she's fine. It's good to let babies cry a little bit. Good for their lungs.'

He frowned.

Sonia finished the last of her coffee and stood. 'I'll go up and get her.'

'Thanks, Mum. I'll prepare the formula.'

James breathed a sigh of relief.

'Babies are a lot tougher than they look,' Bill said. 'And the women seem to know what they're doing.'

The crying stopped and Sonia's voice came through the monitor. 'Hello, my little darling, did you wake up?'

Ella answered with a happy gurgle.

'Come on, everyone wants to see you.' Her grandmother lifted her from the cot. 'It's time to go downstairs and have your supper.'

More happy gurgles rippled loudly and clearly through the system.

James relaxed.

'Hope you're enjoying the sound effects,' Bill commented.

James picked up the speaker from off the coffee table. 'It's a great little device,' he said. 'Must put your mind at ease when you're down here.'

'Yes, it sure does. And we carry it from room to room – even take it outside when we're in the garden.'

'Here we are,' said Sonia. 'Say hi to Grandpa and James.' Sonia leant over and held Ella's face close to Bill's.

'Thank you,' he said as he wiped the remains of an open-mouth slobbery kiss from his cheek. 'Mmm, just what I wanted.'

Sonia turned to James, and as soon as Ella saw him, her little eyes lit up, and she gave him the biggest smile. 'It looks like she's pleased to see you, James.'

'Hello, Ella,' he said, 'I'm pleased to see you too.'

'Now where's that Mummy of yours?' Sonia asked as she turned toward the kitchen.

Just then Claire came in holding the baby's bottle. 'Hello, my little possum,' she said as she shook the bottle.

'Would you like me to feed her before I head off?' asked James.

Sonia looked questioningly toward Claire who gave the nod of approval. 'It's kind of you to offer. Here we go then,' she said and placed the baby in his waiting arms.

Ella reached her little arm toward him and gave a toothless smile. He took her tiny hand in his, lifted it to his lips and kissed it tenderly. With his eyes fixed on the baby, he reached toward Claire. She passed him the bottle.

James tucked the terry-towelling feeder under her chin, tested the temperature of the milk on the inside of his wrist, then offered her the bottle. Ella began to suck contentedly, her chubby cheeks moving in rhythm as an overflow of warm milk trickled from the corner of her mouth. Soon the bottle was empty. James put the cloth over his shoulder, held the sleepy child to his chest and gently rubbed her back.

Burp! Everyone heard it.

'That was a good one!' Claire said and offered to relieve James of his duty.

'I don't mind holding her for a while longer, that is, unless you think she should go to bed,' he said as he looked up with pleading puppy dog eyes.

'All right then,' Claire tutted. 'I suppose she can stay up for another five minutes.'

James rested his head back on the sofa, closed his eyes and rocked the baby gently in his arms.

Picking up the empty bottle, Claire tiptoed toward the kitchen and beckoned to her mother. 'Come and have a look at this,' she whispered.

Sonia followed her through to the lounge room where Bill sat on his recliner, feet up, mouth wide open and fast asleep while on the couch opposite sat James, eyes closed and relaxed with the baby snug in his arms.

'What a picture! Quick, take a photo,' Sonia mouthed.

Claire grabbed her phone from her pocket, focused in on the sleeping duo and snapped, then took a photo of Bill. 'That'll be one for the family album,' she whispered.

Sonia and Claire returned to the kitchen.

Reaching out toward her daughter, Sonia embraced her in a motherly hug. 'Oh darling, I'm so happy for you. I think James is wonderful. He's a real gentleman. And isn't it amazing how Ella has just taken to him like that!'

'I feel like I need to pinch myself, Mum; it's almost too good to be true.' Claire choked back a threatening tear. 'But it is true, Mum, it really is.'

Sonia plucked a handful of tissues from the box, gave a wad to Claire, and totally saturated the rest herself.

'Thanks, Mum,' Claire said, 'but I really must put Ella to bed. And James will be so tired.' She frowned. 'I hope he'll be all right driving back to the hotel.'

'Don't worry, darling. I'm sure he'll be fine.' Sonia stroked Claire's arm. 'I'll make him a strong cup of coffee before he goes.'

Sonia filled the kettle, flicked the power switch on and took four mugs down from the top cupboard.

'I'll put Ella into bed,' Claire said and wandered through to the lounge room.

She tapped James on the shoulder. He stirred. Groggy at first then shaking his head, he focused. 'Sorry, I must have dozed off.' Little Ella stretched her arms and yawned. 'Would you like me to carry her upstairs for you?' he asked.

'Thanks, I'd appreciate that, if you don't mind. That is if you're sure you're awake,' she said with a cheeky grin.

He looked at his watch. 'Of course I'm awake, but do you realise it's actually after midnight back home in Adelaide,' he said as he slowly inched himself from the seat clutching the precious baby girl in his arms.

Together they climbed the stairs, entered Ella's room, and settled her into the cot.

James kissed his fingers and touched Ella's forehead. 'Good night, little princess, I'll see you in the morning,' he said and quietly left the room.

Claire raised the side of the cot, looked around the room, grabbed some of the baby's clothes for the wash, and followed James downstairs.

The smell of fresh coffee wafted through the air.

'Mmm, your Mum sure knows how to make a good cup of coffee,' James whispered in Claire's ear. Bill was still asleep, and Sonia was in the kitchen, so James, seizing the moment, sat himself down, took Claire by the hand and set her on his lap. With one arm around her waist, he brushed a stray strand of hair from her forehead then moved his hand to the back of her head and gently drew her face to his. Her heart skipped a beat and flocks of butterflies fluttered in her stomach. She licked her lips. James touched his lips to hers; gently at first, then little by little the pressure and intensity built. Her lips parted. His tongue touched hers. They both savoured the sweetness of the taste.

Bill snorted.

The kiss ended.

Just then Sonia came in carrying a tray of coffee.

Claire stood and collected two drinks. She handed James his coffee and sat beside him. 'Thanks, Mum,' she said.

'Yes, thank you, Mrs Martin, this should keep me awake until I get to the hotel. You've been so kind to me. I'll have to find some way to repay you.'

'No need. We're more than happy to have you.'

Chapter 20

Claire was almost ready when James arrived early the next day. 'Won't be long she called from upstairs.'

'Would you like a cup of coffee while you're waiting?' Sonia asked. 'Bill's outside giving Ella a tour of the garden – she loves it out there - I'll let him know you're here.'

'Thanks, Mrs Martin; coffee would be lovely.'

She slid the window open. 'James is here,' she yelled, 'and I've made a fresh pot of coffee. Are you coming in?'

'Okay. We'll be there in a jiffy,' he said and stooped to pick a small bunch of everlasting daisies. 'Let's take these in for your Nan. I think she'll like them.'

Hearing a noise on the stairs, James turned, crossed the room and looked up. 'Don't try to carry all that!' he said as Claire struggled down the stairs juggling two over-stuffed bags. 'Wait there, I'll come and get them.' He climbed the stairs two at a time, took the bags from her, placed them down and, wrapping his arms around her, kissed her thoroughly. Then kissed her again.

Pulling away, James looked into her eyes. 'You are beautiful,' he said and told her again how much he loved her.

'I love you too,' she said. 'And by the way, you don't look too bad yourself.'

'Coffee's ready!' came the call.

James carried the bags down, put them by the front door and then went through to the kitchen.

'Hi, mate,' Bill said as he opened the screen door. 'How's it going?'

'Good, thanks, Bill. How about you?'

'Not bad for an old codger.'

James reached toward Ella. 'And how's our little princess?' he asked. She smiled and wrapped her hand around his finger.

'Looks like she's pleased to see you. Here we go, then,' Bill said as he passed the baby over to him. 'Are you staying for coffee?'

'Yes, thanks, then we'll have to head off because we want to make sure we get tickets for the lunchtime cruise.'

'Righto then, but before you go, I'll give you a hand to put the baby capsule into your car. I've got it in the garage ready to go.'

'Thanks, Mr Martin,' he said and immediately corrected his mistake. 'Bill.'

They loaded the car and said their goodbyes. Then, checking that his passengers were both safely secure, James slowly reversed the car up the driveway.

Sonia and Bill waved them off.

'We couldn't have picked a better day,' Claire said as she turned to check on Ella.

James adjusted the rear-vision mirror. 'It's perfect,' he replied. 'Just being with you makes it perfect.'

'I feel like I'm dreaming!' Claire said. 'I think I need to pinch myself. It's too good to be true.'

James kept his eyes on the road. 'Well, it is true, and while I'm here, I want to make the best of our time together.

'Me too,' said Claire. Then a happy little gurgle came from the back of the car. Claire laughed. 'It sounds like Ella agrees with that!'

'Yeah! Good girl, Ella.'

They continued south to Mandurah and, when they arrived, were pleasantly surprised to find plenty of parking and not too many people around.

'It wouldn't be like this if it was a weekend or the school holidays,' Claire said. 'Sometimes we have to drive round and round before we find a place to park. This is great!'

James lifted the pram from the car boot and tried to set it up. 'I can't seem to get the hang of this,' he said.

Claire took hold of the handle and, with one quick flick of the wrist, had it set ready to go.

James scratched his head. 'You make it look so easy.'

'Comes with practice,' Claire said with a cheeky smirk.

'Mmm, well then,' James replied with an equally cheeky crooked grin, 'in that case, it looks like I'll have to have more practice!'

Claire collapsed the pram again. 'Here we go then, now you watch carefully. Number one, hold the handle firmly with both hands – like this.'

'Right. I've got that.'

'Then with one fluid motion, lift and flick, like this. Then all you need do is apply the brakes. Do you want to have a go?'

'Yep!'

With the pram refolded, James placed both hands on the handle. 'Is this right?'

Claire's hands covered his. 'Yes, that seems right,' she said and stepped back.

'Why did you have to take your hands away?' he complained, looking at her with his puppy dog eyes. He sniffed. 'I was enjoying that.'

'Come on now,' she replied sternly, hands on hips, 'you have to concentrate.'

'Okay,' he said and, with one flick, mastered the skill.

'Yeah! You did it! Congratulations,' she said and kissed his forehead.

James swept her off her feet and twirled her round.

'Stop it,' she said with a giggle. 'We've got to get the rest of the things out of the car. Will you do that while I put Ella in the pram?'

'Righto,' he said and lowered her to the ground.

Claire uncoupled the safety harness and lifted the sleeping child from the baby capsule. Ella stretched her arms above her head, opened one eye and gave a big yawn. Claire kissed her soft rosy cheek. 'There's a good girl,' she said and settled her into the pram.

'Do you need all these bags?' James asked.

'Yes, here give them to me.'

Claire put one bulky bag in a compartment under the pram; another she fitted into a mesh basket at the back, then hooked a smaller one, with a long strap, over the handle. And finally slung her own bag over her shoulder. 'Right, we're ready to go,' she said.

James was amazed at the efficiency with which Claire moved. 'You're amazing!' I didn't realise how much stuff one little baby needs. Wow! It's like getting ready for a two-week holiday.'

'Yep, that's right, but you always need to be prepared, it's better to have too much than not enough.'

'That's so true.' James said as he clicked the car lock. 'Now, which way do we go to get the tickets for the boat?'

Claire nodded toward the Visitors Centre and turned the pram.

'Can I push it please?' he asked.

'Sure, be my guest.'

James proudly took control of the pram. Claire looped her arm through his and they strolled toward the ticket office.

Having secured seats on the Dolphin Cruise they wandered out to the point, sat under the magnificent Morton Bay Figtree, and watched two fishermen trying to catch ... something – anything? But they caught nothing.

Ella began to stir.

'I'll give her a bottle now,' Claire said. 'It's a bit early, but if I leave it 'til we get on board, she'll be really hungry.'

'Can I feed her?' James asked.

'If you want to,' Claire said as she added dry formula to the warm water already in the bottle. She shook it well. Tested the flow. 'Just right,' she said and handed it to James.

'Hello, little possum, did you wake up?'

Ella blew a raspberry bubble and dribbled down her chin.

'Well, I guess that's a yes.'

Claire shivered. 'Brrr, it's a bit chilly,' she said as she lifted Ella from the pram and pulled the bunny rug up around her head. 'Are you ready for your morning tea?'

Ella smiled a gummy smile.

James took the baby in his arms. 'Time for dinner,' he said and tucked the bib under her chin. She smiled up at him.

After a good feed, a burp, and a nappy change they headed off to join the queue of waiting passengers.

It was a beautiful day. The sun glistened on the water. The muffled throb-throb of the vessel's engine, the sweet salt smell in the air and the screech of seagulls overhead all added to the excitement of the cruise. But the highlight of the trip was seeing a pod of dolphins darting and turning and frolicking in the wake of the boat.

James held Ella up and pointed. 'Look, bubby, dolphins!'

An elderly lady turned to him. 'What a lovely child!' she said. 'And she's the image of her daddy.'

'Do you think so?' Claire said.

'Yes, definitely,' she replied. 'She is the spitting image of him.'

James smiled. He turned to Claire and whispered, 'And I thought seeing the dolphins was the highlight of the day, but that tops the lot!'

Claire smiled up at him. 'That was nice, don't you think?'

'Yes, it was.'

All too soon, the cruise ended. The Ferry pulled into the dock, and the passengers filed out. Claire and James were the last to disembark. They thanked the pilot, and then James pushed the pram up the ramp.

'That was so good,' he said. Claire caught hold of his arm and snuggled close. 'Come on, let's have a coffee.'

Five minutes later, while meandering along the boardwalk toward the coffee shop, Claire suddenly pulled back. She shuddered. 'Oh no! Look who's heading this way.'

James glanced up. 'Just put your head down and keep walking,' he whispered, 'they might not notice us.' But it was too late.

Francine spotted them. She nudged Eddy. His piercing dark

eyes flashed their way as they came closer. Then he spat out his venom. 'So, it's you!' he said through clenched, tobacco-stained teeth.

'Don't make eye contact,' James warned. 'Just keep walking ahead; don't look back.' He could feel Claire's hand shaking against his arm. 'It'll be all right,' he said, trying to reassure himself as much as Claire. 'It'll be all right'.

Claire did exactly what James said even though her legs felt like jelly, and she could almost feel Eddy's eyes burning holes through her back.

'Come on, Claire, we're almost there,' James encouraged. They veered left and then right and entered the coffee shop. James pushed the pram through to the rear of the café and found a table right at the back. 'Here, we are safe now.' James pulled the chair out for her. 'You just sit here, and I'll order the drinks. What would you like?'

Claire flopped onto the chair, rested her elbows on the table and covered her face with her hands. 'I don't know,' she said, 'I feel sick.'

'You should have something. How about a hot chocolate?'

'Yuk! I couldn't possibly stomach it.'

'What about a cup of tea or warm water?'

'Water will be fine.'

James put in their order and quickly checked outside for any sign of Eddy and Francine. All was clear. Returning to the table, he placed their order number down and sat opposite Claire. She looked pale. He was concerned. 'There's no sign of those two around anywhere,' he said, 'so now we can relax and enjoy a drink.'

Claire excused herself and rushed to the toilet.

She'd no sooner gone than Ella began to stir.

'It's all right, sweetie pie. Mummy will be back soon.'

Minutes passed. James became anxious. Ella started to cry. He picked her up. She wiggled restlessly in his arms. 'Shh,' he whispered softly.

A young waitress served their order.

'Excuse me,' James said, 'my friend wasn't feeling well and went into the Ladies' room. She's been gone for quite a while, and I'm worried about her. Would you mind checking on her for me please?'

'Sure, just give me a moment,' she replied and wiped her hands on her apron.

'Thank you, I appreciate that.'

James tried to remember where Claire kept Ella's bottle of water and the formula powder. Was it in the bag under the pram or in the one at the back? *Umm.* He scratched his head. *I can't do this with one hand.* 'I'm going to have to put you back in the pram, little girl,' he told Ella and laid her down. She didn't like that one bit and let everyone in the café know. But James had to make up the bottle first! And for that he needed two hands! The more he tried, the more frustrated he became.

Just then Claire appeared.

'Phew!' James wiped his forehead.

'I'm sorry,' he said as he jiggled the pram, 'she was hungry, but I couldn't find her bottle.'

Claire wiped her mouth with a tissue and took a sip of water. 'That's all right, I'll sort it out.' Rummaging through the bag, she soon found what she needed while Ella continued exercising her lungs.

'Shall I pick her up?' James asked.

'Thanks, that would help.'

Instantly the crying stopped.

'You've sure got the touch, mate,' a guy sitting at the next table called.

James smiled.

Claire cleared her throat and tried to tip the baby formula into the bottle, but her hand was shaking.

'Here let me do it.' James said and passed the baby across to Claire. He poured the powder into the bottle, screwed the top on firmly and gave it a shake. 'Would you like me to feed her?' he asked.

'It's all right. Just give me the bottle I'll feed her. And I could really do with a drink of hot chocolate now. Do you mind ordering one for me while I feed Ella?'

'Sure, that's no problem,' he said and brushed his hand across her cheek. 'And it's good to see you looking much better.'

'Thanks, James, it's good to feel a bit better too.'

Her heartbeat almost back to a normal pace, Claire stared into the mug. She swirled it round in her hands and watched as the marshmallow sank slowly beneath the chocolate foam.

'A penny for your thoughts?' James said.

'I was thinking about Francine and how awful she looks. I hardly even recognised her at first. Did you see that terrible bruise on her arm?'

'That black thing! I thought it was a tattoo.'

'No, it was definitely a bruise. Eddy would be using her like he used me … as his personal punching bag. He's so cruel. I know if I hadn't left him when I did, he would have killed Ella.'

'What! Don't tell me he hurt her too!'

Tears filled Claire's eyes as she shared with James some of the horror they had encountered with Eddy.

Furious, James banged both fists on the edge of the table and hung his head. 'I could punch his lights out,' he said through gritted teeth. 'That guy should be charged.'

Claire had never seen that side of James before. *Well, he is a normal guy, after all,* she thought, *with normal guy emotions. Good. And he's obviously very protective, that's good too.* 'You had better finish your coffee before it gets cold,' she said.

James sighed, and lifting his head, looked at her with such tenderness that her heart skipped a beat. 'I love you so much,' he said and, reaching across the table, took both her hands in his. 'And I'll love you forever,' he added.

The mood was sombre in the car as they drove home. Neither

James nor Claire felt much like talking, and thankfully, Ella stayed fast asleep.

Claire's mobile phone sounded. She shook herself from her stupor and grabbed it out of her bag. 'Hi, Claire here.'

'Hi, darling, it's Mum. I just rang to see how you're going. Are you having a lovely time?'

'Mmm, um, yes,' she replied hesitantly.

'Are you all right?'

Claire sighed. 'Yes, we're on our way home. We'll tell you all about it when we get there.

'Is Ella okay? And what about James?'

'Yes, Mum, they're all right. We'll see you soon.'

'You don't sound right,' she said. 'I'm worried.'

'No need to worry, Mum, we're fine. Thanks for ringing. Bye.'

Sonia sighed and ended the call. She was worried. *What could have happened? Did they have an accident? Maybe they had a disagreement. Oh, no I hope they haven't broken up.'* Poor Sonia. The more she thought about it, the more worried she became. She felt sick to the stomach and Bill wasn't home from work yet. She checked the time. *Too late to ring him at the office, he would have already left by now. Oh well I'm just going to have to wait 'til he gets home*, she concluded.

She heard the roller door to the garage open.

'Yeah!' she said with much relief and, not waiting for Bill to come inside, she rushed out to meet him.

'Whatever's the matter,' he said as he opened the car door.

'I don't know. When I spoke to Claire on the phone, she didn't sound happy.'

'Oh Sonia, you shouldn't have rung them while they were out.'

'Well, I am her mother and I like to keep in touch,' she said and burst into tears.

Bill pulled a handkerchief from his pocket, wiped her eyes, and put his arms around her. 'It's all right, darling. Everything is going to be fine.' He locked the car, pressed the remote-control button for the roller door and led her into the house. 'Come on, you sit down, and I'll make you a nice cup of tea.'

She sniffed. 'Thank you,' she said and flopped onto the sofa.

They were almost home when Ella began to stir.

It's all right, darling,' Claire said as she turned and stroked the baby's arm.

James glanced across at Claire. 'Your voice sounds a bit husky. Are you feeling all right?'

'To tell the truth, I feel as if I've been run over by a steamroller; my ribs are aching and I'm absolutely exhausted.'

'Mmm, I know what you mean. That would be due to the shock of seeing Eddy again. I feel rather washed out myself.'

Ella started to cry.

'Oh no, darling. Please don't get upset, we're almost home. I can't pick you up now.' Claire did her best to rock the baby's capsule from her seat in the front of the car, but Ella wouldn't be pacified. Then Claire burst into tears.

James pulled the car off the road and cut the engine. It broke his heart to hear his girls crying. Uncoupling his seatbelt, he reached across and took Claire in his arms. 'We can stop here for a while. I can get Ella out of the back and make up another bottle for her if you like.'

Claire forced a smile. 'Thanks,' she said, 'I don't think I could even stand up; my legs feel like jelly.'

'Here we go, little girl,' he said, lifting Ella from her seat. He held her to his chest. Her crying stopped. She took a jagged breath.

'Here's your Mummy,' he said and handed her to Claire. 'I'll just get that bottle ready.'

Keeping the door of the car open, Claire sat the baby upright on her lap and rubbed her back. Ella burped. 'That's better,' Claire said and received one great big smile in return.

'Are you all right to feed her?' James asked.

'Yes, I think it'll take my mind off … you know who.'

'Yep, that's a good idea.'

Ella fed contentedly.

Suddenly Claire caught her breath. 'Oh no,' she gasped, 'Mum will be worried about us. I'd better ring her back.'

'Do you want me to ring?'

'Okay.'

Sonia jumped at the sound of the telephone.

'I'll get it!' Bill called from the kitchen. 'Hello, Bill Martin speaking.'

Sonia strained to hear.

'Mmm, oh, I see,' Bill replied. 'Never mind; can't be helped.' The call ended.

Poor Sonia's heart raced. 'What is it?' she asked. 'What's happening?'

'They've just got a bit delayed. They'll be home soon.'

'But what's wrong? I know there's something wrong.'

'As far as I know there's no problem,' Bill tried to reassure her.

'Well, why didn't you ask more questions? You know it worries me when I know there's something wrong and they don't tell me what it is!'

'There's no need to worry. James rang out of courtesy to let us know they'd be a bit late so we wouldn't worry! So please stop worrying!' Bill took her in his arms and held her close. 'It's all right, darling, they'll be home soon, so, how about you put the kettle on and I'll set the table.'

Sonia smiled through her tears and let the overflow trickle down her cheeks.

'Oh, you're an old softy,' Bill said and wiped her tears with his handkerchief.

Ten minutes later, the car pulled into the driveway.

'They're here!' Sonia yelled and rushed outside to meet them.

The sound of Ella's screeching pierced the air, drowning out the sound of the engine. 'Oh, my little darling,' she said as she opened the car door. 'It's all right. Nanna's here.' It was then that she noticed Claire slumped forward in the front seat. 'Are you all right?'

Claire nodded.

'Well come on, everyone; let's get you inside.'

Sonia lifted the baby from the seat and rested her against her shoulder. Ella shivered. Wrapping the rug around her, Sonia carried her into the house.

James helped Claire out of the car and, taking her by the arm, guided her along the pathway toward the house.

Claire looked back. 'What about the things?'

'Don't worry about them, I'll bring them in later.'

'Did you lock the car?'

'Yes, all done.'

Claire and James slumped down onto the couch and, after catching their breath, explained what had transpired that day.

Sonia gasped. 'My goodness, of all people, fancy meeting them! I can't believe it.'

Claire started to cry.

'Oh, darling, I'm sorry. I didn't mean to upset you,' Sonia said as she sat down on the other side of Claire.

From his recliner on the opposite side of the room, Bill added his reassurance. 'Don't let that jerk get you down – he's not worth it. Forget about him and just put what happened today behind you. Okay, princess?'

She nodded.

Taken aback by how deeply the encounter with Eddy had affected Claire, James tried his best to comfort her. 'I wish I didn't have to go away for work tomorrow,' he said. 'I hate leaving you.'

Claire sniffed. 'I'll be all right. Mum and Dad are here.'

'I'll phone every day to make sure you're all right.'

Claire rested her head on his chest and held him tight. 'I'm going to miss you,' she said with a sad smile.

'Me too.'

Sonia looked across at Bill, jerked her head toward the kitchen and stood up. 'Come on, Bill. I need help in the kitchen.'

'Right you are,' he said and followed.

Ten minutes later, Bill poked his head around the corner and gave an exaggerated cough. 'Excuse me,' he said with a cheeky sideways grin, 'if I can interrupt you two lovebirds for a couple of minutes, I'd like a word with James.'

Reluctantly breaking away, James followed him through to his study. Bill pointed to the chair. 'Take a seat,' he said, 'I won't keep you too long – I just wanted a little word.'

James sat bolt upright on the edge of the chair and stared straight ahead.

'You can relax, mate, it's not the headmaster's office,' Bill said and rested his hand on James' shoulder.

'Sorry, I'm still a bit jittery.'

'That's understandable, but please don't worry about Claire and Ella while you're away. They'll be fine – we'll make sure of that. Okay?'

'Thanks, Mr Martin. I know you will.'

Bill didn't bother correcting James; he figured that eventually he'd get the hang of calling him by his first name. 'And, James,' he went on to say, 'please be patient with Claire; she's been through a lot. She's doing well considering all ...' He paused, turned on his heels and stared out the window, then weighing his words, he continued. 'Seeing Eddy today would have brought it all back to her, like a nightmarish flashback. The specialist warned that this could and most probably would happen. I'm sorry you had to witness the incident and sorry we weren't there with you.'

Bill turned, his eyes awash with tears.

'No need to explain, Mr Mart ... oh, sorry, Bill.' James stood. 'I love Claire, and no matter what has happened and no matter what will happen, nothing can stop me loving her and nothing ever will.'

'It's good to hear you say that James and I believe your love is sincere.' Bill took his handkerchief from his pocket, gave it a shake, and blew his nose then folded it neatly and placed it back in his pocket. 'James, as you know Claire and Ella are all that my wife and I have, and we love them more than life itself and we'll do anything to protect them.'

James knew that love full well – it was what he felt too.

The two men embraced. Unembarrassed. James spoke. 'I promise you with every fibre of my being that I will do everything in my power to always love and protect Claire and Ella. Bill, could I have your permission to marry your daughter?'

Bill choked back tears. 'James,' he said, 'I feel like you are the son I never had and it's like God has brought you into our family. Yes, James, and I'm sure I speak for Sonia when I say we would be happy for you to marry Claire.'

James sucked in a deep breath. 'Thank you, Mr Martin. Now all I have to do is ask Claire, but I might wait awhile.'

'Good idea, mate. I don't think tonight would be the best time.'

Bill pulled the curtains across and opened the door. 'After you, sonny boy,' he said with a wink, 'smells like dinner cooking.'

'Shh,' Sonia whispered when she heard the fella's coming. She pointed at Claire who lay curled up on the sofa fast asleep.

James leant over, touched her face and placed a gentle kiss on her forehead, and then, taking a rug from off the chair, covered her.

'It's best to let her sleep … best way to recover,' said Bill when James joined them in the kitchen.

James couldn't wipe the grin from his face. And Bill seemed to be in a jovial mood.

'What have you guys been talking about all this time behind closed doors?' Sonia asked.

'Can you keep a secret, Mrs Martin?' James whispered.

'Of course I can. What is it?' Sonia's eyes sparkled with excitement. 'Come on, don't keep me in suspense.'

Bill looked across at James. He rubbed his chin in contemplation. 'Aw, I'm not sure that we should tell her just yet,' he teased.

Sonia jiggled her leg in frustrated anticipation. 'Oh, you can't say there's something and then just leave me dangling in mid-air like that. Come on, please tell me.'

'Now, Sonia,' Bill emphasised, 'if we tell you, you must promise not to breathe a word of it to Claire. Promise?'

'Cross my heart, I won't say a word.'

'Okay then, let's go out into the backyard – we don't want Claire to hear.'

Sonia was so excited she could hardly wait. 'Come on then, be quick before Ella wakes up,' she said and, grabbing the baby monitor from the bench, she tiptoed to the door.

The evening breeze swept her hair across her face. She tucked it behind her ears, sat down on one of the wicker chairs and adjusted the cushion at her back.

Bill took the seat beside her, and James sat opposite.

'Go on, James, you tell her.'

'Um …' *How do I word it? Perhaps I should ask her; not just tell her,* he surmised. He cleared his throat. 'Could I, um, would it be all right if I, um, with your permission, ask Claire to marry me?' *Did that come out right?* he thought.

Sonia was lost for words. She put her hand to her chest, her head down and wiped a tear from her eye.

Oh no, she's not happy, James thought, then he looked at Bill and frowned.

'Don't worry, son. Enjoy the silence. It's a rare treat for Sonia to be lost for words. She'll come around soon.'

'But she didn't answer my question,' James mouthed.

Sonia jumped to her feet, wrapped her arms around his neck and sobbed. 'Yes, yes, yes,' she said. 'These are just tears of happiness.'

'Oh, I see. Thank you, Mrs Martin.'

'When are you planning to ask Claire?'

'Soon I guess, but I'll have to wait for the right moment. Besides, I haven't bought a ring yet. I might have a look for one over the next few days, while I'm away up north. If I have time that is; the schedule's quite busy.'

'Do you know what size ring to buy?'

'No, I didn't think of that. Do you know her size?'

'Not off hand but I can have a look at one of her dress rings she keeps in her jewellery box and measure that for you.'

'Would you? Thanks, that'd be great.'

'I'll sneak upstairs now while she's asleep and check it out for you,' Sonia said with a mischievous grin and shot off.

'When she gets a bee in her bonnet there's no stopping her,' Bill said in answer to James' questioning gaze.

'Well, she certainly seems keen; I'm pleased about that,' he replied.

Bill jumped to his feet. 'How about we have a drink to celebrate. I'm not sure what we've got in the fridge, but I'll have a look.'

'Want a hand?'

'No, you stay there. Sonia will be back in a minute and I'm sure she wants to give detailed instructions as to sizing etc.'

Bill wandered inside, leaving James to his own thoughts. The last of the sun's rays cast a golden glow around him. He looked up. The evening star, visible in the western sky, appeared larger than usual and seemed to twinkle its approval.

James smiled. 'Thank you, Lord,' he whispered.

When Sonia showed James the ring that they'd given Claire for her eighteenth birthday, he slipped it onto his little finger. It went as far as his middle joint. 'Oh, it's so tiny,' he said. 'I'm glad you mentioned about the size, because if I'd have chosen one it probably would have been much too big. Thanks.'

'You wouldn't want it any bigger than that one, because you see, Claire wears it on the ring finger of her right hand and being right-handed that would actually be slightly bigger than her left finger.'

'Oh, I didn't realise that.'

Bill appeared with a tray of sparkling apple cider.

'Here we go,' he said. 'Cheers!'

They clinked glasses.

'Cheers!' echoed Sonia.

She took a sip and thought for a minute. 'Would you like to take the ring with you?'

James sucked in a breath. 'I wouldn't want to lose it,' he said. 'Anyway, Claire will wonder where it is. No, I know how it fits on my finger now and I should be close to the mark.'

'I'm sure Claire won't miss it. She only ever wears it on special occasions, and I've got a little velvet draw-string bag you could put it in.'

'Well, if you're sure that's okay. I could keep it safe in my wallet.'

'Good idea.'

Just then, Claire, blurry eyed and cocooned in a rug, appeared at the doorway. James quickly put his hand behind his back and slipped the ring deep into his trouser pocket.

'Why are you all sitting out here in the dark?' Claire asked.

'Well, it wasn't dark when we first came out and we've been talking, and we didn't want to disturb you,' Sonia said. 'Anyway, it's time for us to come in for dinner.'

'You had a good sleep. Do you feel better now?' James asked.

'I feel a bit drained and spaced out, but I'm okay.'

Bill stood and gathered the empty glasses. 'We just had a drink of apple cider. Would you like me to pour one for you?'

Claire licked her dry lips. 'Thanks, Dad, that'd be nice.'

'After you, my darling,' Bill said as he waited for Sonia.

She picked up the baby monitor and wandered into the kitchen.

James held back. With his hands in his pockets, he felt for the tiny ring lodged deep in the corner of his left-hand pocket.

Claire shivered. 'Are you coming in, James? It's getting cold with the door open.'

Snapping from his daydream, he strode into the house, closed the door behind him and whisked Claire off her feet and twirled her round.

'Put me down!' she demanded with a laugh. 'I can't get my arms out, they're trapped in this rug.'

He lowered her gently to the floor and, looking into her eyes, he said, 'I love you so much, Claire, my honey bear.'

'Shh, Mum and Dad will hear you.'

'I don't think that matters,' he said, an taking a deep breath said it again, louder this time, 'I love you, Claire Martin!'

Claire giggled. 'You're such a dag.'

'Oh, a dag, am I?' he said as he peeled the rug from her shoulders, took her in his arms and kissed her intensely without reserve, in the kitchen, in full sight of her parents.

'Wow!' chorused Bill and Sonia.

'I think you two had better go into the lounge room while I give Sonia a hand to dish out the dinner,' Bill added.

'Come on, Claire. We'd better do as we're told – we don't want to get into trouble,' James said as he took her by the hand and led the way.

Out in the kitchen, Bill and Sonia spoke in hushed tones, both thrilled with Claire's bounce back from the day's upset.

'And what about James?' Sonia whispered. 'Isn't he excited. I don't think he'll be able to wait 'til he gets back from his trip to pop the question to Claire. What do you think?'

'I think he'll wait. He seems dead set on having a ring to give her first. The question is, will you be able keep the secret?'

'Of course I will.'

Bill lifted the lid of the saucepan, picked up a wooden spoon and stirred the Irish stew. 'Mmm, smells delicious,' he said, looked around and then stealthily snuck a sample.

Sonia flicked the rolled-up tea towel at him. 'I saw that,' she said with a cheeky grin. Tonight, nothing could dampen the amazing joy that bubbled in her heart.

Taking her in his arms, Bill kissed her, and then, pulling away, he looked into her eyes and told her how much he loved her.

'I love you too,' she whispered. 'I always have, and I always will.' Then she stood on her tiptoes, reached up, brought his head down, and kissed his forehead.

'Come on now, that's nice, but let's not get too carried away.'

Bill reached up, took the condiments from the top cupboard, and put them on the table. 'Do you want anything else on the table?' he asked.

'Just the bread rolls and the butter,' Sonia said as she drained the potatoes ready to mash. 'Oh yes, you can pass me the milk while you've got the fridge open, if you don't mind.'

'I don't mind, my darling,' he said, and placing the milk on the bench, he stood behind her, put his arms around her waist and nuzzled his face into the back of her neck.

'Excuse me,' Sonia tutted. 'Now tell me who's the one getting carried away?'

'Mmm, um, sorry, darling. I'll try to behave myself; I just got a bit distracted.' Bill scratched his head. 'Um, now what was the other thing you wanted me to put on the table?'

'The bread and butter, and when you've done that, you can call the kids to come for dinner.'

Turning on his heels, Bill bowed his head, did a little salute, and carried out the instructions.

Chitchat around the dining table that evening was light and pleasant, seasoned as always with a good helping of "dad jokes".

'Oh Dad, do you have to?' Claire complained with a resigned rolling of her eyes.

Sonia passed the bread basket around the table. 'Just try to ignore him,' she said, 'maybe it'll go away.'

'I doubt it very much,' Claire replied. 'I think it's an addiction.'

'Reminds me of my dad,' James chipped in, adding his bit to the banter.

Just then the baby monitor sprang to life.

'Sounds like a little princess wants to join us,' Bill said. 'I know she appreciates my jokes — she always smiles.'

'Oh, Dad, that's because she doesn't understand a word you say.'

Bill rolled his bottom lip in a mock pout and, pushing his chair back from the table, looked at Claire. 'Will it be all right if I go upstairs and get her and bring her down?'

'Off you go then,' she said with a dismissive brush of her hand.

'Who's for seconds?' Sonia asked as Bill disappeared from the room.

James rubbed his tummy. 'Um, that was delicious, Mrs Martin, but I'm afraid I couldn't fit another thing in. I'm filled right up to pussy's bow.'

'That was one of my dad's sayings,' Sonia remarked, 'I haven't heard that expression for years.'

Sounds from the nursery interrupted their talk.

A slight squeak as the door opened, followed by a happy gurgle from Ella. Then Bill's voice came through the monitor.

'Hello, little princess, you had a big sleep. Now where's that teddy bear? Oh, here he is! Hello, teddy, did you have a big sleep too? You did. Well, let's go down and see Nanna, and Mum, and James.'

Ella yawned.

'Am I boring you? I'm sorry,' he said with a chuckle. 'Come on now, let's go.'

Meanwhile, downstairs, with the baby monitor relaying the upstairs conversation, Claire put both hands to her mouth to smother her laughter while Sonia took a sip of water trying to quench her blush.

Entering the room with Ella in his arms, Bill stopped and gave them all a strange look. 'What?' he asked.

'I see you brought Teddy with you,' Sonia said in a childlike voice.

'Of course we did. We love our Teddy, don't we, Ella?'

She smiled and gave Bill a big open-mouth kiss.

'Thank you, darling,' he said as he wiped his cheek with the back of his hand.

'Oh, Dad, when you were upstairs in Ella's room, we could hear what you were saying; it all came through on the baby monitor. I thought it was so cute!'

'Oh, so you were eavesdropping, were you? Did you hear that, Ella? They were listening in on our private conversation. Can you believe that?'

'I don't think she knows what you're saying, Dad.

'Of course she does. That right isn't it, Ella?'

Ella rested her head on Bill's chest and, looking up, smiled at him with her big blue eyes.

'See, I told you she understands every word I say.'

'Come on, Grandpa, you had better sit down and finish your meal. Here, I'll take Ella.' Claire took the baby and, turning to James, said, 'You stay and keep Dad out of mischief while I go and feed Ella.'

Sonia busied herself in the kitchen and left the men to themselves to talk.

After they'd finished their meal and tidied the kitchen, Sonia and Bill discreetly left the house to go for a walk.

'We'll be back later,' Sonia called and closed the door behind them.

Chapter 21

Alone once more, and with Ella settled down for the night, James and Claire wanted to make the most of their precious time together. Sitting on the sofa, James cupped Claire's face in his hands and looked deep into her eyes. 'I love you so much,' he said. 'And it's good to see the sparkle back in your eyes again.' He breathed a gentle kiss across her lips. She tilted her head slightly back. He kissed her neck then the top of her chest and, sliding his hand beneath her t-shirt, pushed it off one shoulder and with his lips caressed the soft skin of her shoulder.

Claire's heart rate quickened, and she felt a stirring; her whole being longed for more.

James recovered her shoulder, smoothed the fabric, and then, checking his watch, moaned. 'Oh no, only a few more hours and I'll have to leave. I wish I didn't have to go away tomorrow; I will miss you so much.'

Claire tried to pull herself together. 'I'm glad it's only going to be three days … this time,' she said with a husky voice.

'Are you all right?' he asked.

Claire cleared her throat. 'Yes. I think I need a drink.' She sighed. 'Would you like a hot chocolate?'

'That would be nice. Can I help you make it?'

Claire pushed herself up. 'Okey-dokey,' she said cheerily and, grabbing James by the arm, dragged him into the kitchen. She flicked on the light switch, and the jug, then opened the fridge and took out the milk. 'Jimmy boy, would you get the drinking chocolate down from that cupboard for me please.' She pointed.

As he reached up, Claire pinched his bottom. 'Hey!' he exclaimed, and, turning around, he took her in his arms, lifted her off her feet and twirled her round and round.

'Hey, put me down!' She giggled and thumped his back. 'I'm getting dizzy!'

'Well, that'll teach you for being cheeky,' he said, and holding her tight in his embrace, he kissed her lovingly.

Claire felt his closeness and the assurance of his desire. She didn't want to ever let go.

The jug whistled.

And reluctantly they parted.

'You've got the milk and the chocolate. Is there anything else you need?'

'Well, since you ask,' Claire replied with a cheeky look on her face, 'now let me see?'

'Shall I get the sugar down?'

'Oh, is that what you meant?'

'Yes, that's what I meant. Do you take sugar or are you sweet enough?'

'Now who's being cheeky?' Claire asked.

'I'm sorry, I know you're sweet enough.' And with that, he took her in his arms and kissed her again.

Bill and Sonia stayed out as long as they could. After their stroll along the foreshore, they popped into their favourite café for coffee and cake, where they stayed until closing time before slowly making their way home.

When they approached the house, the porch light came on automatically, illuminating the entrance. Bill rattled his keys and coughed.

'We're home,' called Sonia as she pushed the door slightly open.

'We're in here, Mum,' Claire replied. 'You guys are late; we were thinking of sending out a search party for you.'

'We went down to the foreshore for coffee; we wanted to give you two a bit of time together.'

'Thanks, Dad, we appreciate that, and James was just getting ready to go, he has to be on the road early in the morning.'

'I'll put the kettle on and make a cup of coffee for you before you head off,' said Sonia.

'No need, Mrs Martin. Claire made a drink for me earlier.'

'Okay then, so if there's nothing else you need, we'll be off to bed.' Bill extended his hand toward James and gripped his hand firmly. 'All the best for your trip. When do you expect to be back?'

'Late Friday night, hopefully, if all goes well. It depends on my last appointment; I can't rush the client and if it gets too late, I'll stay in the town overnight and travel back early Saturday.'

'That's wise. It's not worth driving when you're tired and besides there's a greater risk of kangaroos on the road at night,' Bill added and bid them good night.

Sonia leant over and kissed her daughter. 'Night, night, darling.' Then she turned to James. 'See you when you get back. Good night.'

Claire walked James to the door.

He put his arm around her. She fitted snug and cosy and just right under his arm.

'Oh, Claire, I don't ever want to let you go, but I know I have to, and I'll be counting off the minutes 'til I get back.'

'Me too,' Claire said with a sad smile.

He kissed her lips, and she returned the kiss.

'Good night, sweetie pie, sweet dreams,' he said and released her from his arms. 'I must go.'

Claire stood on the doorstep and watched him go. 'Good night, my love,' she whispered, and blew a kiss, her breath a vapour in the still night air.

Tears filled Claire's eyes as she turned and entered the house. Flopping on the still warm couch she breathed in the lingering fragrance from James' musky aftershave. She fluffed one cushion, wrapped the rug around herself, hugged the other cushion close to her heart and snuggled down on the couch. She felt warm and cosy as if she was floating on a cloud.

In her dream, Claire could hear the distant buzz of a mobile. *Why doesn't someone answer that?* she thought. The phone stopped. *Oh, good at last!* She stretched her arms above her head and yawned. The phone rang again. She opened her eyes and, realising it was her mobile, she frowned. *Who would be ringing at this hour? It's not even daylight!* Then she remembered where she was. *Oh, it might be James,* she thought and grabbed the phone. But she didn't recognise the number. Her finger hovered momentarily over the screen; she swiped it and, putting it to her ear, answered.

'Is that Claire?' The shaky voice of a distraught woman crackled across the line.

'Yes,' she answered hesitantly.

There was a pause and a jagged sniff.

'Who is it?' Claire asked.

'It's Francine; oh, Claire, I had to talk to you.'

Taken aback, Claire asked how she got her number.

'From the hospital records,' she explained and quickly told her the reason for the call. 'I want to get away from Eddy, but he follows me everywhere, even when I'm at work – on my lunch break, he's right there waiting in the cafeteria. And he's ...' she hesitated, 'cruel.'

Claire's heart went out in sympathy to Francine; she could feel the pain in her voice.

'Um, there must be someone there at the hospital who could help you – a counsellor or psychologist or someone.'

'Maybe. It was just that ...' She sniffed and blew her nose, 'when I saw you yesterday with James,' she said in a coy voice, 'I thought I'd ask you how you made the break from Eddy. I've tried, but he knows where I work and follows me and drags me back. I don't know what to do.'

'Do you have family or friends that could help you?'

'No.'

'Have you tried getting a restraining order?'

'That's what I mean – I can't get away to do it.'

'Where are you now?'

'At work, I've almost finished the night shift and he'll be waiting in the car – my car!' she said angrily. 'He'll be just outside the door, hovering menacingly, waiting for me when I knock off. I'm scared.'

'Would you like me to contact the police for you?'

'I don't know,' she said with a sob. 'I'm going to have to leave my mobile phone here; I'll have to say I forgot it. He checks my phone every day and if he sees that I rang you he'll be so …' her voice trailed off.

Claire sighed. 'Is there another number that I can contact you on?'

'Maybe the hospital, or it might be best if I ring you when I'm at work tomorrow night.'

'Okay, and meanwhile, I'll talk to my dad; he'll know what to do.'

'Thanks, Claire, you're a pal; I'll be in touch.'

'Mmm. Bye, Francine,' she said and ended the call.

Claire lay awake, the sound of Francine's cry for help echoing in her mind.

As the first rays of morning light streaked through a gap at the edge of the curtain, Ella began to stir. Claire checked the time: it was five-thirty-eight. She pulled the rug up over her head in the hope that either Ella would go back to sleep, or her mother would get up and feed her like she usually did. Claire figured that if her mother came downstairs to prepare the bottle then she would tell her about the phone call from Francine. And so, she waited. But Ella didn't go back to sleep. Instead, her baby babble became a cry which increased in volume by the second until Claire couldn't stand it any longer. She rolled off the sofa, shuffled into the kitchen and flicked the jug on. She yawned, stretched her arms above her head and sighed. Her mind wandered to James. *I miss him already*, she thought. *I wish he was here. I don't know what to do about Francine. He would know how to help her, I'm sure.*

The jug boiled. 'Oh, blow!' she said out loud to no one in particular. Now I'll have to wait for the water to cool. Oh, no, I won't,' she corrected herself. There's some cooled boiled water in the fridge; I'll do half and half.'

While she prepared the baby's bottle, Claire turned down the volume on the monitor. Although she could still hear Ella's cry, it was muffled and, therefore, bearable.

Reaching the top of the stairs, Claire was surprised to see that her parent's bedroom door was still closed. *Boy, they must be tired,* she thought, *but I don't suppose they are used to such late nights anymore.*

Opening the door to the nursery she poked her head around the corner. 'Good morning, darling,' she whispered brightly, and instantly Ella stopped crying. 'What was all that noise about?' She received a big smile in reply.

After feeding and bathing Ella and having her own breakfast, Claire put a load of washing in the machine, cleaned the kitchen and even hung the clothes on the line, but there was still no sign of Bill or Sonia.

'Okay, little princess,' she said, 'let's go for a walk.'

Ella kicked her little legs enthusiastically.

Claire packed the baby bag and strung it over the handle of the pram then, tilting the back of the seat to a slight angle, she settled Ella in and fastened the safety straps. She grabbed her bag, tossed it over her shoulder and manoeuvred the pram over the slight hump in the doorway and closed the door behind her.

'Off we go then,' she said as she tucked a stray hair behind her ear and slipped her sunglasses on.

The sun felt warm on her back as she headed toward the ocean and Claire breathed in the fresh morning air. Scattered clouds floated like tuffs of cottonwool across the bright blue sky and birds chirped happily, welcoming in the new day.

Ella chattered away and Claire smiled. All was well with her, and James, and the world – except for Francine.

By the time Claire returned from her walk, her mum and dad were sitting sleepily at the breakfast table.

'Hi, you two,' she said. 'Looks like you had a rough night.'

'We're not used to late nights, that's all,' said Bill, 'but it looks like you two are as bright as the morning!'

'Yep, we've been up for ages; we've done all our work and been for a walk. It's such a beautiful day,'

Claire poured herself a cup of coffee and told them about the early morning phone call from Francine.

'Oh, the poor girl,' Sonia said with a frown. 'I wonder how we can help her?'

'She said she'd ring again tonight. And if she can talk to you, Dad, I thought you might be able to advise her.'

Bill swirled the coffee in his mug. 'I'll have a think about it,' he said as he drained the last of his drink.

James left his hotel early to avoid the worst of the Perth morning peak hour traffic. And he succeeded! The hire car purred along beautifully.

Clearing the city, he saw the sunrise lighting dewdrops and flickering through the branches of gum trees that stood like sentinels on the side of the road.

Two and a half hours into his journey, James stopped at a roadhouse service station in Jurien Bay for a late breakfast snack. He pulled out his mobile phone and was just about to ring Claire when he had second thoughts. *It's not quite eight o'clock, she might still be asleep after her … our … late night. I'll wait 'til I get to Geraldton; that'll only be another couple of hours.* With his first appointment in Geraldton not scheduled until eleven o'clock he figured he'd have plenty of time to make the phone call.

James sipped the last of his coffee and thought about Claire. She was truly the love of his life. He opened his wallet, unclipped the catch on the coin section and pulled out the tiny ring he'd tucked securely, deep into the corner. *My number one project, other than work,* he reminded himself – not that he needed reminding – *is to buy the engagement ring.* James twisted the ring around on his little finger contemplating the future with Claire.

Shaking himself from his daydream, he replaced the ring in his wallet, gathered his bits and pieces and headed back to the car, breathing in deeply the fresh salty air. *This is lovely … be a great place for a holiday. I'll have to keep it in mind,* he noted. The rest of the journey was fine, and he was able to take his time to enjoy the scenery along the way.

Arriving early, James decided to check out a couple of the local jewellery shops before phoning Claire. He looked at every diamond ring, which were all very nice, but he didn't find one that he thought was good enough for Claire. He wasn't too concerned. *It's early days,* he thought. *There's plenty more towns and plenty more shops.* So instead, he found a small coffee shop, ordered his cappuccino, and took a seat by the window.

Claire's mobile rang. 'Yay! It's James,' she yelled with delight. 'Hi, James, good to hear from you. Where are you?'

'I'm in Geraldton. I've got about twenty minutes before my first appointment, so I thought I'd give you a call.'

Claire let out a long breath. 'That's great. And did you have a good trip?'

'Yep, it was great. I had a good run, just made one stop at a lovely place called Jurien Bay. Do you know it?'

'Yes, we love Jurien Bay. We've often stayed there for holidays.'

'I thought it would be a nice place to stay.' James looked at his watch. 'Anyway, how are you?'

Claire hesitated.

'Are you all right?' James asked.

'Um, yes … it's just that I had a phone call from Francine this morning.'

'What!'

'She rang from the hospital, and was extremely upset; apparently Eddy's been violent toward her. She wants to get away from him, but she doesn't know how. Sounds like he tracks her every move.'

James listened with utter disgust.

'How did she get your mobile number?' he asked.

'From the hospital records.'

'She had no right to contact you.'

Claire was taken aback by James' seeming insensitivity.

'Don't you care?' she snapped.

'I care for you!' he retorted. 'If you only knew what a conniving, nasty, self-centred person she is, you'd have nothing to do with her. Claire, I'm telling you, please, keep well away from her. She's as bad, or worse, than Eddy, and you know what he's like.'

'How can you say that? You don't even know her.'

'Oh, yes, I do. I didn't tell you before because I didn't want to upset you, but she came over to Adelaide and tried to get her claws into me!'

'What! When! When was that?'

'Oh, Claire, it's a long story.' He checked his watch. 'I haven't got time to explain, I have to go to work. I'll ring you tonight, okay? But please, please, please don't go anywhere near her.'

Claire could hear the desperation in his voice. She sniffed. 'Okay, I'll wait for your call.'

'Just promise me you'll be careful.'

'I promise.'

They exchanged kisses through the phone and ended the call.

James' heart pounded, his head throbbed, and his hands wre moistened with perspiration. He clenched his fists and hit the table. 'God,' he cried in desperation, 'I need your help … please protect Claire.' His lip quivered. 'All I want to do is turn around and head back to Perth, but I can't; I have these work commitments. Please help me concentrate, I can't do it myself, I need you.' He wiped his hands down the sides of his trousers and stood up.

The café owner approached and placed a glass of cold water on the table. 'Are you all right, mate?' he asked. 'Can I get you anything?'

Pulling a handkerchief from his pocket, James blew his nose and cleared his throat. 'Thank you. I will be all right. It's just that I received some unexpected news, and I just need a couple of minutes to, um … recover.'

'Take as long as you like and call me if you need anything.'

James forced a sad smile and took a sip of water. 'Thank you,' he said and bowed his head.

A calm assurance washed over him. He finished the glass of water and went to the men's room to freshen up. And, thankful to be alone, he said a short prayer, used the facilities and left feeling much better.

His eleven o'clock appointment went well and was finished within twenty minutes so instead of going straight to his second appointment James took the opportunity to check out another jewellery shop. Disappointed again – there still wasn't a ring good enough for Claire. 'I'll know it as soon as I see it,' he told the lady behind the counter.

'I'm sure you will, sir,' she replied as she slid the fourteenth tray of diamond rings back into the cabinet. 'Good luck.'

The bell above the door tingled as he left the shop.

The remaining three appointments for the day went relatively smooth, except for the last one. Just when he was in a hurry to get to the hotel and phone Claire, the managing director chose to call a meeting of the board to discuss their current order. The meeting went on and on.

'Would you like me to come back tomorrow for your final decision?' James asked.

'No, we're almost through. If you don't mind stepping outside for a moment, there's just one last thing we need to discuss.'

'Of course, no problem at all,' James said, and he stood up, gathered his folders, placed them in his attaché case and went out into the corridor.

Not daring to phone Claire while he was waiting, he tapped his foot nervously and watched the clock on the wall.

To James, it seemed to take forever when, in fact, it was only five minutes, and the result was excellent.

Not wanting to wait until he got back to the hotel to ring Claire, as soon as he left the building, he scurried across the road, darted into the closest café, and made the call.

Although the room was crowded James managed to nab the last table-for-one at the back near the toilets, but he didn't care. Slipping his case under the table, he quickly grabbed his phone and pressed the automatic dial.

Claire answered on the second ring.

'Wow, that was quick,' he said. 'You must have had your mobile in your hand.'

'I did! I was waiting for you to ring.'

'Sorry I'm a bit late. I got held up with my last appointment, I thought I'd never get away. But never mind, here I am. And Claire, I miss you so much.'

'James, you've only been gone one day. What's it going to be like when you go back to Adelaide?'

'Oh, I dread thinking about it.'

'Me too.'

'Anyway, this morning I didn't even ask you how Ella's going.'

Claire chuckled. 'Yeah, you did seem a bit preoccupied.'

'I was worried about you. You haven't heard anymore from Francine, have you?'

'No, she's not going to ring until she gets to work tonight.'

'What time will that be?'

'I don't know.'

'Did you tell your dad what I said about her?'

'Yeah, sort of.'

'What did he say?'

'Not much. You know Dad; he never says much – except if

he's telling dad jokes.' Claire laughed.

'Can I have a chat with him now if he's there?'

'Yep, he's outside; I'll just go get him for you, just a minute.'

'Dad! You're wanted on the phone; its James,' Claire yelled.

On the other end of the line, James pulled the phone away from his head, stuck his little finger in his earhole and gave it a jiggle to stop the buzzing.

'Hi, Jimmy boy, how's it going?'

'Workwise fine, but I'm worried about Claire. I don't want her to get involved with that Francine – she is a dangerous woman! She's manipulative, conniving, and vicious. I plead with you, Bill, please do whatever you can to protect Claire from her.'

Bill paused. He could hear the urgency in his voice.

'James,' he said, 'I believe she's supposed to be phoning sometime tonight. I'll take the call and direct her elsewhere for help. Now don't you worry, I won't let anything happen to Claire. Everything's going to be fine.'

'Thank you, Bill,' he said and heaved a sigh of relief.

'You're welcome, mate. Here, I'll hand the phone back to Claire. Bye for now.'

Claire grabbed the mobile and, with a smile on her face, put it to her ear and walked back into the house.

Sonia gathered fragments of the paper serviette that she'd been shredding while listening to Bill's end of the conversation. 'What was that all about?' she asked with a puzzled frown.

'It was James.'

'Yes, I know it was James,' she answered in a frustrated tone. 'But what did he say?'

'He's worried about Claire. He doesn't want her getting involved with Francine. He says she is dangerous.'

Sonia blinked her eyes in disbelief and splayed her hands. 'That's what Claire told me he said to her when he rang this afternoon. What puzzles me is, how on earth James knows so much about this Francine!'

'Mmm, not sure, but he was adamant and forceful in his request. And I'm sure he'll explain more when he sees us.'

Claire sat on the sofa with both feet resting on the coffee table. 'Just a minute James,' she said, 'there's another call coming through.'

'No! Don't answer it! It might be Francine. Let it go to message bank.'

'Okay,' she replied and continued to ignore the beep.

'Oh, it's all right,' she said. 'It's stopped now.'

'Good,' replied James with relief. 'And when we finish this call, if your phone rings again, will you get your dad to answer it?'

'Yep, okey-dokey.'

'Promise me?'

'I promise,' she said and meant it.

The beep started up again.

'Can you hear that?'

'What's that?'

'Someone's trying to ring me again. Very persistent, whoever it is.'

'Just ignore it, Claire.'

'I will.'

James kept Claire on the phone for as long as he could, while, on and off, in Claire's ear, the beeping continued.

They talked about their day and what they got up to. Claire told him that, while they were out walking, Ella said "dog" for the first time.

'Wow, what a clever little girl,' James replied.

Finally, with the promise of phoning again the next day James blew a kiss to Claire. 'I love you,' he said. She replied with her love, said her goodbye and ended the call.

Claire placed the mobile phone down on the coffee table, then, resting one hand on each shoulder, she rotated them each in turn to relieve the tension in her neck.

Suddenly the phone rang and vibrated vigorously on the

wooden table. Claire jumped with fright. She backed away not daring to touch it. It moved across the table like a live adder.

'Dad!' she called.

Hearing the commotion, Bill rushed downstairs. 'Don't answer it,' he said as he pulled his dressing gown around his waist and tied the cord. He reached out in a desperate attempt to try and catch the mobile phone before it toppled off the edge of the table. He caught it, but just as he did, it stopped ringing. He checked the screen. It registered eleven missed calls, but no identification.

'Right,' he said and checked the time. 'It was probably Francine trying to ring again and I suggest that you turn your phone off and call it a night.' Bill put his arms around Claire and hugged her close. 'What you need, what we all need, is a good night's sleep. You go up and get ready for bed and I'll make you a nice mug of hot chocolate and bring it up for you.'

Claire sighed. 'Thanks, Dad. You're the best!'

Claire didn't bother having a shower, it was getting too late, and she was too tired.

The glow from the night-light in Claire's room cast a gentle beam from the slightly open door.

'Is it all right if I come in?' he whispered as he tapped one knuckle softly on the door. He waited. 'Claire, are you there?' With no reply he slowly opened the door, tiptoed across the room, and put the drink on the bedside table. Claire had fallen asleep on top of the doona. Not wanting to disturb her, he pulled a rug over her and kissed her forehead. 'Good night, my princess,' he said, and left the room.

Chapter 22

James had all but given up hope of finding that elusive engagement ring. Only by chance on his way back to Perth did he stumble upon a little out-of-the-way jewellery shop in an out-of-the-way arcade in the back blocks of a little country town. There in the window he saw it.

'That's it! That's the one!' he said aloud to himself and, cupping his hands around his eyes, he leaned in closer.

The ring was beautiful. Its large central white diamond glistened brilliantly under the down lights. Smaller diamonds on the outer edge straddled shiny pink gemstones, all of which were set in a yellow gold band. *Perfect!*

James scanned the other rings on display, but nothing compared to the one he'd chosen. 'This is definitely it,' he whispered. 'I've found it at last.'

He turned to go into the shop and pushed the door, but it wouldn't budge. He looked for a handle to pull. There wasn't one. He glanced up. The sign above his head said "Closed."

James frowned. He checked the time: it was 1:52 pm. *Perhaps the Jeweller has gone for lunch,* he thought. *I can wait.* So, he squatted down on the step outside the shop.

Minutes passed. Two o'clock came and went, and still James waited. However, after three quarters of an hour and with still no signs of life, he stood, rubbed his rear-end and hobbled to the door. The inside of the shop was in darkness. James grunted in disbelief.

There was just one shop toward the other end of the arcade that appeared to be open. James crossed his fingers. The door was open. *Good*, he thought, and went inside. An elderly lady was stacking shelves. 'Excuse me,' James said with a little cough.

'Oh, hello there. I didn't hear you come in. Can I help you?'

'Yes, actually I was wanting to buy something from the jewellery shop, but it's closed, and I was wondering if you could tell me when it will be open again?'

'He always shuts the shop at lunch time on a Friday, and he opens again on Monday morning.'

James sighed. 'That's a blow,' he said. 'I'm just passing through town on my way back to Perth and I can't stay until Monday.'

'Don't worry, dear,' she said when she saw the disappointment on his face. 'Umm, now let me see what I can do for you.' She thought for a moment then rummaged through an overstuffed box of papers. 'Here we go,' she said and handed him a tattered business card. 'If you give him a call and tell him your predicament, I'm sure he'll do what he can to help you. Here, use my phone.'

James' hand shook as he dialled the number. 'Thank you,' he mouthed as he waited. The phone rang and rang and rang with no answer.

'Seems like no one's home,' he said.

'Oh, no. Alexander Goldsworthy lives out of town on an acreage; he could be out and about somewhere. You just sit yourself down and try again in a while.'

'How far out of town does Mr Goldsworthy live?'

'Aw, not far.'

James took a seat and jiggled his leg nervously.

'Don't worry, son. Would you like a cup of tea while you're waiting?'

'That's kind of you Mrs ...'

'Wilson. But just call me Barb.'

'Thank you very much, Barb,' he said as she disappeared through to a back room.

'Was that tea or coffee?' she yelled.

'Coffee please; milk with one sugar.'

In next to no time Barbara returned carrying a tray laden with a selection of homemade goodies.

'I thought you might be hungry,' she said with a smile and handed him a mug of steaming coffee. 'The scones are fresh out of the oven, I made them myself this afternoon.'

'Mmm, they smell delicious. I don't mind if I do,' he replied.

'Jam and cream?'

'Sounds great!'

Just as James opened his mouth to take a bite of the scone, the phone rang.

'Hello, Barb Wilson here.'

Listening to the one-sided conversation, James realised it was the Jeweller, Mr Goldsworthy.

'Thanks for ringing back, Alex. No, there's no problem, everything's fine. It's just that I've got a young man here from out of town who's interested in one of the items in your shop and ...' Barb stopped mid-sentence.

'Look here, just a minute and I'll put him on.' She handed the phone to James.

'Sorry to disturb you on your afternoon off,' he said.

'That's quite all right. What was it you wanted?'

James explained his situation and described the ring he was interested in.

'You mean the one on the top shelf right in the middle?' he asked incredulously.

'Yes, that's the one.'

'Well, young man, you certainly have an eye for quality.'

James thought of Claire. 'Thank you,' he replied.

'If it's the one I think you're describing,' Mr Goldsworthy continued, 'it is the most valuable piece in the entire shop.'

James' heart missed a beat. 'Can I ask the price,' he said hesitantly.

'Look, how about I come in, give you a private viewing and we can discuss it, and possibly negotiate further?'

'Would you do that for me? I'd really appreciate it if you could.'

'I don't usually open the shop Friday afternoons, but since you're only in town today, I'll make an exception. I'll be there soon.'

They ended the call.

And now it was Barb's turn to be curious. 'Sounds like you convinced Alex to come back and open his shop!' she said bright-eyed. 'I think you had better show me the famous ring you've chosen. But I'll let you finish your scone first.'

'Sure,' he said and stuffed it in his mouth, took a swig of coffee and swiped his hand across his lips. 'Let's go,' he said as he headed for the door.

'Hang on, hang on,' said Barb as she wiped her hands on her apron. 'We've got plenty of time, don't rush me.' She pulled the door to and hurried along behind James.

He turned around. 'You forgot to lock your shop,' he said with a frown.

'You're in the country now, James. There's no need to lock up when you're just going around the corner!'

James felt at home in this little country town and, even though he hadn't met Alex, it seemed like he already knew him. And dear Mrs Wilson was like a mother hen to him. *That's strange*, he thought, *how come I feel like this when I've only been here a couple of hours?*

He pointed out the ring in the window.

'Wow, that is beautiful. Your girlfriend must be something special.'

'Yes, she is. Her name's Claire.

James took the tiny dress ring from his wallet, put it on his little finger and showed Barbara. 'Her mother suggested I bring this with me to get the size right.' He squinted and looked closely at the ring in the window. 'Do you think it's about the right size?'

'Aw, it's hard to tell,' she said, 'But they can be re-sized you know?'

'Mmm.'

'Anyway, James, I'd better get back to the shop. It's been lovely meeting you, and I wish you and your special lady all the very best. I'm sure Alex will be along shortly.' She extended her hand and, as he reached to shake it, enfolded him in a friendly hug.

'Thanks for taking me in, and feeding me, and helping me get in touch with Mr Goldsworthy, you are a God send.' Tears filled his eyes.

'You're welcome. I hope I see you before you leave town.'

'Me too,' he said and sniffed.

James watched the elderly lady wander back along the arcade and into her shop, his heart full of thanks to God for her help and His.

Now all he had to do was wait.

It was sometime later when Alexander Goldsworthy pulled his car into the parking area at the rear of his shop. He unlocked the back door, stepped inside, and disarmed the alarm system, and after locking the door behind him, switched on the lights, and walked through to the front of the shop.

James heard a noise and noticed the fluorescent lights flicker. He turned. The front door of the shop opened.

'Hello there. I'm Alexander Goldsworthy. You must be James. I'm pleased to meet you,' he said with a warm smile. Sorry if I kept you waiting.'

'Not at all,' James replied. 'It's so good of you to come back and open your shop again just for me.'

'Well, I hope I can help you,' he said, 'Come on in.'

Alexander showed him through to a plush leather seat. 'Here, you sit down, and I'll bring the ring out for you. Would you like a drink?'

'No thank you,' he chuckled and rubbed his tummy. 'I've been well looked after by Mrs Wilson. She gave me coffee and scones and biscuits and cake.'

'That's good,' he replied as he placed a black velvet-covered tray on the table in front of James. 'So, let's get down to business.'

Alexander gently lifted the ring from the front display window and carried it ceremoniously across to James. 'It truly is exquisite,' he said and placed it on the tray.

James was awestruck. He sat speechlessly staring at the magnificent creation. Tears flooded his eyes accentuating the sparkle of the diamonds. A lump formed in his throat. He swallowed and tried to talk.

'Is it not to your liking?' Alexander asked.

'Oh, no, it's not that. It's just that it's far more beautiful than I could have envisaged.'

'That's good. I'm glad that you like it. Now let me explain to you its quality. It's a one-of-a-kind uniquely designed and made in Western Australia by a renowned artisan (he gave the name). The ring is of 18carat yellow gold with argyle diamonds. As I said to you on the phone, this diamond ring is the most valuable piece in this entire shop. Are you still interested?'

James had done his homework, having checked out many jewellery shops in Adelaide and, of course, a few in Geraldton. He had priced engagement rings from the top of the range right through to the lower end and had budgeted for about the upper middle range. So, yes, he was interested. Holding his breath, he asked the price.

'Mmm.' He pondered and bit his lip. 'That is more than I planned to pay, but …' he hesitated.

'It is negotiable. Would you like to discuss it further?'

James released a long slow breath.

'To be honest, it is triple the amount I had planned to pay. Would you mind giving me a little time to think it through?'

'Sure, James, that's no problem. Look, I'll go and do some calculating myself and work out the best price I can offer you.'

Alex moved behind the counter, pulled out his calculator and began punching numbers.

Picking up the ring again James slipped it onto his little finger. It seemed about the right size, and it looked superb. *Yes, this is the one,* he reassured himself, *and I know it's more than I wanted to pay, and I'll be biting into my extra savings, but Claire's the love of my life and she is worth it!*

Alex wandered over and sat down beside James. He handed him a sheet of paper. 'This is the best I can do for you. What do you think?'

James, taken aback, couldn't believe his eyes. 'Wow! That's a huge discount. Are you sure you're not cutting yourself short?'

'Actually, it's cost plus a small margin. I wouldn't normally make such an offer, but …' This time it was his turn to hesitate. 'But I … I really don't know why. I just felt that this ring is meant for you.'

'Really! Thank you.' James opened his wallet and pulled out two bank cards. 'I hope you don't mind me using two different cards; I will need to divide the payments between my savings account and the credit card.'

'I don't mind; that's all right. But you don't necessarily have to pay it all up front. You could do a layby and pay it off over time if you prefer.'

'Oh no, that wouldn't work for me. I don't expect to come back this way anytime in the foreseeable future. But thank you for the suggestion.'

Having finalised the transaction and, holding the treasured purchase in his hand, James thanked Mr Goldsworthy once more and headed for the door. Turning back, he asked, 'I'll need to stay in town for the night. Can you recommend a good place to stay?'

'Why not come home with me. You could have dinner with us, stay the night and head off early in the morning.'

Once again James was surprised that he would make such a generous offer to a stranger. 'That is very kind of you, but I can't really impose upon you like that.'

'Why not? We'd be happy to have you. I'll just give Deb a call and she'll set an extra place at the table.'

Before James could answer, Alex was already on the phone to his wife.

'We've got a visitor for dinner, love, and an overnight guest. Be home in forty.'

A shrill of excitement echoed along the line and James, being a city boy, recognised this was country hospitality to the max.

'It's all arranged,' Alex announced as he opened the door for his customer. 'I'll bring my car around and you can follow me in your vehicle.'

James thanked him and made his way to his car.

The country drive was exhilarating and, as the sun sunk lower in the indigo-blue sky, Alex flicked his indicator and slowed down. Turning into the driveway, they stopped. Alex got out of his car, opened the wide gate to his property and drove through. Then, waving his arm from the open window, he signalled for James to follow.

'Shall I close the gate?' James shouted.

'Thanks, mate.'

James took a deep breath, savouring the fresh country air.

The gate secured, the two vehicles made their way along the narrow road leading to the farmhouse, gravel crunching beneath the tyres.

Alex parked his car in the carport at the side of the house, and James pulled in beside him. No sooner had Alex cut the engine than three curly-haired children emerged from the house and ran to greet him, followed closely by his wife, a toddler at her side and a baby in her arms.

'Daddy, Daddy!' called the smallest of the three, her chubby arms reaching to him.

Lifting her high above his head, he twirled her round. 'How's my special girl,' he said, kissed her cheek and lowered her to the ground.

'My turn, my turn,' said the next child, jumping up and down on the spot.

Alex sighed and ruffled the boy's hair.

'Jake, you're getting such a big boy. Soon, I won't be able to lift you up, and you'll have to carry me.' Then, with an exaggerated groan, he took hold of the boy's hands and spun round and round 'til his feet lifted off the ground.

'Wee,' exclaimed the boy, 'that's fun.'

They all giggled.

The oldest child simply gave her father a hug. 'I love you, Daddy,' she said and turned to James. 'Hello, I'm Matilda and I'm nine.'

James extended his hand. 'I'm pleased to meet you, Matilda. My name's James.'

'Sorry, James, how remiss of me,' Alex said. 'This is my wife Debra and our youngest son George.'

'Very pleased to meet you and thank you so much for inviting me to stay with you.'

'You're most welcome,' she said with a smile.

The toddler clung to her mother's skirt and hid her face.

'And this is our little Katie,' Alex continued. 'She's a bit shy, but she'll soon warm to you. And you met Matilda, and this is Jake and Olivia.'

Olivia held up three fingers.

'Are you three years old?' James asked.

She nodded and smiled widely.

'Wow! You certainly are a big girl.'

'And I'm six,' announced Jake, his chest expanding at least a centimetre. 'And Kate's only two.'

Alex frowned. 'Never mind giving James our family history, let's all go inside. And Jake, since you're such a big boy, I'll get you to help James bring his things into the house.'

'I'll help too,' said Olivia, smiling up at James as she took hold of his hand. 'I like you, Mr James.'

'And I like you too, Olivia,' he said, handing her a small tote bag. 'Do you think you could carry this for me, or is it too heavy for you?'

Holding the bag high under her chin with both hands, she turned around. 'Not too heavy for me,' she said and waddled off beside Jake, who looked very official carrying a maroon attaché case with its gold embellishments.

James closed the boot of the car, picked up his suitcase and followed the kids into the house.

'Your room is this way,' Matilda indicated with a sweep of her hand.

'I'll show him where it is,' said Jake, grabbing the tote bag from Olivia.

James followed the boy.

'This is the bed. This is the cupboard. This is the light switch, and you open this door to go to the loo.'

'Thank you, Jake; you have been very helpful,' James said and swung his case onto the bed. 'And do you know what? I think I'll use that loo now.'

Jake giggled.

'Jake! Matilda!' Debra called from the kitchen.

'I've got a go now. Mum wants me.'

'Okay mate, see you later.'

After freshening up, James sat on the edge of the bed. Although old-fashioned, the room's furnishings were neat and clean, uncluttered, and gave a welcoming feeling of warmth and homeliness.

I wish I had some gifts for the children; they're such great kids. He scratched his head and opened his attaché case. Inside were a pen, a pencil, a torch, a keyring, and a folder containing loose sheets of paper.

I suppose I could teach them some origami, maybe make a paper aeroplane for Jake, a crane for Matilda, a chatterbox for Olivia – since she's quite a little chatterbox herself! Then there are the two little ones? he mused. *Oh, I don't know, perhaps I'll wait until I get home and send them all a little gift in the post. They'd probably like that better. Yep, that's what I'll do.*

There was a knock at the door. It was Jake. 'Mum wants me to feed Kitty and Dog. Want to come?'

'Sure. Be with you in a minute.' James closed the case, tucked it under the bed and joined the boy.

Out in the backyard, a floppy-eared, silky-haired pet dog came running to them. Jake knelt beside the excited pooch and vigorously rubbed behind his ears. The pup licked him on the cheek.

'She's very friendly. What's her name?'

'This is Miss Kitty.'

James bent down and stroked the top of her head. 'Hi, Miss Kitty, I'm pleased to meet you.'

The boy filled her plate with off cuts of raw meat and put fresh water in her bowl. 'Good girl, Kitty,' he said, and turning around he cupped his hands to his mouth, whistled then called, 'Doggy, here boy.'

James looked around expecting to see another dog, but to his surprise from behind a bush a large tabby cat came running toward them.

'And who is this?' he asked.

'This is Dog.'

'Dog? That's an unusual name for a cat.'

Jake laughed. 'Well, that's what he's called, and he doesn't mind.'

'So, you've got a dog called Kitty and a cat called Dog. Don't they get a bit mixed up?'

'No,' Jake shook his head, 'they know who they are,' he replied, amused at the idea that they would ever get mixed up.

James gave a chuckle and rubbed the top of Dog's head. The tomcat responded with a solid head-butt to his leg.

'Wow! You sure are one tough guy,' he said, 'but I guess you have to be with a name like that!'

After feeding the cat and dog Jake showed James around the house paddock. He took him to see the chooks.

'Do you name the chickens? Or do you call them pigs?'

'Of course not,' Jake replied with an amused frown, 'that would be daft.'

'Yes, I suppose it would. And what about the sheep, do you call them cows?'

Jake, in tears of laughter, tried to catch his breath.

'Www, what about the horses? … www, will we say that they're … rhinoceroses!'

'You don't have rhinoceroses on a farm.'

'How about calling them goats then?'

'Oh, Jake, I think we should just leave them as horses, what do you think?'

'Aw, yeah! Okay.'

James ruffled the boy's hair. 'Thanks for showing me around, mate. 'But you'll have to excuse me while I make an important phone call.'

'Rightio.'

James returned to his room, pulled out his phone and rang Claire's mobile number.

Claire paced the room waiting for James to phone. *I hope he's all right*, she thought. *Hope nothing's happened to him*. She answered on the first ring. 'James, where are you?'

'Sorry, Claire, I got a bit held up and I'll have to stay another night.' There was silence on the end of the line. 'Claire, are you there? Can you hear me?'

'Yes,' she sighed with disappointment.

'I'm so sorry it couldn't be helped, but I plan to leave early in the morning, and I should be back by lunchtime at the latest, and I'll come straight over to see you. Okay?'

Claire sniffed. 'Okay.'

A knock came to the door. 'James,' said Matilda, 'dinner is ready.'

'Thank you, I'll be there soon.'

'James,' Claire said in an angry voice. 'I heard a girl's voice! Where are you?'

'Staying the night at a country homestead with a lovely family.'

'Well, that's unusual when you are supposed to be on a business trip!'

'What's the matter, Claire? You sound upset. Are you all right?'

'Not really.'

'What's wrong?'

'I've been worrying about you and now you tell me you're living it up in the country somewhere. Why didn't you ring earlier? And how come you're not staying in a hotel?'

'As you know, I expected to be back in Perth by tonight, and I hadn't booked any accommodation. I met one of the locals in town and asked if he could recommend a place where I could stay the night. He kindly offered me a room at his place. That's how country folk are – they're very obliging. So that's how come I'm here. And the little girl you heard is one of their children, she is nine years old and her name's Matilda; she's the eldest of five and they are a lovely family.'

James took a breath and softened his voice. 'I'm sorry, Claire. I wish you were here too, I'm sure you'd love it.'

Claire sniffed. 'Sorry for being so stroppy.'

'That's all right. It's my fault; I should have rung you earlier, and I can't wait to see you and Ella tomorrow.'

'Me too, I've missed you so much. I love you,' she whispered, then added, 'Well, you'd better go and have your dinner before it gets cold.'

'I'll ring you later.'

'Okay. Bye.'

'Talk soon. Bye.' The call ended.

James felt flustered and sad that he'd disappointed Claire. *Hope she's not too mad at me*, he thought as he made his way down to the dining room.

The table was set beautifully. Everyone had waited for him to come before being seated.

'This is your place,' Matilda said, and Jake pulled the chair out for him.

'Why thank you, madam, and sir,' he said with a bow, 'you are so kind.'

Olivia climbed up onto her chair, covered her mouth and giggled. 'I like you, Mr James.'

'I like you too, Olivia, and I think you are all such lovely, kind people.'

The table was a long solid jarrah-wood setting with matching high-back chairs, each child having his or her special place; even little Kate's highchair was pushed up to the table, so she was on the same level as all the others. The only one missing from the family table was baby George, who sat bright-eyed in his baby bouncer, watching all that was going on.

'Right then,' Alex said and cleared his throat, 'shall we pray?'

They all bowed their heads, clasped their hands together and closed their eyes.

'Can I pray, Dad?'

'Sure, son, you can start.'

'Me too?' asked Olivia.

'Yes, you can go after Jake.'

'Dear God, I'm glad tomorrow is Saturday, and I don't have to go to school. I like being home best. Amen.'

Olivia opened her eyes. 'Is it my turn now, Dad?'

'Yes Olivia, your turn.'

'Hello, God, it's me. Umm. I forgot.'

'That's all right, Ollie – you can just say thank you.'

'Thank you.'

After a slight pause, Alex asked if anyone else wanted to pray.

'If I may,' James began. 'I'd like to say thank you, God, for this lovely family who have invited me, a stranger, into their home. I feel totally blessed indeed. Thank you for their love and hospitality, and for this food, we say thank you. Amen.'

Everyone at the table chorused their 'amen' then began to eat.

The meal was delicious and had been prepared using their fresh homegrown produce. All the children had hearty appetites, and none needed coaxing to eat.

The setting reminded James of the old TV program *The Waltons*. It was as if he had been transported back in time. The Goldsworthy family was old-fashioned and quaint, but he felt privileged to have been invited to join them.

Conversation around the table was light and fun. During one lull between banter, James asked a question that had been on his mind.

'Alex,' he asked, 'I'm curious as to just how your cat got to be called Dog and the dog named Kitty?'

They all laughed. 'Tell him, Dad,' said Matilda.

'Well, it's a long story, but I'll get Deb to tell you; she tells it better than me.'

Debra blushed. 'It was a few years ago. We only had two children at the time; Matilda was about five or six years old, and Jake was just a little toddler. Matilda's favourite book character was Miss Kitty. So, when we brought the dog home, who was only a puppy at the time; the prettiest little thing you could imagine, like a little ball of fluff with big blue eyes and cute floppy ears, we asked the children what we should call her. Matilda jumped up and down. "Can we call her Miss Kitty?" she said excitedly, "pleeease?" And that is how Miss Kitty got her name.'

'And the cat?' James asked.

'Well, since we had called the dog Kitty it seemed logical to name the cat Dog!'

'Oh, I see,' said James. 'I guess that makes sense - well, I think it does,' he added with a crooked smile.

They chatted on about this and that, interested in hearing some aspects of James' life.

Jake jumped to his feet. 'My turn to clear the table,' he announced with enthusiasm.

'I'm washing,' added Matilda.

'Me too!' chipped in a little voice.

'No, precious, you can help Mummy wipe the table.'

Kate pouted. 'But I'm a big girl too.'

'And that's why I need you to help me,' Debra said, lifting her from the highchair.

A flurry of activity followed.

'Can I help?' asked James.

'Oh, no,' replied Olivia. 'You are our guess.'

Jake laughed at her. 'No silly, James is our guest, not our guess.'

'I don't care. I like him anyway.'

With all the chores done, the family retreated to the lounge room. James excused himself, returned to the guest room, and called Claire. Thankfully, all was forgiven, and James was once more in her good books.

Not wanting to seem rude, he cut short the call, grabbed a few sheets of paper from his briefcase and re-joined the family.

The two little ones had already gone to bed, and young Olivia sat snug on her mother's lap, trying very hard to keep her eyes open.

'Have any of you done origami?' James asked.

Jake screwed up his nose and frowned. 'Orug ...? What's that?'

'It's paper folding. Making things out of paper.'

'You mean like paper aeroplanes?'

'Yes, that's right. Can you make a paper aeroplane, Jake?'

'Yep.'

'Well, how about we have a competition and see who can make the best plane. Do you want to join us, Matilda?'

'Me too!' came a little voice and Olivia slipped down from Debra's lap.

'Okay,' said James, 'but first of all let's watch how Jake does it.' He handed him a sheet of white paper.

With care and concentration and tongue protruding from the corner of his mouth, Jake creased, folded, and fashioned the sleek aircraft.

'It's a beauty!' James exclaimed. 'Now let's see if it flies.'

Jake turned toward the dining room and, making final adjustment to the wings, lifted his arm above his shoulder and let fly.

It soared high above the table, circled the hanging light, made a slight turn, and came in for a gentle landing nearby.

'How about that!' Jake screeched with delight.

James stood; his mouth wide open. 'Wow!' he said with a sigh. 'What a beauty! That's amazing. Now, how about you decorate your aeroplane while the girls and I have a go at making ours.'

'Okay, I'll go get my felt pens and coloured pencils,' he said and dashed off down the hallway.

'Come on, girls, let's see if we can make one as good as Jake's.'

Matilda smoothed the already flat paper and waited.

'Here we go then. Now, Olivia, this is your paper.'

She took it in her hand and waved it in the air excitedly.

'The first thing we do is fold the paper across like this.'

'Is this right?' asked Matilda.

'Yes, that's it. Now fold the extra piece over, like this, and cut that part off, and that leaves a square.'

'I didn't see Jake do that.'

'No, he designed his a bit differently; ours is going to be a different model.'

Little Olivia scrunched her paper.

James looked up. 'You're doing a great job, Olivia; can I see your aeroplane?'

She tossed the ball of paper to James. He caught it. Shrieks of joy pieced the air and three-year-old Olivia jumped up and down. 'I did, I did; I made my eduplane go.'

'Good girl, Ollie. Why don't you take it over and show Mummy.'

Jake returned with a large pencil case and a box full of coloured felt pens. He settled himself at the table and started decorating his aircraft.

Olivia climbed onto her mother's lap and began unfolding her creation. 'See, Mummy, my eduplane.'

Debra stroked her daughter's hair. 'It's a beautiful aeroplane.'

Olivia smiled up at her mother, and clutching the re-scrunched paper to her chest, snuggled her head and closed her big blue eyes.

Jake, Matilda, and James finished off their paper planes and then tiptoed to the family room and tested their machines, where all three passed with flying colours.

By the time they returned to the lounge room, supper awaited them – hot chocolate complete with marshmallows afloat in each mug, gingernut cookies and fruitcake. Yum, yum.

After supper, Matilda and Jake were allowed to stay up a little longer while James demonstrated a couple more origami pieces. The children watched wide-eyed with every fold.

'Here, Matilda, pull this bit.'

Carefully following instructions, Matilda gazed in wonder when she saw how the crane's wings flapped when she pulled its tail.

'Will you make one for me?' Jake said.

'Of course I will, but before I do, I'll show you one more.' And with only a few quick folds and tucks, out came a cute little puppy dog.

'Aw, that's great!' Matilda exclaimed, still working the bird in her hand.

'Can you do some more for us, James?'

'Not tonight, it's getting a bit too late. But here, I'll make another crane for you, Jake, and two more dogs, one for Oliver and one for Kate. And you can give them to them in the morning. Okay?'

'Yep. Thanks, James.'

As quickly as a meerkat lifts its head, James worked his magic and soon another crane and two puppies appeared. 'Look, I'll show you how to draw a face on the puppy.' He took a black felt pen, coloured the nose and drew two eyes.

'I could do that!' Matilda said.

'I'm sure you could. And how about you, Jake, could you finish this one in the morning for me and give it to Kate?'

'Yeah.'

Debra came from the kitchen, wiped her hands, and tossed the towel over her shoulder. 'Come on now, you two; it's time to go to bed. Say good night to James. And did you thank him for showing you how to do origami?'

'Ohh, do we have to go to bed right now? Can't we stay up a little bit longer? It's Saturday tomorrow.' Jake wiggled his leg in anticipation.

'No, Jake, you've already taken too much of James' time. Anyway, you'll see him in the morning.'

James chipped in. 'Actually, I was planning to get away very early, so I'll probably be gone before anyone else is awake.'

'Oh, no we won't hear of that. We'll all be up early. The children wouldn't want to miss seeing you before you go, besides, you'll need to have a good breakfast. You can't drive all that way on an empty stomach.'

'You have all been so kind to me. I really do appreciate it.'

Alex reached his hand out to James. 'It's been our pleasure to have you and anytime you're up this way drop in and see us. And next time, please bring Claire and Ella with you; we've heard so much about them we'd love to meet them.'

James sighed. 'I can't promise anything. I head back to Adelaide on Monday, and I don't know when, or even if, I'll be up this way again.'

Matilda and Jake lingered.

'Come on now, you two, if you don't get to bed soon you won't wake up in time to say goodbye to James in the morning.'

After stretching out their "good nights" as long as possible, the children reluctantly headed to bed.

Two minutes later, Jake reappeared. 'I need a drink of water,' he announced sheepishly.

'You go back to bed right now, mister. I will bring a glass of water in for you,' his father said sternly.

James looked at his watch. 'I must be heading off to bed myself. Would you like me to take the water in for Jake on my way through?'

Alex thought for a moment. 'Yes, but don't let him keep you – just put the glass on the table and go. In fact, I think we'll be heading off to bed ourselves. Is there anything else you need, James?'

'No thank you, I'll just get that glass of water.'

By the time he reached the boy's bedroom, Jake was fast asleep. James smiled. It seemed the boy wasn't thirsty after all.

The next day, after a hearty breakfast and friendly goodbyes, the whole family followed James out to his car.

Olivia tugged on his trousers.

'Don't go. I like you, mister James.'

'I like you too, Olivia. But I must go and see my little girl.'

James could hardly believe his own words. *I called her my little girl!* he thought with a jolt.

Debra took hold of her daughter's hand. 'Sorry about that, James,' she said as she pried Olivia's hand loose from his leg.

Olivia buried her head in her mother's skirt and sobbed.

'Do you mind if I pick her up?' James whispered.

'No, that's all right. Go ahead.'

Crouching down, he spoke tenderly. 'How about I give you an aeroplane ride before I go?'

'Yes please,' she said, then wiped her nose with the back of her chubby little hand and ran over to him.

'Just a minute,' said Debra, taking a tissue from her pocket. 'James doesn't want your slobber all over him.' She mopped her tears, cleaned her hand and wiped her nose. 'That's better, now you can have an aeroplane ride.'

'Wee,' she said as she spun round and round.

'Can I have a go?' asked Jake.

Alex placed his hand on the boy's head and ruffled his hair. 'Come on now, we mustn't keep James any longer; he's got a long way to go and we don't want to wear him out before he leaves.'

'Oh, Dad.'

James brought his plane to a gentle landing.

Olivia staggered off, flopped to the ground, and giggled.

'Oh, my goodness now I'm giddy too,' said James with puff.

James opened the car door and sat down. 'Thank you so much for having me stay with you,' he said. 'I've had a great time.' He reached out and shook Alex's hand. 'Thanks again for everything.'

'You're most welcome. And all the best for your coming engagement and whatever the future holds.'

'Thanks, mate.'

'Do keep in touch. We'd love to hear what Claire thinks of the ring.'

'Will do. Bye, everyone,' he said with a wave, and drove the car slowly toward the gate.

From the rear-vision mirror, he could see the children running along behind the car, their arms waving vigorously. He paused at the gate, but before he could get out of the car Jake had climbed onto the bottom rail, unlatched the chain from the post and swung the gate open.

'Thanks, buddy,' James said and drove through.

As soon as Jake fixed the gate shut, the other children joined him on the fence to wave their final goodbyes. Even little Olivia clutched the fence with both hands and peered through the wire.

James wound the window down. 'Bye, kids,' he shouted over the sound of gravel crunching under the tyres. 'Have fun.'

A cloud of dust followed as he drove away.

Once away from the farm James pulled the car to the side of the road, cut the engine, and tried to phone Claire. The phone rang out. He checked the time. She should be awake by now. *Hope everything's all right.* He tried her number again. *No luck.* He put his phone away and drove on. *I'll try again when I get to Geraldton.*

It seemed such a long way back to Geraldton. Much further that he remembered it being when following Alex to the farm.

Hope I haven't taken a wrong turn, he thought. He looked up and noticed the trees were leaning. *Ha ha! I am on the right track,* he assured himself, *now I remember, the trees in Geraldton grow almost horizontal due to the prevailing winds.* He breathed a sigh of relief.

Although he hadn't planned to stop for morning tea, by the time he reached Geraldton James' mouth was dry and in need of coffee. This always happened when he felt anxious. He knew he shouldn't worry, but he loved Claire and somehow, in a strange way, felt responsible.

Parking the car near the foreshore, he wandered across to the Dome café and placed his order. Being a Saturday, the place was busy. He'd hoped to find a table in the alfresco area overlooking the water but had to settle for inside. It didn't matter; he wasn't intending to stay long anyway; just grab a coffee and go.

After two more unsuccessful attempts to contact Claire, James phoned Sonia.

She picked up on the first ring. 'Hello,' she whispered in a croaky voice.

'Hi Sonia, it's James. Are you all right?'

She cleared her throat. 'Yes ... haven't been up long – we had a bit of a rough night.'

'Is something wrong? I tried to ring Claire, but she's not answering her mobile.'

'Yes, she's still asleep. She was up most of the night with little Ella.'

'Oh, I hope they're not sick.'

'The baby's been a bit miserable; she's got a little runny nose, teething, I think.'

'I'm sorry to hear that. Look, I'm on my way back … should be there in a couple of hours, depending on traffic. I'll see you then.'

'James, did you get that ring you wanted?'

'Yes, I hope Claire likes it.'

'I'm sure she will. I'm so excited. Can't wait to see Claire's reaction.'

'I was planning to take her out for dinner tonight, but if Ella's unwell it might not be the right thing. I'll wait and see what Claire wants to do.'

The waitress placed the coffee mug on the table in front of him. 'Was there anything else, sir,' she asked with her hand on the order number stand.

'No, thank you. That's all.'

'Sorry about that, Sonia. I'm at the Dome in Geraldton. Just dropped in for coffee.'

Sonia cleared her throat. 'Well, I'll let you go. I think I need a coffee myself.'

'Rightio, I'll see you soon. Bye.'

'Goodbye, James. I'll tell Claire you rang.'

The call ended.

James picked up a sugar sachet, gave it a shake, tore off the top and watched the crystals trickle slowly into the foam. *I wish Claire was here with me,* he thought as he stirred his cappuccino.

Chapter 23

The trip back to Perth proved trouble-free; it was only when he hit the outskirts of the city that the traffic began to thicken. The car slowed to a crawl. James tapped his fingers on the steering wheel, anxious to reach his destination.

With the city behind him the traffic began to flow freer the further south he travelled. A smile crept across his face as the distance between him and Claire narrowed.

His heart rate quickened with mixed emotions; on the one hand he was so looking forward to being with Claire and Ella again, but sad and worried about little Ella. *Please let her be all right,* he prayed silently.

Just then a suburban train passed by him on his right. James was impressed with how the railway line, both north and south from Perth, ran down the centre of the freeway. Each station with its unique design, and the trains all clean-looking and modern.

I do like Perth, he mused. *I could live here.* Then he thought about home, his mother, and the family in Adelaide.

As he drove past Cockburn Central Station, he noticed the train that had sped by him back further was now stationary at the platform.

Caught up with you at last, he thought, but all too soon the train left him behind once more.

About ten kilometres further on, the train disappeared from sight, the railway tracks veering right, into a tunnel under the northbound side of the Freeway.

James scratched his head. *Oh, well, no more chasing trains today.*

Pulling into the driveway at the Martin house, James stopped the car and checked the time. 10:08 am. Anxious to see Claire, he left his gear in the car and rushed to the door.

Sonia answered. 'Hi, James, it's so good to see you. Come on in, Claire's in the lounge room.'

The room was dim, the curtains drawn, and Claire, bedraggled and still in her pyjamas, sat trying to comfort the miserable child. Ella lay sobbing and listless in her mother's arms, her head resting on her shoulder.

James' heart ached as he walked slowly across the room.

'Oh, my little princess, I'm sorry you're sick.'

At the sound of his voice, Ella turned her head toward him and, with flushed cheeks, a runny nose, and tear-filled eyes, gave him a big smile.

He kissed the top of her head.

She gurgled.

'She seems happy to see you,' Claire said with a sigh of relief, 'and I'm happy to see you too.'

James opened his arms, enfolded them both in a loving hug and kissed Claire's cheek. 'I missed you both so much,' he whispered and kissed her again.

Claire wiggled free from his embrace, grabbed a tissue from the box and wiped Ella's nose. Ella squirmed in protest.

'Oh, look at her, James. Her little nose is so red, and I'm worried about her. She hasn't been able to drink her milk or even drink water. Poor little thing, her nose is all clogged up and when she tries to drink, she can't breathe. She just fusses and pushes the bottle away.'

'Have you tried putting a drop of cooled boiled water in each nostril before she has a drink? That's what my mother told my sister to do when her children were little, and it seemed to work.'

'No, I've never heard of that.'

'Have you got a little dropper?'

'Yeah, I think so.'

'Would you like me to hold her while you make up another bottle and get the dropper ready.'

Claire happily handed Ella across and dashed through to the kitchen.

Holding the baby close, James walked around the room jiggling her gently in his arms and showing her the pictures on the wall.

Claire returned. 'I couldn't find a dropper, but will this syringe be okay; it's very fine?'

'It should be all right,' he said.

'Would you be able to do it for me, James? I don't think I could do it.' Claire shivered and looked away.

James sat on the couch, laid Ella on her back and tilted her head. She squirmed. 'It's all right, little one,' James said. 'It will only take a second and you'll feel better.'

He quickly inserted the drops in her nose.

She coughed and spluttered then had a big sneeze.

'That's better,' James said and, taking a clean white handkerchief from his pocket, dabbed it gently under her nose.

Claire turned back and handed the bottle to him. 'Seeing you're doing such a good job do you want to try feeding her?'

'I'll just let her settle down first,' he said as he lifted her to his chest and patted her back.

Ella relaxed and rested her head on his shoulder.

While still savouring the warmth of her tiny body, James lowered her carefully in his arms, tucked the feeder bib under her chin and offered her the sweet warm milk.

Claire, surprised and relieved to see Ella taking the bottle, leaned against the doorframe; she couldn't help but wonder at the scene; Ella, hardly shifting her eyes from James, and James looking lovingly at the child in his arms. *What a contrast*, she thought. *Here's James, so kind, patient and gentle and then there's Eddy, violent, cruel and* ... She shuddered at the thought.

Bill came in from the garden. 'Hi, mate; sorry, I didn't hear you come in.' He blinked. 'Why is it so dark in here?' he asked and pulled back the curtains. 'That's better, a bit more light on the subject.'

Claire frowned. 'Shh, Dad, don't talk too loud, you'll disturb Ella.'

'Sorry,' he whispered sheepishly then glanced across to his granddaughter. 'She certainly seems to be a lot more content now. Looks like you have the magic touch, James.'

'I had plenty of practice with my older sister's three children.'

'Well, I think you're a natural,' Bill said with a grin.

With Ella asleep in his arms and an almost empty bottle nearby, James signalled to Claire. 'Shall I put her in the rocker, or do you think she'd be better in her cot?'

'She looks so comfortable, it's a shame to disturb her, but I guess she'd be better in her bed.' Claire slid her hands under the sleeping child.

'It's all right. I'll carry her upstairs for you,' James mouthed.

Claire slowly moved her hands away and, leaning close, whispered in his ear. 'Thank you, my darling. I'll just pop up and fold the blankets down for her.'

James placed the baby in her cot, covered her with a light bunny rug and felt her forehead with the back of his hand. Satisfied she was okay and seeing her snug and content in her cot, he and Claire backed slowly out of the room.

'Do you think she'll be all right?' Claire whispered.

'She is a little bit warm, but don't you worry. I'm sure she'll be fine.'

He took her in his arms and held her close, their bodies blending as one.

Claire began to cry. Her body shook with a shuddered breath and her tears flowed freely. James held her tight, her hot tears soaking the front of his shirt.

His plans to take Claire out to dinner that night and propose to her didn't eventuate. With Ella sick and Claire tired, he thought it best to put it on hold – for the time being anyway.

There's always tomorrow, he thought. And crossing his fingers, silently hoped for tomorrow.

The next day took a different twist. Instead of going to church with Bill and Sonia as planned, Claire, still feeling a bit bedraggled, decided it best for her and Ella to stay home.

James arrived a bit earlier than expected.

Sonia answered the door.

'Hi James, it's good to see you again. I'm glad you came early. Claire's still in the shower and I've been dying to hear all about your trip up north, and especially about the ring! Come on in. Bill is in the kitchen.'

James kissed her cheek.

She blushed.

With the sound of the shower running, and with Ella still asleep, James gave Bill and Sonia a quick rundown on how he came to find the engagement ring.

'Well, that's great, mate,' Bill said, and patted him on the back.

Sonia drew a long deep breath. 'And when are you going to give her the ring?'

'Actually, I had planned to take her out last night, but that didn't happen.'

'Why don't you go out this afternoon? We can mind Ella.'

'I'll see what Claire says when she comes down.'

Bill looked at his watch. 'Time for us to go,' he said and headed to the door.

'I'll be with you in a minute.' Sonia turned to James. 'You'll be here when we get back, won't you? You will stay for lunch?' she added hopefully.

'Yes, thank you, that would be nice.'

'That's good. We'll see you later then.'

She turned to go. 'Oh, and by the way, the baby monitor is on the kitchen bench.'

'Thanks, Sonia. Yes, I did notice that. See you later.'

'Bye.'

The door closed behind them.

Claire ran down the stairs and into his arms. She laughed as James lifted her off her feet and spun her round and round.

'Put me down, I'm getting dizzy ...' Claire complained.

James lowered her gently to the floor and kissed her forehead. She swooned.

'I think you had better sit down before you fall,' he said as he led her across to the couch.

Claire caught her breath. 'I thought you were going to church with Mum and Dad,' she said cheekily.

'Nah, thought I'd give it a miss today.' He looked into her eyes. 'You sure look a lot better than you did yesterday. You must have had a good sleep, ay.'

'Yeah, and Ella slept better too; she only woke up once and I did what you said before she had her bottle – and it worked! Thanks, James, you're a genius.'

James took her hand in his. 'Your Mum and Dad invited me to stay for lunch, and I was wondering if you would like to go for a drive this afternoon and maybe we could have dinner out somewhere. What do you think?'

'Yep, sounds good.'

His heart skipped a beat. *Today's the day!* he thought.

The baby monitor crackled.

'Sounds like our little princess is awake,' James said as he leapt to his feet. 'Shall I go get her?'

'There's no rush. I like to let her have time to wake up properly. She's not always hungry when she first wakes, and I like to let her have a bit of time to herself without me rushing straight to her.'

James sat on the sofa next to Claire. 'I'm sure you know best,' he said and put one foot on the coffee table.

'Would you like a coffee?' Claire asked, leaning forward.

'That'd be great. I am rather thirsty. Do you want me to come and help you?'

'Okay, you can get the mugs, and I'll put the kettle on.'

They sat at the breakfast bar, coffee in hand, sun streaming through the window.

'This is nice,' James said, his hands wrapped around the mug. 'And it's good to see you looking so much better today.'

'Yeah, it's good to feel better too. I'm sorry I wasn't much company yesterday. You saw me at my worst.'

Ella started to fuss. The sound through the baby monitor changed from happy baby talk to 'I'm hungry and I need some attention – right now!'

Pushing his stool back from the breakfast bar, James jumped up. 'You finish your coffee; I'll go get her.'

'Okay, I'll fix her bottle.'

James took the stairs two at a time and dashed into the nursery, Claire smiling as she listened in from the kitchen.

'And how's my little princess today?' James' voice came gentle yet clear through the monitor.

A baby giggle resonated.

'Well, you're a happy little girl today … want to go down and see your Mummy?'

'Mummm.'

'Did you say Mum? What a clever little girl you are. Come on then, let's go.'

When they returned to the kitchen, Claire was shaking the baby's bottle vigorously.

Ella looked at her mother then turned to James; a brilliant smile spread across her face.

'I think she wants me to feed her,' he said in a pleading voice.

'Okay then if you must,' Claire quite happily conceded and, although she knew he wouldn't change his mind, quickly passed the bottle to him.

They retreated to the lounge room. Claire flopped onto the couch, tucked her feet up under herself and sipped her second cup of coffee.

'I think I'll call her Snuffleupagus, she's still got a bit of a snuffle, but she's a lot better than yesterday,' James said.

'Yeah, she seemed to turn the corner when you gave her the bottle last night, and after that she had a decent sleep.'

'That's good,' he replied, then hesitated before continuing. 'Claire, your mother offered to mind Ella for us when we go out this afternoon, if you like. Or would you rather we take her with us?'

'I think it'd be nice for just the two of us to go on our own, and I think it best for Ella to stay home. I wouldn't want her cold getting worse in the night air.'

James agreed wholeheartedly. 'Right then, it's a date.'

It was a beautiful afternoon. The clear sky and light westerly breeze were just enough to keep the late November heat bearable.

Walking hand in hand along the shoreline, suddenly Claire bent down scooped up a handful of water and threw it at James, and slipping her hand from his took off up the beach.

'Oh, so that's how it is, hey!' he shouted after her with a cheeky smirk, and the chase was on.

With shrills of laughter, Claire endeavoured to escape, but breathless and no longer able to laugh and run at the same time, she gave up and fell into his arms.

James lifted her into the air and twirled her around until the earth seemed to spin like a crazed kaleidoscope around her.

'Stop, stop!' she yelled.

James scooped her up into his arms. 'So, you want a dunking, do you?' he said as he carried her toward the water.

Claire kicked her legs and screamed. 'No! I haven't got a change of clothes.'

'Oh, it's all right, you'll soon dry off.'

James lowered her to within centimetres from the water. Her skirt touched the surface.

'James! Stop it!' she yelled in desperation.

Back on dry sand, he lowered her gently down and kissed her forehead.

Claire gathered up the edge of her skirt, squeezed out the salty water and shivered.

'You're cold, I'm sorry,' James apologized. 'Look I'll go back to the car and get a jacket for you.'

Claire grabbed her sandals and headed for the car in a mock huff.

'I didn't mean to upset you. I was only mucking around.'

A cheeky grin crossed her face. 'So was I,' she said as she slipped her hand into his.

Shadows lengthened as afternoon gave way to dusk.

After dropping Claire off at her home, James went back to the hotel to freshen up and get ready for their big night out. A wave of nervousness mixed with excitement surged through his whole being. 'Tonight's the night,' he said. His voice echoed through the empty room.

James took the velvet box out of the gift bag and opened the lid. Shafts of light shot like arrows from the lustrous diamonds. He lifted the precious ring from the box, held it to his lips and kissed it. Then, slipping it into the red velvet drawstring pouch, he closed the top securely, pushed it deep into the side pocket of his trousers and placed a folded handkerchief in his pocket to cover the hidden treasure and keep it safe. And, with a little pat to his pocket, he was ready to go.

To James' surprise, when he arrived at the Martin's house, Claire was ready to go.

'You look beautiful,' he said when she opened the door to him.

Claire kissed him on the cheek. 'You don't look bad yourself,' she said. 'Come on in.'

James stepped across the threshold and enquired after Ella.

'Sorry, James, she's already in bed. She couldn't keep awake any longer.'

He rolled his bottom lip, in a mock pout, but the sparkle in his eyes told a different story.

'Hi, Mr and Mrs Martin,' he said excitedly then quickly corrected himself. 'Oh sorry, I mean Sonia, Bill.' James flushed with embarrassment.

'That's all right, mate; I'm sure you'll soon get used to it.'

Sonia gave James a motherly hug. 'Would you like to have a coffee before you go?' she said hopefully.

James looked at Claire. 'It's up to you, babe. I don't mind either way.'

'How about we have a coffee with you when we get back, Mum. We shouldn't be too late because James must get away early for work in the morning, so we had better not make it a late night.'

'Oh, okay, we'll wait up for you then,' said Sonia.

'Don't know about that,' Bill chipped in. 'Let's just wait and see.'

Claire grabbed her evening coat and shoulder bag, looped her hand around James' arm and threw a kiss to her mum and dad. 'We'll be off then,' she said with a giggle. 'Lead on, James.'

James spared no expense for his beloved Claire. They dined by candlelight at a most exquisite restaurant overlooking the ocean. The soft background music blended with the gentle swish of the waves.

Claire adjusted her shoestring shoulder strap and rested her glass on the table. 'You're spoiling me you know; making me feel like a queen.'

'You are a queen,' he replied and, taking her hand in his, placed a gentle kiss on the back of her soft hand.

Lingering momentarily, he luxuriated in the sweet fragrance of her skin, and then looking up, their eyes met. 'I love you, Claire,' he said.

'I love you too,' Claire replied and, pulling her hand from his, wiped a tear from the corner of her eye.

James felt for the precious ring in his trousers pocket and leaned closer. 'Claire, um …' He licked his lips and cleared his throat. 'There's something I want to ask you.'

At that precise moment, the waiter sidled over.

'Is there anything else I can get for you, sir, madam?' he asked.

Claire tilted her cup over. 'Yes, please, could I have another chai latte?'

'Certainly. And you, sir?'

James shifted uneasily in his chair. 'A cappuccino, mate,' he replied sharply.

Sensing his intrusion, the waiter gathered the empty cups and backed away.

Claire turned her attention to James. 'Sorry, you were saying?'

'Oh, never mind, it mustn't have been important.'

He tried to recapture the moment, but it was lost. *Perhaps another time,* he mused.

After settling the account, James and Claire strolled along the ocean path. The air was cool and fresh, and the moonlight danced like silver glitter on the water.

'This is beautiful,' Claire said and breathed in the salt-infused air.

The sound from a party wafted from the third-floor balcony of one of the beachside apartments.

'Sounds like someone's celebrating,' James said as he squeezed Claire's hand.

A shiver of anticipation rippled down his spine with the thought that, hopefully, they, too, would be celebrating before the night was out.

Back at home, Sonia couldn't sit still. She paced back and forth from the kitchen, through the dining room and into the lounge room.

'Come on, Sonia, sit down, why don't you? You're making me tired and besides, you'll wear out the carpet if you keep going,' Bill said with a yawn.

Sonia checked the time once more. 'I thought they'd be home by now; I hope nothing's happened to them.'

'Oh, my goodness, you are a worrywart. The kids are probably having the time of their life. They'll be back when they're ready.'

'But James has to leave early for work tomorrow.'

'So what? He's young and fit and could stay awake all night and still keep going. Anyway, I think we should go to bed.'

'No way! I want to stay up and see the ring.'

'How do you know he'll give her the ring tonight?'

'Because of the way he looked at me before they left.'

Bill sighed. 'Even if James does give Claire the engagement ring tonight, it will still be there in the morning.'

'No, I'm staying up. You can go to bed if you must.

'Oh, I think I heard a car pull into the driveway.'

Sonia crossed the room and was about to look through the side of the curtain when Bill stopped her.

'You can't do that! They'll see you.'

'Well switch the light off then.'

'Then they would know that you are spying on them. Just sit down. I'll go and put the kettle on.'

James cut the engine and switched the courtesy lamp on low. He reached into his pocket, pulled out the red velvet pouch and slipped the ring into his hand. Then, taking Claire's hand in his, looked into her eyes. 'Claire,' he said as he held out the ring, 'I would like you to be my wife. Will you marry me?'

Claire took her hand from his and covered her mouth.

'I … I … I don't know. I don't know what to say.'

'Just say "Yes".'

'But …' Claire paused.

'Don't you like the ring?' James asked.

'Yes, it's beautiful. But I don't know. I just wasn't expecting this right now. I haven't thought about it.' She shrugged.

'What's wrong?' James said with a heavy heart.

'Well, how would it work? You live in Adelaide, and I live here in Perth. And what about your job? Your promotion, and all that?'

'I love you, Claire. That's all that matters, and I'd move to the other end of the earth for you. So don't worry about the details. They'll all sort out.'

Claire swallowed the lump in her throat and hung her head.

'I do love you,' she sniffed. 'But I just need time to think about it.'

James was quiet. Claire tried to explain.

'Sorry, James, I'm not saying no, but it's just that I need a little more time to think things through.' Her voice quivered. 'I hope you understand. I do love you. Please don't be upset.'

James slipped the ring back into the pouch, tucked it in his pocket and smiled a sad smile.

'I'm sorry if I rushed things. I didn't mean to put you on the spot, and I understand there are a lot of things to work out — if it's to be.'

James reached across and put his arm around her. He held her close and kissed her tenderly. Then, looking deep into her tear-washed eyes, whispered, 'It's all right, my darling. You take your time.'

Claire rummaged through her purse, pulled out a tissue, daubed her eyes and blew her nose.

'James, I promise I'll give you my answer when I see you Wednesday. Okay?'

'Thanks, Claire.'

'You coming in for a coffee?' Claire asked, trying to lighten the mood.

'I won't if you don't mind. I had better get back to the hotel and get myself organised for work tomorrow. Say "Hi and Bye" to your Mum and Dad for me, and I'll catch up with them when I get back.'

Chapter 24

Inside the house, Sonia re-boiled the kettle, again. 'Why are they taking so long?' she asked.

Bill looked at her over his glasses. 'Sonia, don't you remember how hard it was to say good night?'

'Yeah, I suppose so,' she said and jiggled her leg impatiently.

'I told you we should have gone to bed ages ago,' Bill grumbled. 'And by the way, where's that cup of tea?'

Sonia sauntered into the kitchen and made them coffee.

'Coffee! We'll be awake all night,' he complained when Sonia handed him the mug.

'We both need to be alert when they come in.'

'Whatever you say, dear.' Bill replied and sipped his coffee.

James got out of the driver's seat, walked around the back of the car, and reaching the front passenger's door, opened it for Claire. He took her by the hand, wrapped her coat around her shoulders and drawing her into his arms, kissed her tenderly.

Claire swooned. The warmth of his strong body enveloped her. She felt like their whole beings were merging as one. *How can I let him go without giving him an answer?* she thought.

'Good night, Claire,' James said, 'I'd better be going.' He took her by the hand and walked her to the door.

'Good night, James,' Claire replied. 'See you Wednesday.'

The porch light came on and the front door opened.

'Come in, come in,' Sonia said, her eyes wide with anticipation.

The sound of a car reversing from the driveway startled her.

'Where's James?' she asked. 'Isn't he coming in?'

'No, he's going back to the hotel.'

'Aw.' Sonia frowned. 'I thought you were both going to come in for coffee.'

'Nah, not tonight, Mum.'

Sonia shut the front door and took hold of her daughter's hand, expecting to see an engagement ring. There wasn't one.

'Oh, is everything all right?' she asked.

'Yeah, why do you ask?'

Sonia shrugged. 'Aw, no particular reason.'

'Is that you, princess?' Bill called from the lounge room.

'Yes, Dad, but how come you're still awake? I thought you'd be in bed long ago,' Claire said and, leaning over, planted a kiss on his forehead.

'Well, it's like this, your mother insisted I stay up until you and James came home. So, being the obedient husband I am, I'm here.'

'Oh, Dad, you didn't have to wait up for us. Anyway, James decided not to come in but he said he'll catch up with us on Wednesday.' Claire yawned. 'I think I'll head off to bed myself,' she said and kissed him again. 'Night, Mum,' she called as she wandered through to the kitchen.

Sonia poured milk into the steaming coffee mug. 'I've made you a drink. Aren't you going to stay and talk to us for a while?'

Claire sighed. 'Mum, I'm pretty tired. Can't we talk in the morning?'

Sonia's disappointment palpable, she twisted the corner of the tea towel in her fingers.

Claire leaned over and kissed her. 'Mum, there's nothing to talk about. We had a good time. The food was great. That's all. Okay?'

'Okay. Good night.' Sonia sighed.

'Thanks for looking after Ella,' Claire added as she turned on her heels and walked off.

As tired as Claire was, sleep evaded her. She tossed and turned, unable to get the picture of James out of her mind.

I'm such an idiot! she thought. *I do love him, he's the best thing that's ever happened to me, and I didn't mean to upset him.* She thought about the ring and how beautiful it was. *Why couldn't I have given him an answer?* Claire pummelled her pillow. *I'm stupid, stupid!*

She sat up in bed and looked at the luminous numbers on the digital clock. 3:57 am. *Should I phone him? No, he'll be asleep. I don't want to disturb him.* So, she lay awake.

In the master bedroom, Sonia also lay awake. 'Bill, are you awake?' she asked.

He opened one eye and rolled over. 'I am now,' he mumbled.

'I can't go to sleep; I know something's wrong. Do you think they've had a fight or something?'

'I don't know.' Bill sighed. 'Let's ask in the morning.'

Sonia sat bolt upright. 'Oh, my goodness, I hope they haven't broken up?'

'It's no good worrying about what you don't know; just go back to sleep.'

'I can't sleep; I haven't been asleep. Oh, Bill, what are we going to do?'

Bill reached over and switched on the bed lamp.

'Darling, how about I make a cup of tea for you?'

Sonia sniffed. 'Yes please, that might make me feel a bit better.'

Bill rolled out of bed, wiggled his feet into his slippers, yawned, stretched his arms up and scratched his head. 'I'll have to go to the loo first,' he announced.

'Thank you, darling,' Sonia said and snuggled beneath the blankets.

By the time Bill came from the en suite back into the bedroom, having left the toilet unflushed so as not to disturb the household, Sonia was asleep.

'So much for a cup of tea,' he said and with a smile crawled back into bed.

The clock clicked over to 5:00 am. Claire couldn't wait any longer. She jumped out of bed, grabbed her dressing gown from the hook behind the door, slipped her mobile phone into her pocket and made her way downstairs.

The house was quiet. Closing the sliding door between the kitchen and dining room, she turned on the light and flicked the switch on the kettle. Then, taking the phone from her pocket, she called James.

He answered on the second ring. 'Good morning, Claire. Did you sleep well?'

'No, I didn't sleep all night. I just had to ring you to apologise for fobbing you off how I did last night. I'm sorry.'

'That's all right. I probably did it all wrong and I'm sorry.'

'No, you did it beautifully, James. It was me that did it all wrong. And I didn't want to leave it any longer to give you my answer: it's YES! Yes, James, I will marry you.'

There was silence on the other end of the phone.

Claire added. 'That is if you still want me.'

James choked back the tears. 'Of course, I still want you.' He sniffed. 'But this doesn't seem the right way to do it over the phone. I wanted to slip the ring onto your finger and seal it with a kiss. This isn't how I planned it to be.'

'It doesn't matter, James, as long as you know my answer.'

'I wish I could be with you today, but unfortunately, I have early appointments down south and I can't change them. So, let's plan a date for Wednesday and make it all proper and official then. Okay?'

The kettle boiled and Claire, bubbling over with joy, danced around the kitchen. 'It's a date,' she said.

'I can't wait,' James replied. 'Thank you for ringing, and I know it sounds like a cliché but, you have made my day, and all my days forever. Thank you, Claire.'

The call ended. Claire whirled around the kitchen her arms outstretched, her head high and her heart aglow. 'Yippee!' she yelled.

Ten minutes later, Bill wandered into the kitchen. 'You're up early,' he said. 'You must have had a good sleep.'

Claire couldn't wipe the smile off her face. 'No, I didn't sleep a wink. And I don't think I'll ever need to sleep again,' she said and grabbed hold of her father's hands and waltzed him around the room.

'What's got into you?' Bill asked with a questioning frown.

'I'm happy.'

'Yes, I can see that, but what's gotten into you? You certainly didn't seem so happy last night.'

Claire did a little jig, and then, throwing her arms around her father's neck, planted a kiss on one cheek, then the other and, standing on her tippy toes, kissed his forehead. She took a deep breath and, releasing him from her grip, sighed. 'Oh, Dad, I can't tell you just yet …' She paused, then took another breath, 'but you'll know, very soon, I promise.'

'Rightio then. Now let's have breakfast.'

'I'm not hungry, Dad. I couldn't eat a single thing!'

Bill touched the kettle with the back of his hand. 'Ouch!' he said then shook his hand and flicked the switch.

The baby monitor crackled to life.

'Sounds like Ella's awake. I'd better get her bottle ready.'

Humming a happy tune, Claire busied herself preparing the baby formula. When it was ready she skipped up the stairs and greeted Ella. 'Good morning, my darling,' she said as she opened the blinds. 'What a lovely day.'

Ella gurgled.

Claire lifted her from the cot, held her tight and danced a happy dance. The baby giggled.

'Shh, we mustn't wake Nanna. Come on, let's go down and see Grandpa.'

Bill sat at the dining table, his hands wrapped round his coffee mug and the newspaper spread open in front of him. He looked up. 'Good morning, and how's my little princess today?'

Ella answered with a smile and reached her arms toward him.

Bill put his mug on the table, swivelled the chair around and taking her in his arms, kissed her soft hair.

Late that morning, after Bill had gone to work, Sonia emerged sporting a morning-after-the-night-before demeanour, surprised to see that the washing had been done and hung on the line, the kitchen was sparkling clean, and the house had been cleaned from top to bottom and smelt like a floral garden.

'Wow! Someone's been busy,' she said as she looked for signs of life. The house was empty. She looked in the garage. It was empty. *That's strange, wonder where everyone is?*

The sun streamed through the kitchen window. Sonia blinked, and turning around, noticed a handwritten note on the bench. She picked it up and read:

Dear Mum,
Gone for a walk to the beach with Ella.
See you soon.
Love,
Claire xxx

Sonia folded her arms across her chest and huffed. *So much for our talk,* she thought and flopped down on the nearest chair.

When Claire arrived home, with Ella fast asleep in her stroller, she found her mother sitting at the kitchen table still in her dressing gown.

'Are you all right, Mum?' she asked.

'No, not really,' came the abrupt reply.

Claire felt her mother's forehead. 'What's wrong? Are you sick?'

'No, I was just worried about you, Claire. I couldn't sleep all night and when I got up, you'd gone.'

Claire chuckled. 'Oh, Mum, look at the time; I'm sure you've caught up with any lost sleep. Have you had breakfast?'

Sonia shrugged.

'Right, I'm going to make you a delicious brunch and then we'll talk.'

Claire filled the kettle and turned it on, and then, opening the fridge, took out bacon, eggs, a tomato, sourdough bread and a tub of butter.

The frying pan sizzled to life and the kettle boiled. Claire cut the tomato in half and placed both pieces skin down in the pan and added the bacon. She then poured two coffees and, grabbing a couple of coasters from the rack, slid one of them across for Sonia and placed the other on the table opposite and set the mugs down.

'Now, Mum,' Claire said, 'why were you worried about me?'

Sonia raised the coffee mug to her lips, blew a gap in the froth and took one sip then put it back on the coaster.

'I was worried because when you came in last night you seemed to be upset and you wouldn't talk to me.'

'I'm sorry, Mum. I didn't mean to worry you.'

'Did you and James have a fight or something?'

'Not really.'

'Well, why didn't he come in for coffee? Dad and I were expecting you both. We waited up all that time for you to come in, and then, when you did come in, you just stomped off to your room without a word of explanation.'

Claire jumped up, went over to the stove, and turned the bacon and tomatoes, then cracked two eggs into the pan. She couldn't hold her secret any longer. 'Oh, Mum,' she said, her heart almost burst with excitement, 'James asked me to marry him!'

Sonia pulled the front of her dressing gown across her chest and sighed. 'At last!' she said, and then jumping to her feet, pulled Claire into a bear hug. 'I'm so happy for you,' she said with tear-filled eyes. 'I'm happy for both of you.'

'Thanks, Mum, but it's not actually official yet. James is going to do it properly on Wednesday.'

'Oh, that's exciting, darling, I can't wait. Does your father know? Did you tell him?'

'No, Mum, I was trying to keep it a secret, but I just had to tell you.'

Sonia, almost beside herself, wondered how she could possibly keep the news from Bill.

Claire read her mind. 'It's all right, Mum, you can tell Dad.'

Sonia grabbed the cordless phone from its cradle and dialled his work number. The receptionist put her through.

Bill answered. 'Hi, darling, is everything okay?'

'Yes, everything's fine. Just a minute I'll put Claire on.'

Sonia thrust the phone at Claire.

'Hi Dad, I've got some news to tell you.' But before she could go any further Sonia squealed in the background.

'Yeah! Exciting news. The best!'

'Umm,' said Bill, 'sounds good, but you'd better tell me now Claire; don't keep me in suspense, or else your mum will burst, and you don't want a mess to have to clean up.'

'Dad, first of all, can you guess my news?'

'Maybe. You did seem very happy this morning, but I think you'd better tell me.'

'Last night, James asked me to marry him.'

'And?'

'Yes, Dad, we are engaged!'

'Well, that's great, darling. I'm so pleased for both of you.'

'But Dad, it's not official yet. We plan to announce it properly on Wednesday.'

Sonia reached for the phone.

'I think Mum wants to talk to you, here just a minute.' Claire passed the phone to Sonia and then went over to the stove and turned off the gas. She frowned. The eggs looked a bit dry and the delicious meal she was making for her mother didn't look so delicious after all.

'Well, Bill, what do you think about that?' Sonia asked, but without giving Bill a chance to get a word in she continued. 'Isn't it the best news ever?'

'Yes, it sure is.' Just then another call came through for Bill. 'Sorry, darling, I'm going to have to go. I've got a call coming. That's great news and I'll see you tonight, bye.'

The call ended and Sonia gave a sigh. 'Dad had to go. He said he'll see us tonight.'

Claire busied herself in the kitchen trying to salvage what she could of the fry up. She added some lettuce, capsicum, and a few miniature grape tomatoes to the plate, but it still didn't look very appetising. 'Sorry, Mum, this doesn't look the best. I think I'll toss it out and start again.'

'How about I take you out for lunch to celebrate.'

'That sounds like a good idea.'

An hour later while mother, daughter and granddaughter were enjoying a light lunch at their favourite restaurant, Claire's mobile rang. She took it from her bag and saw that the incoming call was from James. With one swipe of her finger across the screen and a smile as broad as the man in the moons, Claire answered.

'Hi, James. I'm just having lunch out with Mum. How are you going?'

'Aw, I had a great morning, but I thought I'd let you know, that my mum rang a little while ago, and I couldn't help it … sorry, Claire, I let the cat out of the bag and told her we are engaged. I think if I hadn't told her, she would have guessed anyway.'

Claire chuckled. 'It's all right, my darling; I'll forgive you if you forgive me. I told Mum and Dad too. Anyway, what did your mum say?'

'She was over the moon – ecstatic. She says to pass on her love and congratulations, and she can't wait to meet you.'

'That's so nice, James. Next time you're talking to her would you say thanks from me and tell her I can't wait to meet her too.'

'Will do. Anyway, I'd better get going. Say hi to your mum and give Ella a big kiss from me. See you Wednesday.'

'Thanks for ringing. Bye.'

Ella was fast asleep in her grandmother's arms; her empty baby bottle rested on the table. Sonia wiped a dribble of milk from Ella's chin and laid her down in the stroller. 'Well, what did he have to say?' she asked in a whisper as she covered the baby with her bunny rug.

Claire slipped her phone back into her shoulder bag and put the baby's bottle in the carry-all. 'As you probably guessed from my side of the conversation, James couldn't keep our secret from his mother either, and when he told her she was really happy for us.'

The rest of the day passed in a blur. They talked and shopped and talked some more before returning home where they continued to talk. And when Bill returned from work, they were still talking.

Chapter 25

Meanwhile, back in Adelaide, James' mother was equally excited. She kept watching the clock; waiting for an appropriate time to phone her son back again.

Then, at the first possible chance, she rang.

'James,' she said when he answered, 'are you going to ring your sisters or shall I?'

He thought for a moment and sensing the excitement in his mother's voice and knowing that she'd want to share the news of his engagement with them, he suggested she be the one to call them.

'Are you sure you don't want to tell them yourself?' she asked, hoping against hope that he wouldn't change his mind.

'No, Mum, I would really like you to do it for me, if you don't mind.'

'That's all right, darling. I don't mind doing that for you. Is there anything else you'd like me to tell them?'

'That'll be fine, Mum; just tell them that I'll talk to them when I get home.'

'Okay, darling, goodbye.'

'Love you, Mum, thanks for calling. Bye.'

No sooner had Gloria finished the call than she dialled Laurel's number.

'Hi, Mum, you're ringing early tonight … are you all right?'

'Yes, dear I'm fine, and I've got some great news. Your brother is engaged!'

There was silence on the other end of the line.

'Did you hear me, darling?'

Laurel cleared her throat. 'Yes, Mum, I heard you, but it's a bit of a shock – they hardly know each other.'

'But aren't you happy for your brother? He really loves Claire and the baby. Ever since he met her, he's been like a different man. I know she is right for him.'

'Okay, Mum,' Laurel tutted. 'If you think it's right, what can I say?'

'Oh, darling, please be happy for him. He said he'll catch up with you when he gets back.'

'Right-o, I'll talk to him then,' she said and ended the call.

Surprised by her response, Gloria made a second call to her youngest daughter, Melanie. But sadly, her reaction was much the same and it left Gloria feeling deflated. *Oh, that's a shame*, she thought as she placed the phone back in its cradle. *If only they knew what I know. If only they'd seen James' face when he talked about Claire. Oh, never mind, they'll come around.*

Late Tuesday afternoon there was an unexpected knock on the Martin's front door.

'Can you get that, Claire?' Sonia called from the kitchen. 'I'm making rissoles … got my hands in the mix.'

Claire pattered down the stairs and hurried to the door. 'Okay, Mum, I've got it.' She unlatched the lock.

'James!' she screeched with delight and threw herself into his waiting arms. 'What a surprise! I wasn't expecting you until tomorrow.'

James lifted her off her feet and held her in a bear hug. 'I finished work early and drove straight back,' he said, lowering her to the ground, looking deep into her eyes, and kissing her passionately.

Hearing the commotion out front, Sonia washed the sticky mix from her hands and hurried to the door.

'James, you're back early,' she said and wiped her damp hands on her jeans. 'Welcome. Come in, I'll put the kettle on. Bill will be home soon,' she said and dashed back into the house.

James took Claire by the hand and started to follow Sonia through to the kitchen but was sidetracked by a familiar little sound coming from the lounge room.

'Hello, sweetie pie,' he said and tickled her on the tummy. 'How's my little princess?'

Ella looked up at James from her baby bouncer and gave a knowing smile. She kicked her feet excitedly, blew a big raspberry bubble through her rosebud lips and reached her hands toward him.

'Claire, is it all right if I pick her up?'

'Yes, of course,' she said as she uncoupled the catch. 'You bring her into the kitchen while I get her bottle ready.'

'Okey-dokey, we won't be long.'

He carefully lifted the baby from her bouncer, took her tiny hand in his, and waltzed her around the room.

'Wee!'

Ella giggled.

James carried her into the kitchen and, holding her firmly in one arm and, with the other hand, grabbed the back of one of the stools from under the breakfast bar and beckoned for Claire to sit down.

With baby's bib in one hand and burp cloth slung over her shoulder, Claire sauntered across the room shaking Ella's bottle vigorously. 'Here we go,' she said, 'dinner time!'

Ella ignored her mother and, with eyes only for James, lifted her hand and touched his chin.

Sonia placed mugs of hot coffee on the bench and slid the sugar bowl to James. 'Here, let me take her while you have your coffee,' she said and endeavoured to pry the baby from his arms.

Ella started to fuss.

'Aw! Looks like you've won a heart,' said Sonia.

'I'll give her the bottle, I don't mind,' he pleaded.

'All right then, if you must,' she said, tongue-in-cheek.

He pulled out a stool, wiggled into it and began to feed Ella.

Claire tucked the bib under the baby's chin and left James to the task at hand. 'You're a natural, James. I can't believe how good she is for you.'

'Yeah, I'm glad too,' he said and kissed her tiny hand. 'She's such a dear little thing. Who could help but love her?'

Claire's mind wandered back to Eddy. *What a contrast*, she thought again, *James, so kind and gentle and Eddy, so cruel.*

She shivered.

The sound of the garage door opening distracted her from her thoughts. 'It's Dad,' she said, announcing the obvious. 'He'll be surprised to see you, James.'

'I don't think so. He's sure to recognise the car out the front.'

'Yeah, I suppose so.'

Just then the door flung open.

'Hi, everyone. Good to see you, James. We weren't expecting you back 'til tomorrow. Are you staying for dinner?'

James looked across to Sonia. 'If it's not too much trouble.'

'Of course it's no trouble – you're family now, remember,' she said with a twinkle in her eye.

'Well, not quite; not officially anyway.' He looked at Claire. 'What do you think? Should we make it official tonight?'

Claire rushed to him, flung her arms around his neck, and kissed his cheek. 'Yes,' she said and then looked down at what she was wearing. 'Oh no, just look at me! I'm not dressed at all appropriately for such an occasion.'

James turned to her and with his eyes full of love, said, 'You are the most beautiful girl in the world, and it doesn't matter to me what you are wearing – to me you're absolutely wonderful.' And with Ella fast asleep in his arms, he leant over and kissed Claire thoroughly.

Bill coughed. 'Excuse me, you two. I was only asking if you were planning to stay for dinner, James. Can I take that as a "yes"?'

'Yes, thank you.'

'Yes!' Sonia said as she punched the air.

'Yes, yes,' echoed Claire.

'Well, that settles it then,' Bill added as he picked up his coffee and made his way into the lounge room.

Claire settled Ella down for the night, had a shower, washed, dried, and styled her hair as best she could, and then got dressed in the lovely frock; the one she wore the night James proposed to her – the night she let him down so badly. She made her way down the stairs.

James looked up. 'Wow! You look amazing,' he said and extended his hand to her. 'May I escort you to the table?'

'You may, dear sir,' Claire replied and slipped her hand into the crook of his arm.

James guided her across the room, pulled out the chair for her and, when she was seated, he spread the napkin on her lap.

'Why, thank you,' she said and smiled up at him.

Alone in the room, James leant over and whispered in her ear. 'I love you, Claire,' and kissed her neck.

'Dinner's ready,' Sonia called from the kitchen. 'Can someone come and give me a hand out here?'

Claire went to jump up, but James placed his hand on her shoulder. 'You stay there, I'll go and help.'

With the lights turned low and music playing softly in the background, the four of them enjoyed the meal together.

During dinner Bill dropped the odd 'dad joke' here and there, and the others tried to laugh politely at most of them.

Sonia apologised profusely. 'James, if I'd have known you were coming, I would have cooked something more fancy than just plain old rissoles!'

He wiped his mouth on the serviette. 'The meal was delicious, Mrs Martin; I couldn't have wished for anything better. Anyway, thank you for having me at such short notice.'

Sonia stood and started to gather the dishes.

Reaching across the table, James touched her arm.

'Don't go,' he said. 'There's something I want to do.' He stood, pushed back the chair and, turning to Claire, took her by the hand, knelt on the carpeted floor beside her and, in a voice soft and low asked, 'Claire, will you marry me?'

Claire threw her arms around his neck. 'Yes, yes, yes!' she replied.

James looked into her eyes. 'Thank you,' he said and, slipping the ring on her finger, kissed her tenderly.

Sonia caught her breath and, choking back the tears, whispered, 'Congratulations, you two, that's so lovely.'

'Excuse me, mate,' Bill said as he tapped James on the shoulder, 'do you mind if I cut in?'

James stepped aside.

Bill pulled his daughter into a bear hug. 'Congratulations, darling. I love you so much and I know you will be happy with James, and he will love you and take care of you.'

'Thanks, Dad; thanks for everything.'

Bill took a handkerchief from his pocket and wept unashamedly, and then, turning to his future son-in-law, extended his hand in a warm welcome. 'Congratulations, mate,' he said with a pat on his back.

Claire held her hand at arm's length and, for the first time, had a good look at her engagement ring. She wiggled her fingers. The tears that filled her eyes magnified the diamonds' glow; a myriad of sparkles flashed in all directions.

'Oh, James, it's gorgeous!'

'Glad you like it,' he said and, taking her hand in his, kissed her slender fingers.

'Look, Mum, what do you think?' Claire said, brushing the tears from her eyes. 'Have you ever seen anything so beautiful?'

Sonia took her daughter's hand in hers and, with Bill gazing over her shoulder, took a closer look at the ring. 'Yes, darling, it really is the most beautiful ring I've ever seen.'

'You've got good taste, mate,' Bill said with pride.

Claire cleared her throat and frowned. 'But how did you know my size?'

'We have ways and means,' he replied with a sideways glance at Sonia.

She grinned.

'Oh, you two! Mum, you mean to say you knew all about this?'

Sonia bit her bottom lip. 'Mmm,' she said and then confessed sheepishly. 'Actually, James asked your dad and me before he went north on his business trip. And I gave him one of your rings, so he'd have the right size.'

'This calls for bubbly,' said Bill and he turned and headed for the kitchen.

'There's some sparkling grape juice in the fridge,' Sonia called after him as she began to clear the table.

James led the way into the lounge room, plonked himself on the sofa and patted the spot on the seat beside him. But instead of taking the seat, Claire sat on his lap and wrapped her arms around his neck.

'Hello, fiancé,' she said with a cheeky grin and kissed his ear.

James slipped his arms around her waist and held her close. 'I love you so much, you've made me the happiest man in the world.' He looked at his watch. 'And I can't wait to spend the rest of my life with you, but I won't be able to stay very long tonight, because I've still got today's reports to write up and get them sent off to my boss. Then, once that's done, we'll have the next five whole days to spend together.'

Claire rolled her lower lip. 'But you don't have to go too soon, do you?'

'No, I can stay for another hour, but then I'll have to go. I do need my beauty sleep, you know,' he said with a crooked grin. 'And by the way, when I was talking to Mum last night, she said she'd love it if you could come over and spend Christmas with us. She so wants to meet you and Ella. What do you think?'

Claire hesitated. 'I don't think so. I always have Christmas with my family, and besides, it's Ella's first Christmas.'

'Why don't you all come? My mum would love to meet the whole family.'

The muscles in Claire's neck tightened. 'Oh, I don't know,' she said and shifted to the seat beside him.

Just then Bill entered the room followed closely by Sonia carrying a tray of four mugs of steaming coffee.

'Who's for coffee?' she asked and, placing the tray on the low coffee table, handed Bill his favourite mug.

'Thank you, Mrs Martin,' James said and passed a mug across to Claire. 'I'd better have a coffee to keep awake because I'll have to be heading off shortly.'

Sonia handed around a plate of cookies. 'Do you have to leave so soon, James? I was hoping to have a little catch up.'

'Sorry about that, but I'll be back tomorrow and then we'll be able to catch up.'

Claire shifted a little uneasy in her chair and looked at James. 'Tell Mum and Dad what you told me,' she said abruptly, 'about Christmas.'

James explained his mother's suggestion.

Looking over his glasses, Bill placed his coffee mug on the table beside him and glanced at Sonia. 'It sounds lovely, but I think it would be a bit difficult to get flights and arrange accommodation for that time of year, school holidays and all. It's very kind of your mother to invite us.' He looked at Sonia. 'What do you think, dear?'

Sonia straightened in her chair. 'I think it would be lovely. I'd like to meet your mum, James. That's if we wouldn't be intruding.'

'No way! Mum would love to have you come. And you won't have to worry about accommodation, we've already arranged where everyone can stay, so there's no problem.'

Seeing her parents so excited, Claire started to warm to the idea.

'Well, how about I make enquiries about flights tomorrow?' Bill suggested.

James pulled out his mobile phone from his pocket. 'I could check online now if you would like me to.'

'Could you?' Sonia said, her eyes aglow with excitement.

Quickly James checked flight schedules; he needed seats for three adults and one baby. He scrolled through the options. But, as expected flights were heavily booked, with the odd one or two seats here and there.

'Looking at Christmas Day,' he said 'there's one seat available on the midnight flight. And Boxing Day, on the early flight, there's two seats. But other than that, you must go back to the 18th to get the three seats – that's a week before Christmas.'

'Book it, book it!' cried Sonia.

'Wait a minute,' Bill cautioned, 'that may not be suitable for your mother, James. You had better ask her first.'

'I'll phone her now.'

'You sure it's not too late over there?'

James looked at his watch. 'No, Mum will still be awake.'

He pressed the automatic dial.

Gloria answered on the second ring. 'James, lovely to hear your voice. How did your trip go?'

'Good thanks, Mum. I'm back in Perth at the Martin's place, and I told them that you had invited them to come for Christmas.'

A shrill of delight came over the line. James pulled the phone away from his ear. 'Are they coming?' Gloria asked.

'Maybe. But there's not many flights to choose from and we were wondering if it would be all right if they came a week before Christmas, on Tuesday the 18th?'

'I'm sure that will be fine. Hang on … I'll check the calendar.' There was a short pause. 'Yes, yes, the 18th is fine.'

James gave a nod around the room. 'And Mum, there's something else we'd like to tell you. Do you mind if I put the phone on speaker?'

'No, that's all right. Go ahead, son.'

James pressed 'speaker'. The light flashed.

'Hi, Mrs Cowan, it's Claire.'

'Hello, honey, how are you?'

'I'm good, thank you.' Claire stretched her arm in front of her and flashed the ring. 'And James and I have some news to share. My Mum and Dad are here too.'

'Say hi to them for me.'

'They can hear you, Mum; remember, I put you on speaker.'

'Oh, silly me, I'm not used to this modern technology.

'Hello, Sonia. Hello, Bill.'

'Hi, Gloria,' they chorused.

'I'm so excited about you coming over.'

Bill walked across the room and leaned in closer to the phone. 'It hasn't been arranged yet, Gloria. We just wanted to check if it's still all right with you. James will try and book it online for us.'

'I'm looking forward to meeting you all. James has told me so much about you.'

Sonia jumped up and joined Bill. 'We're looking forward to meeting you too, Gloria – that is if it all works out.'

James chipped in. 'Hey, Mum, guess what?'

'I don't know, you'd better tell me.'

He put his arms around Claire and pulled her close. 'Claire and I are officially engaged. I gave her the ring tonight.'

Another shrill of joy filled the room.

'Oh, that's so exciting. Congratulations to both of you,' she said and wiped a tear from her eye.

'Thanks, Mum. I know you're going to love Claire.'

'I already do, son. I feel like I know her. I'm happy for you.'

'Thanks, Mrs Cowan,' Claire said. 'You should see the beautiful ring James gave me. I'll send you a photo.'

James checked the time. 'Mum, sorry to interrupt but I'll need to hang up soon so I can try to book the airline tickets for the Martins, so we'd better say goodbye and I'll talk to you again tomorrow. Okay?'

'Okay, darling. Bye.'

'Bye, Mum.'

They all sent their love and the call ended.

After James secured the booking for their flights to and from Adelaide, Bill and Sonia thanked him and then headed off to bed.

The next hour stretched on to two and passed too quickly. Claire and James found it harder than ever to say goodnight.

'I'll see you in the morning, gorgeous,' James said as he waved through the window of the car.

'Good night, handsome,' Claire whispered in the night air and blew a kiss.

The next few days passed in a flash, each day crammed with activity, Claire and James making the most of their precious time together. But all too soon Sunday arrived – the day James said his goodbyes and returned home to Adelaide.

His heart weighed heavy knowing that he wouldn't see his beloved Claire and Ella for two months. He missed them more than ever.

Claire began to count off the days until they would see each other again – 58, 57, 56 … It seemed forever!

James phoned every night at 7pm, give or take a minute. And Claire waited eagerly for his calls.

A lot happens in two months; a lot can happen in one day, especially with a growing baby.

'I don't know how they can find enough to talk about for a couple of hours *every* night,' Sonia said to Bill. 'That much can't happen in one day surely, can it?'

Bill lowered his newspaper and looked over his glasses. 'Young love, dear. Don't you remember?'

'Yeah, I suppose so.'

Chapter 26

Weeks passed and the 18th of December came at last. After a smooth flight from Perth to Adelaide, the Martin family disembarked from the plane. Claire, holding Ella in her arms, and Bill and Sonia beside her, walked through the sliding glass doors into the arrival lounge at the airport.

Smiling widely, James rushed up and threw his arms around Claire and Ella. Ella squealed with delight and James kissed her chubby cheeks.

'Look at you,' he said. 'What a big girl you are.'

Bill tapped James on the shoulder. 'I'll take Ella; you and Claire have a little time to yourselves. We'll go for coffee, and you can join us later. Okay?'

'Thank you,' he said, then he placed another kiss on Ella's forehead and handed her to Bill.

He hugged Sonia and shook Bill's free hand. 'Welcome to Adelaide.'

James took Claire by the hand and led her across to a private little corner – well, as private as one can find in a busy airport lounge.

'Mum didn't come with me to meet you, but she'd like you all to go to her place for afternoon tea, that is if you are not too tired after your flight. She's so excited about meeting you, Claire; she said she can't wait.'

Claire rubbed her ears and yawned. 'I feel a bit spaced out,' she said, 'and my ears are still blocked from the flight.' She swallowed hard to try to clear them.

'It's all right. Mum will understand if you don't feel up to it.'

'But I'd really like to see her. How about we go and have a coffee and talk to Mum and Dad and ask what they want to do.'

'Good idea, honey bun,' he said and, taking her in his arms again, squeezed her tight.

By the time they finished their coffee and headed down to collect their luggage, the area was all but deserted. The carousel continued round and round, and the only items left were Ella's stroller and car seat, three suitcases, and an overstuffed carry-all bag.

James grabbed a trolley and loaded it up.

'Shall I open Ella's stroller?' he asked.

The baby looked comfortable in Bill's arms, her head resting snuggly on his chest, her eyes heavy with sleep.

'No, don't bother. I'll carry her.'

James steered the trolley toward the exit, Claire by his side and the others following close behind. When they arrived at the car James fixed the baby capsule firmly in place before loading the luggage. Then, closing the boot as quietly as possible so as not to wake Ella, he whispered, 'Sorry, it will be a bit squashy, but there's room for everyone. I think it'd be best for you to sit in the front; Bill and the girls can sit in the back.'

'Right you are,' Bill agreed and carefully settled Ella in her seat.

'I'll fasten the straps,' Claire said as she slipped into the seat behind the driver's seat.

James closed her door, walked around the other side of the car and held the door open for Sonia.

'Thank you, James, you are a true gentleman.'

Bill looked across the roof of the car and winked. 'That's the way to win a heart,' he mouthed.

James shrugged and bit his bottom lip. 'Shall I open your door for you, too, sir?' he said in jest.

'I think I'll be able to manage it, mate.'

James climbed into the driver's seat, fastened his seatbelt, and started the engine.

'I know you're all tired, but do you mind if we go via Mum's place on the way home, I'm sure she would love to see you. We won't stay long; you don't even have to get out of the car. How about we just say hello?'

Claire ran her fingers through her messy hair. 'That's fine, if she doesn't mind seeing me like this.'

'Darling,' he said adjusting the rear-vision mirror so he could see her, 'you are beautiful just as you are.'

Bill cleared his throat and brushed his fingernails on the front of his shirt. 'And what about Sonia and me, are we presentable enough?'

'I think you'll pass,' he said with a smirk, 'Besides, I didn't mention it before, but my mother's short-sighted,' he added in jest.

Sonia gasped.

'Sorry, Mrs Martin. I was only joking.'

'Oh, James, you are wicked!'

By the time James stopped the car on the street outside Gloria's house, Ella was still fast asleep in the back. James wound down the windows to make sure everyone was comfortable and then raced up the path, knocked on the front door and waited.

The door burst open, and Gloria rushed out, quickly hugged her son, and hurried to the car.

'A big welcome to all of you,' Gloria said as James opened the door on Claire's side. 'I've been so looking forward to you coming. She took a deep breath and threw her arms around Claire. 'Let me look at you,' she said as she released her from the bear hug. 'You are even more beautiful than James described you. And this is Ella, what a darling! And she's just as beautiful as her mother.'

'Thank you, Mrs Cowan. That's very kind of you.'

Gloria took hold of Claire's hand. 'Oh, dear, the ring is superb!' Tears filled her soft blue eyes. She sniffed. 'I'm so happy for you both.'

Claire felt accepted. The love and warmth from Gloria were palpable.

'I know you'll all be tired after your flight, but I'd love you to come inside. Why don't you stay for dinner?'

'Thank you so much,' Bill said from the front seat, 'it's kind of you to offer but I think it would be best for us to get some rest and freshen up, and hopefully catch up with you tomorrow.'

'Yes, I understand, and it'd be a shame to disturb the baby.'

Gloria said her goodbyes, hugged her son, and then whispered in his ear. 'Oh, Claire is such a dear. I can see how you fell in love with her.'

'Thanks, Mum. I love you,' he said, then kissed her on the cheek and gently closed the car door. 'See you soon.'

Tears of joy pooled in Gloria's eyes as she stood waving from the front verge, watching until the car disappeared.

She turned toward the house, pulled a handkerchief from her pocket, dabbed her eyes, and whispered a prayer of thanks to God for having brought Claire into their lives.

James had comfortably set up his place for the Martin family to stay until Christmas Eve, when the big shuffle would take place. He'd planned every detail, right down to enough food for all. James would stay with his mother until the rest of his family arrived on Monday, December 24.

'Oh, this is lovely, James,' Sonia gushed when he showed them through to the master bedroom. 'You shouldn't have put yourself out for us. We could have organised our own accommodation.'

'No way! I wouldn't think of it. Besides, Mum is looking forward to having me stay with her.'

Bill sidled over, placed a hand on James' shoulder and expressed his appreciation.

'Well, I'll leave you guys to settle in. Do make yourself comfortable and I'll go and put the kettle on. Just let me know if there's anything else you need.'

'Thanks, mate. Much appreciated.'

Meanwhile, Claire settled Ella in the port-a-cot, sorted out her bits and pieces, and then wandered into the kitchen.

Alone at last, James drew Claire into his arms and held her tight. 'I love you so much,' he said, holding back tears.

Claire looked into his eyes. Words failed her. She touched his face. A tear ran down his cheek. She gently brushed it aside and kissed his soft, moist skin where the tear had escaped.

The kettle whistled shrilly and, without shifting his gaze from Claire, James reached behind him and switched it off.

On hearing the call of the kettle, Bill and Sonia wandered into the kitchen, then hesitated.

'Sorry you two, are we interrupting something?' Bill said with a cheeky grin.

'Well, yes, but do come in … I was just about to make coffee, or would you prefer a cup of tea?'

'Actually, tea would be nice,' Sonia replied as she pulled out one of the cream-coloured wicker-back kitchen chairs from the table.

'And what about you, Bill? Tea, coffee?'

'Mmm, I think I'll have tea, too, thanks. I feel all coffeed out! Coffee-log syndrome.'

James took four fine china mugs from the back of the overhead cupboard, rinsed them in the sink and, after drying them thoroughly, laid them out on the bench.

'Sorry, I don't have a teapot to brew the tea, but I can offer you English Breakfast tea bags, Earl Grey or Chai Latte?'

'Oow! Chai Latte sounds lovely,' Sonia replied. 'I haven't had a chai for ages.'

James turned to Claire, put his arms gently around her waist and with a loving smile asked, 'And you, sweetie, what would you like?'

'A big kiss,' she said cheekily.

'What? Now? In front of your Mum and Dad?'

'Yeah!'

He swept her off her feet, twirled her around, then set her down and kissed her thoroughly.

'Yeah!' their audience chorused with accompanying applause.

'Good on you, mate,' Bill added. 'But how about our tea? I, for one, am parched.'

'Sorry about that, got a bit distracted,' he said and proceeded to serve his guests.

As they sat around the kitchen table, James explained his schedule for the week and the plans of what would happen when his sisters and the kids arrived on Christmas Eve.

'Mum's happy to have me stay with her this week while you guys camp here,' he said. 'And when Laurel and Matt and the kids arrive with their caravan, we'll do a bit of a shuffle; I'll move into the van with the two boys – they'll love that – then my sisters and brother-in-law, Matt, and young Emily will stop here and the four of you can stay at Mum's.'

Bill was horrified. 'Oh no, we don't want to put you all out like that! I'm sure we'll be able to organise some other accommodation.'

'You're not putting us out at all. We've talked about it and worked it all out. It'll be fun. Mum is looking forward to having you.'

Bill shifted in his chair and cleared his throat, but before he could say another word, James continued. 'Now look,' he said as he ran his fingers across the edge of the table, 'I'm sorry I won't be able to spend much time with you over the next few days, but I've made a list of some places of interest around Adelaide that you might like to see.' He reached across the table and handed the sheet of paper to Bill.

'Thanks, mate,' he said. 'Sounds good to me. I did check out a few of the popular touristy spots before we came over, but this will be great.'

Sonia leaned over and scanned the list. 'We were planning to hire a car, at least for this week while you're still working.'

'You can do that if you want to, but the public transport is very good, and the bus stop is just around the corner.'

James continued, 'Anyway, if it's still all right with you guys, I'm happy to come over in the morning to pick you up and take you across to Mum's before I go to work. She'd love to spend the day with you. And then in a few days' time, when I'm free, I can take you around and show you a bit more of our beautiful state.'

Claire tilted her head and looked at James. 'So that's tomorrow sorted, but what about the rest of today? Don't you have to go in to work?'

James looked at his watch. 'Only for a short time, that is if you guys will be okay on your own for an hour or two.'

'Of course, you do what you need to do; we don't want to put you out too much.'

'Okay, I've just got a couple of phone calls to make and a report to finish off and then I'll be back, and I'll take you all out for dinner tonight.'

James pushed his chair out from the table, excused himself and put his mug in the sink. 'Please make yourselves at home and I'll be back as soon as I can.'

Sonia looked around the room, admiring his taste in decor. 'James, you've certainly got an eye for quality,' she said.

He smiled at Claire. 'Yes, she is lovely, isn't she,' he replied and kissed her silky hair.

'I was talking about your furniture, silly,' Sonia quipped.

'Well, I'm glad you like it, but my most precious treasure is …' He took Claire by the hand and pulled her close. '… your lovely daughter Claire, my fiancée. I love her to bits,' he said and kissed her tenderly.

'Yippee!' Bill cheered. 'But hey, mate, don't you think you had better get going?'

'I suppose so,' James conceded reluctantly, 'duty calls.'

He grabbed his jacket from the back of the chair, picked up his attaché case and gave Claire one last long kiss. 'Bye, sweetie, see you when I get home. Bye, Sonia, Bill.'

'Bye.'

The door closed.

'I suggest we all try to get a little shut-eye while Ella's still asleep and before James gets home.'

Claire yawned. 'Good idea, Dad.'

No sooner had the words passed her lips than Sonia gave a long, drawn-out yawn, closely followed up by Bill.

Over-tired, Sonia giggled. 'Catching, isn't it?' she said and yawned again.

'Come on, dear. Time for sleep.'

And off they went.

Ella began to stir.

Still heavy with sleep, Claire reached over, grabbed the top of the rail, and started to rock the cot. 'Shh,' she whispered sleepily, 'please go back to sleep; just a little longer.'

But Ella's tummy clock said, 'Dinner time' and she listened to her tummy.

Claire stumbled out of the lovely warm, soft, and cosy bed, ran her fingers through her hair and shook her head to blow the cobwebs away.

'Hello, my darling,' she said and checked the time. 'Oh, my goodness, you must be hungry.'

The baby girl smiled up at her mother and with a gurgle of agreement, kicked her legs excitedly.

With Ella in her arms, Claire pattered along the hallway and into the kitchen. She took a deep breath, luxuriating in the lingering fragrance from James' musk-scented aftershave. 'I love you, James,' she whispered to the air around her.

Claire slid the baby's feet into the portable highchair that was attached to the table and fastened the safety straps.

'Look at you, sitting up like a big girl!' Claire said and slipped the bib over Ella's head.

Ella bounced happily, waving her hands in the air.

The digital clock on the microwave flicked over to 4:45 pm. Deducting two and a half hours, Claire realised that it would only be 2:15 back home in Perth.

'My goodness,' she said, 'our time clocks are really out of whack.'

Ella smiled.

'Never mind, you must be hungry, so how about custard and bananas? Does that sound good?' she said as she tried to unscrew the lid from the jar. But it wouldn't budge.

Claire flicked the kettle switch on and waited. It seemed to take forever to boil. So, tapping the teaspoon on the lid of the jar, she began to sing: *I'm a little teapot short and stout, here is my handle, here is my spout. When I get all steamed up, hear me shout. Tip me over, pour me out!*

Ella laughed.

Claire rested the jar on the kitchen bench. 'You like that one, don't you?' she said, and taking Ella's hands in hers, she sang the song again, this time with actions.

The kettle's shrill interrupted their chorus, and Claire excused herself, picked up the jar of baby food, lent it over the sink, and carefully poured boiling water over the metal lid—a trick her father had taught her that worked every time. Tea towel in hand, she twisted the lid. It popped open with ease.

'Here we go, my darling,' She stirred the soft custard. 'Mmm.'

Ella opened her mouth as wide as her big blue eyes and swallowed the first spoonful.

Click! The metal spoon touched something new on her gum.

'You've got a tooth!' Claire stuck the spoon back into the jar and ran her little finger over Ella's bottom gum. 'Yes! It is a tooth! Wow, what a clever girl you are.'

Just then the sound of keys in the front door announced James' arrival. He entered the kitchen and hurried over to Claire's side.

'This is so nice; coming home to my two favourite girls.' And before Claire could say a word, he took her in his arms and waltzed her around the room. 'You have no idea how many times I have dreamt of this day,' he said and planted a long and loving kiss on her soft lips.

Breaking away from the embrace, Claire caught her breath.

'Well, hello to you too,' she replied. 'Were you able to get all the things you wanted to do done?'

'Yes, and I don't have any appointments until 11:30 tomorrow. Isn't that great?'

'Aw, good. And guess what?'

'I don't know. What?'

'Ella's cut her first tooth. Today! Yeah!'

'Well, we'll be able to remember the date, won't we?'

'Yep. Tuesday, December 18, 2018.'

James turned to Ella. 'Hey, little princess, are you eating your lunch, or is this dinner, or just a snack?'

'She was hungry when she woke up, so I'm giving her a little in-between snack just to keep her happy until dinner time. Would you like to give her the rest?'

'Of course,' he replied as he washed his hands over the sink.

James sat on the chair beside Ella and, picking up the jar of baby food, checked its contents. 'Mmm, I'm feeling a bit peckish myself,' he said with a lick of his lips.

'Open wide, here comes the aeroplane, *broom, broom, broom.*'

Ella gave a little giggle, and then quickly consumed the remainder of her custard.

James scraped the inside of the jar. 'All gone,' he said and went to wipe her hands and face.

Ella protested.

'I think she's still hungry. What else can I give her?' he asked.

Claire popped the top off an airtight plastic container and handed him a baby rusk. 'That should keep her content for a while,' she said and replaced the lid.

Ella reached out and grasped the rusk, which went straight into her mouth.

'Looks like she can manage that herself,' James said as he pushed his chair out from the table. 'Anyway, where are your mum and dad?'

'Still asleep,' Claire answered with a whisper. 'So, it's just us.'

James swept Claire into his arms and looked deeply into her eyes. 'How I've longed to have you to myself,' he whispered, and kissed her waiting lips.

The kiss was long and passionate, interrupted only by the thud of the rusk hitting the floor.

Ella cried in protest.

'Shh, bubby,' Claire said, putting her finger to her lips.

Ella quietened.

And then, reluctantly breaking from James' loving embrace, Claire retrieved what was left of the gooey rusk. 'Sorry, we've made a mess on your nice clean floor. Do you have a cloth I can use to wipe it?'

'Don't worry about that,' he said as he tore a sheet of paper from the kitchen towel dispenser. 'I'll sort it out, you just take care of Ella.'

Claire wiped the baby's face and hands and then folded the grubby bib inward and pulled it off over her head. 'That's better, now you're a nice clean bubby girl,' she said and placed her favourite plastic squeaky toy on the table in front of her.

Bash, bash. Squeak, squeak.

'Oh no, I shouldn't have given her that, the noise will wake Mum and Dad.' Claire snatched it back.

Ella screamed.

'Oh no, that's worse,' she said and relinquished the decision. 'Here we go, darling.'

The screaming ceased and the squeaking resumed.

James laughed. 'So much for our few quiet moments together,' he said as he sidled up behind Claire, placed his hands around her waist and gave a gentle squeeze. 'Never mind, that's life – and I wouldn't have it any other way.'

By dinnertime, Bill and Sonia, still too tired to go out for a meal, opted to stay home with Ella and let James and Claire have some quality time on their own.

'Don't worry about us, we'll order in. You two just go and enjoy a nice meal together,' Bill said with a yawn. 'This travelling sure takes it out of us youngies.'

Chapter 27

During the following week, the Martin family visited many of the popular tourist spots in and around Adelaide. Bill liked what he saw. He discussed the possibility of selling their house in Perth and relocating to Adelaide.

'I don't see why not,' said Sonia, 'since I've only got my sister, Joan, over there and we hardly ever see each other, and she's got her family.' Sonia rolled her eyes. 'Besides, Joan's always busy with her circle of snobby friends.'

Bill pushed his cap back and scratched his head. 'Of course, it all depends on what James and Claire decide to do; for all we know, they might be thinking of living in Perth.'

'That's true. We'd better just leave our options open. But whatever, wherever they decide to live, I want to be nearby.' Sonia sighed.

'Ditto,' replied Bill, 'we'll just have to wait and see.'

Christmas Day arrived.

Gloria had prepared a beautiful traditional Christmas dinner for them all: her own family, plus Sonia, Bill, Claire and Ella, a total of eight adults, three children and baby Ella.

The food was amazing, and Gloria was the perfect hostess. Laurel and Matt's three children had an instant rapport with Claire and were in absolute raptures over Ella. But the atmosphere in the room that day hung heavy. James' sisters were giving Claire the cold shoulder.

After the first course was finished, Gloria stood and began to collect some of the empty plates. Sonia pushed her chair out from the table and started to help.

'No, no, you sit down,' Gloria insisted. 'Melanie and Laurel will help me – won't you, girls?' she said.

'Okay, Mum,' Laurel replied reluctantly, 'we'll be with you shortly.'

Gloria gave them *the look*. 'I need both of you in the kitchen – now!' she said in no uncertain terms.

They followed her into the kitchen.

Gloria closed the door behind them and, taking them aside, spoke her mind. 'I am utterly disgusted with you two!' she said sternly. 'You are being rude, and you're treating Claire terribly. And you are embarrassing me, and James, and I can't imagine what Bill and Sonia must think of you. Whatever has gotten into you? This behaviour is so out of character.'

Laurel hung her head. 'Mum,' she said, 'it's just that we don't want to see James get hurt. We don't know anything about this Claire.'

And then Melanie spewed her venom. 'She's a single mother with a past – and if she gets her claws into our brother, she might ruin his life, take everything he has and leave him crushed!'

'Stop right there, you two. What happened to Christian love, respect, and acceptance? Can't you see how happy James is?'

Melanie tutted. 'Acceptance! Why should we accept her?'

'Because, for one thing, your brother loves her, and after all it is his life, and it is his choice.' Gloria paused for just a moment and then, looking her daughter straight in the eye, continued. 'And Melanie, my dear, please don't you talk to me about acceptance. As much as I do not approve of your choice of lifestyle, nor do I agree with it, but because you are family and I love you I accept that it *is* your choice.'

'What! What are you talking about?' Melanie replied, her eyelids flickering like a faulty fluorescent light tube.

'You know perfectly well: your so-called flatmate, Chris, the way you try to pretend that she is a he. I'm not stupid, you can't pull the wool over my eyes.'

Laurel's face paled. She caught her breath, and her hand covered her mouth as she stared in disbelief at her younger sister. 'What! You mean ...?'

Gloria wrapped her arms around Melanie. 'It's all right, darling. I'm only sorry you didn't tell me earlier.' She reached out her hand toward Laurel and drew her into the warm embrace. 'Come on, darling. We're family and families love and accept each other whatever the situation.'

Laurel shivered, stricken with disbelief. 'I'm just,' she sniffed and swiped the back of her hand across her nose, 'I'm absolutely and utterly shocked to the core is all; please just give me some time,' she mumbled, and then grabbing a wad of tissues buried her burning face in their softness.

Melanie smiled through her tears. 'I'm sorry,' she whispered in a husky voice. 'I didn't mean to hurt anyone. It's just that, I guess, I don't know,' she shrugged, 'I am what I am.'

Gloria stepped back, grabbed a handful of tissues and pushed a bundle into her daughters' hands. 'I'd better not leave our guests any longer,' she said. 'They might think we've run away or something. So, I'll leave you two to talk and I'll serve dessert. You just take as long as you need. Okay?'

'Thanks, Mum,' Melanie mouthed as she glanced over her older sister's shoulder, 'you're the best.'

Gloria walked into the dining room balancing two plates of wobbly jelly, one in each hand: red in her right hand and bright green jelly in her left.

'Yeah!' shouted eight-year-old Christopher. 'Ice cream and jelly, my favourite!'

'Who said anything about ice cream?' James teased. 'I don't see any ice cream.'

'Cause Nanna always makes the bestest ever ice cream and jelly, that's why, Uncle James.'

James ruffled the boy's curly blond hair. 'Yes, you're right but what if I eat it all first?'

The boy laughed. 'No way, 'cause I'm gonna eat it all up.'

'Now boys, back up a bit, there's plenty for everyone and there's still more to come. Hand up who would like plum pudding with custard?'

Several hands shot up instantly.

Most, that is, except for six-year-old Emily who, puckering up her nose, protested. 'Yuk! I don't like plump pudding; it stings my mouth.'

'It's not plump pudding, silly,' corrected Christopher, 'it's plum pudding.'

'I don't care,' she replied tilting her head to one side and looking down her nose at her brother, 'I still don't like it.'

'Nah, nah! You're just a baby,' he teased mercilessly.

Tears pooled in Emily's eyes and trickled down her pink cheeks.

At the far end of the table Bill and Matt where engrossed in man talk, voicing their solutions for the world's problems, both totally oblivious to the unfolding drama at the other end of the table.

Sonia, while half listening to the men's conversation, became alert to the accelerating sibling spat, but not wanting to interfere; she looked first at Claire and then turned to James. 'Can you sort that out, James? I think I'm needed in the kitchen.'

James stood, pushed back his chair, and went across to the teary child.

'Come on, my pumpkin pie,' he said and reached out his arms. The young girl smiled up at him through her tears, and James took her in his arms; dried her eyes and, holding her tightly, whirled her gently around the room.

'Whee!' Emily threw back her head and giggled with delight.

'That's my girl,' he said, and then, slowing to a stop, he caught the twinkle in her eyes. 'Now, how about we go get that ice cream?' he added.

'Yeah!' she shouted enthusiastically. Putting her arms around his neck, she landed one big sloppy kiss on the side of his face and then whispered in his ear, 'I love you, Uncle James.'

Out in the kitchen, Gloria had just finished pouring hot creamy custard over the last plum pudding when James entered the room.

'Oh, good darling, you're just in time. Could you take this tray of puddings through to the dining room please?'

'Actually, we just came out to get the ice cream to go with our jelly. I thought the girls were helping you. Where are they?'

Just then James noticed his sisters sitting outside on the back step. He frowned. 'What's with them?'

'Oh, just leave them be. They haven't seen each other for a long time, and they are just catching up.' Gloria replied.

'But they'll have all next week to catch up, they should be in with our guests.'

'It's all right, darling. I'm sure they'll join us shortly.'

'Hey, Uncle James, what about our ice cream?' Emily piped up.

James looked at his mother with those sad puppy dog eyes that no mother can possibly resist.

'Oh, go on you two, get your ice cream.'

'Thanks, Nanna,' said Emily.

'Yes, thanks, Mum.'

After the meal was finished and everyone full-as-a-goog, and with Ella fast asleep, Claire and Sonia started to clear the table.

Bill looked up, paused his conversation, and smiled at Sonia. 'Thanks, dear,' he said. 'My compliments to the cook.'

'I think you had better go and thank her yourself.'

'Of course I will, and hey, don't you wash the dishes. How about you leave the cleaning up to us guys? What do you think Matt, think we could handle it?'

'Right then, let's go!' Matt pushed his chair back, grabbed the stack of dishes from Sonia's hands and marched into the kitchen.

'Come on now, mother-in-law dear,' he said with a cheeky grin, 'it's time for you to sit down, put your feet up and have a good talk with Sonia. Bill and I will do the dishes.'

Gloria dried her hands on her apron. 'All right,' she said, 'but just let me …'

'No way. We can take care of that – you go into the lounge room – I'll make the cups of tea and bring them in for you.'

'Thanks, Matt, you're a champion.'

By the time Gloria went back into the room, the kids, having already coerced Claire and James into playing UNO, sat cross-legged in a circle on the floor.

'Right then, who has played UNO before?'

'Me,' replied Christopher self-importantly. 'I played UNO with my best friend, Oliver, at his house one day.'

'Right then, you must be an expert,' James said as he shuffled half the pack, while Claire shuffled the rest. 'So, tell us the rules.'

'Um … I don't know, you just play it.'

'Well, how about you read what it says on the side of the packet?'

Christopher grabbed the box and turned it over several times. 'It says, *easy to pick up, impos … impossible to put down, UNO is the wor… worl … world's no 1 family game.*'

'You're doing well, mate,' James said, ruffling his hair again. 'So, it's the world's number one family game, hey. What else does it say?'

'Can you read the rest, Uncle James?'

'Sure, here, throw me the box.'

Suddenly, James shot his hand out instinctively and caught the packet just in the nick of time as it flew past Claire's ear. 'Wow, you've sure got a good toss there, mate. You should sign up to be on the cricket team.

'Now let me see.' James read from the front of the package, 'It says it's for *2-10 players, age 7+.*'

'Emily can't play, she's only six,' Christopher chided.

'I'm nearly seven!' she said, fluttering her eyelids indignantly.

'Me too,' little Jake piped up.

'You're not nearly seven, you are only three,' said Emily.

James had an idea. 'I know what, how about if Jake helps me, I think that's a good idea.'

Sitting on James' lap, the boy looked up and, with great admiration, said, 'Me help you, Uncle James.'

'Thank you, Jake.'

'And what about me?' Claire asked, 'Who is going to help me?'

'If Emily sits next to you, I'm sure she will help you.'

'Would you, Emily?'

Bright eyed, the little girl nodded enthusiastically. 'I will be your helper, Aunty Claire.'

'Thank you, darling.'

James read the rules and Christopher dealt the cards, and then placed the remaining 'stack' face down to one side and turned the top card over.

'Now, don't forget when you've only got one card left you need to yell UNO!'

'Me no!' shouted Jake.

'No, silly. It's not 'me no', it's UNO,' Christopher corrected him.

And so, the game began.

Meanwhile, Gloria and Sonia sipped their tea, shared anecdotes, and continued to be entertained with the antics of the kids.

'They never really grow up, do they?' Gloria chuckled.

Sonia agreed.

The next day, Matt arrived early to pick up his boys. They'd had a great time staying the night in the caravan with Uncle James. But of course, Laurel missed them and worried all night, especially about young Jake.

'There was no need to worry,' James assured him. 'They were right as rain, they slept all night, I think they wore themselves out yesterday. But thanks for coming early and taking them off my hands, because I want to spend the day with Claire.'

'I don't blame you, mate,' he said and, leaning over, he added. 'You've got a winner there, James. You don't want to let her go.'

'Thanks, Matt, I'm glad you said that, because I wasn't really sure about the girls; I got the impression they didn't approve.'

'I think they have a bit of an issue between themselves, I don't know what it's all about, but the air was thick when I left the unit this morning. Laurel tossed and turned all night; she had something on her mind, and I don't think it was that she was just worried about Jake. Anyway, I'd better say hello/goodbye to my best mother-in-law and get back to the others, or else I'll be in strife. Have a great day and,' he paused mid-sentence and smirked, 'don't do anything that I ... mmm, I'll say no more.'

James said goodbye to his nephews and reminded them to make sure they came back tonight and stay in the caravan with him again.

'Yes, Uncle James,' they said excitedly.

It was a beautiful Adelaide day, quite hot really, expected to reach 34 degrees centigrade with a light breeze. James decided to take the girls, his two girls, for a lovely drive up into the hills where, hopefully, they would visit The Big Rocking Horse and Toy Factory, that is if it was open on Boxing Day.

Gloria had already prepared a picnic basket for them, and after their morning pleasantries, she bustled them out the door and sent them on their way.

'We'll be fine,' she said. 'You young people need to spend as much quality time together as you possibly can while you have the opportunity.'

James landed a kiss on his mother's face and waved a quick goodbye to Sonia and Bill.

'Bye, Mum; bye, Dad; bye, Mrs Cowan,' Claire called through the ever-narrowing crack in the front door.

'Bye, pet. Have a great day,' came a muffled reply as the door closed on them.

'Well, looks like we're not wanted around here,' James said as he reached out to take Ella.

Claire smiled and handed him the baby then, reaching up she stood on tippy toes, enfolded them both in her arms and kissed him intentionally.

The three of them had a wonderful day in the Adelaide Hills. They took a guided tour of the toy factory, enjoyed the animal enclosures, and managed to climb to the top of the largest wooden rocking horse structure in the world, receiving a certificate to prove it. Of the many photos Claire took that day, her favourite one was of James holding Ella astride the giant rocking horse.

Claire threw her head back and laughed. 'I love it!' she said. 'Who would have ever thought there was such a place as this?'

'I knew you'd like it; there's so much to see and do; I think one could spend a whole week here and still not experience everything there is.'

James checked the time. 'Anyway, my darling,' he said and slipped his arms around her waist, 'I think it's time for us to head home, so we'll have time to get organised for tonight.'

Claire kissed the tip of his nose. 'So, what's the plan for tonight?'

'Remember, your mum and mine offered to mind Ella for us and I'm taking you out for dinner – it'll be just you and me.'

'Sounds great, let's get going.'

With tension still raw between Laurel and her sister, they parted company for the day. Melanie went over to her mother's place and offered to take her, Sonia and Bill out for the day, leaving Laurel, Matt, and family to do their own thing.

'Is there anything particular you would like to do, or anywhere special you'd like to go?' she asked.

'Well actually, this might seem like a strange request, but I wouldn't mind having a little nosy at some real estate,' Bill suggested. 'I know it doesn't sound very exciting, but I wouldn't mind getting a bit of an idea of prices.'

Sonia rolled her eyes and tutted. 'Here we go again. Wherever we go he must look at real estate.'

Melanie looked from one to the other, shrugged and then answered, 'Yeah, that would be fine, but I don't think any Real Estate Agencies will be open today, being a public holiday and all that.'

'Actually, I don't mind that, I'd just be able to take my time and browse.'

'Right. Well, in what area would you like to look?'

'Glenelg seems nice.'

'Well, you've certainly got good taste, Bill. You know that's one of the most sort after areas in Adelaide.'

Melanie thought for a moment. 'Okay then, I'll tell you what, I can drop you off on the main drag … no, on second thought, I'll park the car, then we can wander down the main street, choose a coffee shop and us girls can stay there and talk, and we'll let you window shop to your hearts' content and, when you've finished, you can come and find us when you're ready. How does that sound?'

'Sounds fine to me.'

'Right, Glenelg it is.'

The remainder of the week passed quickly. Claire and James discussed wedding plans, Bill and Sonia put a deposit on a lovely two-bedroom unit with water views and Laurel came to terms with her sister's alternate life choice.

By the time the Martin's holiday ended, Claire and James had set February 16th as the tentative date for their wedding. Claire was to confirm the date and make the final arrangements when she returned home to Perth.

So much had happened in such a short space of time.

Chapter 28

The Martin family's first week back in Perth was a flurry of activity. Having arrived home on Thursday, by the following Monday, a large *For Sale* sign stood prominently on the front lawn of their house. Putting first things first, Claire had booked the church and the minister for their wedding.

Breathing a sigh of relief, Claire started on her list of "things to do", placing them in order of priority. With just under six weeks before the big day, the number one thing Claire had to finalise was the guest list, then choose the invitations and get them sent out ASAP. They didn't want a big wedding, just family and close friends. But … by the time she tallied up the basic list, there were already thirty-five, not counting kids!

Claire raced downstairs frantically waving the sheet of paper. 'Oh, Mum,' she said, 'this is just crazy, and it's already gone way over what we planned.' She slammed the guest list down on the dining room table and burst into tears.

'It's all right, darling; you're just experiencing the first throes of pre-wedding jitters; it happens to everyone. Don't worry, it will all fall into place. Here, let me see the list.'

Regaining her composure, Claire pulled a tissue from the box, wiped her eyes, and sat down next to her mother.

'I've divided it up into two columns.' She ran her finger over the first section. 'This is James' side, and across here is our side of the family and some friends.'

'Okay, darling, let's go through it.'

Claire began. 'First of all, there's James of course …' she sniffed.

'Of course! Well, that's a good start so far,' Sonia said with a grin.

'Yes, and then there's his mother, and her two friends; there's Laurel, Matt and their kids, Melanie and her partner, James' boss, or business partner and his wife, three of his close friends. Then there's his two aunties and uncles, who are not likely to come, but we still must invite them, and if we invite them, there's all the cousins and their partners, etc. etc. And that comes to at least twenty! Without counting my side.'

'That's all right, darling. We haven't got many on our side anyway, so don't worry.'

'At least another fifteen, Mum!' Claire's forehead creased in a frown.

Sonia put her arm around her and, with an understanding smile, drew her close. 'Claire, my darling, this is going to be your special day. It's a once-in-a-lifetime event, and remember you are our only daughter, and we want your wedding day to be a day for us all to remember, so please don't stress and don't worry about the cost. Dad and I have put aside plenty to cover any expenses.' Sonia put her arm around her daughter's shoulder, and with a reassuring pat, kissed her tenderly. 'Darling, you've done such a lot in one day, and you're probably still feeling the effect of jetlag, so have a break now and look at it again tomorrow.'

'Thanks, Mum.'

By the time James phoned at seven o'clock that evening, Claire was feeling more relaxed and on top of things again. She answered on the second ring. 'Hi, James; how was your day?'

'Hello, sweetie pie,' he replied with that familiar smile in his voice. 'My day was fine, but I missed you and our little princess. How was your day?'

'Busy, and guess what?'

'Good news I hope.'

'Yes, our wedding date has been confirmed, the church is booked, and our Pastor is happy to do the ceremony and,' she paused and caught her breath, 'he'll organise all the paperwork and stuff and he wants us to do a pre-marriage course via Skype, but he said he'd line all that up for us, so we don't have to worry.'

'Great. Sounds like you've been a busy little bee. I'm sorry that you have to do most of the organising, and I can't do too much from over here.'

'That's okay; there's still a lot more to be done. I've made a list, and Mum is going to help me. Although I can't write the invitations until we finalise the reception. Pastor Steve did make mention that the church hall is available, and there's a group of ladies who are willing to decorate the hall and cater for a three-course sit-down dinner at a reasonable fee if we would like to take up that offer. I wasn't sure about it so I talked to Mum and wanted to mention it to you and see what you think.'

'What's the hall like?' James asked.

'Just a regular church hall.'

'What does your Mum think about it?'

'She said she'd go with me to find out more details and she thought it would be a good idea to look at other options as well.'

'Okay, I'll leave it to you guys to decide.'

They chatted about this and that, the wedding and the honeymoon, which James was going to book and organise from over there. They talked about their future dreams and wishes, and before long, the clock struck midnight in Perth, and it was time to say good night or, rather, good morning and end the call.

The next day, Sonia and Claire checked out two of the most popular Wedding Reception venues. Both were fully booked for the next twelve months.

Frustrated, they decided to go for coffee before looking at the next venue on their list, a new place they hadn't heard of before.

In the café, Claire plonked herself down on the nearest chair and sighed. Ella began to fuss. 'Oh no, not now, bubby,' Claire said and stuck the dummy in her mouth.

Returning to the table, Sonia placed the order number on the table, pulled out a chair and sat down on the other side. 'Oh, what a lovely spot,' she said. 'I'm glad you picked the bay window, it's nice to be able to look out on the street and watch all the activity.'

Just then Ella lost her dummy and started to whinge.

'Looks like our little lady is ready for her morning tea, too,' Sonia said, leaning over the stroller to unfasten the safety strap. 'Would you like me to feed her for you, darling?'

Claire, almost in tears, exhaled one long exaggerated sigh and thanked her mother. 'I really do appreciate your help, Mum; sorry I don't always show it.'

'That's all right. We understand, don't we, bubby?' Sonia said as she lifted Ella from the stroller.

Ella smiled up at her grandmother and Sonia's heart melted with love for her one and only little granddaughter.

'Coffee for two,' the waitress announced as she placed one medium-size latte' on the table in front of Sonia and a large mocha in front of Claire.

'Thank you, dear,' Sonia said and, not wanting to risk little hands knocking the hot drink over, she pushed her mug a bit further in from the edge of the table.

'I'll bring the cakes over shortly,' the waitress added with a smile and headed back to the counter.

Having each consumed a generous helping of the most delicious fresh black forest cake, piped with lashings of thick cream, they drained their coffee mugs and then headed off for their next destination.

Claire caught her breath. 'I can't believe it,' she said as they drove under the archway, along the circular drive and then came to a stop at the front of the magnificent *Palicia Fashone*.

They ascended the white marble staircases, stepped onto a spacious landing, and turned to take in the panoramic view. The building overlooked lush green lawns, colourful gardens and a winding stream that flowed over rocks, through a grove of willows and under an arched wooden footbridge.

'Wow! This place is amazing; even nicer than the other two we looked at. Fingers crossed it's available on the sixteenth,' she added hopefully.

Sonia agreed.

'Well, come on,' she said, 'we'll never find out unless we ask.'

The glass doors opened to a huge foyer featuring antique white ceramic floor tiles, plush black leather lounge chairs, potted palm trees that reached almost to the high ceiling and a golden spiral staircase leading to a second floor.

'Hello, can I help you?' came a pleasant voice.

They turned around.

'Oh, hello,' said Claire apologetically, 'sorry we were just admiring your lovely building.'

'Don't be sorry,' she said, 'I'm glad you approve. We haven't been open long and it's taking a while for people to get to know we're here.'

Claire moved closer to the reception desk. 'I've heard that you do wedding receptions, is that right?'

'Yes, we do. How can I help you?'

'I was wondering if you'd be available on the sixteenth of February for an early evening wedding dinner?'

The receptionist clicked her fingers over the keyboard and looked up. 'Yes, my dear, we have nothing booked for that day; would you like me to hold it for you?'

Claire's eyes sparkled with joy. 'Yes, please!' She looked at Sonia and gave a silent 'yay!'

'Sorry ladies, I didn't introduce myself – I'm Heather McFarland and in what name shall I register the booking?'

'I was just about to say Martin; that's my name, Claire Martin, but I'll be married then and so you had better list it as Cowan.'

'Congratulations, Claire, that's wonderful. But before I fill out the rest of the details, I'll show you around our facilities.'

Claire lifted Ella out of her stroller and jiggled her on her hip.

'Wow, you're getting quite heavy, little lady,' she said, and Ella smiled up at her.

'Do you want me to take her for you?' Sonia offered, her arms already extended in readiness.

'No, we're fine, Nanna,' Claire replied and gave a little whirl.

After the guided tour was complete, Claire and her mother were over the moon with excitement. Heather returned to her desk, clicked the mouse, and her computer sprung to life.

'Now,' she said, 'how many guests will we be catering for?'

'About thirty-five, give or take a few.'

Heather looked up from the computer. 'I'm sorry, dear, the minimum we cater for in the smallest room is fifty.'

Claire's eyes teared. She sniffed. 'Ow, can't you please make an exception?'

'Regrettably, that's not possible. You see, our chefs are professionals and won't cook for any less than fifty.'

Sonia spoke up. 'Could you pencil in a booking and hold it for us. I'll talk with my husband this evening and see if we can get the numbers up to fifty. I will get back to you by the end of the week if that's all right?'

'Yes, I can hold it for you, and if someone else enquires and wants to make a booking for that date, I'll contact you and give you the first option.'

'Thank you so much, Heather.' Claire sighed with relief. 'That would be great.'

'Look, I'll give you the price list, menus, and extra optional services that we offer. Take them home, have a browse, and if you have any questions, feel free to give me a call.'

'Thanks again; we so appreciate your help,' Sonia said as she settled Ella in the stroller. Bundling up the brochures, they headed off.

Mixed emotions surged through Claire like waves of the sea and her heart raced like a pack of wild brumbies.

Sonia tried to calm the storm. 'Darling, it's not about where you hold the reception, it's not about numbers, it's about you and James getting married and having the wedding you want.'

'You're right, Mum, I don't want to just pluck names out of the air and invite people just to get the numbers up; I'd rather have a quiet wedding with the people we want there to celebrate with us.'

'That's right, and I'm sure James would agree. Your dad and I had a simple wedding with a handful of close family and friends, and that made happy, lasting memories for us.'

Claire took a deep breath. 'Mum, what about the church hall? We could always check that out again.'

'Yes, I was thinking the same. Why don't you talk it over with James tonight, see what he thinks, and we can always phone and make an appointment at the church to discuss it further.'

'Actually, Mum, I did mention it to James earlier on, and he said he'd leave it up to us; he'd be happy with whatever we decide. But I'll still tell him about the other places we looked at today.' Claire flipped open her phone and swiped her finger across the screen. 'I will ring the church right now and see if I can organise an appointment.'

7 pm, on the dot, Claire's mobile phone sounded; it was James. She shared with him her frustration in not having been able to settle on a suitable venue for their wedding reception.

'Don't worry about trying to get the number of guests to fifty just to satisfy that fancy place, it sounds nice, but the church hall sounds good too.'

'Mum and I have got an appointment for Thursday to see the lady who heads up the church catering committee, so we'll find out more and let you know. I'll be so relieved when I can get those invitations sent out,' she said with a sigh.

'It's all right, sweetheart; we've still got thirty-nine days.'

'Thirty-nine days! Who's counting?'

'Me. I've started marking off the calendar, I just can't wait for that day to come and I can call you my wife.'

There was silence on the line.

'Are you still there?'

'Yes,' Claire replied in a broken voice. 'It's just that …' she paused, 'there's so much to do.'

'Claire, sweetie pie, I love you so much; you are my greatest treasure and joy and if there was any way I could be there to help you I would, but please don't stress, please take care of yourself. I love you.'

The next morning, Bill and Sonia sat alone at the breakfast table. After crunching the last mouthful of his Vegemite toast, Bill wiped his mouth with the serviette and, turning to his wife, asked, 'What are you girls planning to do today?'

Sonia placed her knife on the plate. 'I'm not sure; depends on what Claire has in mind.'

'My advice would be that you both take it easy today, you've been flat out since we got back from Adelaide, and I think it would do you good to stay home and have a rest.'

'You know, I think you're right, Bill. I am pretty worn out and I'm sure Claire could do with a quiet day, so hopefully she will be in for it.'

Just then the baby monitor crackled to life.

'Sounds like Ella. I'll go up and bring her down before she wakes Claire.'

Sonia hurried upstairs and pushed open the nursery door. 'Hello, how's my little girl?' she whispered.

Ella gurgled her reply and Sonia lifted her from the cot and kissed her chubby cheek. 'Let's go down and see Grandpa before he goes to work,' she said and tiptoed from the room. Not the slightest stir of life emanated from Claire's room as Sonia passed by, so she continued downstairs with Ella in her arms.

'Hey, my little princess,' Bill said as he reached out his arms to take her. 'Who's my girl?'

Ella blew a raspberry bubble then landed an open mouth sloppy kiss on his freshly shaven chin.

'Thank you, darling. I just needed an extra wash.' He laughed, and as he did, his chest expanded with love for the child.

'But I can't stay and play all day,' he said. 'Someone must go to work. Has your nanna got your breakfast ready for you yet? I think she has.' Bill popped Ella into the high chair and fastened the shoulder straps. 'There we go,' he said and kissed the top of her head. 'I'll be off then. See you tonight.'

Bill grabbed his briefcase, kissed Sonia, and headed out the side door. Ella's bottom lip dropped.

'It's all right, bubby; Grandpa will come home again.'

Sonia enjoyed the morning with her granddaughter. After breakfast they went for a long walk along the beachfront, watched the cheeky seagulls swooping down, hopeful for a feed, and then walked slowly home. By the time they returned home Claire, still in her PJs, was sitting on the sofa, her knees up under her chin, sipping coffee.

'Good morning, sleepyhead,' said Sonia when they walked through the doorway.'

'Hi, Mum. I read your note. Thanks for taking care of Ella and for letting me sleep in; I really needed that.'

'You're looking better, darling. So do you think you've caught up with all your beauty sleep?'

'Yeah, but I still feel a bit rung out.'

'I know what you mean – I feel much the same. What say we take a day off wedding arrangements and just chill out?'

Claire sighed. 'Well, I had planned to go and look at wedding dresses, but I just can't be bothered trying on those cumbersome gowns, not today anyway.'

Sonia glanced up at the clock on the wall. 'What say I give Ella an early lunch, put her down for a nap and then we can do a sort of review of our program?'

'Sounds good to me,' Claire said as she unfurled herself from the sofa.

Following what turned out to be a late brunch for Claire and an early lunch for Sonia, they spent the rest of the day pottering around the house, doing a little bit of this and a little bit of that. By late afternoon, having achieved nothing, they certainly felt refreshed.

When Bill arrived home from work, he found his wife and daughter lounging on the sofa watching a soapie, and Ella sitting contented in the baby bouncer chewing her toe.

'Well, hi, everyone. I hope I'm not disturbing you,' he greeted them tongue-in-cheek as he loosened his tie and undid the top button of his shirt.

Sonia looked up. 'Oops, sorry, darling, I forgot the time, I haven't even thought about dinner. How about we order pizzas?'

'It's fine with me. Shall I put the kettle on?' he asked as he wandered through to the kitchen.

'Thanks, darling,' Sonia replied, her eyes glued to the television screen.

The kitchen was a mess; the sink stacked with the whole day's dirty dishes. He smiled. Obviously, the girls had taken his advice.

Bill filled the kettle and flicked the switch then, while he waited for it to boil, began to stack the dishwasher.

'You don't have to do the dishes,' Sonia called from the lounge room. I'll see to that later. You just come and sit down. I think Ella wants to see you.'

'Be with you soon,' he replied and quietly continued with the task at hand.

Mission completed, and having phoned through the pizza order, he carried a tray of tea and coffee through to the lounge room and placed it on the low coffee table in front of the girls. 'Here we go then,' he said with a wink, 'Tea for Nanna, coffee for Mum and a big hug for Ella!'

Bill snatched Ella from the bouncer and danced her around the room. 'Who's my little princess?' he asked and was rewarded with a shrill and a giggle.

Carrying her on his hip, Bill wandered back into the kitchen and warmed the baby's dinner. Then, placing her in the high chair, buckled the safety strap and fastened a brightly coloured terry-towelling bib around her neck.

Ella waved her little hands with excitement.

'Here comes the aeroplane,' Bill said as he aimed the first spoonful of chicken and vegetable mash, in ever-decreasing circles, toward her open mouth.

'Yum. You like that, don't you,' he said and continued the process until the plate was empty. 'All gone! And what a good girl you are.'

Bill stood and went to take the dirty plate over to the sink, but Ella protested. 'Don't tell me you're still hungry,' he said with a chuckle. 'Well now, let me see what else I can find.' He scratched his head, opened the pantry, and selected a jar of banana custard. 'I know this one is your favourite.' He popped the lid, found another spoon and once again, very soon found himself scrapping the bottom of the jar.

With Ella finally content, and after wiping her hands and face, Bill carried her through to the lounge room and placed her back in the bouncer.

Claire thanked him just as the doorbell chimed. 'That will be the pizza guy,' she said but didn't budge or make any attempt to answer the door.

Bill looked around.

Sonia didn't move.

'I'll get the door then, shall I?' he said since there seemed no other alternative.

'Would you? Thanks, honey,' Sonia replied.

By the time they had finished their last slice of pizza, it was ten to seven, almost Ella's bedtime, but little bright eyes showed no intention whatsoever of going to sleep.

It was close to the time when James usually phoned Claire, and, being such a lovely warm evening, Sonia suggested to Bill that they go out for a walk and take Ella with them in her stroller, to leave Claire and James time to talk with no interruptions.

'Good idea, dear,' Bill concurred cordially, and within three minutes they were out the door and on their way.

No sooner had the door closed behind them than Claire's mobile phone chimed, and the call ID announced, *James*.

'Hi, darling, you're five minutes early; great timing; Mum and Dad just took Ella for a walk.'

'That's good, it must be a nice evening over there.'

'Yep, still twenty-six degrees, and it's been another really hot day today.'

'Well, I think our temperature only reached twenty-six, in fact it's quite cool over here tonight,' James said with a shiver.

'Anyway, darling, I don't want to just talk about the weather. How was your day?'

'I had a lazy day. Did nothing. Mum and I just sat around.'

'Good on you. I'm glad you took a day off; you've been racing around every day since you got home. How's Ella?'

'She's great, as cheeky as ever and growing every day.'

'I miss you both so much. Only thirty-eight days to go.'

Claire gave a chuckle. 'So, you're still counting the days?'

'Yes, sure am,' James paused, reached for his notepad, and opened it at the first page. 'Claire, there's something else we should have done while you were here, but I forgot, I'm so sorry.'

Claire shook her head in wonderment. 'What was that?'

'The wedding rings, we should have bought them together while you were here. Looks like I'll need to arrange to get them myself. I would have loved to take you to the jeweller's shop where I bought our engagement ring; unfortunately, we didn't have the opportunity. I'd still like you to meet Mr Goldsworthy, the jeweller, and his lovely family. Maybe we could drop in and see them on the way home from our honeymoon.'

'Mmm, maybe.' Claire stretched out her left hand and wiggled her fingers. The diamond ring sparkled. 'Anyway, about the wedding rings, I trust you to make the choice since you did such a good job at selecting the engagement ring.'

'All right, sweetie, you can leave that to me. And by the way, I still have the business card that Alex Goldsworthy gave me, the one with your ring size written on the back of it.' James paused, ran his finger down the things-to-do list and then added; 'and the other main thing I've decided is for the groomsmen and me to buy our suits rather than hire them. I've seen some nice ones and have arranged to meet the boys this Saturday to have them fitted. That gives us plenty of time for any alterations that might be needed.'

'And I thought I was busy. Sounds like you have quite a lot to do and think about too, what with work and everything.'

'Yes, I suppose so, but not as much as you. It's a good thing you have your Mum there to help.'

Claire agreed and they chatted on until after midnight once more, and before their final goodbye James reminded her that it was now only thirty-seven days until their wedding.

Thursday morning Claire woke bright and early. First one up, she jumped out of bed, slipped her arms into the sleeves of her robe, wrapped the tie around her waist and pattered bare foot downstairs. She felt alive. Happy. An overwhelming feeling of contentment and peace washed over her.

The house was quiet until she switched on the kettle and opened the kitchen blinds. A tiny wattlebird alighted onto the windowsill and chirped his cheeky song, welcoming in the new day.

'Hello, little fellow,' said Claire, 'and a good morning to you too.'

The sound of running water coming from her parent's bathroom alerted her that they were awake. Wanting to surprise them, she bustled around the kitchen, prepared a nutritious breakfast; she set the table, and packed her dad's lunch for him to take to work.

Confused, Bill did a double take. Sonia was still fast asleep under the covers, the sheet pulled over her eyes. *That's strange*; he thought he detected the smell of freshly brewed coffee wafting through from the kitchen.

Opening the bedroom door a smidgen, he peeped through the opening to see Claire humming softly to herself. He smiled as he finished dressing in readiness for work.

'Good morning, Father,' Claire said. 'Breakfast is served.'

'Well, this is lovely, daughter dear. How is it you're up so bright and early today?'

Claire heaved a sigh of happiness. 'I don't know really, I just feel so …' She hesitated, ran her finger around the rim of her coffee mug, 'Mmm, I feel excited for some reason, sort of like something good's going to happen today.'

'So, what have you got planned for today?'

'Mum and I are going down to the church to see about hiring the hall for our wedding reception. Anyway, Dad, you sit down and drink your coffee and I'll serve your breakfast.'

'Thank you, darling. This is so nice of you. I left your mother sleeping. I think she's still getting over all the excitement of the trip, putting the house on the market, and helping with the wedding plans. But I'm sure she'll enjoy going with you today. What time is your appointment?'

'Ten thirty.'

'Aw, that's good – it's not too early.'

Claire placed a plate laden with goodies on the table in front of him.

'Wow!' Looks like a banquet.' Bill said with a smile. 'Thank you, darling.'

Claire kissed the top of his forehead and sat down at the table opposite him, and they enjoyed a quiet meal together.

Just before ten thirty, Claire and Sonia arrived at the church and parked the car, and, with Ella in her stroller, wandered in through the main entrance.

Pastor Steve welcomed them. 'I'd like you to meet Jean Baldwin; she heads up our catering committee,' he said and guided them through to the hall. 'Here she is, busy as usual. Claire, Sonia, this is Jean.'

'Pleased to meet you,' Jean greeted them with a warm and friendly smile. 'What a beautiful baby. What's her name?'

'Her name is Ella.'

'Ah, that's nice. Look, come in and take a seat and I'll get you a cup of tea or coffee. Which would you prefer?'

Orders were taken and Pastor Steve excused himself. 'I'll leave you two in Jean's capable hands,' he said and returned to his office.

Jean called to them from the kitchen. 'You can look through those albums on the table. It'll give you a bit an idea of some of the wedding functions we've done.'

Claire shifted her chair closer to her mother and opened the photo album. Page after page showed the church hall exquisitely decorated. Some photos showed the ceiling draped with softly coloured sheer fabric that billowed like clouds. Tiny lights hung in scallops around the walls, creating a fairy-tale atmosphere. Behind the bridal table stood a beautiful white latticework archway intertwined with fresh ivy, baby breath, and roses. The tables, all beautifully arranged, were set with silverware, crystal, and fine china.

Sonia raised her hand to her chest and sighed. 'You couldn't wish for anything better than this.'

Jean returned carrying a tray of tea, coffee, hot chocolate and homemade scones with strawberry jam and freshly piped cream. 'Here we go,' she said.

'Thank you, you've gone to so much trouble; we do appreciate you coming in especially for us today.'

'It's no trouble at all; I'm pleased you came.

'And what do you think of the photos?'

'They are beautiful,' Claire said as tears pooled in her eyes.

Jean showed them more photos of some of the weddings they had catered for, a few with crowds of about a hundred guests as well as other smaller groups, all set in this beautifully decorated church hall.

Claire was excited and before she had finished her hot chocolate drink agreed to book the hall for the wedding.

Sonia threw her arms around Claire. 'I'm sure James and Dad will be happy; you couldn't get anything better.'

'Would you like another cup of tea?' Jean asked, noticing Sonia's cup empty.

'Yes, please, I think it's all the excitement making me thirsty.'

'Well, I'm so excited that I can't even drink the rest of my chocolate,' Claire said with a giggle. 'Not that there's anything wrong with the drink, it's quite delicious. It's just that my tummy is full of dancing butterflies.'

After filling out the paperwork and also booking the dates for the pre-marriage counselling course, Claire and Sonia left the church just before mid-day, Ella still fast asleep in her stroller.

'What say we leave the car here, wander up to the corner café, have lunch and then, maybe, we could look for dresses. What do you think?'

'I think that sounds great,' Sonia said, 'let's go.'

That afternoon, they not only put a deposit on Claire's wedding dress, chose the bridesmaids' outfits and accessories, and ordered the bridal bouquets, but on the way home, they also picked up the wedding invitations.

Claire stretched her arms and yawned. 'Wow! What an amazing day. I would never have thought that we could achieve so much in one day.'

'And Ella was so good,' Sonia agreed. 'She only started to grizzle that once and soon settled down again when I took her for a stroll around the block. She seems to like shopping as much as we do.'

'Yep, seems that way. She's such a good girl.'

When James phoned that night, he hardly got a word in. Claire chatted on and on detailing all the things she had done that day.

James smiled, thrilled to hear the excitement in her voice. He jotted down the dates for their Skype pre-marriage counselling sessions and checked his calendar. 'Looks good to me,' he said and continued listening to Claire's news report. 'Sounds like you had a good day – only thirty-seven more to go.'

'I'm going to make a start on writing the invitations tomorrow. I want to try to get them all away by Monday. Can I check that I've got the addresses right for your family and friends?'

'Sure, fire away.'

One by one Claire read out the ones she had, confirming postcodes and spelling. 'Thanks, my darling,' she said and signed off with love.

Over the next few days, Claire sent out the wedding invitations and arranged with her friend, Emily, and cousin, Jessica, to get their bridesmaid dresses fitted. Everything seemed to be falling into place nicely.

Days flowed into weeks. Pre-marriage counselling sessions progressed well bringing up a few issues that neither of them had considered. Pastor Steve threw in a few challenging scenarios here and there that made them stop and think … such as 'James, how would you feel if Claire decided to pursue a career and earned more money than you?' 'And you, Claire; what if James had to move interstate or overseas for work, would it be hard for you to move away from family and friends?'

Fortunately, they scored well in the compatibility test and were able to talk through some of the curlier issues that arose.

Claire shrugged. 'I just thought we'd live happily ever after once we were married,' she confessed, 'and I suppose I expected the pre-marriage course would confirm that. But I'm glad we sort of faced those issues.'

'Me too,' said James.

The week leading up to the wedding was hectic for the Martin household.

While most of the interstate visitors had settled into their pre-arranged holiday accommodation, on Sonia's insistence, James' mother, Gloria and five other members of his immediate family, stayed with them. The lounge room became a makeshift dormitory. Inflatable mattresses, suitcases, toys, and bags strewn across the floor made for a cosy nook.

Early Thursday morning, the telephone rang. It was the Real Estate Agent wanting to bring an older couple through to view the house. 'They are genuinely interested,' she said.

Sonia tried to put them off. But the agent persisted.

'I will explain to them the situation and I'm sure they'll understand. They only want to have a quick look at the house. Will it be all right if I bring them around in about ten minutes?'

'Oh, please, can you make that twenty minutes?'

'Very well, thank you, Sonia, I really appreciate this.'

Everyone bustled around. Soon, the house looked like an orderly mess. With five minutes to spare, Sonia pulled the front door shut behind her, and they all took off for an unscheduled walk to the beach.

When they returned home there was a note on the kitchen bench to phone the agent.

Bill rang.

'Hi, Mr Martin, thank you for getting back to me. The couple that viewed your house today would like to put in an offer that I'm sure you will be more than happy with. They're still with me here in the office now, but I was wondering if I could drop the forms in for you to have a look at some time this afternoon?'

'Just one moment please.' Bill covered the mouthpiece of the phone with his hand and turned to Sonia. 'The people want to put in an offer! Is it all right with you if the agent comes over this afternoon with the paperwork?'

Sonia sighed and slumped forward. 'What, now?'

'No, darling, later on this afternoon.'

'Oh golly, it's such bad timing - but I suppose so.'

Bill confirmed the appointment with the agent and then replaced the phone.

He wiped his forehead. 'Everything happens at once. Cliché, I know, but it never rains, but it pours.' And taking Sonia in his arms, he added, 'We'll get through it, my darling, and everything will be fine.'

With the offer accepted and the settlement date confirmed on both properties, Bill and Sonia focused on the wedding.

Chapter 29

Saturday, the sixteenth of February, arrived. Rays of sunlight glistened on the bride's tiara as she walked the cobble path toward the little stone church. Claire caught her father's arm and smiled up at him. Bill patted her hand reassuring her of his love and support. The fragrance of jasmine filled the air as they stepped into the foyer.

Claire's friend and bridesmaid, Emily, smoothed out a fold on the front of Claire's gown and adjusted the train. 'You look radiant,' she said, choking back a tear.

The bridesmaids took their place and the congregation stood as the organ started to play the Bridal March.

Emily stepped forward and began her slow walk down the aisle followed closely by Jessica in her matching full-length sky-blue satin dress.

'Are you ready, my princess?' Bill asked. Claire nodded. Then, arm in arm, father and daughter passed under the arched entranceway and into the chapel.

The Best Man, Matthew, stood proudly by James' side, hand in pocket, feeling nervously for the rings, while the groomsman, Tyler stood on the other side.

James smiled briefly at the bridesmaids and then, looking up, tears filled his eyes as he gazed upon the most beautiful being he had ever seen. His Claire.

Bill took hold of Claire's tiny hand, placed it in James' hand, and then enfolding them both in his hands, blessed them.

Sonia sobbed. Bill took his seat beside her and, wrapping his arms around her, comforted her.

Little Ella sat wide-eyed on her grandmother's lap, her pretty, white tulle and lace dress scrunched when she clapped her hands to the music.

One highlight in the ceremony happened during the pause following the statement, 'Anyone showing just cause why this couple cannot be married let him say so now or keep quiet. The silence was broken when Ella said, 'Mumu'.

Gazing into each other's eyes, Claire and James voiced their love for each other as they recited the vows, including the ones they had written themselves.

The service went without a hitch and even Matthew presented the rings at the right time.

Claire could hardly keep a straight face, especially at the romantic part where James lifted her veil to kiss his bride, she had to hold back the giggle that threatened to erupt.

With the register signed and the paperwork completed, Pastor Steve invited the congregation to stand as he presented Mr and Mrs James Cowan.

The triumphant sound of organ music drowned out the cheers and applause as the newly wedded couple mingled with family and friends.

As the bridal party stepped out into the sunlight, a light breeze caught Claire's veil and whisked it across her face. Brushing it aside, James kissed her tenderly. The photographer captured that exact moment along with many other candid shots and the more formal photographs.

A short while later, the guests formed a guard of honour to welcome the bride and groom and their attendants into the beautifully decorated reception hall. The aroma of roast chicken, lamb, vegetables, and mint sauce wafted from the kitchen.

When all were seated and Pastor Steve had once again welcomed everyone, he said a short prayer of thanks and then introduced the catering staff. A round of applause broke the silence, and soon after, people began to chatter amongst themselves.

The kids thought it was great having their own special table where the head caterer's daughter, Jenny, supervised and entertained them throughout the meal. She even set up a high chair for Ella. Following the second course, Jenny took the children to the games room for their ice cream cones, marshmallows, and lots of fun.

In the main reception hall, the speeches began. First, the father of the bride gave a warm and tender speech about his little girl, throwing in a few tasteful anecdotes. Bill choked back a tear and wiped his eyes, and then, leaning over, he kissed Claire on the cheek. She pushed back her chair and stood; arms outstretched to her dad. An 'ooh' and 'ah' rippled through the hall as father and daughter locked in a loving embrace.

James tapped Bill on the shoulder. 'Excuse me, sir, may I cut in?'

Everyone laughed.

'No, not yet. You'll get your turn,' Bill said cheekily before whisking her away.

Frivolity over, James took the microphone. 'But, Dad, you said "yes" when I asked you if I could marry her,' he began. James paused and cleared his throat. 'But seriously now ...' he continued, 'on behalf of my wife and myself, I would like to thank you all for joining us here today as we celebrate our marriage ...' The speech was short and sweet followed by the Best Man's talk, after which Tyler read the messages.

Tray-in-hand, the caterers stood ready to serve the sweets: pavlova with fruit salad or apple pie and ice cream.

Standing, Claire caught Pastor Steve's attention. 'I'd like to say a few words if that's okay,' she asked.

'Of course, my dear, it is after all your day.'

He tapped the microphone. 'Excuse me, ladies and gentlemen, if I could have your attention, please. Our lovely bride, Claire would like to say something. Here we go,' he said and handed her the microphone.

'Hi, everyone. First, I'd like to thank my Heavenly Father for blessing me with such a wonderful man. I know I don't deserve him. But for those of you who know a bit of my story, my life was a wreck until Jesus Christ, my Saviour, rescued me, forgave me, and gave me a second chance. And with the support and help of Mum and Dad, I recovered physically and emotionally. Then I met this most amazing man.' She turned to James. He lowered his head and wept.

'And so, I would like to thank you all for joining us as we celebrate this, the first day of the rest of our lives together.'

Claire went on to thank Pastor Steve, Jean, Karen, Bev, and their husbands, who helped in the background, for putting on such a lovely dinner and Jenny for taking care of the children; that was an extra-unexpected bonus.

The music played the bridal waltz. James took Claire by the hand and guided her to the dance floor.

'What a lovely couple they make,' Pastor Steve said. 'Let's put our hands together for Mr and Mrs Cowan.'

James whirled her around, paused and kissed her tenderly.

As the music continued, Bill and Sonia joined them on the dance floor, followed by Matthew and Gloria. Tyler went out, took little Ella in his arms, and waltzed her around the dance floor. Others joined in, including the children, who, leaving their shoes behind, had fun sliding across the polished floor in their socks. The kids were having the time of their lives.

During the next hour or so, the young ones continued dancing while the older guests were happy to sit out the livelier movements.

Matt and Tyler slipped outside, and were conspicuously absent from the party for quite a while. With Bill close on their heels, the boys were careful not to damage the hire car.

Before they returned to the hall, Tyler pulled Matt aside. 'Matt, do you think it would be all right if I ask Melanie for a dance?'

Matt scratched the back of his head. 'Don't see why not.' He paused. 'But you do know she's in a … relationship?'

'Mmm, that's the problem. I don't want to just leave her partner sitting there by herself feeling like the proverbial wallflower.' He hesitated. 'Do you think it'd be okay?'

'Go for it, mate, be brave. What's the worst thing that can happen? She turns you down. So, what.' Matthew thought for a moment. 'Hey, I'll tell you what. How about we both go up to them together; you ask Mel to dance, and I ask Christine?'

Tyler's eyes lit up. 'Would you? Thanks, mate.'

'Look, just give me a minute to explain to Laurel, so she won't wonder what we're up to.'

'No worries,' he said, and they returned to the hall.

Tyler had been spending quite a bit of time with Melanie and Chris since they had arrived in Perth. They were on the same flight from Adelaide, were staying at the same hotel and had shared meals together.

As he took her in his arms and the music slowed, their eyes met and they began to dance. Melanie smiled up at him. Tyler's heart skipped a beat. He gently squeezed her hand. Her finger twitched beneath his touch.

She felt guilty for enjoying his closeness, the fragrance of … it wasn't only his aftershave; it was the very essence of who he was. A surge of passion, like a kaleidoscope of butterflies, fluttered in her stomach. She felt faint. 'Excuse me, Tyler, I need to sit down,' she said and swooned in his arms.

'Are you all right?'

'Yes, just tired I think.'

Tyler escorted her to her seat and sat down in the empty chair beside her. He signalled the waitress for drinks and handed Melanie a glass of sparkly. 'Here, sip this. It'll make you feel better.'

'I don't know what came over me,' she said, but in her heart, she knew.

Christine was still having fun on the dance floor, Matt whirling her around. She ducked and dived and displayed some very unconventional moves.

Melanie was pleased to see her friend enjoying herself.

All too soon the music stopped, and Pastor Steve announced the final farewell.

Everyone, including the children, formed a circle, held hands, and sang Auld Lang Syne. After that, the bridal party made their way out through the courtyard toward the brightly decorated hire car.

Tears filled Sonia's eyes. She kissed her daughter and held her tight. 'Goodbye, my darling, we'll see you when you get back. Have a great time.' She took Ella's little hand and waved it. 'Bye, Mummy,' she said.

Bill extended his hand to James. 'Goodbye, son, take care.'

The two men embraced.

'I will, Dad,' James replied, 'I will take care of her.'

'Thank you.'

Claire's eyes misted over. She hugged her dad and sobbed on his shoulder. 'I'll miss you, Daddy,' she whispered.

Bill took a handkerchief from his pocket and patted her eyes gently. 'I'll miss you too, princess. But we'll see you soon. And don't worry about Ella, she'll be fine.'

'I know she will, Dad. Thank you for everything.'

James hugged his mother and kissed her cheek, then turned to his sisters and said his goodbyes. He looked around for the kids, but they were busy playing tag on the lawn. 'Bye, Chis, bye, Em, Jake,' he yelled.

Christopher gave him a backwards wave over his head and continued chasing his sister.

'Goodbye, Uncle James,' Emily screamed as she fell to the ground laughing.

Laurel called to them. 'Come on, you three, come over here and say goodbye properly.'

'Don't worry, sis, just leave them play; they're fine,' said James, eager to leave the party.

With confetti flying and bubbles floating in the air, guests bid the happy couple farewell.

Opening the passenger side door, James helped his wife into the car, closed the door and climbed into the driver's seat. Then, with seat belts fastened, he fired up the engine. And with streamers flying and tin cans clunking on the road, James sounded the horn, and they were off.

Gloria turned to Sonia. 'That was the nicest wedding I've ever attended,' she said. 'Thank you so much for all you've done to make it so …' She was lost for words.

The two women hugged.

'And thank you for welcoming James into your family.'

'James is the best thing that ever happened to Claire. We couldn't have wished for a better son-in-law.'

Young Emily came running over to her mother. 'I like it when Uncle James and Aunty Claire get a wedding. Can we come next time?'

Laurel laughed. 'Weddings aren't like birthdays; people only get married once … usually.'

Emily rolled her bottom lip. 'Oh,' she whimpered, 'it was fun, I want to do it again.'

After a brief stop off at the house for a quick change of clothes, James and Claire headed north on their honeymoon. They stayed the first night at Geraldton then, following a late checkout, headed on to beautiful Kalbarri.

Chapter 30

Just before 8:30 the next day, they were awakened by the sound of the telephone. Sonia moaned. Blurry-eyed, Bill, staggered out of bed, made his way down the hall, and answered the call.

'Good morning,' came the cheery voice on the other end of the line. 'It's Madeline Jones, from Bailey and Brooke's Real Estate Agency. I'm sorry to disturb you so early on Sunday morning, but I have some exciting news for you!' she said and took a deep breath. 'The couple that are buying your house are anxious to settle as soon as possible. I just wanted to check with you if the 28th would be a suitable settlement date?'

Bill rubbed his eyes and yawned. He looked at the calendar, turned the page over and ran his finger down to the last Thursday. 'The 28th of March should be okay,' he said.'

Madeline cleared her throat. 'Actually, they were thinking the 28th of this month.' She waited.

'That's only next week,' Bill retorted, suddenly wide awake. 'Oh no, that would be impossible. Our daughter's not due back from her honeymoon until early March and we've got the baby and …' Bill's mind boggled.

'That's all right, Mr Martin. You have a think about it, talk it over with Sonia, and I'll call you back later.'

The call ended.

Still in a daze, Bill wandered into the kitchen, made a strong coffee for himself, a cup of tea for Sonia, and a bottle of baby formula for Ella.

Sonia had fallen asleep again and when Bill entered the room she turned over, pulled the covers over her head, and gave a grunt. Not wanting to disturb her or Ella, who was still fast asleep in her cot, he sat sipping his coffee and worried alone.

A short while later, Bill heard movement in the family room – the kids were awake.

'Shh,' said Matt, 'keep the noise down, people are still asleep.'

'Can we watch TV?' Jake asked in a loud whisper.

'No, just read your books quietly.'

'But I need to go wee-wees.'

Reluctantly, Matt dragged himself out of bed and took care of it. By the time he returned to the family room, the rest of his family was up, and everyone was a bit grumpy.

Laurel slipped her dressing gown on. 'What time is it?' she asked.

'Ten to ten,' replied Matt. 'How about I put the kettle on and get the kids their breakfast while you have your shower.'

She stretched her arms above her head, scratched her head, squeezed her eyes closed and yawned. 'Okay.'

And that was the start of the day after the night before.

When Sonia came to and heard about the early morning phone call from the Estate Agent, she sprang to life.

'No way!' she said. 'We need more time than that. We must sell some of the furniture, pack our stuff and arrange to have it shipped to Adelaide, and that's just for starters. There's so much more to do. And I'm so tired.'

Overwhelmed, Sonia began to cry.

Bill took her in his arms. 'It's all right, darling. We don't have to go along with what they say. We'll just sit down together and work out a date that suits us.'

Sonia sniffed. 'Oh, Bill, it's all too much.'

'It will be all right. You are just tired. It's been a big build up; what with the wedding and visitors and the house selling so quickly. Everything's going to be fine. You wait and see.'

Snuggling her head against his chest, Sonia felt the warmth of his strength. She looked up into his eyes and, in a husky voice said,

'Thank you. I love you, darling.'

With the house still a mess, that afternoon there came a loud knock on the front door. Bill answered it.

It was Eddy, drunk as usual.

He swayed and staggered forward. 'I 'eard she married that bloke from east. No way she gunnu take my kid outa the state,' he slurred.

'Excuse me,' Bill replied. 'Just who do you think you are coming around here making demands? You go home. Sober up and behave yourself.'

'I got my rights. I'll take 'er to court I will. She ain't goin' nowhere,' he slurred.

Bill grabbed the front of his shirt, held him steady and eyeballed him. 'Listen here, mate, you show up in court, they'll lock you up and throw the book at you. And if you don't leave this property immediately, I will call the police, right now!' Bill turned him around and marched him to the front gate.

'Yu arnt urd the last of this. Jist you wait n see.'

With his heart pounding in his chest and his hands shaking, Bill wandered back into the house, closed the door, and sighed.

Having heard the commotion, Sonia sidled up to him. 'What was that all about?' she asked.

'It was just Eddy, making idle threats.'

'What! What's he saying?'

Bill turned to face her. He clutched his chest. The room spun, everything closed in around him and he fell to the floor.

Sonia screamed.

Startled, Gloria rushed to her side. Matt followed close behind. Laurel ushered the children into the family room, switched on the TV, turned the volume down, and told them to stay there and be very, very quiet.

'Call triple O,' Gloria instructed as Sonia lay slumped across her husband's limp body, weeping bitterly.

With the phone to his ear, Matt relayed the instructions given by the woman on the other end of the line. 'Turn him onto his side. Tilt his head back slightly.'

Gloria lifted Sonia off Bill and, with Laurel's help, rolled him over. He was a dead weight.

Matt continued. 'She asked if he's responding?'

'No, but he is breathing.'

Matt's mind went blank. 'Um, I'm not sure, just a minute.' Feeling stupid, he covered the mouthpiece with one hand. 'What is the address here again?' he asked.

Calm as usual, Gloria filled in the details. The only question she couldn't answer was the name of the nearest crossroad. And Sonia was incoherent and beside herself with worry.

'Don't worry,' the lady replied, 'the ambulance is on its way.'

'Ambulance is on the way,' Matt repeated and sighed with relief.

Gloria put her arm over Sonia's shoulder and whispered a short prayer. 'Try not to worry, dear,' she said. 'I'm sure everything is going to be okay.'

Sonia smiled a sad smile. 'Thank you.'

Bill stirred and blinked his eyes.

'Oh, Bill,' Sonia cried, 'are you all right?'

'Mmm,' he mumbled, 'a bit groggy. What happened?'

Sonia leaned over and kissed his forehead. 'You passed out and collapsed on the floor. How do you feel? Can you sit up?'

'Mmm, I think so,' he said and lifted his head, but his limbs refused to cooperate. 'I think I'll just stay here for a little while,' he said, not wanting to worry her.

Laurel brought them a rug and pillow from the family room.

Sonia smiled. 'Thanks, dear,' she said and tried to make Bill comfortable.

The sound of a distant siren brought them comfort and reassurance. Matt opened the front door and stepped out onto the porch.

'The ambulance will be here soon, dear,' Sonia said. 'They'll check you over and see if you need to go to the hospital.'

Matt waved the ambulance down. The driver came to a stop and reversed the vehicle into the driveway.

'How is the patient?' the first officer asked.

'He's come to and is coherent, but we haven't moved him.'

'That's good.'

Matt held the door open. 'He's just through here,' he said and pointed the way.

After checking his vital signs, the medical officer gave Bill a tablet to put under his tongue and after fitting an oxygen mask on his face, asked him what happened.

Sonia answered for him.

'Sorry, madam, we need your husband to answer the questions for us.'

Embarrassed, Sonia backed off. 'I'm sorry, sir.'

'It's all right, Mrs Martin.' The second officer smiled understandingly. 'It's a natural response. You're probably still in shock, but don't worry your husband is in good hands.'

'Thank you.'

Just then Gloria came in carrying a tray of teas and coffees. She handed Sonia a mug of tea. 'Here, dear, have this it will make you feel better.'

Sonia wrapped her shaking hands around the warm mug and began to sip the sweet tea. 'Thank you, Gloria. I don't know how I would have managed without you.'

As Bill was being loaded onto the stretcher trolley, the head medical officer asked Sonia if she was going to accompany her husband to the hospital.

She looked at Gloria.

'Go on, dear. Bill needs you with him. Don't you worry about a thing, we'll look after Ella. Everything will be fine.'

Sonia grabbed a few things, dashed out the door and followed the two officers to the ambulance.

'Ella's formula is on the middle shelf in the pantry and the nappies are in our room and …'

'Go on, don't you worry now; we'll soon find everything. And you just phone us if you need anything more. Okay?'

'Thanks, Gloria, I'll be in touch.'

The door closed behind them and they were off.

Ella laughed with the kids, enjoying their company.

Having the children there was a pleasant distraction for the adults as they tried to cope with the seriousness of the situation.

Gloria's phone rang. 'Hello,' she answered tentatively.

'Hi, Gloria, it's Sonia here. They've just taken Bill down for a routine chest x-ray and I thought I'd give you a quick call to let you know what's happening.'

'How is Bill?' Gloria asked.

'Well, he has improved, and he looks a much better colour now. He's not in any pain and he's been giving the nurses a bit of cheek. I think that's a pretty good sign,' she chuckled.

'Well, that is a relief. You had us all worried there, and actually, you're sounding better yourself.'

Sonia took a deep breath and released it slowly. 'Yes, I am — now,' she said, 'but golly, it was a huge shock. I tell you I've never felt so frightened in all my life.'

Gloria cast her mind back a few years to the time when she sat grief-stricken by her late husband's bedside. 'I understand,' she said and, clearing her throat, asked, 'Sonia, do they know what caused him to collapse?'

'Not now, we have to wait for test results. He's had an ECG and one blood test, but they need to do another blood test in a few hours' time to measure something or other. And they're wanting to do an ultrasound on his heart as well. Anyway, Gloria, I'll let you know as soon as we find out anything definite. By the way, how is everything at home?'

'Everything's fine. Ella is having the time of her life with her three cousins. It's lovely to see them interacting so well.'

'Aw, that's good. Please give her a big kiss from me and, thank you so much for all your help.'

'It's my pleasure dear. Just let me know if there's anything you need or anything you want me to do.'
'Thanks, Gloria.'
'You're welcome. Bye for now.'
'Bye.'

Later that evening, the Martins telephone rang. Laurel shrugged and turned to her mother. 'Do you think we should answer it?'
Gloria hesitated a moment and then lifted the cordless phone from its cradle. 'Hello?'
'Hi, Mrs Cowan, Sorry, I should say Mum … it's Claire here. We just wanted to let everyone know that we've arrived in Kalbarri and are having a great time. '
'That's lovely, dear, thanks for ringing.'
'How is Ella? I miss her so much.'
'She is fine. She's already asleep, and I think the other kids are nearly ready to go to bed too. They have had a great day together and I think they have worn themselves out.'
'Aw, that's good. Could I speak to Mum?'
Gloria trembled. 'Actually, your Mum and Dad are both out at the moment. Would you like me to get them to ring you when they get back?'
'Oh no, don't worry. I'll call them tomorrow night, just give them our love. Would you like to speak to James?'
'Sure, dear.'
'Hi, Mum, how are you going?'
'Good thank you, darling; how are you?'
'Great, couldn't be better. Claire wants to know what you thought of the wedding.'
'We all thought it was wonderful. A funny thing happened after you guys had gone. Young Emily asked Laurel if we could come

back again for your next wedding!'

James cackled. 'Sounds like she really enjoyed herself then.'

'Yes, they all did. We all did. It was one of the nicest weddings I've ever had the privilege to witness.'

'Thanks, Mum. I thought it might have been just because it was our wedding that we enjoyed it so much.'

'No, darling, it truly was a special day.'

They said their goodbyes and finished the call.

Gloria breathed a sigh of relief. She hadn't actually told a lie; she just hadn't told them everything. For good reason, too: she didn't want to worry them and there was no need to spoil their holiday. *If things should change for the worst, we will let them know*, she reasoned.

'Phew! It was a good thing she didn't ask you where Bill and Sonia were,' Laurel said. 'You really handled that well, Mum. If it was me, I wouldn't have known what to say.'

'Well, I did say a short prayer under my breath and hoped I could get away without telling them. I don't want them worrying unnecessarily. Or think they need to cut their holiday short.'

A little while later, Gloria's phone rang again. It was Sonia with good news.

'They seem to think he might have had a slight heart attack likely brought on by stress. All the tests have come back good, but they want to keep him overnight for rest and observation. And he may be able to go home tomorrow. Fingers crossed,' she added.

'That's great news. So do you plan to stay with him tonight?'

'No, I'm going to book a taxi and head on home.'

'Oh, don't do that. Matt will pick you up in the hire car. He has been waiting to hear from you.'

'That's very kind of him; I wasn't expecting anyone to come out for me.'

'That's no problem at all. Here, I'll pass the phone over to him so you can give him the directions.'

'Okey-dokey will do,' he replied and, picking up his keys, shot out the door.

After a restless night of tossing and turning Sonia woke early the next morning and unable to go back to sleep, rose, took a shower, and prepared for another day.

Unlike Sonia, Ella slept right through the night and woke up bright and chatty.

'What a joy you are little one,' Sonia said as tears pooled in her eyes.

'Na, Na, Na, Na,' replied Ella, reaching her chubby arms toward her grandmother.

'Did you say Nanna? What a clever girl you are.'

Very soon, everyone was up, and the whole household became a hive of activity. Matthew kindly offered to drive Sonia to the hospital, and once again, Gloria volunteered to babysit Ella for her.

Just as Sonia and Matt were about to leave the house, the telephone rang. Sonia looped her bag over a hook on the hallstand and dashed to the phone. It was Madeline from the Real Estate Agency wanting to know if they had decided on a date for settlement.

'Sorry, Madeline, we haven't had a chance to discuss it yet. You see Bill's in hospital. He's had a bit of a heart scare. I'm just about to head off to see him now. Could I give you a ring when I get back? We should know more of what's happening then.'

Madeline was very understanding and sympathetic. 'I'm so sorry to hear that,' she said. 'Don't you worry; just get back to me when you can.'

The call finished and Sonia and Matt headed off.

On the way to the hospital, Matt asked Sonia to let him know when they were ready to leave the hospital so he would know when to pick them up.

'Oh no, we wouldn't expect you to do that. It's your last day and you'll need to take your family out to see a bit more of Perth. Bill and I can take a taxi home, that's no problem. Besides, you've already done more than enough for us. But thank you for the offer.'

'Well remember, I'm just a phone call away if you need me.'

'Thank you, Matthew.'

Sonia entered the room to find Bill out of bed, gazing through the window, oblivious to her presence. 'Hi there,' she said, 'it's all right to be some people living it up in the lap of luxury.'

When he turned, Sonia saw the familiar sparkle was back in his eyes again. She threw her arms around him and hugged him tightly. 'I love you so much,' she said and lingered in his embrace.

'Looks like I'll be going home today,' Bill said. 'I just have to wait to see the cardiologist when he calls in sometime this morning to give the final okay.'

'That's good, darling. And Matt offered to come in and pick us up when we're ready to go home, but I said we could order a taxi. I didn't want him to be hanging around all day for us, especially since it's their last day in Perth before they head back to Adelaide.'

'Good.' Bill nodded, and then turned toward the window again. 'So what do you think of this lovely view?'

'Sonia rested her head on his shoulder and snuggled close. 'It's beautiful. I think you must have the best room in the entire hospital.'

He agreed.

Bill was released from the hospital that day under strict instructions to take things easy for the next few days, keep on the medication, and to see the cardiologist again the following week.

When they arrived home, the house was quiet. Everything sparkled. Sonia breathed in the sweetness of a freshly cleaned house. And through the kitchen window she could see the clothesline full and spinning in the breeze. A note on the kitchen table explained. Laurel, Matt, and the family had gone out for the day and Gloria had taken Ella for a walk down to the waterfront.

Sonia switched on the kettle. 'This is lovely,' she said. 'Gloria must have been working flat out all morning! She's such a treasure.

'Now, Bill, you go and sit out on the patio, and I'll bring lunch out to you.'

'Actually, I'd love a cup of coffee,' Bill said with those pleading puppy dog eyes.

'Oh no. You heard what the doctor said: you must cut down on the caffeine.'

'He said, "cut down" not "cut out." And I'm dying for a proper coffee. The so-called coffee in the hospital was awful.' Bill screwed his nose. 'It was weak and milky and cold and yuk.' He shivered at the thought.

'All right, just this once.' Sonia sighed as she shooed him out of the kitchen.

With joy in her heart and a skip in her step, Sonia balanced the tray on her upturned hand. 'Here we go, my dear,' she said and placed a plate of leafy green salad on the table in front of Bill.

'What's this? It looks like rabbit food! I can't be expected to survive on this. Surely not,' Bill said cheekily.

'I'm just following the healthy heart food guidelines the dietician gave us.'

'How long do I have to stick to this?' Bill groaned.

'Forever,' Sonia replied. 'It's to keep us fit.'

'Aw, do I have to?'

'Yes, you and me too.'

Just then the telephone rang. Sonia raced inside.

'Hi, darling,' It was Claire. 'How are you going? Are you having a lovely time?'

'Yes, and yes and yes again, it's beautiful up here; we're having a great time. We're sitting on a bench outside the Interpretative Centre at the Pinnacles enjoying a picnic lunch.'

'Well, Dad and I are sitting out on the patio, in the lovely sunshine having our lunch too.'

'How is Ella?'

'She's not here at the moment. Gloria's taken her for a walk to the beach. But she's been a good girl.'

'Oh, that's good, Mum, but I miss her so much; we miss her so much.' Claire laughed.

'Well, darling, enjoy your time together while you've got the opportunity because you'll be hitting the ground running when you get back. The couple who are buying our house want to finalise quickly.'

'Really? How quickly?'

'Like – yesterday if they could.'

'Wow, I hope you put them off a few more weeks.'

'Yes, the Estate Agent has given us more time to think about it and we haven't come up with a final date yet. But the sooner the better because once you and James have gone to Adelaide with Ella, I'll be counting the days until we see you again.'

'Yes, I guess so, Mum. But you still need to take your time; you don't want to overdo it, you know.'

Sonia knew all too well.

'Anyway, Claire, do you want to chat to Dad?'

'Thanks, Mum, that'd be great.'

Sonia took the cordless phone out to Bill who was dozing in the sun. 'Just a minute, Claire, I think your dad's asleep.'

'That's unusual … Dad never sleeps in the day. Is he all right?'

Sonia swallowed hard. 'Yes, he's fine. Oh, he is awake, he must have been resting his eyes. Just a minute I'll pass the phone to him.'

Sonia shook her index finger and mouthed a message. 'Don't tell her you were in hospital.'

'Hi, how's my princess?'

'Good thanks, Dad. We're having a great time. But how are you? It's not like you to doze off in the sun.'

'I'm fine, thanks, darling. What about you and James?'

Bill could hear the smile in her voice when she replied. 'We're both very well, thanks, Dad. We are having a great time, but we miss everyone, especially Ella.'

'Well, you guys just forget about everyone else and enjoy your holiday.'

'Yeah, we will, Dad. Now promise me you won't work too hard with the packing and everything. You must look after yourself. And Mum,' she added.

'We will, darling. Did you want to speak to your mother again?'

'No, just give her a big kiss and hug for me and lots of love to everyone from James too.'

'Will do. Bye, darling. Enjoy.'

Just then, Gloria returned with Ella who was fast asleep in the pram.

Sonia sighed. 'Oh, you just missed the kids,' she said. 'They rang to ask after everyone, but we didn't say anything about the troubles. Didn't want to worry them. They send their love.'

'How are they?'

'Good. Having a great time. Missing everyone especially Ella, of course.'

Gloria turned to Bill. 'Well, I must say you're certainly looking a lot better than the last time I saw you.'

'Yeah, and I'm sure feeling a lot better than the last time I saw you too,' he chuckled.

Sonia began to clear the table and then looked up at Gloria. 'Oh, by the way, have you had your lunch yet?'

'Yes, I took a picnic lunch with us and had it down by the ocean. It's such a pretty spot. Now,' she said, 'here, give me that tray, you just sit down and take it easy; I'll do the dishes.'

'Thank you, you've been a real godsend. I don't know what we would have done without you.'

'It's my pleasure. I'm glad to help. And …' she paused. 'I'm happy to stay longer if that will be of help to you. I talked to my friend and neighbour who is house-sitting for me, and between her and another friend, they'll look after my place and my dog, Buddy, if I do decide to stay on.'

'That's kind of you and your friends,' Bill replied, 'but what about your return flight?'

'That's okay. I checked with the airline, and I would be able to change the date without too much trouble. So, you two have a little think about it. Just know that the offer stands.'

'Thanks, Gloria. We'll have to agree on a final settlement date for the sale of the house and take it from there.'

Gloria went indoors and left Bill and Sonia to talk things over. They checked the calendar and made a list of things they needed to do before settlement could take place.

Bill looked at his watch. It was just after two. 'Mmm,' he mused. 'It will be past four thirty in Adelaide, I suppose I should try to phone the Estate Agent and find out how soon we can finalise the purchase of our unit over there.'

'Are you sure you're feeling up to it?' Sonia frowned. 'Or do you think it would be better to wait until tomorrow?'

'Aw no, I think the sooner the better.'

'All right, but you stay there, and I'll bring the phone to you.'

The next day, the Estate Agent from Adelaide phoned back, proposing Tuesday, March 12th, as the proposed settlement day for their two-bedroom unit in Glenelg.

'That's three weeks. Do you think we can do it?' Bill asked Sonia.

She shrugged. 'I'm sure we could but let's wait and see what the cardiologist says when you see him next week.'

Bill chatted some more with their agent who was totally understanding of their situation. She suggested they start things in motion toward that date and make any adjustments necessary along the way.

They agreed.

Bill notified Madeline Jones, their Perth Agent, of the proposed settlement date and explained that they still needed time to sell a lot of their furniture because they were downsizing to a two-bedroom unit in Adelaide.

'Really!' exclaimed the agent on the other end of the line. 'That's wonderful because my clients are interested in buying your furniture.'

'We don't want to sell all of it,' Bill hastened to say. 'There are some pieces we want to keep.'

'I'm sure they would be more than happy to negotiate. When would be a good time for me to bring them through again?'

Bill checked with Sonia. 'How about either tomorrow afternoon or anytime Thursday?'

'I'll tell you what I'll do, I'll get in touch with the Weatherby's and get back to you with a suitable time. Okay?'

'Yes, that'll be fine. Thanks, Madeline.'

'You're welcome. Cheerio.'

The next day, most of James's family headed back to Adelaide and Melbourne – all except Gloria, who stayed on for an extra week to help with the packing, sorting, and cleaning and, of course, enjoy time with her new nine-month-old granddaughter, Ella.

Bill continued to rest and recuperate while Sonia and Gloria got stuck into the packing and cleaning. Room by room, they meticulously made three main piles: things to keep, things to give away, and items to be discarded.

'We won't touch Claire's room. She'll sort it out herself when she gets home. It won't take her long, she's very efficient, not like her mother.' Sonia huffed.

Gloria turned to Sonia. 'I'm sure James will help Bill sort out his garage and the shed and anything else that might be a bit heavy for him.'

'Oh, my goodness,' Sonia threw her hands in the air. 'I'd forgotten about the shed and g. I don't know what I would have done without you, Gloria. You're my lifesaver.'

'It's my pleasure, dear. I'm glad to be of assistance.'

On the Wednesday morning, after a good night's sleep, Bill and Sonia took an inventory and rough valuation of the furniture they wished to sell. They erred on the side of generosity and were ready to negotiate further.

When Liz and Darrel Weatherby went through the house, they were more than happy with the price of the furniture. They stayed on and chatted a while after the estate agent had left.

Bill took Darrel into the garage and showed him the tools and equipment he had no intention of taking to Adelaide.

Darrel's eyes lit up. 'Want to sell some of your gear to me?' he added.

'I'll tell you what, mate, how about I give it to you, as is?'

'Oh man! Really?'

Bill nodded.

'That would be like a dream come true.' Darrell threw his arms around Bill in a spontaneous reaction.

'That's okay, mate, you'd be helping me out because I have to downsize and won't be needing all this stuff.'

Bill thought about the shed, which contained mostly gardening tools and a few odds and ends of no significance or value.

'Don't suppose you'd want to check out the back shed while you're here?'

Darrel pushed the cap back on his head. 'Yes, if you don't mind, that'd be great.'

They did and then shook hands on the deal, a deal which included the old tom cat!

Meanwhile, back in the house Sonia had negotiated an arrangement with Liz that any food they hadn't used could be left in the pantry when they vacated.

That would make the final packing and sorting a lot easier for Bill and herself and would also be a blessing for the new owners.

Chapter 31

James slowed the car and turned left. Claire tilted the road map sideways. 'Where are we going now? This isn't the way to Geraldton!'

'Just a little detour.'

James glanced across at Claire and gave a cheeky grin. 'It's a secret. I've got a surprise for you.'

'I hope we don't get lost,' she said shifting uneasily in the passenger seat. 'And I don't like surprises.'

'It's all right, you're going to love this one.'

She sat in silence, head down fidgeting with the corner of her scarf.

A couple of kilometres along the country road, James could stand it no longer. He pulled the car to the side of the road. Dust swirling in their wake.

'What's wrong? Please tell me. I didn't mean to upset you.'

Claire sniffed. 'I just like to know what's going on is all. We're a couple now and we need to make decisions together.'

James shook his head and hot tears pooled in his eyes. 'I'm sorry, darling. I haven't been married before; I'm still learning.'

'I haven't been married before either,' she huffed.

'Oh, I didn't mean …' James paused. He felt uncomfortable. He'd said the wrong thing again.

Reaching out, he took Claire's hand in his. 'I love you so much. I never want to hurt you. Please forgive me?' He raised her hand to his lips and kissed it tenderly.

How could she hold a grudge? 'Oh, James, I feel bad; I shouldn't have reacted that way.' She sighed. 'I'm just tired, and I'm missing Ella, and I just want to get home.'

James unclipped his seatbelt and leaning across, took Claire in his arms and held her tight. 'We are both tired, my darling. Just one more day and night and we'll be heading home tomorrow.' He rubbed her back.

Turning her face toward him, she realised he'd been crying. She brushed his tears with the back of her hand and kissed his eyelids.

'You are the best thing in my life, and I don't mean to be nasty. Please forgive me and let's start again.'

'Of course, I forgive you,' he said and wondered if he should tell Claire where they were heading.

'I'm taking you somewhere special for lunch,' he began. 'Do you want to know where?'

'Yes, please.'

James gently twisted the rings on Claire's hand. 'Do you remember me telling you about the jeweller where I bought your engagement ring?'

Claire nodded.

'I wanted you to meet him and his lovely family. When I phoned to ask if they would be home, Alex's wife, Deb, was thrilled and insisted that we come for lunch.'

Claire splayed her arms. 'But I'm not dressed to go visiting for lunch; look what I'm wearing!'

'Darling, we're in the country, these are country people, casual is fine. Besides, you look beautiful.'

Pulling the sun visor down, she flicked the courtesy mirror cover across and raked her fingers through her hair. Her cheeks blushed.

'Do you really think I look all right?'

James chuckled. 'My darling, you are absolutely wonderful.'

Arriving at the property, James opened the passenger's side door for Claire. But before she got out of the car, four excited children, an energetic dog and Alexander's wife, Debra with their baby son, rushed out to greet them.

Three-year-old Olivia raced to him and, wrapping her arms around his legs, shrieked with pure delight, 'Mr James, Mr James, I love you, Mr James.'

'Woo, Olivia, you almost knocked me over. Well, thank you. I love you too. Hey, you guys, there's someone I want you to meet.'

Olivia stepped back as the other children, wide-eyed with excitement, inched closer.

Taking Claire's hand, James helped her from the car. 'Hi, everyone, I'd like you to meet my wife, Claire.'

'Hi, Miss Claire,' they chanted in unison.

A warm glow saturated her whole being. 'What a welcome! Thank you,' she said. Looking up, she saw Debra cradling her baby son in her arms. Claire felt an instant rapport.

'Just call me Deb,' she said and wrapped her one free arm around her. 'It's lovely to meet you at last; we have heard so much about you.' She paused and smiled. 'And you are just as beautiful as James said you were.'

Claire blushed. 'Thank you.'

Following the introductions all around Alexander came from the house, gave James a hearty slap on the back and kissed Claire. 'I'm pleased to meet you, Claire. And congratulations to both of you.' He looked at James and winked.

The children all tried to talk at once.

'Hey now, everyone,' Alexander chided. 'There's plenty of time for chit chat later, let's get our guests inside.'

Claire and James walked together beside Alex and Deb, and four animated youngsters trailed close behind.

The lunch was delicious. Roast chicken with vegetables followed by freshly baked Apple pie and custard. And when the meal was finished, the children jumped up, eager to get stuck into their chores. One cleared the table, another washed the dishes, another dried and, in next to no time, the entire kitchen sparkled.

Claire was amazed to see how happy the children were and how well they did their allocated tasks. 'You have a lovely family, Deb; they're all so well-behaved and good-mannered. They're a credit to you.'

'Thanks, Claire. Now tell me about your little girl.'

With the rest of the family outdoors and Alexander and James down in the men's shed, the women had a heart-to-heart talk.

Claire opened up about her previous relationship with Eddy, the birth of Ella and how she met James.

She felt comfortable to share with Debra; it was as if she'd known her all her life. Was it because her baby George was the same age as Ella? Or was it something much deeper – a kindred spirit?

Tears filled Deb's eyes. She cleared her throat. 'James must really love you, Claire.' She hesitated. 'I don't mean to be speaking out of place, and I hope I'm not, but I want to tell you that he spent an awful lot of money on that ring of yours, I mean a *huge* amount! That diamond ring was the most valuable one Alex has ever carried in his shop. It cost much more than James had budgeted for and he moved heaven and earth to scrape together enough to buy it. He said that nothing was too good for his Claire.'

Now it was Claire's turn to cry. She held out her arm and wiggled her fingers. 'Thank you for telling me that.' She sniffed and patted her eyes. 'I knew it was beautiful and now I'll treasure it even more.'

Debra checked the time. 'Look, it's getting a bit late, why don't you guys stay here tonight?'

'That's most kind of you, Deb, but we have booked in at the Ocean Centre Hotel. And we plan to leave early tomorrow morning to head back to Perth. I can't wait to get home and see Ella again; we've been away two weeks and I miss her so much.'

'I totally understand. I'd be the same.'

When it came time to leave, it was Claire who found it hard to break away. In the car, she rolled down the window.

Debra leaned in and kissed her cheek. 'Don't forget about us when you move to Adelaide. Please keep in touch. And remember, you are always welcome to stay with us. Come for a holiday! We have the spare room, and we'd love to have you.'

'That's very kind of you, Deb, but we don't know if or when we'll get back to WA. Anyway, I'll keep in touch.'

The men shook hands, and the children said their goodbyes.

'I love you, Mr James, and I love you, Miss Claire.' It was Olivia's little voice they heard as they drove away.

Claire smiled. 'James, I'm sorry I made such a fuss about coming here. It turned out to be a lovely afternoon, and I wouldn't have missed it for anything. You were right about the Goldsworthy family. Having met them has enriched my life somehow. Thank you, my darling.'

A wave of excitement surged through her. They were heading home. Claire could hardly suppress her joy. *Only tonight, and by this time tomorrow I'll be home, oops, we'll be home*, she corrected her thought. And glancing across at her handsome husband, she sent up a silent prayer of thanks.

After delaying her departure a week, Gloria's return flight to Adelaide was rescheduled for Thursday February 28 - the day before Claire and James were due back from their honeymoon.

'What a shame you can't stay one more day and catch up with the kids.' Sonia sighed.

'No, I'm best to leave you to enjoy their company. There'll be plenty of time for me to see them when they get back to Adelaide. Besides, you're all going to be busy enough with all those last-minute bits and pieces, and you wouldn't want another hanger-on-a-er.'

Sonia chuckled. 'My dear, as if you would be any trouble! You've been amazing.'

Gloria insisted on taking a taxi to the airport much against Bill's protest.

'Bill, remember you are still convalescing, and you have an early appointment with the heart specialist tomorrow. So, it's an early night for you both tonight. And not another word.'

Bill gave a jestful salute.

Sonia smiled. 'Thanks, Gloria. I'm really going to miss you when you go, but I guess you're looking forward to getting back to your own place again.'

'Mmm, it'll be good to get home and see Buddy again.'

'Aw, yes, he's a lovely dog; he must be great company for you.'

Gloria nodded and looked off into the distance. 'Yes, he is.'

Just then a horn sounded at the front. She quickly snapped back to the present. 'Oh, that's for me, the taxi's here.'

After tearful goodbyes all around, the cab pulled slowly away from the kerb, Gloria's small hand waving from the slightly open window.

'Bye, Gloria.'

The flight from Perth to Adelaide went well, and as Gloria walked through the arrival door and into the passenger lounge, she quickly scanned the crowd, hoping to see Melanie. She checked the time. *Oh, the flight is a bit early – perhaps she's not here yet.*

Uncertain as to whether she should tag along and follow the crowd to the baggage collection area or just wait around where they had planned to meet, she waited.

The welcoming area emptied quickly. Gloria struck up a conversation with an elderly lady who had also come from Perth. She had travelled on her own and was waiting anxiously for her son to come for her.

Gloria patted her hand. 'Now don't you worry, my dear. I'm sure he'll be along soon. What's your son's name?'

'Steven,' she replied.

'That's a nice name. Tell me about him. How old is he?'

Her eyes lit up. 'He'll be fifty-one next month, I've come over for his birthday.'

'Really, that's lovely.'

'Steven's married; he's got three children; all grown up and gone their own way. So now he and his wife are left with one big, empty house.'

'Well, it's good that you can come across and stay with them.'

'Yes, I suppose so,' she replied unconvincingly.

Just then their conversation was interrupted.

'Hi, Mother. Who's your friend?'

The elderly lady stood and wrapped her arms around his shoulders. 'Oh, Steven, you came.'

Without any further introductions they turned, said goodbye, and were gone, leaving Gloria alone in the vast emptiness.

'Mum! Sorry we're late, we were held up in the peak-hour traffic.'

It was Melanie. She wasn't alone.

Gloria blinked and swallowed. The young man with her looked vaguely familiar. But who was he? 'Hi, darling, umm ...'

Before her mother asked, Melanie spoke. 'Mum, you remember Tyler, at the wedding, Tyler was James' groomsman.'

'Of course. Hello, Tyler; lovely to see you again.' Turning to her daughter, she frowned the unspoken question.

Melanie held her mother in a long embrace and whispered. 'I'll explain later, Mum.'

Tyler looked at his watch. 'Would you like a coffee, Mrs Cowan?'

Still rather stunned, she turned to Melanie. 'I'm fine, but what about you, dear?'

'It's totally up to you, Mum.' She shrugged. 'I'm easy.'

'Umm...' *Now what have I got in the house to offer them*, she mused. 'Well, why don't you come to my place? I'm sure I'll find something for supper.'

'Thanks, Mum, that'd be great. So much has happened since you've been away. I've, we've,' she grinned, 'got so much to tell you.'

'It seems like you have, my dear.'

Tyler took Gloria's bag in one hand and held the other toward Melanie, who eagerly grasped hold of it and, looking up into his eyes, mouthed her thanks.

Over supper that evening the story emerged. Melanie and Tyler had fallen in love. The sparks began when they danced together at the wedding.

'But, what about Christine?'

'As it turns out, unbeknownst to me, she had met a fellow at work. He'd asked her out, she liked him, but she didn't want to let me down. And when I met Tyler, I felt the same, I couldn't let her down.' Melanie reached across and squeezed his hand. 'It was Chris who saw the sparks between me and Tyler, and she encouraged me to follow my heart. So, we were both happy to end our relationship, move on and pursue our newfound friendships. When Chris and I talked about our relationship, we knew it had been wrong, it was experimental in a way, and we should never have gotten involved like we did. We were just stupid. Anyway, it's over now; she's happy, I'm happy and we still want to be good friends.'

Gloria exhaled a long slow sigh. 'Wow, I've never heard of that happening before. But I'm happy for all of you.' She turned to Tyler. 'And how do you feel about it, Tyler?'

'All I know is I love Mel, and she loves me, and that's all that really matters.' Staring contemplatively into the distance he added, 'We all have a past, and the past is past and must remain in the past.'

'Wow, that's deep,' Melanie chuckled, and they had another coffee.

Claire and James strolled along the beach taking in the golden sunset.

'This is spectacular! I don't ever want this day to end.' Then

Claire corrected herself. 'On second thought I can't wait for tomorrow to come. I just want to get home and see everyone, especially Ella, and there are our wedding photos. Mum said the package arrived yesterday. I'm so excited, I can't wait to see them.'

Before Claire could say another word, James covered her lips with his and kissed her long and passionately.

'Mmm,' she murmured and melted in his embrace.

Early next morning the newly married couple set out for home. Claire could hardly wipe the smile from her face.

After only one short stop on their trip back to Perth, James pulled the car into the driveway at his parents-in-law's house.

Before he had time to switch off the engine, Claire jumped out of the car and raced to the front door.

'Hey, what about me?' James called to her through the open window.

Not looking back, Claire waved her hand dismissively.

Sonia opened the door and threw her arms around her daughter. 'Oh, darling, it's so good to see you. You're back early; I wasn't expecting you until this afternoon.'

'We left Geraldton when it was still dark and virtually drove straight through.'

James sidled up behind Claire and peered over her shoulder. 'Good morning, mother-in-law,' he said with a mischievous grin.

'Well, good morning to you too, my favourite son-in-law,' she retorted. 'Welcome home. Come in, I'll put the kettle on.' Sonia hugged James and called to Bill. 'Guess who's here?'

Hurrying from the yard, Bill wiped his feet on the doormat and walked in. 'The honeymooners, I guess,' he said with the biggest smile. 'Yes, it is! Welcome home, you two.'

Claire threw her arms around his neck and kissed his cheek.

'Oh, Dad, we had a wonderful time. I've got so much to tell you. But, hey, where's my girl?'

'Hah hum!' James coughed. 'You mean *our* girl.'

'Sorry, James.' Claire tutted. 'I'm still getting used to this "our" business.'

They all chuckled.

'I remember well that time. But you'll soon get into the swing of it and it will become second nature.' Sonia looked across at Bill. 'Won't she, dear?'

He nodded. 'Yeah, guess so.'

Sonia checked the time. 'I put Ella down for her morning nap about ten minutes ago. I haven't heard a peep out of her since, so I assume she's asleep. But if you want to pop up and check on her, you do that while I make the tea and coffee.'

In a flash, James followed Claire up the stairs. They crept into the nursery and oohed and aahed over their sleeping child.

James put his arms around Claire's waist. 'She is so beautiful,' he whispered, 'just like her mother.'

Claire turned in his arms, stood on her tiptoes and kissed his waiting lips.

Downstairs, the baby monitor relayed the sound effects. And, in response, Bill held Sonia, and enfolding her in a loving embrace, kissed her tenderly.

Breaking away, Sonia snatched a tissue from the box, wiped her eyes and blew her nose. Bill did likewise. Sonia smiled through moistened lips. 'That is an answer to all our prayers.'

Bill reached over and taking her by the hand, offered a short, heartfelt prayer of thanks.

Ten minutes later, Claire and James returned.

'Ella has grown so much in the two weeks we were away. Whatever have you been feeding her?' Claire said with a cheeky smirk.

Seizing the opportunity to put his bit in, Bill bragged. 'Oh, we forgot to tell you, she's now eating steak and kidney stew, steamed potatoes with the skin on and raw onions!'

'Right, now pull the other leg.'

Sonia reached for the envelope marked Mrs Claire Cowan and held it to her chest possessively. 'I don't suppose you'll be wanting to see what's in this,' she said and turned away.

'Oh, the wedding photos!' Claire reached out excitedly. 'Thanks, Mum, I can't wait to see them.'

Placing the envelope on the kitchen table, she ceremoniously unsealed it and then carefully slid the inner package from the envelope. The photo proofs were further wrapped and sealed in a soft layer of thick tissue paper.

Sonia was beside herself with excitement. 'Hurry up! Can't you go any faster?'

'Leave her be,' hastened Bill, who was just as excited to see the photos as Sonia.

Claire sat down and folded back the paper. She gasped. 'Oh, look, they're beautiful! And look at this one.'

The photographer had included one enlarged photo as a sample. It was of her and James outside the church following the ceremony just before the formal photos were taken. The photographer captured that moment just as the wind caught Claire's veil and James brushed it back from her face. Claire's head thrown back in laughter and James looking lovingly into her eyes. The outer edge of the photo fogged and faded softly into oblivion.

Claire pushed her chair back and stood up.

'What are you doing now?' Sonia frowned.

'I have to wash my hands; I don't want to smudge the photos.'

Sonia rolled her eyes and tutted. 'You are so pedantic.'

'Well, I don't want to spoil them,' Claire replied.

Bill suggested that he and Sonia go for a walk and leave the kids to study the photos by themselves.

'Oh, no,' Claire chided. 'I want you guys to see them too.'

Sonia exhaled a sigh of relief and smiled. 'You and James sit down at the table and Dad and I can stand behind you and look over your shoulders.'

James protested. 'No way, you and Claire sit down, and Dad and I will stand. We don't mind, do we, Bill?'

'Of course not.'

And so, Bill shuffled from one foot to the other with each new sheet. The women oohed and aahed.

The last few sheets were dedicated to candid shots. One photo attracted a lot of attention. It was a casual shot, taken during the wedding reception, of James' sister, Melanie, dancing with the groomsman, Tyler.

Claire was the first to comment. 'If I didn't know better,' she said pointing to the picture, 'I'd say those two are in love. Look at the way they are looking at each other.'

James shrugged. 'Yeah, I know what you mean, but … it couldn't be – you know the situation.'

'Yeah, but I wouldn't want Christine to see this photo; she might get jealous.'

Sonia leaned across and pointed to another photo. 'Look, there's one of Christine dancing with Matt. You can't possibly read anything into that. They're all just having fun, that's all.'

'Yeah, I suppose so.'

There was a crackling sound through the baby monitor. 'I think I hear Ella starting to stir. I'll go get her,' Claire said, and turning to James, reminded him to phone his mother.

'Well, I'll put the kettle on,' Sonia said.

When Claire returned, jiggling Ella on her hip, James offered the phone to Claire. 'Mum wants to speak to you, my darling,' he said and reached out to take Ella. 'Hello, how's my little princess?'

Ella leaned into her new daddy and landed a dribbly open-mouth kiss on the side of his cheek.

'I love you too,' he said and held her tight.

'Hi, Mum,' Claire said into the phone, 'how are you?'

Claire stood wide-mouthed almost speechless.

'Really! Wow! But what about Chris? How does she feel?'

A long pause followed.

'Oh, I can't believe it. That is amazing.'

Sonia's curiosity aroused; she questioned James. 'What is so amazing?'

'You guys were right. What you suspected about Melanie and Tyler, it's true. They are an item.'

Sonia frowned. 'But …'

'I'll let Claire fill you in with the details.'

Sonia waited, impatient for Claire to finish with the phone call. 'I'll, um … pour the tea,' she said needing to do something to fill the time.

'Actually, I'll have coffee, thank you,' James interrupted when Sonia poured tea into his mug.

'Oops, sorry, I was a bit distracted, I wasn't thinking properly.'

'That's all right, Mum. Shall I do the coffees while you pour the tea?'

'You're a treasure, James.'

Claire's face beamed with joy as she relayed the story of how the two new romances came about.

'Melanie and Christine are happy for each other and still remain good friends.'

Sonia shook her head and blinked her eyes in amazement. 'I've never heard of anything like that happening before,' she said, 'But I'm pleased for them and wish them all the very best for their future.'

James sat on the sofa and bounced Ella on his lap, and Claire snuggled up beside him.

Sonia looked through the wedding photos again. Tears filled her eyes; she sniffed and rubbed her nose. 'They are beautiful,' she said and slipped them back into the envelope.

Chapter 32

The following week was like a whirlwind as Claire and James prepared for their move to Adelaide.

With everything sorted, Bill and Sonia took them to the airport and said their goodbyes, knowing that in just over a week, they too would be leaving Perth to start their new life in the beautiful state of South Australia.

Packing boxes lined the hallway and Sonia's footsteps echoed as she walked into the seemingly empty house.

Bill closed the front door behind him. 'I miss the kids already; it just doesn't seem like home without them.'

Sonia shivered. 'Well, we can mope around like a couple of old fuddy-duddies, or we can get busy organising ourselves.'

'Yes, you're right. Where shall we start?'

'I'll clean the upstairs rooms and make sure the kids haven't left anything important behind.'

'How about we do it together; you start on the bathrooms, and I'll clean the walls and the inside of the windows and vacuum the floors.'

'Good thinking. If we can get that done today then we'll be able to forget about upstairs and just concentrate on the downstairs area tomorrow.'

And so, with buckets, cloths, and plenty of elbow grease, they rolled up their sleeves and got stuck into it.

Bill whistled as he washed and polished the windows while Sonia emptied the last bits and pieces from the cupboard under the vanity unit in the upstairs bathroom.

At five o'clock Sonia wandered downstairs and put the kettle on. 'Bill, she shouted over the sound of the vacuum cleaner, 'it's time to knock off, I think we've both done enough for today.'

'Just give me five,' he yelled back, 'then I'll be done.'

On the six o'clock news that evening a report came through of a horrific accident. A car had veered off the road and hit a tree at high speed. One person was killed and the driver was in hospital with life-threatening injuries.

Bill had a sickening feeling in the pit of his stomach. The vehicle, or what remained of the vehicle, seemed familiar. He drew a deep breath, turned to Sonia, and voiced his fear.

'That car looks like Eddy's car.'

'No, I don't think so … Anyway, how can you tell? It's just a mangled mess of twisted metal.'

She could tell Bill was worried. 'Why don't you phone the hospital and find out?'

'I don't think they would divulge that sort of information.'

'No, I don't suppose so.' Sonia shook her head and, under her breath, thought, *No such luck*. Feeling guilty, she added, 'Anyway, it's probably not his car.'

Bill wasn't so sure. 'I'm going to phone Sergeant Jones,' he said and rose from the chair.

He punched in the numbers and waited. A young constable answered.

'I'm sorry, Mr Martin; Sergeant Jones is not in now. He should be back soon. If you give me your number, I'll get him to contact you when he gets in.'

'Thank you, son,' Bill replied and gave him his contact details. He rested the phone back in its cradle and sauntered back into the lounge room.

'Any luck?' Sonia asked.

'No. Sergeant Jones wasn't in. He'll ring back later.'

Bill slumped down in his chair.

'Don't worry, it might never happen.' Sonia said, trying to ease the tension.

Almost an hour passed before the phone rang. Bill rushed to take the call. It was Claire, ringing to let them know they had arrived safely.

'That's good, darling, I'll put your mother on.'

Claire was taken aback at her father's abruptness. *He's never like that*, she thought, and then concluded he must be tired after their busy day.

'Hi, darling,' Sonia greeted cheerily.

'Hi, Mum. Is Dad okay?'

'Yes, he's fine. I think he might have overdone it a bit this afternoon; he cleaned all the upstairs windows.'

'Oh, Mum, Dad's supposed to be taking it easy. Remember what the heart specialist said? You could have got someone in to clean the windows.'

'I know, but we wanted to finish off upstairs today, so we don't have to think about that part of the house anymore.'

'I understand. Anyway, please don't wear yourselves out before you get here.'

'Don't worry, darling, we'll be careful.' Sonia could hear another call coming in. She ignored it and kept talking to Claire. 'Tell me, dear, did you have a good trip?'

Claire yawned. 'Yep, it all went well. Ella was good, but I tell you, it was great having James share the care. He was great.' She yawned again. 'Sorry about that; I think it's all catching up with me, and besides, my body clock still has to adjust to the time difference.'

'It's all right, darling, I'll let you go. Thanks for phoning. I'll be in touch tomorrow. Bye.'

'Bye, Mum, I love you.'

The call ended. Sonia rested the phone in its cradle and turned to go. The phone rang again.

'Hello. Sonia speaking.'

Sergeant Jones identified himself and asked to speak to Bill.

'Just one moment I'll get him for you.'

Sonia shook Bill's arm waking him from sleep. Startled, Bill hurried to his feet.

'It's all right, don't worry. It's the phone for you, Sergeant Jones returning your call.'

Bill squeezed his eyes shut and open three times and cleared his throat. He picked up the receiver and answered.

Sergeant Jones wasn't at all surprised to hear from Bill. Of course, he remembered him and, sadly confirmed his fears.

'I attended the scene of the accident. It was horrific. The passenger died at the scene and Eddy is in a really bad way. It's a wonder he survived the impact and I doubt that he will make it through the night.'

Tears welled in Bill's eyes. He blew his nose and coughed. 'As much as I hate the things he did to our Claire and the baby, I am really sorry for the guy.'

'Yes, I know what you mean,' replied the hardened policeman, 'but he lived that way, and it looks like he'll die that way. The level of alcohol in his system was enough to kill anyone.'

Bill sniffed and swallowed the lump in his throat.

'Sir, do you think the hospital would allow me to visit him?'

'Do you think that's wise?'

'I can't let him die alone.' Bill agonised. 'Besides, the man is my only granddaughter's biological father.'

'True.' Sergeant Jones thought for a moment. 'I'll tell you what, Bill, how about I come over and pick you up and we go to the hospital together. That way they're sure to let you in.'

Bill sighed. His heart pounded in his chest. 'Thank you, I would appreciate that.'

The call ended and Bill wandered in and told Sonia what was happening.

'What! You're going in to see him? That's stupid. I can't believe you'd even think about doing such a stupid thing. You must be crazy!'

Bill took her in his arms and held her close. 'I know it's hard for you to understand, dear, but this is something I must do. Please try to understand.'

Sonia pushed him away and said nothing.

The police car siren beeped in the crisp night air when the vehicle pulled into the driveway.

Bill went to the door. 'Bye, Sonia. Don't wait up for me, I'll see you when I get back.'

She gave him the cold shoulder.

When they arrived at the hospital, Sergeant Jones introduced Bill to the night staff in the Intensive Care Unit and explained Bill's family connection with the patient.

'Thank you for coming, Mr Martin. It's good that he will have someone with him.' Concerned, the nurse added, 'You do realise Mr Simpson is in a critical condition? He's not expected to survive the night,' she whispered. 'In a coma; on life-support, it's only the machines keeping him alive.'

Bill took a deep breath. 'I understand,' he said as he was led to Eddy's bedside.

Moments later, he gazed at the motionless form in the bed, unrecognisable except for the spider tattoo on his forearm. The sight, together with the rhythmic beep of life-sustaining machinery in the cold sterile room, sent a shiver down his spine.

The nurse put her hand under Bill's elbow and guided him to the chair. 'Are you all right, Mr Martin?'

He cleared his throat and swallowed. 'Yes, I'll be fine, thank you,' he replied as he inched the chair closer to the bed.

'You can talk to him; he may be able to hear you.'

Bill felt uncomfortable. *How can I talk to him when he's asleep? I might as well talk to the wall,* he thought.

The young nurse touched Eddy's arm. 'You have a visitor, Mr

Simpson. Bill Martin's here to see you.'

There was no response.

Cautiously, Bill reached his hand toward Eddy. He touched his arm. It was warm. Then, lifting Eddy's dry callused hand, fingernails packed with grease and skin cracked and blackened, he held it in his and tried to talk.

'I'm sorry to hear about your accident, Ed, but you're in the best place. They are looking after you really well.' Tears pooled in Bill's eyes and trickled down his cheeks. He sniffed as he brushed the tears away with the back of his other hand.

Bill's head flopped forward and resting it on the edge of the bed, he wept unashamedly.

The young nurse sidled close, touched him gently on the shoulder and offered him a box of tissues.

'Thank you,' he said through quivering lips.

'It's all right. I'm here for you. If there's anything you need, just let me know.'

Bill nodded.

Hours passed and Eddy's breathing became more laboured.

Oh, God, I feel so useless; Bill prayed silently. *What can I do? Pray for him.*

Pray for him? Bill frowned and, holding Eddy's limp hand in his, shifted restlessly in the chair.

'Eddy,' he whispered, 'would you like me to pray for you?'

Eddy's finger twitched.

'Ed, would you like to make your peace with God?'

His finger twitched again.

'He's responding!' the nurse said excitedly, 'I saw it on the monitor.'

Bill's heart quickened and, not quite knowing what to say, he began to pray.

'Dear heavenly father, I thank you that you are kind and merciful and you love Eddy. Please help him. He needs you. Everyone needs you. Have mercy on Eddy, I pray, forgive his sins, and give him your peace. Now father, if it pleases you, take him to yourself. This I pray in Jesus' name, Amen.'

Bill opened his eyes. Eddy smiled softly, took a deep breath and, with a final twitch of his finger, Edward Simpson exhaled his final breath.

The heart monitor registered three small blips and then the line flattened on the screen. There was a gentle hush, and peace filled the room.

Time of death: 2:42 am. Date: Saturday, March 9, 2019.

The digital clock flicked over 3:25 am. Bill's side of the bed remained empty.

Sonia tossed and turned, unable to sleep. Her thoughts troubled her. She cried into her pillow.

Suddenly startled by a car's headlights as it turned into their driveway, Sonia lifted her head. It must be Bill, she thought. She heard the car door shut, followed by footsteps, which triggered the front security light. The sound of keys rattling and then of one engaging the lock followed. The front door opened.

'Bill, is that you?' she asked as she leaned over and switched on the bedside lamp.

Closing the door behind him, Bill followed the light. 'Yes, it's me. I thought you'd be asleep. I hope I didn't wake you.'

'No, I haven't been asleep, I was worried about you.'

Bill walked around to Sonia's side of the bed and kissed her tenderly. 'You shouldn't have worried, my darling. I did what I had to do.' He held her close.

Overwhelmed with sorrow, Sonia wept aloud. 'I'm so sorry,' she said with shuddered brokenness.

Bill rubbed her back, every stroke gently reassuring her.

Sonia smiled and, through tear-filled eyes, noticed a soft, warm glow around Bill's face. She listened as he unfolded the events of the evening to her, little by little, including the death of passenger Francine Myer.

'I'm happy and sad at the same time,' she said, 'Happy, and relieved, that Eddy's out of our life and can't cause any more trouble, but sad for him in a way, I suppose, because he had such a sad life, and that Ella will never know her real father.'

Taking her in his arms, Bill wiped a stray tear from her eye and smiled a soft smile. 'I know what you mean, darling. I feel mixed emotions too.' He shrugged. 'How about I make us a nice cup of tea?'

'Yep, that sounds good.'

After their cups of tea and a short prayer, Bill and Sonia closed their eyes and fell asleep just as the first hint of a new day filtered through the darkness.

Following a hectic week, and with the settlement of their house behind them, Bill shut the front door of the family home behind him for the last time. He and Sonia dropped off the house keys to the Real Estate Agent's office, expressed their appreciation and, with a sigh of relief, said their final thank you and goodbye.

When Claire heard the news of Eddy's death, she felt nothing—no shock, no sadness, no sorrow, no emotion whatsoever. *That's weird*, she thought, blinking, and trying to conjure up some sort of response, but still, nothing came.

She shivered and thought about Eddy's deprived childhood. Abandoned by his mother before he was three, he never knew his father and was shuffled from one foster home to another and branded "the naughty boy" and "a no-hoper."

Yes, Claire did feel sorry for Eddy, not sorry because he was dead, but because he didn't really have a chance in life.

Looking back over her own somewhat sheltered and privileged life, Claire wondered again how she'd become involved with Eddy. *I thought I loved him, but I probably just felt sorry for him and thought I could make his life better somehow.* She shrugged. *I don't know. Maybe I wanted adventure, to break away from my mundane,* predictable, "goodie-two-shoes" lifestyle. One thing I do remember is that the "bad boy" image Eddy portrayed seemed attractive to me at the time.

Claire shuddered as she visualised afresh the violence Eddy had afflicted on her and her newborn baby, how he had deprived them of the necessities of life, and how he had used her. No, I don't feel sorrow over Eddy's death, and I don't have to cry and I don't have to feel guilty.

James understood. 'It's all right, Claire. I'm glad you've forgiven yourself for not being grieved over Eddy's death. It's sad news, but don't' think about his life as wasted. Come with me.' Taking Claire by the hand, he led her through to the nursery where Ella lay fast asleep in her cot. 'Look, my darling, something good did come from Eddy's life. If it wasn't for him, we wouldn't have our precious little girl, and I may never have met you.'

Pulling a tissue from her pocket, Claire dabbed her eyes. 'That's true, my darling, thank you for reminding me and thank you for rescuing me from …' She paused, '… from the gutter – literally. On that cold and stormy night, if you hadn't stopped and called for help, I probably would have died there on the side of the road.'

'I'm so glad I found you, my darling,' he said, whisking her off her feet and carrying her out to the kitchen. He sat her up on the bench, hugged her, and loved her thoroughly.

After one night's stay at a Perth hotel, Bill's good friend and work colleague, Phil Haynes, met them and drove them to the airport for their midmorning flight to Adelaide.

In the departure lounge, just before they boarded their flight, Phil slung his arms around Bill, pulled him into a manly bear hug and slapped him on the back. 'I'm going to miss you, Bill. You've been a great mate.'

'Likewise,' Bill replied with a tear in his eye. 'It's been thirty years – thirty good years. Thanks for everything.'

Phil released Bill from his grip and pulled a handkerchief from his trouser pocket. 'I know you're doing the right thing, mate – the family must always come first. Enjoy your l-o-n-g, long service leave, Bill. You sure earned it. Keep in touch and let me know when you start that new job of yours.' He shook out the folded hankie, blew his nose and then kissed Sonia on the cheek. 'Bye, you two.'

When they arrived in Adelaide, Bill and Sonia received a warm welcome. Their ten-month-old granddaughter, Ella, leaned over and reached for them. 'Na, pa,' she said with a big smile.

Sonia lifted her from Claire's arms, squeezed her tightly and kissed her chubby cheeks. 'Did you say Nanna and Pa? You are a clever little tyke.'

'Yes, we've been telling her over and over that Nanna and Grandpa are coming soon.'

Bill ruffled Ella's golden curly hair and placed a kiss on the back of her hand. 'And here's me thinking you might have forgotten us.'

'No way! We've been counting down the days,' James added, 'and we're glad you arrived safely.'

With more hugs and kisses all around, they headed for the baggage pickup area, chatting all the way.

'Hey, slow down you two,' Sonia called as she shifted Ella across to her other hip. 'This little princess of ours is getting heavy.'

James spun around. 'Oh, I'm sorry, Mum, here let me take her.'

Ella went to her daddy and laid a slobbery kiss on his cheek.

'I love you too, little princess,' he said as he wiped the kiss away.

After their two-week stay with Gloria, during which time they ordered and arranged delivery of their new furniture and household appliances, Sonia and Bill shifted into their new unit.

Another three weeks passed before the bulk of their personal freight arrived from Perth. It was like Christmas as they opened boxes and unwrapped parcels. Everything was just as they'd packed it. Sonia placed family photos about and, stepping back, admired her handiwork. 'This makes it feel more like home. What do you think Bill?'

'Yep, that's lovely, dear,' he said lifting his head from the newspaper.

Bill's car still hadn't arrived; there'd been some sort of delay with the shipping. But that hadn't bothered them at all. There was plenty for them to do, including setting up the flat, unpacking boxes, sorting, and culling even more of their possessions. Besides, the shops were close by, and public transport was great.

Sonia stepped out onto the patio and breathed in the fresh sea air. The early autumn sun highlighted a tinge of yellow, orange, and red on the leaves of the English plain trees in the street below. A seagull squawked. The distant sound of waves gently lapping on the shore awakened her senses to the sheer beauty that surrounded her.

Claire quickly settled into a steady routine. She kept busy with a one-year-old, going-on-three socially active youngster, and her weeks were full and fun, leaving not much time for her to think about herself. On Tuesdays, they visited Nanna and Grandpa Martin; Thursday mornings were playgroup, and they took a bus trip to Nanna Cowan's; Saturday was always Daddy's special day and Sunday was family day with church and crèche in the morning. After church, they all went back to Gloria's place for lunch and a leisurely afternoon together.

Chapter 33

Claire woke early one Saturday. James was still asleep beside her, and Ella hadn't woken up yet. Claire slowly rolled over in the bed, but as she did, a sudden wave of nausea swept over her. She lay perfectly still and held her breath hoping it would pass, but it didn't. Pushing back the covers she quietly slid out of bed and rushed to the bathroom. Another wave of nausea hit. Her stomach heaved and then a stream of bright yellow acid bile poured into the toilet bowl. She shivered, coughed, and spat a mouthful of the bitter spew into the loo.

Yuk, that was sudden, she thought as she flushed the toilet. *I hope I didn't wake the others up.* Claire padded out to the kitchen, poured herself a glass of water and wandered across to the calendar on the wall. Gulping down a mouthful of water, she scratched her head and frowned as she turned the calendar back to the previous month. She ran her finger along each line, but there was no usual red circle around any of the dates. She flipped back another month, and there it was, on the 25th, that distinct mark. *Oh, I must be pregnant*, she concluded and counted the days. *Forty-one days. I am pregnant!*

James wandered into the kitchen blurry-eyed and hair-tossed. He yawned, ran his fingers through his hair, and sat next to Claire. 'Good morning, sweetie pie. You're up early for a Saturday.'

'I was sick,' Claire replied in a slightly husky voice.

'That's no good,' James said with a worried frown. He reached across and put his arm gently over her shoulder. 'You just pop back into bed, and I'll bring you in a nice cup of tea.'

'No, it's not that sort of sick, and besides, I'm all right now. It's just ... well, um … I think I'm pregnant. No,' she corrected herself. 'I am pregnant!'

James' eyes lit up. 'Really? How? When? Wow!' he stuttered.

Claire smiled. 'Well, I think we know how and I'm not sure about the when, but, yes, wow!'

James wrapped his arms around her and helped her from the chair. He lifted her off the floor and started whirling her around. Suddenly he stopped, lowered her cautiously to her feet and shuddered. 'Oh sorry, darling, I didn't mean to ...'

'That's okay. I won't break. And there's no need for the cottonwool treatment.'

He softly touched Claire's tummy and sighed. 'So, what do we do now? Should we get one of those pregnancy test kits, or what?'

'We don't really have to do anything. And we won't need a pregnancy test because I'm quite familiar with the symptoms. But I probably should make an appointment to see the doctor soon.'

James did a little jig around the kitchen table. 'I'll phone Mum. She'll be so excited.'

Claire gave a chuckle. 'Oh no, I think you should wait.'

'But I need to tell someone.'

Just then the nursery-monitor sprung to life as Ella gurgled her good morning greetings.

'Why don't you go in and tell Ella. I don't think she'll be telling anyone.'

'Great idea!' James called back when he was already halfway to the nursery. 'I'm coming, my little princess.'

The monitor continued to relay the following conversation intermingled with goo's and giggles.

'Bub, bub, bub,' James sang.

'Bup,' replied Ella.

'It's Ella and Daddy's Day today. What should we do?'

'Bup, bup, bup,' she answered.

'Good girl,' he said as he bounced the youngster on his hip, 'but let's have breakfast first.'

Claire appreciated the way James looked after Ella for her on a Saturday. He would dress and feed her in the morning, and then they would go out for the day, sometimes to the park, the beach, or shopping. Whatever they did, they enjoyed having quality fun together. Claire enjoyed having the break and a little time just for her.

That afternoon James arrived home much earlier than usual. With a grin from ear-to-ear and Ella asleep in the stroller, he wandered into the kitchen and slipped a package onto the table.

'What's this?' Claire asked.

James cleared his throat.

'Well,' he said, 'we passed a Chemist shop, and decided to pop in and pick up a pregnancy test kit.'

'We did, did we?' she tutted, 'You didn't have to do that.'

'But I did. So, please, please, please take the test. Go on, just for me,' he pleaded with those big blue puppy-dog eyes.

'Oh, all right.'

Claire took the packet from the bag, turned the box over and read the instructions.

James jiggled his foot and waited.

'I think I might have to wait until morning to do this test,' Claire tutted.

'No, no, it can be done any time of the day. I checked the label. Look, see here?' James ran his finger along the line to emphasise his point.

'Well, I don't need to go to the toilet at the moment.'

'Okay then, I'll put the kettle on, we'll have a cup of tea.'

'But I'm not really thirsty,' Claire said with a teasing smirk.

James filled the kettle anyway, hit the switch, and waited. And waited. *They say a watched kettle never boils*, he mused, *it sure seems true today*.

After a leisurely afternoon tea, Claire felt she could delay it no longer. Grabbing the package from the table, she rushed off to the bathroom; James, shadowing closely in her wake.

'I can do it by myself,' she said.

'But can't I go in with you?'

'Oh, all right then.'

Claire completed the test and, in trying to hold the plastic strip close to her chest, spilt some of the contents. 'Oops,' she said as she righted the container.

'Yippee!' exclaimed James when he glimpsed the two tell-tale pink lines on the result panel. 'We're pregnant! Yeah!'

Sunday morning, Claire was too unwell to go to church. James wanted to stay home and look after her.

'Don't fuss, James.' She brushed his hand from her shoulder. 'I'll be okay as soon as this stupid nausea settles. Please, just take Ella and go.'

James backed away. 'I don't like seeing you like this, Claire. I feel so helpless. What can I do?'

'Get used to it, James! This is what pregnancy is.'

As James drove toward his mother's house to take her to church, wave after wave of mixed emotions surged through him – happy that they were expecting another child – but sad for how it was affecting his precious Claire. He drove into the driveway, stopped the engine, and turned to see Ella fast asleep in her car seat. 'You darling little princess,' he whispered. And with tears threatening to cascade from his eyes, he sniffed and brushed his hand across his cheeks.

Gloria tapped on the car window.

'Hi, son. Where's Claire?'

'She's not feeling too well today. I told her to stay home and rest,' he replied with a slight frown.

Noticing the baby asleep, Gloria climbed into the car, closed the door as quietly as she could, slid the seatbelt slowly across her shoulder and locked it gently into place.

'Thanks, Mum,' James whispered.

The drive to church was quieter than usual. Gloria expressed her sadness in hearing of Claire's sickness and hoped she was not coming down with the latest virus going around.

James wriggled in his seat and re-assured her all was well.

'Will you still be coming home for lunch after church?' she asked.

'I'll give it a miss today, Mum. Thanks all the same. But I guess Bill and Sonia will be joining you as usual.'

'I hope so, son.'

The church service was lovely. Ella enjoyed playing with her friends in the crèche, but James' thoughts were elsewhere.

As soon as the last hymn ended, he rushed out, collected Ella, and tried to say a quick goodbye to Claire's parents after arranging for them to give Gloria a lift home.

'Sure, son. No problem at all. Give our love to Claire and tell her we hope she's soon feeling better,' Bill said with a knowing glint in his eye.

Sonia pulled James and Ella into a tight hug. 'Every little thing will be fine, James, just look after our girls.'

He was stunned. 'You guys know, don't you?' he said with a telling smile.

'You mean Claire's going to have a baby?'

'What's that?' Gloria chirped in. 'A baby!'

Bill smiled and patted James on the back. 'Congratulations, son, and do give Claire our love and we'll call in for a visit this afternoon.

Arriving home James crept sheepishly into the kitchen. 'Hi, darling,' he said and kissed her on the cheek. 'Your mum and dad sent their love and will call in to see you this afternoon. My mum says she hopes you feel better soon.'

'Thanks, darling,' she smiled. 'Yes, I'm feeling better now, let's eat, I'm starving.'

By the time Sonia and Bill arrived at James and Claire's place that afternoon, Claire was feeling much better. Little Ella was sound asleep, and the house was quiet.

Sonia threw her arms around her daughter. 'When can we expect the new arrival?' she asked.

'Oh, Mum, James shouldn't have told you; it's all too soon; we haven't even had it confirmed ourselves yet.'

Bill kissed his daughter. 'Congratulations, darling; another little princess on the way.

Just then James came rushing from the bathroom, test kit in his hand. 'Aw, what a shame,' he said. 'It looks to be fading a bit, but yesterday both the lines were bright pink.'

'Pink! Does that mean it is a girl!' exclaimed Sonia.

'No, it just means we are positively pregnant,' James replied excitedly.

James took his mobile phone from his pocket and scrolled through. 'Here's the photo I took of the pregnancy test result yesterday. See how bright it is.'

'I suppose that will be the first photo to go in the baby's album,' Sonia said with a faraway look. Her thoughts were momentarily interrupted by Claire's voice.

'Come on, everyone, don't stand here in the kitchen; let's all go into the lounge room. James will put the kettle on, won't you, dear?' Claire said with a pleading smile as she ushered her parents through to the next room.

The golden afternoon sun shone through the open window and a gentle breeze stirred the soft sheer curtains.

Sonia's mind drifted back to the day Claire had visited her with news of her pregnancy to Eddy. Ragged clothes hanging from her emaciated body, bruises on her face and arms, the putrid stink from Eddy's cigarettes and alcohol clinging to her, and a seemingly bleak future ahead.

Sonia sat on the sofa and patted the cushion beside her. Looking around the room, she realised how different things were this time. Her daughter, now glowing with health and happiness, and contented with her new husband and baby girl. 'Come and sit down here beside me, Claire. We're so happy for you, darling.'

Claire smiled. 'Thank you, Mum – we're happy too.'

Claire soon recovered from the morning sickness, and the rest of the year passed with a flurry of activities: Ella's first birthday was in May; they moved into their new four-bedroom house in September, and to top off the year, a grand Christmas celebration was held at Gloria's home in December with the whole family.

Claire counted off the days until her baby was due. The 30th of December came and went, 31st – one day over. New Year came, and a new calendar replaced the old. The days dragged on.

'How many days late can a baby be?' James asked.

'I'm not sure. I didn't have to wait for Ella – she came six weeks early! Anyway, the doctor said he would see me again next week unless the baby comes beforehand. So, I guess we just need to wait.'

The contractions started, gently and infrequently at first. It was Monday afternoon and James was still at work. He'd phoned her during his morning break and at lunchtime, but Claire had no news to report; nothing had happened at that time. But now, it seemed, something was starting. Ella was having her afternoon nap and Claire was feeling quite comfortable relaxing on the recliner with her feet up and her hands wrapped around a warm mug of sweet tea. The curtains billowed in the breeze.

She squeezed the mug tightly. 'Ouch, I felt that one,' she mumbled under her breath. Eight minutes later, her stomach tightened again. *This is it*, she thought. *I'll call Mum.*

Sonia answered the phone on the first ring. 'Are you all right, Claire?'

'Yes, Mum, but I think the labour pains are starting.'

'Have you told James?'

'No, I'll ring him next. But, Mum, I need you.'

'I'll come straight away.'

By the time Bill and Sonia arrived, James was waiting with Claire, her bag by the door, ready to leave for the hospital.

'Hi, Mum,' Claire said. 'Ella's dinner is in the fridge. Just warm it in the microwave. Her pyjamas are under her pillow and …'

'Don't you worry, we'll be fine, you just go!' Sonia kissed her daughter and hurried them out the door. 'We'll be thinking of you, and praying for you, darling.'

As the door closed, Sonia called after them. 'Make sure you let us know as soon as there's news. It doesn't matter what time it is.'

'Will do,' came the reply. And they were gone.

Sonia turned to Bill and frowned. 'I'm worried about her; she had such a terrible time having Ella.'

'Now, remember you told Claire not to worry, so don't you go worrying,' Bill said with a reassuring hug.

'Yes, but …'

Just then, Ella woke from her nap, excited to see Nanna and Grandpa.

'How's my little princess?' Bill said and whirled her around till she giggled.

'Don't do that! Put her down, it might make her sick,' Sonia roused.

'Oh, your nanna is fussing too much,' he said, and lowered her gently to the floor.

Sonia opened the box of toys she had brought from home.

Bright-eyed, Ella quickly rummaged through the toys and found her favourite soft baby doll, Betsie May. She held the doll to her chest and rocked back and forth.

'Isn't she cute,' Sonia crooned. 'She's going to love the new baby.'

That night Bill and Sonia waited up until their eyelids drooped. When finally, they went to bed, sleep evaded them, so they talked. Suddenly the ringing of the phone startled them.

Sonia reached for the cordless extension phone on the bedside table. 'Hello,'

'Hi, Mum, it's me,' James answered excitedly. 'We have a healthy baby boy; Michael William Cowen was born at 1:42 am.'

'That's great, James! Congratulations! How is Claire? Give her our love and tell her we are so proud of her.' Sonia sighed, 'Fancy … a little boy.'

'He's not so little. He weighed 3940 grams!'

'How much is that in ounces and pounds?'

'That's 8 pounds eleven ounces!'

'Phew! That is big for Claire. How did she do?'

'She's fine, no problems, just a few stitches. She didn't need a caesarean. They thought she might have needed one seeing she had a caesarean last time. She's here if you would like to talk to her. Oh, sorry, she has just closed her eyes.'

'Please don't wake her, let her sleep, we'll see her tomorrow.'

James yawned.

'Sounds like you need to go to sleep too.' Sonia said and smothered a yawn herself. 'Are you coming home, or can you sleep there?'

'I'll stay here with Claire and our baby.'

'We'll take Ella to meet her baby brother tomorrow.'

'Thank you. I'll see you in the morning. Oops, it's already morning. I should say I'll see you later today. Bye.'

'Bye, James.'

The next day, the hospital was abuzz with visitors. Sonia, Bill, Ella clutching her baby doll, James' mother, Gloria, and his sister, Melanie, all packed into Claire's small private room in the maternity ward.

Claire couldn't believe how big Ella was. She seemed to have grown overnight. Claire looked at the baby asleep in his crib, and then at her nineteen-month-old daughter. 'Wow, you really are the big sister.'

With her visitors gone and the room fragrant with flowers and decorated with congratulatory cards, Claire gazed down at her newborn son sleeping contentedly in her arms. The close bond she felt was instant. Tears filled her eyes – tears of happiness mingled with sorrow. Happy for how her life had turned out, but sad when she remembered how she had rejected Ella when she was born. *If it hadn't been for Mum and Dad loving Ella and caring for her*, Claire thought, *she could have suffered irreversible emotional damage.*

Claire closed her eyes. 'Thank you, God, for Mum and Dad. Thank you for protecting Ella, and me, from Eddy's violence. And thank you for bringing James into my life, and for blessing us with two healthy children. Amen.'

Following her shift, the midwife called in to see Claire. 'I needed to see you again, Claire. You and your husband are such a lovely couple. I wish there were more like you. We see so many fractured families. Single mum's struggling on their own, women in abusive situations. It's so refreshing to meet a "normal" family these days.'

Claire thanked her for her kind words, and then went on to explain that her life wasn't always like this, that she too was once caught up in an abusive relationship. She told her about Eddy, and how badly he had treated her. 'In my search for love,' she said, 'I made wrong choices and suffered the consequences. Then I realised that there is a better way.'

Claire gazed into the distant past. 'I thought I loved Eddy, but that wasn't love. True love thinks of others and is kind. When I met James, I learned what real love is; he accepted me as I was.' She smiled. 'And would you believe me if I told you that he literally picked me up out of the gutter? But that's another story.'

About the Author

Born in Sydney, NSW, Dianne now lives in Perth, Western Australia, with her husband Jim. They have six children, nineteen grandchildren, and eight great-grandchildren.

Dianne's desire to write was evident from a young age – long before she could read or write! She writes poems, skits, and short stories and has won awards in two National Literary Competitions. Her published works include her memoir, *Fragrance of Life*, a children's picture book, *Ben and the Muddled-up Moon*, and poems and short stories in several anthologies.